QUEEN
OF
SHADOWS
AND
RUIN

BOOKS BY NISHA J. TULI

THE NIGHTFIRE QUARTET
Heart of Night and Fire
Dance of Stars and Ashes
Storm of Ink and Blood

ARTEFACTS OF OURANOS
Trial of the Sun Queen
Rule of the Aurora King

CURSED CAPTORS
Wicked is the Reaper

To Wake a Kingdom

QUEEN
OF
SHADOWS
AND
RUIN

NISHA J. TULI

SECOND SKY

Published by Second Sky in 2025

An imprint of Storyfire Ltd.
Carmelite House
50 Victoria Embankment
London EC4Y 0DZ
United Kingdom

www.secondskybooks.com

The authorised representative in the EEA is Hachette Ireland
8 Castlecourt Centre
Dublin 15 D15 XTP3
Ireland
(email: info@hbgi.ie)

ISBN: 978-1-83618-416-4
eBook ISBN: 978-1-83618-415-7

This book is a work of fiction. Names, characters, businesses, organizations,
places and events other than those clearly in the public domain are either the
product of the author's imagination or are used fictitiously. Any resemblance to
actual persons, living or dead, events or locales is entirely coincidental.

For everyone who wants to 'ride' the dragon—in all ways possible.

CAST OF CHARACTERS

People you already know

Zarya Rai: Queen of our story and our hearts. The chosen one. Aazheri with six anchors and a prophecy inside a magical stone that's shaking up her life. Yasen's second-best friend.

Yasen Varghese: The one and only. Former commander and soldier in Daragaab's army. Enjoying his freedom from his old life. Emotional support companion and king of our hearts.

(Rabin)dranath Ravana: Zarya's destined magical servant who knows how to treat a woman right.

Raja Abishek: King of Andhera, the most powerful Aazheri in Rahajhan, and Zarya's father. Rabin's mentor, which makes things, like, really complicated.

Aishayadiva (Asha) Madan: Zarya's mother, Row's lover, and former queen of Gi'ana. She's been missing for twenty years.

Rani Amrita: Queen of Daragaab. Now a tree and about to give birth. Don't think too much about the details. You don't want to know.

Vikram Ravana: Steward to Rani Amrita and brother to Rabin. About to become a father. Sort of.

Suvanna: Merdeva from the queendom of Matsya. Has water powers and could kick your ass. She's got a thing with Apsara, but she doesn't do commitment.

Apsara: Vidyadhara from the region of Vayuu with powerful ice and wind magic. Definitely does commitment.

Koura: A healer from the region of Svaasthy and powerful wielder of Niramaya—the magic of healing.

Aarav: Gave up his life for Zarya in the fight to save Rani Amrita.

Kindle: Agni from the region of Bhaavana, known for his fire magic and ability to alter emotions in others.

Professor Dhawan: The first villain in our tale. Betrayed everyone to get back into Abishek's good graces, but Zarya offed him. As she should have.

Gopal Ravana: The nawab of Daragaab, powerful rakshasa, father to Vikram and Rabin.

Jasmine Ravana: Third wife of Gopal Ravana, Vikram and Rabin's mother.

Ajay Chandra: One half of the Chandra twins and supporter of the resistance.

Rania Chandra: The other half of the Chandra twins and supporter of the resistance.

Farida: Vanshaj and girlfriend to Rania. Leader of the resistance.

Dishani Madan: Zarya's half-sister and oldest of the Madan siblings.

Kabir Madan: King consort and former husband to Asha.

Advika Madan: Zarya's half-sister.

Miraan Madan: Zarya's half-brother. Oldest brother. Advisor and right hand to his sister Dishani.

Talin Madan: Zarya's half-brother. Youngest of the Madans.

Vikas: Vanshaj member of the resistance.

Ekaja: Commander of Raja Abishek's army. The only female commander in Rahajhan.

Kishore: Raja Abishek's personal mystic.

Rahajhan: Name of the main continent, comprised of seven main regions: Daragaab, Svaasthy, Vayuu, Gi'ana, Andhera, Bhaavana, and Matsya.

Gi'ana: The queendom of knowledge and one of two regions that are home to the Aazheri. Located on the western shore bordering the Saaya.

Ishaan: Capital city of Gi'ana. Located inland, surrounded by forests and distant mountains.

Andhera: Northern kingdom and the second region known as the home of the Aazheri. Home of Raja Abishek.

Saaya: Unceded territory located between Gi'ana and Andhera. Uninhabitable and constantly under dispute between the two regions thanks to its abandoned diamond mines.

Daragaab: Queendom of earth magic, lies in the southeast corner of the continent and is bordered by the Dakhani Sea to the south and the Nila Hara Sea to the east.

Dharati: The capital city of Daragaab. Home to the Jai Palace.

Pathara Vala Mountains: Enormous mountain range in the northeast corner of the continent bordering Andhera and parts of Gi'ana.

Matsya: The underwater queendom of water magic. Lies in the depths of the Dakhani Sea.

Vayuu: The mountain kingdom of air and wind magic, residing high in the Pathara Vala Mountains.

Bhaavana: The kingdom of love and passion, known for fire magic. Located in the northwest quadrant of Rahajhan, east of Gi'ana.

Svaasthy: The queendom of spirit magic and Niramaya and the power of healing. A land of desert sands and residing on the southwestern shore.

Dakhani Sea: Southern ocean of Rahajhan.

Nila Hara Sea: Eastern ocean of Rahajhan.

Ranpur Island: Small island on the southern coast of Daragaab and Rahajhan.

Premyiv: City located on Ranpur Island.

Other Creatures and Magical Things

Aazheri: Mage-like beings who use anchors that represent each element to create magic: fire, earth, air, water, and spirit. There is a sixth anchor known as the darkness.

Vanshaj: The descendants of the Ashvin twins, relegated to positions of servitude and forbidden from using their magic by the application of a magical ring of tattooed stars around their necks.

Paramadhar: A magical servant destined for a specific Aazheri to help control and amplify their magic, protect them, and heal them.

Masatara: The name for the Aazheri portion of the paramadhar bond.

Bandhan: Official name of the binding that joins the masatara to the paramadhar.

Jadugara: Ancient sect of Aazheri hailing from Gi'ana. Responsible for applying the vanshaj star collars.

The Ashvin twins: Two powerful Aazheri brothers who used the darkness to bring misery upon Rahajhan and were banished away.

Chiranjivi: Powerful beings that represent each region of Rahajhan—kind of like the Avengers.

Vidyadhara: Winged beings from the region of Vayuu, capable of wind magic.

Merdeva: Beings of water magic who come from Matsya.

Agni: Beings of fire magic from Bhaavana.

Niramaya healers: Beings from Svaasthy who use spirit to heal.

Rakshasa: Blood-drinking beings who use earth magic. Some can shapeshift into animals.

Khada: Elite force of soldiers whose job is to guard the wall around Dharati against the blight.

Fairies: Colorful beings with various skin and hair tones and known for their beauty.

Peri: Miniature versions of fairies.

Bayangoma: Magical birds that live in secret groves and bestow knowledge on those who are worthy in exchange for a drop of blood willingly given.

Naga: Snakes that live in the swamp, white and gelatinous and without eyes.

Ajakava: Giant bronzed scorpions.

Nairrata: Demon army that once did the bidding of the Ashvin twins.

Kala-hamsa: Red-feathered birds of varying size that are birthed from marble-like eggs that can hatch in the middle of the sky.

Dakini: Bipedal demons with black hides, big teeth, and long claws.

PROLOGUE

ONE THOUSAND YEARS AGO

City of Taaranas

Aravind Ashvin had spent the night with his cock buried inside a courtesan, feeling like a god. He'd barely slept. He'd come with a grunt, sweat coating his skin and a shiver rolling down his spine. As he drove into her perfect cunt, he couldn't help thinking about the world continuing around him.

The people of Taaranas slept in their beds and dined with their families, toasting to their health, none the wiser to what they'd witness this afternoon.

History. Destiny.

Today, he would tap into an unimaginable source of power alongside his twin brother.

It would signal the moment the Ashvins would finally rule the world.

He strode past the wide doors of their dark castle, bracketing one end of the city. The grand boulevards stretched in three directions, paved with silver stones and lined with homes, shops, and businesses. Despite the early hour, many were already awake, preparing for the market or their daily errands.

None of it would matter soon.

The snow had been swept earlier where it gathered along the edges of the street. The biting wind nipped at his nose and ears. It was a cold that would bring lesser men to their knees, but Aravind had always found the chill invigorating.

With a scepter clutched in his hand, he thunked along the stones, his gait sure and steady. It did little but look impressive, but he was nothing if not a slave to appearances. He wore a long robe covered with jewels that dusted the pavers underfoot.

Everyone quickly cleared his path, lining up along the wide street and bowing their heads in deference.

It was a beautiful city. Magnificent, in fact.

Over the centuries, his family had crafted Taaranas to greatness from a humble rocky plain surrounded by the Pathara Vala Mountains, erecting opulent buildings to rival every kingdom. Stretching for miles, it now housed thousands of citizens. Soaring snowy peaks loomed in the distance, casting long, cold shadows over the city when the sun fell below the horizon.

As Aravind passed the onlookers, he dipped his chin, acknowledging their respect but maintaining his steady pace. Though he usually enjoyed mingling with his subjects and basking in their adoration, he didn't have time for their courtesies today.

It was more than likely that Manish was already at the temple. If Aravind knew his brother, he'd probably slept on the floor last night.

Aravind, on the other hand, had chosen to enjoy his lady friend instead. Still reveling in the afterglow, he felt like nothing could stop him. Even now, his cock stirred at the memory of her heaving breasts and the way her tight pussy had clenched around him.

He adjusted himself, grateful that his ostentatious robe

covered the tenting fabric in his pants. Sex and power had always been his greatest vices, and soon, he would have everything he'd ever wanted.

Aravind had spent years studying magic and researching its properties alongside his brother.

Nightfire.

That gift unique only to them. Passed down by their mother, who'd died when they were merely children, she'd left them with this kingdom and its legacy and this wild, untamed power that gusted through their veins.

Their father had met with a 'tragic' accident once the brothers came of age. Or so the story went. No one could prove what really happened to the former king of Taaranas, and now, decades later, there was no one left to care.

Aravind and Manish had taken their crown, happily agreeing to share it to honor their mother's dying wish.

Manish was the only person in this life he trusted implicitly.

Aravind continued his walk towards the giant temple standing sentinel at the opposite end of Taaranas's wide main boulevard.

The brothers had built it as an homage to Andhera, the God of Darkness, their chosen deity. Aravind loved to stand on the wide steps leading to the entrance where he'd recite sermons, interjected with his laudable opinions before receiving his subjects, demanding they bow to their knees and swear loyalty and unwavering faith.

The silver-stepped structure rose nearly as high as the castle, sparkling in the morning light. But its most remarkable feature was the glittering silver star that hung above it, suspended in space.

It spun slowly on an invisible axis, catching flashes of weak winter light.

It was a reminder of their power.

Of what would happen should anyone try to cross the Ashvins.

Aravind continued walking, bounding up the steps, light on his feet. He couldn't remember the last time he'd felt such excitement. He felt like a small boy receiving sweets.

The temple formed a large square made of creamy marble, carved with the likeness of Andhcra. His terrifying horned visage adorned every wall and pillar, whittled to nearly lifelike perfection by an army of sculptors they'd commissioned for the task. He'd never admit to the shiver that crept down his spine whenever Aravind found himself alone here at night.

As he entered, he found Manish standing over the crystal-blue pool burrowed into the center of the room.

"Finally awake?" Manish asked as Aravind approached.

Aravind smirked. "I had things to attend to."

Manish rolled his eyes. Though he also enjoyed the regular company of the fairer sex, he wasn't as governed by his urges, making him the more responsible brother. When Aravind claimed the brothers had been researching ways of tapping into their power, he really meant that Manish had shouldered most of the work. It was his nature, and he thrived on it.

"I think we're ready to begin," Manish said, his unblinking gaze focused on the pool's surface. Lights created through magic illuminated the deep well, giving Aravind a clear view straight to the bottom many feet below.

He nodded as his stomach churned with anticipation.

They'd coveted this for years. Planned for it. Dreamed of it. But now that it was time, he was faced with the enormous weight of this final step they'd take in their quest to seize power across the continent.

"We'll need to create a rip in the world between ours and the demon realm," Manish said, still gazing into the pool.

Aravind nodded. He already knew this, but he sensed that

Manish was nervous, and repeating the familiar instructions was a way to calm himself.

"Then we'll establish a portal to call the nairatta to us."

Aravind nodded. This he knew, too. They'd discussed their plans a thousand times late into the night with several bottles of wine and liquor emptying between them.

"And how will we control them?" Aravind asked, also knowing the answer while allowing his brother to work out his anxiety.

Manish met his gaze, his dark eyes reflecting in the pool's light.

"Our nightfire will call them," he said, his voice low and rich with the unmistakable pull of destiny. "Once they enter our world, our magic will control them. Fuel them. Give them life. They will answer only to us."

Aravind nodded, the corner of his mouth curling up into a smile.

Manish inhaled a long breath before he focused on the pool again.

They'd constructed it to help channel their magic. The water had been sourced from the sacred fountain of Pavitra Jal in Matsya with great difficulty and for an exorbitant amount of gold. Amongst many other traits, such as healing illnesses and curing drought, the holy water also allowed those with strong magic to tap into other worlds, acting as a conduit and helping one connect to the demon realm.

Aravind moved to the far side of the pool, peering across at his brother.

"Ready?" Manish asked, and he nodded.

"Mother will be pleased."

Manish nodded, his eyes glassing over. "I wish we could remember her."

"We will see her again," Aravind promised. "In another life."

Their mother had been possessed of a need for power, too. When the twins were young boys, they loved listening to stories about how she'd conquered territories and brought her enemies to their knees. Manish and Aravind knew she would have loved being here today, and though she'd been lost to the heavens for many years, they wanted to make her proud.

Manish nodded, and they both focused on the pool, stretching their hands out.

Aravind called upon the six anchors spinning in his heart, joining them to create his nightfire. It sparked at his fingertips before channeling out into ribbons of starry night.

It had always been the most beautiful sight.

The brothers focused their magic into the well, forcing it deep, sinking into the earth, questing for the hidden places where only the most sinister creatures dwelled.

Aravind could feel it. His magic burrowed down, funneling into another world where darkness and power reigned.

It took a few minutes before they heard the screams.

Their eyes met, and Aravind smiled before Manish returned it with a grin. They turned and ran for the door, stopping at the temple's steps.

The city had erupted into chaos. The sky was black, churning with smoky clouds as lightning, red as blood, flashed across the horizon.

Stars glowed like a million silver flames.

Taaranas echoed with fear and screams.

Then something appeared high in the mountains.

Light flashed across the stone as a portal of blackness darker than night opened and then spread to form a door large enough to accommodate a monster.

Or rather, a demon. Thousands of them.

Aravind could have wept.

They'd done it. After so many years of planning, they'd done it.

He met Manish's wide-eyed gaze as they returned their attention to the portal. As one, they raised their hands, filtering out streams of nightfire, channeling their magic into the world they sought.

Aravind felt it—the presence existing beyond this plane. The dark things living in a world that had been lost to time and memory but would soon reign again.

He called them. Invited them in.

There was a shift, and then came the moment when he knew everything was about to change.

Finally *they* appeared.

Larger than life, covered in armor, their sharp teeth glinting in the light. Fierce, deadly, and even more terrifying than Aravind's most vivid fantasies could have imagined.

The nairatta marched from the portal, forming a sinuous line as they wound down the mountain. They beat their chests and clanged their swords against their shields, the sound echoing through the barren landscape.

The people screamed—their cries rose over the sounds of thunder and the wet snarls of an army of demons arriving to destroy everything in their path.

Aravind dropped his hands, mesmerized by the sight. Then he looked at Manish, who stared into the distance, his mouth slack.

A moment later, he turned to Aravind, and their gazes met.

"We did it," he whispered.

Aravind nodded. "And now we will rule the world."

ONE

Zarya's hands gripped cold, slick scales as the soaring spires of her father's dark castle appeared in the distance. It stood in miniature, nestled into the mountains, contrasting rivers of pure white snow.

Rabin banked left, swooping over the crystalline landscape, and she clung on tighter as the wind tangled her hair and whistled in her ears. Ducking low, she shrugged deeper into the warmth of her hood.

Yasen and Miraan sat in a row behind her with Miraan's arms around Yasen's waist. They'd been flying for days as the sun had set and risen, taking only short breaks for Rabin to rest. Despite Miraan's best efforts to warm them with his magic, Zarya was frozen inside and out. Even her blood felt thicker, idling through her veins as she dreamed of wool blankets and roaring fires.

Rabin angled into a gentle descent, skimming over ice-capped lakes and an endless expanse of sparkling white. The sun hung low in the sky, a white orb glowing softly against a pale blue backdrop. The barest wisps of clouds hung in the air like the puffs of a giant's breath.

The endless Pathara Vala Mountains surrounded them like a wall—soaring peaks of dark grey stone streaked with veins of shimmering ice and jagged summits climbing so high they were lost to clouds of mist and fog.

Zarya had only viewed them at a distance from her balcony in Ishaan, and though they'd always been imposing, now they loomed larger than life. How could anything so colossal just *exist* without the entire continent collapsing under their weight?

Rabin flapped his wings with a crack, dipping with a stomach-lifting swoop as he arched over a range of foothills, once again revealing a sight that stuck in Zarya's chest.

There, it waited. *Andhera.*

He flapped again, dragging them towards the dubious future awaiting her as she began to make out the castle's dark towers and windows.

Andhera.

A few months ago, the name had meant almost nothing to her. It had been a distant place she'd rarely considered except inside her daydreams when she'd longed to travel and see the world. But then her entire life had been blown wide open, and despite so many warnings and reservations about what she would find here, everything kept pointing her north.

She'd sworn she'd never come.

She'd planned to keep her distance and stay as far away as possible.

But a part of her knew that was never true.

She'd only ever had two choices.

To hide—and she would never do that.

Or to run towards him and force the possible consequences *out* so she could confront her fears and worries.

So that she could get this over with.

Thus, here she was, arriving on his doorstep willingly and into *his* waiting arms.

Would she be welcomed? Would she find something she'd spent her entire life seeking? After the disappointment of meeting her family in Ishaan, would Andhera offer the belonging she sought?

Rabin had found a home here when he'd arrived all those years ago, and maybe none of that had been by chance. He'd been so *sure* about his fated connection to Zarya and her father.

Or was this all a trap?

Zarya no longer doubted Rabin's honesty. He'd bared himself to her, body and soul, and she trusted him implicitly. It had taken some time, but they'd bridged their divides. She believed everything he'd promised. He hadn't meant to betray her. He hadn't intended her any harm. But she still wasn't convinced Rabin saw the king of Andhera as clearly as he should.

She recalled his assurances that Abishek only wanted to know her, and she swallowed a needle of guilt as she thought of Row's warnings. She had planned to discuss it with him before deciding to meet her father, but there hadn't been an opportunity thanks to their hasty escape from Ishaan.

No matter what happened, Rabin would protect her with his life.

She peered over her shoulder at Yasen, watching silver strands whip across his reddened cheeks. He studied the barren landscape, his dark grey eyes assessing everything.

"You okay?" she called, and he met her gaze with a tight smile.

"Sure. I can't feel my balls anymore, but this is first-class travel all the way," he answered with a thumbs up.

She snorted as her attention fell to Miraan next, his features arranged into his signature stoic expression while he also gauged their surroundings with a wary eye.

Her brother. Half-brother.

Until a few weeks ago, she'd never even spoken with

another living soul who'd shared her blood, and now she had a brother and was set to meet the man who had helped *make* her.

She only hoped he wouldn't also ruin her.

Rabin soared over the castle, and Zarya leaned in, trying to get a better look. The formidable structure was made entirely of matte black stone that stood in harsh contrast to its white backdrop. Built with durability in mind, the thick walls were almost featureless except for long banks of windows wrapping around each corner.

From there, the practical design gave way to something more fanciful with hundreds of soaring towers connected through narrow bridges. Each column was inset with dozens of arched windows, likely added to welcome in beams of weak winter light.

She shivered, tucking the collar of her jacket tighter at the thought of the icy wind seeping through every crack on the coldest nights. Before they'd left the Saaya, Rabin had insisted on purchasing proper attire for their journey. She'd called him dramatic and overprotective, but as another blast of cold wind tore through her clothing, she realized he'd been right.

As they drew closer, Zarya made out the walled city surrounding the castle where the people of Andhera made their home. Unlike Rahajhan's other realms, Andhera had no main capital. Most of the region's population lived within these winding streets and its sturdy houses designed to withstand the bite of winter's chill.

Zarya had read enough about Andhera to know that a few mountain clans inhabited the caverns and passes at the Pathara Vala's higher altitudes. They were a hearty bunch who practiced their own customs and worshiped their own gods. They rarely came down to mingle with Andhera's citizens unless necessity forced them out.

Dozens of guards stood on the castle's ramparts, their faces

tipped up to monitor their approach. They traced Rabin's movements as he turned another loop.

He shook his head, his giant wings snapping before he lost
altitude. His trajectory curved downwards in a wide circle as he
aimed for the surface of a large flat tower where someone had
painted a massive black dragon with its wings spread out.

Zarya's heart twisted at the sight.

This really was his home. This really was where he
belonged.

And perhaps... it was where she belonged, too. The thought
eased a trickle of nervousness from the tense set of her shoulders as they continued their descent.

After another moment, Rabin landed softly with a thump,
his wings beating steadily before they collapsed at his sides.
Zarya and the others scrambled off before Rabin dissolved into a
puff of smoke and appeared again in his rakshasa form.

Something about witnessing him standing on this tower
overlooking the mountain valley made her chest ache. His dark
hair tossed in the breeze, and his black armor offered a stark
contrast to the blanket of white, almost like he'd been placed
here by a divine hand from the sky.

As if sensing her distress, he strode over and caught her in
the protection of his arms. He brushed a hand down her face.

"Are you okay?" he asked.

She started to nod and then stopped before shaking her
head. "I'm not sure. I don't know if I'm ready for this.
For... him."

Rabin pressed his nose to her temple and inhaled deeply. "I
swear everything will be fine." He pulled away. "You're sure
you're okay with... everything?"

Zarya pressed her mouth together and nodded.

Before leaving the Saaya, they agreed to keep their marriage
a secret from Abishek until they could find the right moment to
break the news. Rabin was worried about the king's reaction,

given he'd defied his orders to break off all romantic ties with Zarya. She'd been reluctant but also didn't want to ruin her first meeting with the king. They'd tell him when the time was right.

Yasen and Miraan had agreed to go along with their deception if that's what they wanted. Zarya didn't want to lie to anyone, but it was for the best, and this was only temporary.

"We'll tell him soon," Rabin assured her, tucking a lock of hair behind her ear.

"Then you should probably let go of me," she whispered.

He paused with his hand mid-air, his eyes flashing, before nodding and pulling away. The cold hit her then, and his absence left a hollow emptiness that did nothing to ease the tension vibrating through her frame.

He stepped back and gestured. "It will be a challenge not to touch you."

"We'll always have the mind plane," she promised, and he nodded, the softness in his eyes opposing the tense set of his jaw.

Rabin then turned to Yasen and Miraan. "You're both still with us?" he asked.

Yasen raised his hands. "Whatever you need. I'm not sure I understand, but you know what you're doing."

"Thank you," Rabin said, pressing a palm to his chest and dipping his chin.

Then he returned his attention to Zarya again. "Are you ready?"

"Please," Yasen said. "My cock is about to freeze off."

They smiled as he made a show of adjusting his crotch before crossing the roof. The wind howled across the mountains, almost sounding like ghosts. Zarya looked up, studying the pale sky. She squinted up at the castle and its high towers, noting the light reflecting off the windows with tiny flashes of silver.

She couldn't see the city from where they stood, but the

sounds of people going about their day floated up from below. The wind gusted, tearing at her long wool coat, screaming in her ears, almost as if it were trying to deliver a message. Or maybe a warning.

She shook off the sensation. She was just nervous.

A pair of sentries guarded the entrance. They bent at the waist, aiming their welcome at Rabin before turning to Zarya and the others.

"Welcome home, Lord Ravana," one said as they stepped aside and opened the door.

Rabin gestured for Zarya to enter, and they all filed into the dim interior of a small landing.

"This way," Rabin said, directing them towards a narrow spiral staircase. "I'm sure they've seen us coming and are already expecting us."

He inhaled a deep breath and then paused briefly before plunging down the stairs. Zarya hesitated for another moment before following, her stomach twisting with nerves as she spiraled lower.

Warm air drifted up, almost like an embrace. The black stones were hard under her feet, and she dragged a hand along the wall to steady herself, feeling the deep chill living in every crack and crevice.

She heard the clatter of Yasen and Miraan behind her, grateful to have them both along. She watched Rabin's dark head circle down, hoping he was right about all of this.

Hoping she hadn't made a huge mistake.

When they reached the bottom, they were greeted by a vanshaj man with silver hair who wore a tailored black sherwani. He stood with his hands behind his back and his nose up. Surrounding him were more guards.

Zarya swallowed at the sight of the stars collaring his throat, suddenly thrown off. She'd spent so many months around people who supported vanshaj freedom, but this was a reminder that their actions had only been a tiny fracture within a much larger battle they'd have to reconcile soon enough. She couldn't abandon what they'd started. And she'd never give up on this fight.

"Omar," Rabin said, his tone polite but devoid of emotion.

"My lord, you've brought guests," Omar replied, assessing Zarya and her party with a critical eye.

"I apologize for not alerting you," Rabin replied.

Omar sniffed. "What's done is done, though I hope we won't be making this a habit. I shall see to their rooms."

"Will you please place them in my wing? We've all been through a lot, and I'd prefer everyone remain close."

Omar tipped his chin in agreement.

"Thank you. Where is the king?" Rabin asked.

"In his throne room, my lord," he answered, eyeing Zarya, Yasen, and Miraan again. "He is most eager to meet your companions."

"This way," Rabin told them, and he turned left, leading them through the straight and orderly corridors.

Black stone stretched underfoot, and Zarya studied the dark walls covered with an array of colorful tapestries, some embroidered with geometric patterns, some with organic styles like flowers and vines, and others depicting a great city nestled within the mountains, the streets crowded with people, buildings, and life. Her eyes caught on a giant silver temple with a star floating above it, but they passed before she could examine it more closely.

The high ceilings were capped with curved glass, the edges covered in snow, offering a view of the watery blue sky. As they walked, Zarya caught a closer glimpse of Andhera's bustling city and the market below.

Rabin gave her a sidelong look. She wanted to reach out and take his hand, but to keep up this charade, they'd have to maintain a physical distance in both the king's presence and any of his people. She curled her fingers against her palms, her nails digging into flesh.

She understood Rabin's reservations, but it also stung in a way that she was trying to move past. This wasn't about her. This was far more complicated than her feelings.

Finally, after several minutes of walking, they turned a corner into a hallway so wide it could easily accommodate half a dozen wagons side by side. A massive black arch stood at the end, framing the entrance of a large room beyond.

"Ready?" Rabin asked, and Zarya swallowed the itchy lump in her throat.

Ready as she'd ever be.

They continued their stride, passing under the arch into a sprawling chamber lined with tall windows stretching several stories high. Black velvet curtains puddled on the silver-tiled floor, and the vaulted ceiling was adorned with thick beams of silver and painted with hundreds of colors, depicting what must have been a great battle.

She couldn't help staring up, wondering who had spent so many hours creating such a masterpiece. It was stunning, but she didn't really care about ancient battles, and her interest was feigned as she avoided the inevitable.

With a deep breath, she forced her gaze forward. The air and sound in the room suddenly evaporated. She took a step, and the click of her boots against the tiles was so loud she could feel it to the backs of her teeth.

At the far end of the room sat a massive black throne carved from what looked like marble veined with silver and gold. Given the grandness of the room, it was simple but regal, suggesting great power and influence.

Zarya stopped walking.

Suddenly, she couldn't will herself to take another step.

There he was.

Sitting on his throne, his posture casual, with one knee tossed over the other.

Abishek. King of Andhera. *Her father.*

He sat up straighter, his hands clutching the armrests as they assessed one another from across the room.

She wasn't entirely sure what she'd been picturing.

Someone with the same features. Someone with the same dark hair and eyes. What she *wanted* to see was something that proved she belonged to him. Something that confirmed beyond a shadow of a doubt that she belonged *here.*

She could sense Yasen and Rabin on either side, half a step back as they waited for her to react. She placed one foot in front of the other as the king slowly rose from his seat. Zarya briefly noted the woman dressed in fighting leathers standing on his left, her arms folded and her stance wide, before returning her attention to Abishek.

As the king watched her intensely, she slowly approached— another step and then another.

She stopped a few paces from the dais, and they stared at one another.

Tracing the shape of his nose and his mouth, she realized these *were* the pieces she'd inherited. This man was a part of her.

Maybe she still hadn't believed any of it was true.

Maybe a tiny part of her had still doubted until this very moment.

But suddenly, she understood that her arrival had always been inevitable, no matter her reservations or Row's warnings. She'd spent too much of her life wishing for a family to ignore that he lived and that he'd been *waiting* for her.

"Father," she whispered.

TWO

The word seemed to hang in the air, coalescing into something solid and malleable, dense but shapeable depending on what direction the wind blew. It tethered her to the floor, cementing her to the snow and mountains and gusts of cold air howling across the tundra.

Father.

There he stood, blinking as if also trying to convince himself she was real. He wore black leather pants and a black kurta, his wavy hair brushing the tops of his shoulders. Like all Aazheri, his appearance belied his age, but they *did* age, albeit slowly, and the finest lines hugged his forehead and the corners of his eyes. He was at least as old as Row—nearly ancient—a fact that became obvious in the bottomless depth of his assessing stare.

"We bring news from Gi'ana," Rabin said, bending at the waist and pressing a fist to his heart. "And as you can see, I also bring a few visitors who I think you will be pleased to meet."

"Is this... her?" Abishek asked, raking Zarya from head to toe. "Zarya?"

She nodded, tears pressing her eyes as she suddenly felt the strangest urge to cry.

Abishek took a slow step down the dais and paused, almost as if he was worried about approaching too quickly. She responded by moving an inch closer.

"Pleased indeed," he whispered, descending another step and then another before his boots hit the floor. Slowly, he neared, studying her face. She felt his assessment in how he took in each of her features.

Eyes. Nose. Mouth.

Hair. Head. Face.

He stopped and cocked his head.

"You look exactly like her," he said, but she couldn't determine the essence of that sentiment, good or bad.

She offered him a rueful twist of her lips. "So, I've been told."

Abishek huffed out a small breath that might have resembled a laugh. "Remarkable. Absolutely remarkable. When Rabindranath told me you existed, I couldn't quite believe it. Perhaps I didn't dare. A *child*. Though, you are already a grown woman."

Zarya nodded. "I didn't know of you until a few months ago, either."

"Because of Row," the king said. "And Asha, I suppose. Yes. I understand. Rabindranath told me everything."

She looked at Rabin, who dipped his chin.

"He took good care of you?" Abishek asked next.

She couldn't make out the tone of that question, either. "He did. He is my father in everything but blood."

She didn't know why she said it, but the subtext didn't go unnoticed, as demonstrated by a tightening around the king's mouth.

Maybe she was testing him already, wanting to understand how far she could push. He hadn't willingly abandoned her, but he had bridges to cross to earn her trust. She must remain on her guard despite her desire to build a family connected through blood.

Rabin trusted him, and she trusted that he believed no harm would come to her, but she couldn't be naive. Row and her mother had believed those terrible things for a reason, and she'd be a fool to disregard them entirely. But she couldn't deny the liquid pit in her heart that desperately wanted to know her only living parent. Anyone would feel the same.

"I'm grateful to him, then. And I'm... very glad you're here," Abishek said.

Zarya didn't miss the raw emotion in his voice. Was he happy to see her? Did he feel this longing ache in his chest, too?

"Please tell me you're staying. I would like to get to know you better very much."

Zarya exchanged a look with Rabin.

"Yes, but for a short time only," she answered. "I am needed back in Ishaan very soon. For now, though, it's best we keep our distance from Gi'ana."

Abishek finally turned his attention to the rest of their motley entourage, his dark gaze already calculating and assessing the situation.

"I hear reports of unrest," the king said. "Whispers of rebellion."

"That and so much more," she answered. "Please meet Prince Miraan Madan of the Gi'ana royal family. And my half-brother."

She stepped back as Miraan bowed and pressed his hands together before his heart.

"Your Majesty," he said. "We thank you for sheltering us in our time of need."

Abishek's brows pinched together in a gesture she could only interpret as unease before Zarya gestured to Yasen.

"And this is Lieutenant Yasen Varghese. Former Commander of Daragaab's army and my friend."

Abishek studied Yasen and then nodded before bowing to him with his hands pressed together. "Any friend of my daughter's is welcome in Andhera."

Daughter.

It felt strange to hear him say it so casually, like it was something they'd been to one another from the very start.

Yasen bowed. "Thank you."

Abishek turned and gestured to the woman waiting on the dais. "And allow me to introduce Commander Ekaja Bhari, chief of my armies."

Somehow, Zarya wasn't the least bit surprised to hear this fierce woman was Abishek's commander. Ekaja sauntered down the steps with a hand wrapped around the hilt of the sword belted at her hip and stopped, regarding Zarya with an arched eyebrow.

Her midnight hair was pulled into a high, braided ponytail. Her dark eyes were ringed in black kohl, and she wore fitted black leather that showed off just how many hours she'd spent in the training ring. Those sharp angles and high cheekbones would turn heads in any room she entered.

"So, you're the one he's been so moody about," Ekaja said with a smirk as she thumbed in Rabin's direction.

Zarya caught Rabin's scowl as she opened her mouth and then closed it. "I suppose?"

Ekaja barked out a laugh full of wicked mirth at Rabin's expense, and Zarya decided she liked this woman already.

"Well, it's nice to finally meet you in person," she said before deferring to her king again.

"I'm afraid we didn't have time to prepare a more welcoming feast," Abishek said. "Omar is rather put out, but he'll survive. I hope you'll join us for a humble dinner."

"We'd love that," Zarya said, confirming with nods to Yasen and Miraan.

"Wonderful." Abishek clapped his hands sharply twice, and

Omar materialized, almost as if from nothing. Again, Zarya couldn't tear her eyes from his star collar.

Abishek noticed her scrutiny, a deep furrow forming on his forehead. She quickly looked away, offering him what she hoped appeared to be a genuine smile. She sensed she'd have to tread carefully when revealing her part in the vanshaj rebellion.

After another moment, he addressed Omar. "We're ready for dinner."

Omar dipped into a deep bow and pressed his hands together. "Yes, Your Majesty. The solarium is ready for you."

"Come," Abishek said, "let us get to know one another over food and drink and fascinating conversation."

They all filed into a group with Abishek at the front. Behind him, Rabin and Ekaja walked next to one another, sharing looks Zarya couldn't interpret.

Zarya walked alone behind them while Yasen and Miraan followed. She kept glancing over her shoulder at Yasen, who offered her a series of cautious looks. Everything appeared fine. Abishek didn't *seem* like the monster she'd imagined, and if he meant her harm, why bother welcoming her? He had enough guards to easily overwhelm all four of them upon their arrival if that had been his intention.

As they walked, Abishek regaled them with details about the castle and the art surrounding them, explaining where he'd acquired each piece. It was obviously something he was very passionate about. They passed more tapestries of the same city she'd seen earlier. She again noted the great stepped building made of silver stone with the sparkling star suspended over it. She blinked as something sharp tugged in the layers of her subconscious. Almost like she'd stood on those very streets herself.

As Abishek continued speaking, she wanted to ask more about the images, but she couldn't get a word in edgewise. What had started as moderately interesting became wearisome as his monologue dragged on, and her thoughts drifted off.

She stared at Rabin's back and his stiff shoulders, trying to cast her mind into his. She wished she'd practiced more in Ishaan, but there wasn't much need. If she'd known they'd find themselves in Andhera, keeping their love a secret, she might have put more effort into communicating without fully entering the mind plane.

She recalled the helplessness she'd felt lying on the floor, being tortured by her sister, when she'd tried to reach for him and had been met with only silence. Her hand drifted to her throat, clutching at the emptiness where her mother's necklace had once hung. Dishani still had it—or so Zarya presumed. She wondered if there was any chance of recovering it. It felt like a piece of her was missing.

Now she could sense Rabin at least. His presence was there, buried deep in the layers of her subconscious. She couldn't quite reach him—there were too many distractions here—but at least it felt possible.

Finally, they arrived at a set of doors. A guard opened them, and they entered a large solarium with a glass ceiling and walls. Frost coated the panes, and snow gathered in the corners. Zarya looked up at the pale blue sky and the gentle wisps of clouds floating across the horizon.

Dozens of plants lined the space, surrounding them on every side, softening the stinging chill. In the center, a large table sat surrounded by six chairs, groaning with an abundance of food and drink.

She wondered what he considered a feast if *this* was a simple meal.

They all sat around the table, and she landed between Rabin and Abishek. She gave Rabin a questioning look, but his expression was unreadable. He seemed even more broody than usual.

When they were seated, a rush of servants entered the room to pour wine and dish out food. More vanshaj bearing the collar. They piled their plates high with coconut-dusted chicken, spiced potatoes, and poached fish swimming in saffron broth. Everything looked and smelled delicious, but Zarya was much too anxious to eat.

"Now, tell me everything," Abishek said. "I want to know every detail about you from the very beginning."

Zarya blinked nervously around the room. "I'm sure they don't want to hear all that."

"Nonsense," he said. "This is my table, and I will decide."

She pressed her mouth together and nodded before recounting the more salient parts of her upbringing. Abishek asked many questions, probing for more and delving into the pieces of her life. She noted Miraan's interest as he sat forward, nodding here and there. Ekaja also hung on her every word but in a cool and detached way, like she was cataloging every fact, should she need them later.

Rabin listened intently while Yasen looked like he might fall asleep. He already knew all of this, and she didn't blame him one bit.

When she was done, Abishek chewed on her words, his expression pensive. The sun was setting now, and servants entered to light the tall candelabras circling the room's perimeter.

When his questions focused on her time in Ishaan, she confessed a few details about what they'd been doing and their role in the rebellion. She mentioned the collars but not how they were specifically related to her magic or the sixth anchor. She hoped to discuss it with him in private so that she might ask about her visions, too.

Surrounded by the others, she wasn't ready to reveal this secret.

She studied his reaction to freeing the vanshaj but couldn't read his expression. In the short time she'd been here, she was already discovering that he was a closed book unless he chose to reveal himself. Vanshaj servants surrounded them, and that alone told her where he stood on the issue. But was he like the Madans, clinging to this archaic practice by the very edges of his fingernails, or was he open to being convinced there was another way?

She also confessed that they'd fled to Andhera because they feared Dishani's wrath and what she might do to Zarya and Miraan.

Abishek took it all in stride, almost as if he'd heard it before.

"Tell me about being masatara and paramadhar," he said, folding his hands on the table and leaning forward. Zarya and the king glanced at Rabin as she waited for him to take the lead. How did he want to reveal this, and how much did he want to share?

"What would you like to know?" Rabin asked.

"Do you intend to perform the Bandhan? Kishore could start preparations as soon as he returns from an errand he is currently tending for me." He turned to Zarya. "He is my personal mystic."

Rabin's gaze jumped to Zarya, the corners of his lips pressing together before he met his mentor's gaze. "We have already completed it," Rabin said. "In Ishaan."

Abishek's eyebrows pulled together as his gaze traveled over Rabin's face. "I see. Did you not think to consult with me on this first?"

Rabin exchanged another look with Zarya. She squeezed her thighs, her defenses rising at Abishek's tone, almost like he was chastising a toddler and not speaking with a grown warrior.

"It was necessary to aid the rebellion. And we did not want to delay."

Abishek leaned on his elbows. "I'm not sure I understand."

Rabin was about to speak, perhaps to apologize or explain

everything, but Zarya interrupted. She had already sensed that she might need to intervene when it came to Rabin and the king, and that was already being confirmed.

"It was *our* decision to make. We chose this. Together. And our reasons are our own."

Abishek's gaze moved to her, his expression flattening.

She stared at him, refusing to feel anything but indignant that he thought it was his place to question *their* choices. He'd met her all of ten minutes ago, and Rabin wasn't even technically his subject or a citizen of this realm. She was beginning to understand why Rabin insisted on keeping their marriage a secret.

"Of course," Abishek said, his expression softening. "I am only surprised as I thought you would take some time to consider it." He looked at Rabin. "It is a rather big decision to make. One that could have far-reaching consequences."

"One I made willingly," Rabin offered immediately, and Abishek nodded.

"I'm sorry," he said, addressing Zarya now. "I'm new to being a parent. It seems I have much to learn."

She returned his nod, trying to rein in her annoyance. "I've managed on my own so far."

"Forgive me," Abishek said, pressing both hands to his heart. "I did not mean to overstep."

Zarya studied him for a moment, sensing his remorse was genuine, before tipping him a small smile. "It's fine. I'm sure we both have a few things to learn."

"Kishore is considered the most skilled of his kind. I would have been happy to offer his services," he continued.

She did her best to affect a pleasant smile. "That's kind of you, but again, we managed fine."

"Would you allow him to examine the bond once he returns? I'd prefer if he ensured it was done properly."

Zarya's mouth opened. Thriti had seemed more than

competent, and Zarya was sure the mystic had known exactly what she'd been doing.

"Please," Abishek asked. "It would make me happy."

She found herself nodding. "Sure. Of course. As long as Rabin is okay with it."

Rabin nodded, and Abishek smiled. "Wonderful—he's eager to meet you."

Zarya waited for him to elaborate on why that was or why it mattered, but instead, he swept out a hand and called for dessert. They spent the next hour drinking and eating while Abishek asked questions of Yasen and Miraan, delving into the details of their lives. He seemed genuinely interested and concerned for all of them.

As they ate, Zarya finally felt herself relaxing.

She'd been so nervous about arriving, but the king wasn't what she'd expected at all. Yes, he was a bit overprotective and perhaps a little autocratic, for lack of a better term, but he was a king, and that was his nature.

But he also seemed genuine in his eagerness to know her, and she didn't sense anything sinister or amiss despite all of Row's warnings. How he engaged with Miraan and Yasen also suggested a sincere person living under his somewhat abrupt exterior.

When everyone had eaten their fill, Abishek turned to Zarya again.

"I would love to talk more about your nightfire," he said. "I'm still somewhat in awe that Asha's prophecy was fulfilled after all this time."

Zarya hesitated, searching for any hidden meanings in the question. Row had been so sure Abishek would want her nightfire.

"What would you like to know?" she asked carefully.

"More about how it works. If you are willing, I'd love to see it. I've read the accounts of the Ashvins and the way they described it. As Rabindranath has probably explained, I've always been fascinated with magic of all kinds. Particularly a gift as rare and ancient as this."

"He did. I also have some questions to that end."

"Of course. I'm happy to share whatever I can." He clapped his hands together. "I do hope you'll all stay for a while. You're welcome to remain for as long as you need, and you'll be safe within my walls."

Zarya swallowed the sudden knot in her throat.

She'd expected to feel every emotion when meeting her father. She hadn't been given much time to prepare for this, and they all crowded for space in her heart.

Abishek looked at Zarya again, a soft smile crinkling the corners of his eyes. He raised a glass and tipped it to everyone seated around the table, finishing with her.

"Welcome, my daughter. I am so very pleased that you've finally come home."

THREE

Rabin was tense, his shoulders tight and his guard up. A return to Andhera usually expanded his lungs with relief and fresh, clean breaths, but when those mountains had come into view hours earlier, he'd been seized with a sense of ominous premonition.

He'd nearly turned back at that very moment but convinced himself he was being ridiculous. Row's warnings had crept under his skin, and he was letting them get the best of him.

Besides, they truly had nowhere else to go right now.

He took a sip of his drink, studying his mentor. Rabin had convinced Zarya to come, but something itched at the back of his intuition. He'd been so focused on finding her. On bringing her to this place where he'd felt such peace that maybe he'd talked himself into something he never should have.

But Abishek was more than pleased to see Zarya, and there was a light in the king's eyes that Rabin had never seen before. Immediately, he felt guilty for his uncharitable thoughts. Abishek had saved his life. He was a complicated man, of course, but he wasn't a monster.

The group continued chattering around the table in Abishek's solarium, but Rabin could see how exhausted Zarya, Yasen, and Miraan were thanks to the dark circles ringing their eyes.

As Rabin took another sip of wine, Abishek gave him a look that suggested he was displeased. Rabin wasn't surprised by the king's reaction to their completing the Bandhan without his input. But if he'd wanted them to wait, why hadn't he said so when Rabin left to find Zarya? Did Abishek think Rabin couldn't or wouldn't make his own decisions?

"Zarya," Abishek said after another few minutes. "You and your companions must be exhausted, and I've kept you talking for much too long."

Zarya shook her head. "Oh no, it's fi—" A yawn cracked from her mouth mid-sentence, and she covered it with the back of her hand. "I suppose we could use some rest."

Abishek gave her a soft smile. "Of course. Omar will see you to your rooms." He then glanced at the door where Omar was already waiting with his hands behind his back.

"Good night, then," Zarya said, standing up. "It was nice to... meet you."

She stared at Abishek for a moment and then blinked before her gaze met Rabin's. He could see the shine of tears in her eyes, and he inhaled a deep breath.

Then Omar turned as Ekaja joined the four of them, leaving the king alone in his solarium.

Ekaja marched alongside Rabin, her posture erect as she stole curious glances his way. She knew he was hiding something. She could read him like a book. Honestly, he was surprised Abishek hadn't picked up on it already, but he'd been so captivated by Zarya that perhaps it had thrown him off.

Rabin left Omar to see Zarya and the others to their rooms before ducking into his own. He unbuckled his weapons and stripped out of his leather armor, leaving him in a thin cotton shirt and leather pants. He shook out his hair and rolled his neck before toeing off his boots and striding over to the window.

Scanning the snowy landscape sparkling under the light of the stars and moon, he inhaled a deep breath, trying to find that calming place. But he couldn't relax.

Something was nagging him, but he didn't understand what.

He was just nervous. He'd wanted their meeting to go well. And mostly, it had. Abishek had always been quick to anger when he didn't get his way, even if the other side had no way of knowing they'd caused offense.

Rabin was just feeling the weight and the responsibility of bringing Zarya to Andhera. He'd said he'd protect her and meant it with every breath. Now he lived with his duty to never let her down.

A sharp rap came at his door, and he spun around.

Ekaja didn't wait for an invitation. She never did. This impatient knock was actually more than she usually bothered with. The door swung open, and she strode in, sauntering towards the window as he turned to face the glass again. She stopped beside him, and together, they stared into the dark, starry night.

"So," she said.

"So?"

"You brought her here."

He looked over to meet her gaze. "And?"

Ekaja shrugged. "You're hiding this from him?"

"I'm not hiding anything," he said a little too quickly, and she smirked.

"Sure."

He ran a hand along the back of his neck and exhaled a long breath. He'd already told Ekaja too much about Zarya, but he trusted her to keep his secrets to herself.

Unfortunately, the king was far too versed in sniffing out

treachery, and Rabin hoped they could keep their marriage a secret long enough to break the news to the king gently. After his reaction to completing the Bandhan without his consent, Rabin was more worried than ever about defying Abishek's orders.

"It's our business alone and has nothing to do with the king."

Ekaja nodded. "Then I hope you understand what you're doing. I *know* he gave you an order."

"One that was completely unreasonable," Rabin growled.

She shrugged again before saying, "She's pretty."

Rabin blew out a sigh. "I know. I don't deserve her."

"Relax," she responded with a scoff. "It's obvious she's in love with you, for whatever reason."

Rabin's heart twisted with those words.

"But now I see why she's had you so moody. Even more so than usual, I mean."

He snorted a dry laugh as they fell into a comfortable silence.

Another knock came at the door, this one more tentative. Rabin spun on his heel and crossed the room, whipping it open to find Zarya standing on the other side.

"Spitfire," he breathed, the tightness in his chest suddenly loosening.

"I wanted to say good night," she said, her gaze moving past him.

Ekaja stood with her arms crossed and her hip cocked regarding them with her usual piercing scrutiny.

"Hi," Zarya said. "We didn't get much chance to talk at dinner. It's nice to meet you."

"You too," Ekaja replied. "I've heard a lot about you."

Zarya's gaze went to Rabin. "That's... nice?"

Ekaja laughed and then strode over to clap him on the shoulder. "Zarya, Rabin tells me you're good with a sword."

Zarya arched a brow and assessed Ekaja from head to toe. "I can hold my own."

"Care for some sparring after some rest?"

Zarya grinned and nodded. "I'd love that."

"Perfect." Then Ekaja pressed the tips of her fingers to her mouth and blew them both a kiss before leaving and closing the door behind her.

"She seems intense," Zarya said, and Rabin snorted another dry laugh.

"You have no idea." Then he grabbed Zarya's wrist and hauled her against him. "I missed you," he said, and she smiled.

"I missed you, too."

"Are you okay?" he asked. "Everything is okay?"

"Yeah. I think so. It was a little overwhelming, and he's *also* intense, and I have no idea how the three of you live here together without this place imploding, but..." She paused and searched his face. "It was also nice."

Rabin brushed a lock of hair off her forehead and cupped her cheek.

"And what will you tell him about your magic when he asks? I know what Row said about your nightfire..."

Something wary moved behind her eyes. "That's part of why I agreed to come here. If he knows as much about magic as you say, I have some questions I'd like to ask."

He thought often about what she'd done to his flowers in Daragaab. She was obviously struggling to explain it, but Rabin wasn't hurt that she hadn't confided in him yet—he understood what it was like to carry something inside you that you weren't ready to share.

"And what about the vanshaj?"

She chewed her bottom lip. "How do you think he'd react if I told him everything? The secret is out now. I'm not sure why we need to hide what the sixth anchor or my nightfire are capable of."

Rabin blew out a breath. "I don't know how he'll react."

Zarya cocked a head. "Can you guess?"

"Honestly, I think he'll be fascinated by the process more than anything. That could trump any reservations he might have."

"Then I'll work with that. Anything is better than the outright antagonism of Dishani and the Madans," Zarya said.

She extricated herself from his hold and turned to face the room, her gaze sliding over the bed and the windows, the fire crackling in the hearth. She took a few steps. "This is where you brought me that night."

He didn't reply as she approached the desk they'd used as a shield between them. She picked up the same dagger she'd threatened him with, a small smile playing on her lips.

Holding it up, she twisted it left and right, admiring the gleam in the firelight. Then she looked over with a spark in her eyes.

"What's on your mind, Spitfire?" he asked, his voice dropping low.

She winked and then turned towards the window, staring out as he watched her. Her midnight hair fell in soft waves down her back, reflecting orange in the firelight. She lifted a hand and pressed it to the glass.

"It's so cold," she whispered, and Rabin walked up behind her, laying a hand on the curve of her waist. "But... beautiful."

"That's how I've always felt about it, too," he answered.

They stood silently for a minute, staring at the sparkling landscape together. This was all he'd wanted. Zarya in this place beside him. Eventually, they'd tell Abishek everything, and there would be no more secrets between any of them.

"What did you think of him?" Rabin finally asked.

She looked up. "He's not what I expected. He seemed genuinely pleased to meet me."

"He is," Rabin said, meaning it. "You made him very happy today."

"He behaved a bit strangely when he asked about the Bandhan."

"He likes to be the one in control. And I can tell he's already possessive of you."

She nodded. "I guess I'm used to men thinking they know what's best for me," she said wryly. There wasn't any bitterness in it, but he understood why she felt that way.

"And now what?" she asked. "You wanted to keep this a secret. How will he react if he finds out we were also married without him?"

Rabin gave her a rueful look. "Possibly the same."

She shook her head. "So, I guess we should decide *how* we tell him because we can't keep this a secret forever."

"*If* we tell him."

Zarya frowned. "You don't want to?"

"Let's just play it by ear, okay?"

She gave him a searching look. "This whole thing feels a little strange."

He nodded. "I understand. It will take us all some time to adjust."

"Does Ekaja know?"

He tipped his head. "She... suspects."

"And she'll keep it to herself?"

He nodded. "We've been friends for many years. She can be trusted."

"Okay. So now what? I suppose I should return to my room for appearance's sake."

He captured her chin between his thumb and finger. "I'll hate every moment you aren't by my side."

She gave him a tipped smile and then stretched up to kiss him. "Good thing we have our dreams. I love you."

When she was gone, Rabin returned to the window, staring out before exhaling a long breath.

This is what he'd wanted. This is what he'd planned for months.

So why did everything he was doing suddenly feel wrong?

FOUR

After leaving Rabin's room, Zarya crossed the hall to her own. It was similar to his, furnished with a large black bed and velvet upholstered chairs and divans, along with plush rugs made of colorful threads, woven with gold to cushion her feet.

She unlaced her boots and stretched her toes before warming her hands by the fire. Someone had turned down the bed and left a pile of clothing on the end. She found a warm pair of pajamas, socks, and a thick robe, all clearly designed for this climate.

After a hot shower, she changed and tucked herself under the covers, preparing to find Rabin in the mind plane. She was exhausted and still recovering from what she'd suffered at her sister's hands, but she craved the reassurance of reaching him in her dreams, even if only for a moment.

Instead of their usual forest, she took a page from his book, imagining the same cold, snowy mountains where he'd summoned her weeks ago. She pictured the same fur rug and visualized them in heavy, warm clothing.

It didn't take long to find herself standing under the sky, the wind tugging at her hair. Rabin already waited a few feet away, his head cocked, and his brow arched in that way that always made her a little weak in the knees.

"When you said you'd see me later, I was hoping it would be in an environment a little more conducive to being naked," he said, and Zarya laughed.

She strode towards him before he folded her into his arms.

"I hope you don't mind. I'm tired, and I just wanted one more goodnight kiss."

He smirked. "Anything you need, Spitfire."

He leaned down, pressing his lips to hers. Despite the cold and the icy breeze whipping at wayward strands of hair, his warmth filtered into her blood, heating her from the inside. His kiss was slow and soft but also deep, his tongue probing her mouth and their lips sliding together. It was the kiss she needed after all the uncertainty of the past week. It was a kiss that reminded her of what was solid and real—unshakeable and constant as the stars sparking against the velvet night.

Then she felt the strangest... *tug.*

A hook jerked behind her navel, yanking her back with a snap. Rabin flashed away, the world around her dissolving into smears of muted color.

Suddenly, she was standing somewhere else.

But this wasn't the mind plane. It wasn't anything she recognized.

She stood in a small round room, the edges caked with dust and grime. A woman was huddled on the floor, leaning against the wall, her knees drawn up and her arms wrapped around them.

She shivered in her threadbare rags, and her dark hair hung thin and limp over scarred, bony shoulders. Zarya blinked, attempting to reconcile the strange sight. She tried to move closer, but all she could do was watch. Slowly, she turned in a circle, hoping to orient herself.

A bright golden glow flashed in the corner of her eye. She

spun around to catch the shape of a woman wearing a golden sari with dark flowing hair, her burnished skin like she'd been lit within by the sun. Zarya blinked, and then she was gone.

Again, she turned to find herself facing the huddling woman.

Zarya tried to reach for her, but she couldn't.

"Hello?" she called, her voice distant and hollow, echoing into nothing.

Then the woman looked up, staring straight through Zarya with dull, empty eyes.

A sharp breath snagged in her chest.

Her heart almost stopped.

She *knew* that face.

A moment later, someone was shaking her.

"Zarya?" came Rabin's rough voice. "Are you okay?"

Her eyes flew open, and she was now back inside her father's castle. Rabin leaned over her, dressed for sleep, his eyes wild with worry.

"Are you okay?" he asked again. "What happened?"

She clutched his arm, her fingers digging into his skin. They'd been torn from the mind plane right before that strange dream. She rubbed her stomach, remembering that hook ripping her away. "I'm not sure. Did you feel that, too?"

He sank next to her, stretching out on the blanket. "I did. Like something was pulling us apart."

She exhaled a short breath. "Do you remember reading about anything like this in the handbook?"

He shook his head. "Never. Try entering again. See what happens."

She nodded and closed her eyes, searching for that glimmering spot in the mind plane indicating his presence, but she couldn't find it. All she saw was darkness. Her eyes opened a second later. "It's gone."

"What do you mean, it's *gone*?"

Her brows drew together. "It's like when I was in the palace with Dishani. I can't feel it anymore. It's just blank."

"But your magic is fine?" he asked.

She checked in with her anchors. "It's fine."

He ran a hand over his face. "What does this mean?"

"Maybe we can ask the king about this, too."

Rabin blew out a breath, running his hand along the back of his neck. "Yeah, I suppose." His expression was guarded, his eyes dark with distress.

She took his hand and squeezed it.

They sat quietly for a long minute, both stewing in their thoughts.

"I don't like this," she said. "I hate being separated from you."

He reached over to cup the side of her face. "I'll just be across the hall. I swear nothing can hurt you here."

She sighed and shook her head. "Yeah. I'm just a little shaken. That felt... awful."

"We'll get to the bottom of this." He pressed his lips to hers and then shuffled off the bed. "Good night," he said, leaning down to plant another kiss on her temple, his lips lingering as though he couldn't bear to leave, before he stood and turned around, giving her one last look before he closed the door.

Once he was gone, she stared around the dark room for a long while. The curtains hung open to reveal a gentle fall of snowflakes drifting from the sky. She rubbed her stomach again.

It felt like everything was going wrong lately.

Finally, she lay back down, tucking the blanket up to her chin.

It was then she recalled the vision of that stone tower with the woman huddling in the corner. She'd been covered in scars, starved, left for dead, or worse.

Someone had *hurt* her.

Zarya remembered the moment the woman looked up. She

knew those dark eyes with that groove between her brows. That face that resembled hers so much.

It sounded impossible.

Ludicrous.

But she was almost certain the woman had been... her mother.

FIVE

Zarya awoke to the sound of frantic pounding on her door. She'd slept surprisingly well, given all of her worries and reservations. She'd fallen asleep to the image of her mother's haunted eyes and the sound of the wind howling off the mountaintops, lulling her into a deep, dreamless sleep.

"Zee!" came Yasen's voice. "Zee!"

"What!" she shouted. "I was sleeping!"

The door swung open, revealing Miraan and Yasen. Her half-brother clutched a piece of paper.

"I didn't say come in," Zarya grumbled as she tucked the blankets around her to ward off the morning chill. When she'd fallen asleep, the fire had been roaring with the crackle of logs, and now, it sat smoldering with glowing embers.

"We received a letter from Ishaan," Miraan said. He scanned the page while pacing back and forth, running a hand through his dark hair. He'd been so stoic and composed the first time she'd seen him, but she was learning that was all a front. He wore his emotions as strongly as she did.

"And?" Zarya asked. "What's wrong? Has something happened?"

"The city is in chaos. They're tearing down buildings. My family fears for their lives." The distress in his voice was evident as he continued pacing, still reading the note as if he could find answers hidden between the lines. "I did this. I caused this mess."

Resigned to the end of her slumber, Zarya pushed off her blanket and stood from the bed, reaching for her robe. "You didn't. This is all a result of *their* actions, not yours. We were only reacting to the situation *they* created."

"But I was a part of building that," he mourned. "I allowed this cruelty to flourish unchecked for years before I tried to do a damn thing about it. I am complicit, too, and when things couldn't possibly be any worse, I upped and *left*."

"I'm no expert, but I *probably* wouldn't say stuff like 'couldn't possibly be any worse,'" Yasen said as he dropped into a chair by the fire.

That earned him a glare from Miraan while Zarya blew out a breath, conceding that some of what Miraan was saying *was* technically true. But he was already beating himself up enough.

"So, what do you want to do?" Yasen asked, sitting forward in his seat.

"We must return," Miraan said, running a hand down his face. "I understand our initial reasons for fleeing, but I can't abandon my home to this chaos. None of this would have started if I hadn't been funding the Phoenix."

Yasen's mouth pressed into a line, and Zarya noted the worry flashing across his grey eyes. Miraan had come to mean something to him, even if he'd probably refuse to admit it.

"Dishani will kill you if you go anywhere near Ishaan. You *confessed* your role in funding the resistance. Like a complete fool, I might add," Yasen said.

Miraan gave him a miserable look. "I had no choice. I couldn't hide it anymore, and I can't sit here like a coward while my home is on the brink of collapse. I couldn't live with myself if the city falls or if anything happens to my family."

"It's too dangerous," Yasen argued. "You'll get yourself killed."

Miraan exhaled a breath of frustration as he dropped into the chair opposite Yasen. He tipped forward and planted his elbows on his knees before gripping his hair, the letter crumpling under his grip.

Another knock came at the door, and they all looked up before Miraan fell back, covering his eyes with a hand.

Zarya walked over to find a vanshaj servant on the other side.

She had to discuss their situation with Abishek. What would he say when he understood the true strength of nightfire? How would he react if she asked to start freeing vanshaj while she was in Andhera?

"Breakfast, Your Highness?" the woman asked, standing behind a cart laden with silver-covered dishes and a pot of tea.

Zarya nearly tripped on her tongue. "Highness?" she croaked.

The woman blinked, a wrinkle forming between her brown eyes. "You are the king's daughter, yes?" she asked, her question somewhat tentative. "That's what they're claiming in the vanshaj wing."

Zarya exhaled a breath. "I... yes... I suppose I am. But that doesn't make me anything."

The woman straightened her shoulders and lifted her chin. "It makes you a princess of Andhera," she said matter-of-factly.

Without awaiting further instruction, she pushed her cart into the room. Yes, technically, Zarya *was* a princess, she supposed. But that was only on paper. The very thought was too far-fetched and bewildering to comprehend.

The woman stopped the cart in the center of the room,

placed her hands at her heart, and dipped her chin. "If you need anything, I am here to assist."

"What's your name?" Zarya asked.

"I'm Urvi."

Zarya returned her bow by pressing her hands together. "It's nice to meet you, Urvi."

"Your Highness," Urvi repeated firmly before she departed the room.

When Zarya turned around, Yasen wore a shit-eating grin, his eyes dancing with amusement.

He pressed his hands together and adopted a high-brow expression. "Your Highness," he said in a snooty voice.

"Oh, shut up," she said. "We're just visiting. I'm not staying here, and I'm not a princess."

Yasen snickered. "Whatever you say, Zee."

"Tea?" she asked.

Miraan was still slumped in his chair, an elbow propped on the arm as he stared listlessly at the fire. She brought him a cup, and he turned to look at her, blinking as if shocked to discover he wasn't alone. Then he accepted it.

"Thank you."

Zarya finished passing out cups and food and sat on the divan.

"What do you want to do, Miraan?" she asked. "I want to return, too, but I'd like to spend at least a few days here. I have some questions for my father."

Finally, he sat up. "I know we said we should keep our distance from Dishani, but I didn't expect things to turn this bad. I hoped the rioting would settle, and we'd have time to let her cool off." He rubbed a hand across his face.

"Have we heard from Vikas and the others? How are things with the Phoenix?" she asked.

"He confirms the same," Yasen said. "But their situation is tense. It turns out someone within the Phoenix's ranks betrayed us to the Jadugara. It wasn't an accident they discovered the collars the morning of the execution."

"Gods," Zarya breathed. "Why?"

"Money," Yasen said. "The reward was too much to resist, I suppose."

"What about Operation Starbreak?"

Yasen shook his head. "They're currently evacuating vulnerable vanshaj out of the city and setting up a temporary encampment. Ishaan isn't safe for them. The Jadugara have been conducting sweeps, trying to track down any Taara Aazheri."

"Taara Aazheri?" she asked.

"That's the name Vikas came up with," he said. "To refer to those who once wore the collar."

"What about those without magic?"

"They all have it," Yasen said. "Vikas said it's just taken time for some of them to find it."

Zarya expelled a quiet breath at that. They *all* had it.

Taara Aazheri. Something to signify their change and honor the lives they'd escaped. Something that heralded the people they'd been and the people they now were. She loved it.

"Are they still breaking collars, then?" Zarya asked.

"They're pausing for a bit," Yasen said. "Vikas and Farida thought it best."

Zarya bit the corner of her lip, worried for everyone left in Ishaan.

"We'll find somewhere safe to hide," Miraan said. "I have friends in the city. At least until we understand what's happening and figure out how to approach my sister."

"Have you heard how she's doing?" Zarya asked, her tone somewhat uncertain.

She couldn't get the image of Dishani's ruined face and body out of her head. Rabin had done it to avenge Zarya, and anyone might argue that Dishani deserved it, but Zarya couldn't deny her complicated feelings for her half-sister.

"In bad shape," Miraan answered. "But they aren't in immediate danger despite the target on their backs. The palace is well-guarded to withstand any sort of attack. Still, I worry because even the nobles are withdrawing support. I'll be the first to admit they're fickle when the winds of power change, and no one wants to be left on the wrong side of history. My family has earned everything they're getting and worse. We all do, but I still worry for them."

They sipped their chai silently for a few minutes, lost in their thoughts.

"I'm to meet with the king today," Zarya said. "I want to discuss my magic and tell him more about the collars."

Miraan gave her a skeptical look. "Do you think that's wise?"

She shrugged. "Honestly, I'm not sure, but I have questions I need answered, and I think he might be the only one who can give me that. If he doesn't react the way I hope, we'll leave and return to Ishaan. How does that sound? I also understand our reasons for fleeing, but you're right, and we can't abandon them."

Miraan nodded. "And what if he's amenable to it? What if he agrees with our cause and is willing to do something about it?"

Zarya took a sip of her tea and peered up at her brother. "Then perhaps a powerful king on our side would help us end this once and for all."

SIX

Yasen and Miraan stayed for breakfast, but it was a quiet affair with everyone lost in their thoughts.

Amongst her many worries about Ishaan, Zarya couldn't stop thinking of how she'd been cut off from the mind plane or the strange dream with her mother. And who was that glowing woman she'd seen in the corner?

She considered sharing the details of her dream with Miraan but stopped herself. He was already distressed, and what if she was wrong? What if it was someone else?

Besides, something about saying it out loud felt ludicrous. He'd *known* Asha. She'd been his real mother. He'd loved her and been loved by her, while Zarya had little right to claim a connection with the woman who had borne them both. *Miraan* had been the one who'd lost her, while Zarya had never even met her.

When they'd all had their fill, Yasen and the prince stood, prepared to return to their rooms, though Miraan was still clearly agitated and struggling with his guilt.

"Why don't you check out the city?" Zarya suggested. "Take your mind off things?"

"Maybe," Miraan said.

Yasen offered Zarya an *I'll take care of him* look and steered the prince out. She understood why he wanted to return home, but they had to be careful. Dishani undoubtedly had people searching for them, and the princess would have endless reach and resources to draw upon.

Still, Miraan wasn't without power. Perhaps he could shield the rebellion for long enough to bring Ishaan under control. But could he do that from so far away? And what did control even look like? Zarya was sure this couldn't end without a complete and total overthrow of everything they'd ever known.

She dressed in a dark blue salwar kameez that Urvi had provided and prepared to meet with her father. When she opened her door, Rabin was already waiting, freshly shaven and showered, wearing a black kurta and leather pants.

"Morning," she said.

"Spitfire," he answered in that low, growly voice that did scandalous things to her insides. She wasn't sure how long she could pretend he meant nothing to her, especially without access to the mind plane.

"Rabin," she said. "Before we go, I want you to know that I plan to tell the king some things I haven't shared with you yet. But it's time you heard them because you have a right to know. Plus, after what happened last night..."

He stared at her briefly, and she wondered if he was hurt or angry that she hadn't shared all her secrets with him yet. But he dipped his chin. "Then let's go. The king doesn't like to be kept waiting."

"Why doesn't that surprise me?" she quipped with a roll of her eyes as he held out his arm.

With their elbows looped, he led her through the castle and its many black stone corridors. Almost every surface was overlaid with colorful rugs and tapestries, expertly woven with battle scenes and significant moments in Andhera's history.

She stopped when she noticed one depicting Abishek standing on the dais with hundreds of people surrounding him in his throne room.

"His coronation," Rabin said, catching the direction of her stare. "His father passed away many centuries ago. He, too, was a very powerful Aazheri."

His father. Zarya's *grandfather*.

She blinked, suddenly feeling the weight of her nameless history. She was connected to an entire network of people she'd never known and never would. Who else was out there waiting to meet her?

"How did he die?" she asked.

"He was much like the king and often experimented with magic. He was found dead in his study, and there was barely any of him left. We can only guess how he met his end, but some say he grew careless and played with forces beyond his grasp."

Her brow furrowed at the grisly image before she inhaled a deep breath and nodded. "Let's go."

They continued their way through the castle, passing numerous vanshaj servants and guards, all dressed in black and stationed at various corners. Their expressions suggested they weren't entirely sure what to make of either of them.

"Can we see the city before we leave?" she asked Rabin as they passed a window, revealing the busy streets below. She couldn't bear the thought of missing out on a quick visit.

"Of course," Rabin said. "Yasen and Miraan are headed down there now. We can join them for lunch in a few hours."

"They want to return to Ishaan right away," she said.

"I know. Miraan shared his worries with me. He's... troubled."

"I'd say he's more than that," she answered as they rounded another corner.

"Do you want to join them?" Rabin asked. "Now that you're here, how do you feel about staying for a while?"

The question was guarded, almost as if he was probing for a specific answer.

"I do want to return. I want to spend time here, too, but I'm worried about the Phoenix. I promised Miraan we'd leave once I get the answers I need."

Rabin nodded. "We won't abandon them. We will return to finish what we started."

She squeezed his bicep. "We knew our visit was only temporary. I just didn't count on having to leave so soon."

Finally, they came to a stop before a set of wide doors flanked by two armed soldiers. After bending at the waist, one opened a door, and Zarya and Rabin entered a long, wide hallway made of black stone and adorned with colorful enamel art, directly contrasting the monotone hues of Andhera's landscape.

Rabin led her to another door and opened it to reveal a massive library. She noticed how comfortable he was within these walls. How he entered rooms without invitation and walked the halls like he knew every corner.

Her eyes widened at the sight of dozens and dozens of high shelves crammed with books. They stretched back as far as she could see. It was massive, nearly rivaling the Jai Palace library in its scale.

The sound of footsteps drew her attention to Abishek, also dressed in black with his hair tied at his nape. She stared at him for several long seconds, again searching for a resemblance in his features. Everyone claimed she looked like Asha, but Zarya found herself in the slope of his nose and the shape of his eyes, too.

Her thoughts wandered back to the tormented Asha she'd seen in her dreams before she shook the image away.

"I see you're admiring my collection," Abishek said with a pleased smile. "It's taken many centuries to gather these texts. It's one of the most comprehensive magical resources in the continent."

She scanned the shelves, wishing she could spend hours losing herself in the pages. "How does it compare to Dharati's library?" she asked as she ran her hand along a shelf, reading the various titles stamped in gold.

Abishek chuckled at that. "Let's just say I could give them a run for their riches," he answered. "However, their collection includes a few items I wouldn't mind getting my hands on."

Zarya glanced at the doorway where Rabin stood silently, thinking of the night they'd broken into the restricted section and lost Vikram's trust.

Abishek swept out his arms and then gestured her towards him. "Let me show you around."

After touring the library's different sections, he directed her towards his work area, filled with long wooden tables covered in an array of glass jars and various instruments. She studied the bubbling liquids, the vials, and the packed shelves crammed with an astonishing variety of magical ingredients.

"This is amazing," she said, admiring every inch of the space. This must be where she'd earned her love of learning and reading, and the thought fired a wave of acute longing in her chest.

"I'm so glad you like it," Abishek said. "Come, sit down, and let us talk. Rabindranath, you, too."

Zarya glanced at Rabin and frowned, wondering why he seemed so stiff. He hadn't said a word since they'd arrived, and she wasn't sure what to make of his behavior.

"I want to know everything we didn't have a chance to discuss last night," Abishek added.

Zarya understood what that meant—her nightfire. Row's

warnings flashed in her thoughts, but she reminded herself that Rabin trusted the king. He would never have brought her here otherwise. If Abishek wanted to steal her magic, then he had no reason to spend time getting to know her or answer any of her questions.

"Sure," Zarya said as they settled into the chairs arranged around a fireplace situated a safe distance from the precious books. Abishek sat on her right, and Rabin on her left, where his knee kept bouncing.

Zarya began by explaining the night in Dharati when the kala-hamsa attacked and her nightfire first appeared. The king asked many probing questions about how it worked and what combination of anchors the magic required. They were the clinical questions of a scholar, and with each answer, she was trying not to feel like she was giving up a piece of herself.

"There's something else nightfire gives me the power to do," she said, suddenly nervous about offering up these words. She checked in with Rabin, who gave her a small nod of encouragement.

"Yes?" Abishek asked as he sat up in curiosity.

"I used my nightfire to break the vanshaj collars."

She said nothing else, letting the silence stretch.

Abishek blinked and shook his head. "*You* broke them?"

She nodded and went on to explain the entire process, first by wielding the sixth anchor and then the more efficient route using her nightfire. When she was done, the king silently watched her, saying nothing for so long that she thought he might not answer.

Was he angry?

Finally, Abishek exhaled a sharp, surprised breath before he sat forward, balancing an elbow on his knee and rubbing his face.

"You must cease this madness at once, Zarya. You are upsetting the natural order of things. You see what's happened in Ishaan. If you continue on this path, it will only result in so much worse."

Those words crushed something delicate in her spirit.

"That isn't my fault. *They* started this. *They* are the reason this is happening."

Abishek waved a hand. "Everything was fine until the resistance in Ishaan began stirring things up—"

"Everything was *not* fine. Thousands of people in Rahajhan are forced to work in servitude against their will. They are without rights or freedoms. They are treated as second-class citizens and deserve the same rights we have. In fact, they deserve more."

"Zarya," Abishek said, holding up his hands. "You cannot change this."

She pressed her mouth together, irritated and angry at the dismissal in his tone. "I was hoping"—she said through gritted teeth—"you'd allow me to practice my magic on some of your subjects."

Abishek blinked. "Free the vanshaj in Andhera?"

"Yes."

"No. It is out of the question."

"Don't you want to see how it works at least? Rabin says you have the sixth anchor. I could teach you, too."

He studied her with a pensive look. "I admit I would be curious to see this in action, purely out of professional interest, but if word got out in Andhera, there would be chaos. It's too risky."

Zarya swallowed the tension in her throat, glancing at Rabin, who remained silent, allowing her to argue her case. "But I—"

He waved a hand silencing her, his expression softening. "I can see you are passionate about this." He paused as his brows drew together. "I will think about it. That's all I can promise for now."

A rush of hope flared in her chest. Maybe he could be convinced. Maybe with the right motivation, he could see his way to agreement. She thought of Miraan's words and how powerful people preferred to be on the right side of history. The king's help could mean securing a victory that felt so far out of reach.

"I would appreciate that," Zarya said. "I think if you consider it, you'll understand why things must change."

The king regarded her with a cautious look. "Perhaps." Another pause before he added, "But until I make a decision, I ask that you not bring this subject up anywhere in my kingdom again. Is that understood? Should I agree to this request, it must be done with care and precaution so as not to repeat the mistakes made in Ishaan."

His tone left no room for argument, and *this* was the king she'd been expecting. Someone colder and more ruthless. Someone who gave an order and demanded compliance. Still, it wasn't a no. Maybe he could be drawn to their side. She had promised Miraan they'd return to Ishaan soon, but what if there were other ways to fight this battle?

A demonstration might convince the king, but where might she find a willing subject?

"Fine," she said slowly. "There are two other things I'd like to discuss with respect to my magic."

Abishek folded his hands in his lap and nodded. "Of course. How can I help?"

Zarya swallowed and shared another look with Rabin. He was watching her carefully now. He knew she'd been keeping something from him, and she was grateful he hadn't tried to force out the truth.

Zarya described her visions and what happened in the forests of Ishaan and at Rabin's estate with his flowers. When she was done, Abishek wore a puzzled groove between his brows.

"I see," he said. "And what do you believe this is?"

She blew out a slow breath. "It sounds... crazy." She looked down at her hands before she continued. "But sometimes, I wonder if the darkness is following me."

It took several seconds before she looked back up to find both men watching her with twin looks of surprise and curiosity.

Abishek sighed, shook his head, and asked a few more questions. At first, her answers were halting, but once she started talking, she couldn't get the words out fast enough.

When she was done, they all fell silent. She snuck a glance at Rabin, worried about his reaction, but he was staring at her with that same fierce intensity as always. Nothing wavered in his expression. She gave him a soft smile that she hoped conveyed her appreciation for everything he'd brought to her life.

"I'll be honest," Abishek said. "I'm not entirely sure what you're describing. And I hate the feeling of not understanding something."

Zarya's shoulders fell. "Oh. I was hoping... I mean, that's part of why I came..." She drifted off as the king sat forward and clasped his hands.

"That doesn't mean we can't figure this out," he said. "You *did* come to the right place. If the answers are anywhere in Rahajhan, they're here." He swept out an arm. "And if anyone can find them, it's me."

His certainty loosened some of the tightness in her chest. "Okay, thank you."

He gave her a warm smile and then tipped his head. "And what was the other thing?"

She then described what had happened in the mind plane last night.

"Ah," Abishek said, this time full of certainty. "I was afraid of this."

"Of what?"

"This is why I wanted Kishore to examine your bond."

"Why?"

"You carry the sixth anchor."

Zarya tipped her head. "Yes? And?"

"Did you mention this to the mystic who performed the Bandhan?"

"No, of course not."

Abishek leaned back in his chair and steepled his fingers. "After Rabindranath left to find you, I spoke with Kishore and he mentioned that if an Aazheri with a sixth anchor completes the Bandhan, the bond can be affected in adverse ways."

"Where is he?" Rabin interjected, finally ending his silence.

Abishek's assessing gaze raked over Rabin. "He's in the mountains dealing with an important errand. Had I known your Bandhan was already deteriorating, I would never have allowed him to leave."

"What do you mean, deteriorating?" Zarya asked.

Abishek circled a hand. "Apparently, the magic can, for lack of a better term, go *off*."

Her breath hitched. "I'm not sure I understand."

"Magic is often an inconstant thing. In most cases, the Bandhan will bind the paramadhar to his masatara, but done incorrectly, the sixth anchor can sometimes corrupt the bond, making it toxic—mostly for the paramadhar."

Both their gazes fell on Rabin.

"What do you mean?" Zarya asked, panic already swelling in her gut. "How does it affect him?"

"Rabin may begin to feel ill, and given enough time, you as well. This corruption can cause the bond to weaken over time and eventually break." Abishek pressed his mouth together in a grim line, letting them fill in the blanks. If the bond broke,

Rabin would die. This was the risk they'd taken in completing the Bandhan.

"Had you waited until you arrived, we might have avoided this. As it stands, I suspect the problem you experienced in the mind plane is only the first sign of trouble."

Rabin's jaw hardened at the reproach in the king's voice, and Zarya couldn't believe he was lecturing them after what he'd just revealed.

"Is there anything we can do?" Zarya asked, gripping the arms of her chair, her voice shaking. They'd completed the Bandhan in a rush. She knew it had been a rash decision, but the Rising Phoenix had needed them.

"Perhaps," Abishek said. "May I examine the markings?"

She looked to Rabin for confirmation, and he nodded. His expressionless face gave her no hint about how he was reacting to this news.

"If it will help," he said.

"I would prefer for Kishore to take a look, but I will do my best."

The king stood, and Zarya and Rabin did the same.

"What did you choose for the image?" he asked.

Rabin pulled off his kurta while Zarya tugged down her shoulder, exposing their matching dragons. Something akin to satisfaction lit up Abishek's eyes.

"Ah," he said. "Well done."

He moved closer and held out a hand. "May I?" he asked, and Zarya nodded.

He touched the iridescent black lines, his fingers warm as he traced the edges. His eyes fluttered closed, and she watched his lips move like he was talking to himself.

"This was a very skilled practitioner," he said. "I feel how precise and clean the bond is. It's very easy to botch the process. I really would have preferred for Kishore to handle something so important, but all things considered, it could have been much worse."

Again, his voice held a hint of admonishment, and Zarya resisted the urge to roll her eyes. But maybe he had a point if they *had* messed up by not revealing her sixth anchor to Thriti.

Abishek then gestured to Rabin. "Come."

He laid his hand on Rabin's torso and once again fell silent. He began murmuring to himself again, and after a few minutes, he nodded.

"Yes, I am concerned," he said. "It's early days, but Kishore must examine this as soon as possible. The bond is corrupted and will require powerful magic to rectify."

"Can he do it?" Zarya asked.

"Of course. There is little he cannot do."

Zarya exchanged a wary look with Rabin and then nodded. "When is he coming back?"

"I'll send word to return as soon as possible."

Zarya pulled up her sleeve while Rabin tugged his kurta over his head. "And in the meantime, could I explore your library and see if I can find out anything about my visions?"

Abishek swept out a hand to encompass their surroundings. "What's mine is yours, my daughter. And I will help you, of course. We can get to know one another better, too."

"Thank you," she said again.

"Wonderful," Abishek said. "I hear your companions wish to return home due to the continued unrest in Ishaan."

She blinked. "How did you know that?"

"Not much happens within these walls without my knowing, my dear."

"Oh."

"I'd be happy to arrange transport for them," Abishek said.

"I can fly them," Rabin added.

"I think you should both remain here for your safety. If

something else should go wrong, then I can assist with keeping the bond stable. I'd feel better if you were close."

"Is it really that serious?" Zarya asked, growing increasingly worried.

Had they made a grave error in binding themselves? What if she'd signed Rabin's death?

Abishek smiled and laid a reassuring hand on her shoulder. "I'm not sure yet. But I promise we'll get to the bottom of this."

SEVEN

"I need to go home," Miraan repeated for the hundredth time, pacing the length of the room.

Yasen sat with his feet kicked up by the fire and a bottle of liquor on the table. Perhaps it was a little early to be drinking, but that was entirely subjective.

And it wasn't like he cared what anyone thought, anyway.

Yasen had attempted to take Miraan's mind off things by coaxing him into a walk through the city, but the prince only glared at everyone and everything until Yasen couldn't take it anymore and conceded defeat. They'd returned to his room, where Miraan paced, muttering to himself.

That was when Yasen had gone in search of the liquor cabinet.

"So you've mentioned," Yasen said, and Miraan blew out a sound of frustration. "But let's be smart about this, okay? Your sister will cut you into tiny bite-sized pieces and feed you to her fish."

"She doesn't have fish," Miraan grumbled as he dropped into his seat with his elbows planted on his knees.

"Metaphorical fish," Yasen said. "Have a drink. Or several. I insist."

Miraan grunted, and Yasen poured him a double shot. "It'll help."

Miraan accepted the glass and clasped it in his large hands. He had nice hands. Long fingers, callused from practicing with his sword. But they were also the hands of a noble, Yasen reminded himself. Someone far too good for the likes of him. Not that it mattered. They were just having fun. Enjoying each other's company, though Miraan had been too stressed for much "enjoyment." Once all this madness was over, Miraan would return home and do his princely duties, and Yasen would go wherever the next adventure took him.

Leaving Daragaab had been one of the best decisions he'd ever made. He'd always wanted to travel the world and explore everything it might offer. He wasn't interested in remaining tethered in one spot ever again. It wasn't until he'd escaped Dharati that he realized how much it had felt like living with a noose cinching his throat. He was here to help Zarya however she needed him, and then he'd be on his way.

She had Rabin now to look over her, and she could manage on her own. That meant, as usual, Yasen had become expendable, and he'd have to find somewhere to carve out another life for himself. Maybe a small part of him missed Dharati, but what would he do even if he did return? He refused to join the army —he no longer wanted to fight. And being too close to Vikram would put him under Gopal's thumb yet again. He simply couldn't return to that life.

"Are you listening?" Miraan asked and Yasen blinked.

"Of course I am."

"Then what did I just say?"

"That you want to return to Ishaan, and you're worried about your family," he answered without missing a beat.

Miraan glared at him for a moment. "Lucky guess," he grumbled as he took another swig of his drink.

"I know you better than you'd like," Yasen said as a knock came at the door.

"I want you to know me," Miraan muttered under his breath, just low enough for Yasen to catch it with his enhanced rakshasa hearing. He ignored it. The prince was distraught. Worried. He didn't know what he needed or wanted. He was a royal. He'd be expected to marry someone with power and influence. Not an orphaned soldier with nothing to offer and without a penny to his name.

The door opened to reveal Zarya and Rabin, despite the fact they hadn't been invited to enter.

"Come in, why don't you?" Yasen drawled.

"You mean the way you barge into my room all the time?" Zarya asked.

"But when I do, it's charming," he answered, eliciting a snort.

Unlike most people, she always laughed at his jokes. Never grew weary of his insouciance and sarcasm. Around Zarya, he could be entirely himself in a way he'd never experienced with anyone else. Not even Vikram.

They'd started on rocky footing, but she appreciated him and reminded him of that every chance she got. He'd never been around someone like her before. Someone who wasn't afraid to be open with her feelings. He never wondered where he stood with her, and something about that was reassuring. It filled this weird, empty space behind his heart.

As his gaze slid to Miraan, he tried to ignore that maybe Zarya wasn't the only one who made him feel that way.

"How was your meeting?" Miraan asked, standing up. "When can we return to Ishaan?"

Zarya held up her hands in a slow-down gesture. "Rabin and I can't leave just yet."

"Why not?" Yasen asked as the chime of warning bells rang in his head.

She explained the possible complications with their Bandhan and her sixth anchor.

"So, we've agreed to wait until the king's mystic can take a look at us and perform whatever spell is necessary to ensure the bond is stable. We're no use to anyone if our magic poisons our blood, and if the bond snaps..."

"That's fucked up, Zee," he said, and she nodded.

"Hopefully, we've caught it early enough. Abishek mentioned he could arrange transport for you back to Ishaan if you like; however, I think you should stay here a bit longer. Just until we can be sure it's safe."

Yasen ran a hand down his face, considering the many sides of his conflicted emotions. He wanted to return to Ishaan for all the same reasons as the others, but he worried for Miraan's safety.

He also didn't want to leave Zarya here alone. Something about the king bothered him. Rabin wasn't stupid—in fact, he was brilliant—but he sensed Rabin might have a blind spot regarding his mentor.

Yasen hadn't forgotten Row's warnings about the king of Andhera. He knew Rabin would protect Zarya with his life, but Abishek was a powerful Aazheri, and they had no idea what he was capable of.

Zarya had become one of the most important people in his life, and he wouldn't survive losing her.

"I agree," Yasen said. "Let's get a better read on the situation." When Miraan opened his mouth to protest, he lifted a hand. "Zarya said it would just be a few days. Let's wait for them to deal with this bond thing, and then we all return? I'd feel better if we stuck together."

Yasen looked around the room, seeking approval from Zarya and Rabin, who both nodded.

"Yas is right," Zarya said. "We shouldn't split up. I also want to see if the king might be persuaded to our side." She chewed on her lip. "He's reluctant, but I think he's open to being convinced."

Miraan let out a surprised huff. "Well, that would certainly be something. I think Dishani would be far more willing to listen to the rebellion's demands if the king of Andhera were already a champion for the cause. She's always admired him."

"Then give me a few days to work on him," Zarya said.

Miraan pressed his mouth together, his knee bouncing in agitation.

"A few days won't make any difference in the bigger picture," Yasen said.

Miraan's jaw flexed again, and Yasen was sure he would refuse before his shoulders dropped. "Fine."

"So, what should we do while we wait?" Yasen asked, eyeing the barren landscape through the window. This climate wasn't for him. He liked the sun and warmth. Fresh grass and flourishing flowers. He had no idea how Rabin could stand being here all these years with so few plants and trees around him.

"There are some things I'd like to understand about my magic," Zarya said. "I have some reading to do."

"Of course you do," he deadpanned, which earned him a glare.

"Come and spar with me and Ekaja," Rabin said with a sly grin. "She'll wipe the floor with the likes of you."

Yasen barked out a laugh and lifted his glass in a toast. "Without a doubt."

EIGHT

While they waited for Kishore to return, Miraan brooded in his room, and Rabin introduced Yasen to the Cradle.

Ekaja had created the treacherous sparring ring decades ago atop a mountain near the castle and nestled in the Zamina Valley. She'd spent months slicing off the top with her air and earth anchors, leaving behind a massive plateau.

She'd then spent the better part of a decade carving a spiraling line of stairs up the side before adding storage racks, weapons, and provisions. There was even a small hut with a wood-burning stove and a few palettes scattered on the floor where one could sleep. Most people needed a moment to rest after spending a few hours in the Cradle.

Rabin and Ekaja had been drinking too much wine one night when she'd turned uncharacteristically maudlin. She confessed she'd built the Cradle to silence the tortured voices plaguing her consciousness. During a brutal campaign against a rebelling mountain clan, her army was ambushed by a group of renegade clansmen. She'd been caught off guard. She'd missed the telltale signs and was terrified of disappointing Abishek after making such a rookie mistake.

So, as punishment, she ordered her soldiers to finish off the entire clan. No one was left alive. After returning home, she was riddled with guilt, unable to sleep or function without seeing their faces or hearing their screams.

The arduous task had temporarily taken her mind off the violence and brutality, giving her somewhere to channel her shame. Enough years passed that time dulled her emotions enough that she could exist again. But every once in a while, she would disappear for days at a time, sleeping and living in the Cradle, and he knew those ghosts had returned to haunt her once again.

"Where the fuck are we going?" Yasen asked as he trudged up the stairs behind Rabin.

"You'll see," he replied, ignoring Yasen's grumbling as they made the ascent. The narrow staircase was a test of one's balance and agility in itself.

When they reached the top, a blast of icy wind hit them with the force of a gut punch. This was one of the primary reasons Ekaja had selected this spot. The added distractions of the cold and wind were enough to test even the most battled-hardened warrior.

Yasen came up beside him, taking in the scope of the Cradle. Snowy mountain peaks surrounded them, casting cold shadows under the pale sky.

Ekaja stood in the middle of the plateau, performing a series of drills as she withstood the harsh elements.

She'd never told another living soul her reasons for creating this place—the king would have called her weak and questioned her role as his commander—but Rabin had been honored that she trusted him enough to unburden herself.

"Welcome to the Cradle," Rabin said with a sweep of his arm.

"The Cradle?" Yasen asked.

"You've heard the term 'from cradle to death?' It's a little play on words."

"Well, this is insane," he remarked wryly.

Ekaja noted their presence as a grin stretched across her face. She stalked over with a confident stride.

"You think you can handle this?" she asked Yasen, who narrowed his eyes.

"Probably not."

That earned him a laugh as she cocked her head and gestured towards the center. "Can I teach you a few things?"

"Sure, probably how to get my ass handed to me," he grumbled as he glanced at Rabin. "How often do you come out here?"

Rabin smirked at Yasen, wrapped head to toe in leather and fur, his teeth chattering, and his hands jammed into his armpits for warmth.

"A few times a week," Rabin said.

Yasen shook his head and shucked off his thick outercoat to reveal his fur-lined fighting leathers while muttering under his breath, "I suppose this is what passes for fun on a frozen wasteland."

Over the next few days, they all formed an easy friendship as they bantered and fought until the sun set each day.

Miraan spent much of his time in his room writing and exchanging letters with his brother about the state of affairs in Ishaan. It had taken some convincing, but Yasen eventually talked him into joining everyone outside.

Now he sparred with Ekaja, just barely holding his own.

Yasen scanned the horizon, taking in the snowy peaks. "You like living here?" he asked, and Rabin shrugged.

"It has a certain charm. Not a fan?"

Yasen snorted. "It's positively wretched."

That almost made Rabin smile as his gaze slid to Yasen. He'd always admired Yasen's way of moving through the world with that easy disposition, never letting too much ruffle him. Rabin wished he could exude the same effortlessness.

"You get used to it," Rabin said. "The cold becomes invigorating."

Yasen stomped his feet and rubbed his hands. "Sure, if you're not particularly attached to your extremities, I suppose."

Rabin offered him a wry look, and they watched Ekaja knock Miraan flat on his back before pointing her blade at his throat. She stared him down, arching an eyebrow before Miraan raised his hands in defeat.

"So, what's her story?" Yasen asked as Ekaja held out her hand and pulled Miraan to his feet.

Rabin shrugged. "Abishek found her when she was a child, abandoned by her parents. She was freezing, almost starved to death. He brought her in and raised her practically like a daughter, teaching her everything he knew and creating the most lethal, skilled, and loyal army commander a king could ask for."

Yasen nodded. "I guess the king is good at collecting... orphans."

Rabin snorted a wry laugh. "I suppose he is."

They watched Miraan and Ekaja circle each other for another round.

"We've been friends for years," Rabin continued. "She's the only one I've been able to confide in during my time away from home." He paused before adding, "I regret how I left things."

Yasen didn't respond for a moment as they watched Ekaja and Miraan start fighting again, their blades flashing in the light. "Vikram is... I don't want to say he's angry because that isn't the right word. Disappointed? Hurt? I don't think he understood why you left."

Rabin turned to look at Yasen. "Do you know what my father did?"

Yasen nodded. "Not at first, but the truth eventually came out."

"So, you understand why I had to leave."

"I do. I don't blame you, just so we're clear. I know better than almost anyone what a complete fucking asshole your father is."

Rabin turned to Yasen, noting the hardness in his eyes.

"I'm sorry that he hurt you, too," Rabin said. "One day, I will kill him with a smile on my face."

Yasen shook his head. "As long as you let me help."

"With pleasure."

Yasen met his gaze as a shared understanding passed between them.

"I wish Vik would see it the same way," Rabin said as they turned to scan the horizon.

Yasen ran a hand down his face. "Your father has brainwashed Vik. He still looks up to him despite everything he's done. He lost so much when he was forced to become Amrita's steward. I think he's still mourning a different life, but he's a good man in his heart, and I think he'll eventually realize what he gave up."

Rabin inhaled a deep breath of fresh air. "Thank you. I appreciate that."

Ekaja knocked Miraan down again before the prince scrambled to his feet. "I don't think I can take any more," he said with his hands on his knees as his breath sawed from his chest. "Someone save me."

Ekaja barked out a wicked laugh and flipped her blade. With a hand planted on her hip, she cocked her head at Rabin. "Let's do this, Ravana. It's been ages since I've kicked your ass."

Rabin's face stretched into a grin as he withdrew his sword.

Amidst all the uncertainty of the past few weeks, this was one place where he still felt like himself.

Without missing a beat, he sprinted towards her, their blades ringing against the echo of the mountains and the endless northern sky.

NINE

While the others spent their time at the Cradle, Zarya spent hers combing through Abishek's library, searching for *something* to explain her visions. The king would often join her, sitting next to her while he queried with more probing questions.

He wasn't only interested in her visions. He asked endless questions about her, too. He wanted to know everything. He was even fascinated by her love of romance novels and declared that he'd have to acquire a collection for the castle.

He welcomed her into his life, and though he could be quick to anger and a little bossy, she sensed his heart was in the right place. He'd become a father overnight, and they were both navigating the possibilities and pitfalls of this new relationship.

As she continued to peruse his numerous books, she grew increasingly frustrated when she couldn't find the answers she sought. Abishek didn't seem concerned, confident they'd figure it out, but she'd rested so many hopes on his knowledge.

Maybe she'd convinced herself that her choice to come here was justified if he could help. But they also needed safety. They couldn't return to Dharati, and Dishani wanted her dead. She was using Abishek for his protection as well.

"Tell me again about the visions," Abishek asked as he sat across from her that afternoon. He leaned forward, folding his hands together. "Is there anything else you haven't shared yet? Something you forgot to mention."

"I don't think so. It's like I said—demon armies and ruin. A landscape bent and shattered. Smoke and ashes. I hear the man's voice in a language I don't know. I thought I heard two voices at some point, but it's hard to be sure anymore. I saw him when I looked in the mirror." She rubbed her face with her hands. "Or maybe it's nothing, and I've been imagining things all along."

She couldn't help adding the caveat. What if she were simply losing her mind?

"Do you really believe that's what it is?" Abishek asked.

She bit the corner of her lip and rallied her courage for the next thing she hadn't shared yet.

"When I killed Dhawan, he said something to me," she started.

Abishek sat forward at the mention of the old Aazheri's name. "Yes?"

"He said that *I* caused the blight."

Abishek tipped his head, curiosity spreading over his features.

"And sometimes I wonder if he was right," she continued. "It started on the shoreline where I lived. The demons always responded to my starlight even when it existed in its inert form, and after I left, it sometimes felt like they were calling to me."

She paused and took a long sip of water before she continued.

"And when it happened again in Ishaan..." She recalled the moment in the forest when *something* had moved in her peripheral vision. Something not of this plane. "I'm starting to worry about remaining in one place for too long."

Abishek remained silent as she inhaled a deep breath.

"So no, I don't think I'm imagining anything. I think Dhawan might have been right. For a moment, I wondered if it was the tainted Bandhan, but the visions started long before we performed the bonding. So it can't be that."

"Is the frequency increasing as more time passes?" he asked. "You mentioned it's only happened a few times."

She shook her head. "I don't believe so."

"That seems like a very good sign," Abishek said, giving her a small smile. He sat back and drained his wine glass before setting it on the table.

"Zarya, I don't have an explanation for this, but I assure you I will do everything I can to help you understand what it means."

She felt another rush of gratitude as her shoulders eased from her ears. He wasn't tossing her out. He wasn't looking at her like she was a monster. He was helping her. So many of her reservations about coming to Andhera faded away in the face of his support.

"I wondered," Zarya said. "It sounds like the stories I've heard about the Hanera Wars."

Abishek shrugged. "It's possible. There are some similarities in what you've described."

"What could that mean?"

Again, he shook his head. "Past lives aren't uncommon amongst our kind, though it is rare to carry their memories."

"Memories?" Zarya asked. "Like these might be things that happened to me in some other life?"

"Perhaps," he said with a wave of his hand. "But this is likely all a coincidence. You lived with the blight for so long that your thoughts go there first when confronted with evidence of something similar."

Abishek offered her a scrutinizing look, his gaze traveling over her face in a way that almost felt like he was searching for something.

Then he waved a hand. "But it's far more likely they're simply dreams and nightmares. Nothing to worry yourself over."

"But I *touched* the forest and the flowers. They died under my hand."

"You have strong magic, Zarya, and you're still learning how to control it. Usually, the simplest explanation is the most likely one."

"Right," she said as he pushed up from his seat.

"Kishore will offer insight into this when he returns. Now I must be off."

"When are you expecting him back? Any word?"

He gave her a patient smile. "As I've said—just another day or two."

Then he made to leave.

"I was hoping we could discuss the vanshaj again," she called after him.

He stopped and turned back to face her. "Zarya, we've already talked about this."

"We haven't really, though. You said you'd consider allowing me to break the collars of Andhera's vanshaj, but you haven't mentioned it since."

The smile dropped from his face, his expression turning serious.

"Nevertheless, I *have* given the matter much thought and am still considering the best approach. I'm not unsympathetic to this cause, but the chaos in Ishaan is proof enough of how careful we need to be. I hope Princess Dishani will soon get her people under control so we may avoid further bloodshed. Once that is done, we can move forward."

Zarya let out a tense breath. "But the answer isn't no?"

He tipped his head, the ghost of a smile playing on his lips. "It isn't no. I promise it will remain at the top of my mind."

"Okay," she answered with a nod. "Thank you."

He offered her one more careful look before he spun on his heel and strode out of the room. It wasn't the answer she'd been hoping for, but he wasn't completely shutting her down.

She flipped through the book on the table, but her heart wasn't in it anymore, at least for today. She also fiercely missed Rabin, and it was throwing her off. Keeping their distance was driving them both a little nuts. With the mind plane still blocked, Zarya desperately wanted some alone time, and she was climbing out of her skin.

Deciding she was done with her research for today, she slammed the book shut and went in search of her husband. He'd promised to take her into the city tonight.

It didn't take long to find him entering the castle with Yasen, Miraan, and Ekaja, all windswept, their noses and cheeks pink from the cold.

"How was the Cradle today?" Zarya asked.

"These two are insane," Yasen said, stomping his booted feet to generate warmth. He pointed at Rabin and Ekaja, who both rolled their eyes.

"If you're too weak to handle it, don't blame us," Ekaja said with a cackle.

Zarya was relieved to see Miraan out of his room and actually smiling.

"Are you done in the library?" Rabin asked, and Zarya nodded.

"For today. Are you still up for a visit to the city?"

"Of course."

"Anyone else?" Zarya asked.

"No, thanks," Yasen said. "I'm sitting by the fire to warm my frozen toes for the rest of the night."

"Me as well," Miraan answered. "I have some letters to write home."

"I also have duties I need to attend, but thank you," Ekaja said, and they all said good night before parting ways.

After retrieving their coats and boots, Rabin held out an arm, and Zarya took it before he steered her out of the castle. They'd only briefly had a chance to visit the city, and Rabin promised to take her somewhere special tonight. There was also someone he wanted her to meet.

They descended the castle's wide staircase and then strolled down the path leading into the city, entering a boulevard lined with vendors selling preserved fruit and vegetables, dried meat, and flour.

Zarya had learned it was difficult to obtain fresh ingredients this deep in the mountains, and the spoils from Andhera's hunters were rare and expensive, out of reach for the average citizen.

Most had to content themselves with dried provisions, especially in winter. She contrasted that knowledge with the bounty of food they enjoyed in the castle with a sour kind of bitterness. She'd considered commenting on it several times but felt she was already walking a fine line with her questions about the vanshaj.

The elevation climbed into flat cliffs at the city's far end, supporting several rows of large houses belonging to Andhera's nobility. They were simple in their construction, built to withstand the harsh climate, but were grand in scale. Zarya suspected food could be found in abundance in these homes as well.

They passed stands selling roasted nuts and glass tumblers of steaming chai while Zarya inhaled deeply, taking in everything with wonder.

From her reading, she knew Andhera wasn't particularly noteworthy compared to Rahajhan's other great cities. It was nothing compared to Dharati's opulent streets, Ishaan's intricate architecture, Vayuu's airy sky city, or Svaasthy's massive buildings carved right into the ridges of soaring sandstone cliffs.

Andhera was practical, built to withstand the harsh winds

and driving snow. The extreme temperatures that made you wonder if your very blood might freeze in your veins. But Zarya appreciated it with the same awe she reserved for everything. If there ever came a day when she viewed the world with only cynicism, she'd rather be dead.

"Come," Rabin said, tugging on her hand. "This way."

Zarya allowed him to lead her through the city and past the western gate. Beyond it they found a path lined with a few small homes before branching off.

Rabin gestured for her to follow down an inclined, rocky path. The edges were dusted with snow, and small bushes broke through the crust.

"Where are we going?" she asked as they continued their ascent.

"Somewhere I think you'll appreciate."

She stomped up the path, huffing and puffing. She wasn't used to this heavy clothing, and the fur-lined boots weighed her feet down.

"Almost there," Rabin promised as they curved around another bend and exited the tree line to find an open cliff. He waited for her to catch up before they approached the edge.

Andhera spread before them, mountains and snow and deep green trees scattering in every direction. The setting sun cast the entire range of soaring peaks in soft yellow light, almost like it had been dipped in gold. Hundreds of snow-dusted trees sparkled like fairies had sprinkled them with magic.

She stared at the horizon, needing silence to honor this moment.

She thought of the seaside cottage. Of all those lonely years she'd spent with that unpopulated coastline as her entire world. She recalled standing at the edge of the sea, staring out and wishing for more. Wishing for a bigger life.

And now, she was here at the other end of the world, looking out over a landscape she'd barely known existed. And this wasn't some inconsequential spot where she'd traveled. This wasn't a random occurrence in the fabric of her life. This place was *hers*. It belonged to her. Or maybe *she* was the one who belonged to these mountains and this sky. Either way, she could feel Andhera in her blood.

"It's beautiful," she whispered.

"I thought you'd like it."

She turned to look at Rabin, studying the lines of his profile as the breeze tossed strands of his dark hair. Perhaps sensing her gaze, he looked down and gave her the softest of his rare smiles.

"Thank you," she said. "For all of this. For convincing me to come here and meet him. I might never have done it without you."

He gave her a look she couldn't interpret as the corner of his mouth pressed together. Then he dipped his head. "Of course. You understand I would do anything for you."

It wasn't a question but rather a statement of fact. Immutable. Unshakeable from now until these very mountains crumbled into the sea.

"I would do anything for you, too," she answered, and his expression softened.

"Then how about joining me for a drink?"

She smiled, and he took her hand as they dove down another path, again losing themselves in the trees. It took a few minutes to emerge onto another flat cliff with nearly the same perspective. By now, the sun was moving behind the peaks, lighting them from behind.

A cozy house made of dark wood sat on the cliff, its windows glowing softly with warm light. They entered to find a common room hosting a smattering of customers. The walls and floors were paneled in more dark wood, and every corner was stuffed with plush chairs and sofas. A massive fireplace dominated one wall, and a bar stretched along the other.

"Rabin!" exclaimed the man behind the counter. He was

Aazheri, with kind eyes and a bright smile. "You're back! So good to see you. Who is this, then?"

The man's eyes fell on Zarya, and she gave him a little wave.

"Dav, this is Zarya. The woman I told you about." He gestured to her, and they shook hands.

"So nice to meet you," she said. "You told him about me?"

"Where else could I go to drown my sorrows?" he asked, and she snorted.

"Did you just make a... joke?"

He tipped his head, his brow furrowing as though he was considering the question. "I'm not sure."

At that, Zarya and Dav both started laughing.

"Well, I'm glad she came around," Dav said. "What brings you here this evening?"

Rabin lowered his head, his shoulders curving inwards.

"Zarya came from Ishaan, Dav. You've heard the stories about the rebellion?"

Instantly, Dav's demeanor shifted. "We should not talk about that here," he whispered.

Dav jerked his chin, gesturing for Zarya and Rabin to follow into another room. He closed the door and spun around.

"What's going on?" Zarya asked, her gaze darting between them.

"Zarya," Rabin said, "Dav is part of Andhera's vanshaj resistance, and I thought you should meet."

TEN

Zarya assessed Dav from head to toe while he returned the gesture.

"The resistance? Here?" she asked. "You never said anything about this."

"It's not as organized or as far along as in Ishaan," Rabin said. "And I confess I wasn't sure their fight would ever amount to anything, so I never gave it much weight. But then I saw what you all accomplished in Ishaan, and I thought..."

"Rabin," Dav said, a warning in his tone. "You can't tell anyone who we are."

"It's okay," Rabin said. "I promise you have nothing to worry about. Zarya is a key member of the Rising Phoenix... but I shouldn't speak for her."

He gestured her way, and she inhaled a breath and nodded.

Abishek wasn't convinced that helping the vanshaj was the right thing yet. But of course, others were working towards vanshaj freedom. If the king refused to help, she might have to work without his consent.

Once she'd relayed the entire story of the Rising Phoenix

and what they'd done, Dav's jaw hung slack, his face completely white.

"You broke the collars," he said, obvious shock quivering in his voice. "You freed their magic."

She nodded, twisting her fingers together in nervousness. No matter how often she revealed this secret, it always felt a bit dangerous.

"Could you do it again? Right now?" he asked, practically stumbling towards her. He didn't seem at all interested in her revelations about the sixth anchor.

"Yes. I could do it as many times as you need."

Dav opened his mouth and then closed it. "Give me a moment."

He flung open the door and began shouting orders at everyone seated in the bar. "We're closed! Everyone out!"

Zarya and Rabin exchanged worried looks as Dav insisted everyone leave, pushing people up from their chairs as they grumbled under their breaths.

"One free drink on the house tomorrow!" he promised. "As long as you get your asses out of here now!" That had the intended effect, and finally, everyone stirred into action. After another minute, the bar was empty.

"I'll be right back," Dav said, bounding up a flight of stairs at the room's far end. Zarya and Rabin waited in the main area before Dav returned with a vanshaj woman in tow.

"This is Suria," Dav said. "My wife."

"Your wife?" Zarya asked, her brow furrowing in confusion.

"Not my wife legally," he amended. "But my wife in every way that matters."

He held Suria's hand to his chest, his voice so full of passion that Zarya felt her throat knot up. Now she understood why he hadn't cared about the sixth anchor. He had far more important things to worry about.

"It's nice to meet you," Zarya said.

"Is it true?" Suria asked. "You can break it?"

"It's true."

Suria immediately stepped forward, pulling on the collar of her shirt to expose her throat. "Then help me."

"Really? You're sure?"

"Why?" Dav asked. "Is it dangerous?"

"No. It's not. I just... usually have to work a little harder to convince people."

Dav looked at Rabin. "You confirm she is honorable?"

"Of course," Rabin said.

"Then that's all we need."

Dav took Suria's hand and kissed her knuckles. "We want to be free of this. We want to marry properly someday."

"You understand you *can't* tell anyone," Zarya said. "The collar is only one step on the road to freedom. I've spoken to the king, and he's still considering the consequences of freeing the vanshaj."

"The king?" Dav said. "The king would never agree to this."

"He might," Zarya insisted.

"He will not," Suria said, her mouth flattening. "He would rather see us all dead than see us freed."

Zarya blinked at the venom in her tone. "You really think so?"

"I do." Suria straightened her shoulders, her chin lifting.

Zarya frowned at Suria's apparent certainty. The king was rigid, but she was sure he could be convinced.

"Then, you understand who I am?" she asked.

"We've heard the rumors about the king's daughter," Dav said.

"And you still trust me?"

"We are not the people we are born of," Suria said, her lips set in a firm line. No one would know that better than her.

"We won't tell anyone but those we trust," Dav said. "Will you help them, too?"

Zarya inhaled a deep breath. She reached for her mother's pendant, tears pressing her eyes at the reminder that it was gone. Regardless, she'd never forget the words inside.

She will free them all.

"Of course I'll help them," she whispered.

"Thank you," Suria whispered back, her eyes glassy with tears.

"You will have magic," she said, and Suria nodded.

"I can help her with it," Dav said proudly.

"Okay, then give us some space," Zarya said to Rabin and Dav, who quickly shuffled aside.

Suria stood before her and waited, unblinking, while Zarya pulled out a thread of her nightfire. She twisted it around the other woman's throat, carefully pulling apart the star collar. She'd done this so often it had become an extension of herself.

It took only a moment for the sparkling black ribbons to do their work as the tattoo dissolved off Suria's skin in puffs of shadow. When Zarya was done, she dropped her hands as Suria grabbed her throat.

"Did it work?" She looked at her husband, who was already crying.

"Suria," he gasped, stumbling towards her, cupping her face in his hands. "Suria. I never thought I'd live to see it."

They fell against one another, sobbing while their bodies shook. As Zarya watched, she felt Rabin move beside her before he looped a finger through her pinky and squeezed. She looked up to witness the proud look in his eyes. She would never grow tired of this gift and this ability to change the course of someone's destiny forever.

After a minute, Dav and Suria gathered themselves enough to pull apart.

"How can we ever thank you?" Dav asked. "You've given us our entire *lives*."

"There's no need," she said, shaking her head. "I'm happy to do it."

"I was hoping we could use the cabin tonight?" Rabin said, and Dav's face lit up.

"Yes, of course! That's perfect. You'll spend the night with us."

Then Dav took Zarya's hand and squeezed it. "If they're willing, can we bring others to see you?"

She swallowed hard. Five months ago, she'd arrived in Gi'ana intending to meet her family and had inadvertently stirred up a rebellion tearing apart their home. Was she here, meeting the other half of her lineage, preparing to do the same?

Of course there was no question. Of course she would help. She'd already sworn she'd die trying if that's what it took.

She looked over her shoulder at Rabin, and she could see the worry in his expression. He'd beg her to be careful, but they had long ago been swept into this tide they couldn't have stopped even if they'd wanted to.

"Yes," she said, turning back to Dav. "Bring as many as you can. I will free them all."

The cabin turned out to be a small, adorable house the couple rented out to visitors. Once Zarya agreed to return to the tavern in two days and free as many vanshaj as they could gather, Dav and Suria escorted them out the back door and along a snowy path lined with flickering lanterns.

They entered through frosted glass doors, finding a small single room with a massive bed covered in a patchwork quilt against one wall and a roaring fire against another.

"We'll be right back," Suria said with a sparkle in her eyes before the couple disappeared, leaving Zarya and Rabin alone.

"Do you think anyone will notice if we spend the night?" Zarya asked with a tip of her head.

Rabin walked over and wrapped an arm around her waist. He tucked a lock of hair behind her ear. "I stay here occasionally when I need space, so I don't think anyone will miss us. Seems like a good chance for some alone time." He leaned down to press his nose into the curve of her throat and rumbled, "Not being able to touch you is driving me mad."

He tipped her head up to capture her mouth before he pulled away.

"Come and see the view," Rabin said.

He led her through another set of glass doors on the other side. There, they found a covered balcony overlooking the mountain valley. In the center was a roaring firepit, giving off enough heat to discard the heaviest of their layers.

After dropping her coat on a chair, Zarya walked to the railing, watching the last of the day's light fade as the valley turned from rivers of gold into puddles of twilight.

"This is magnificent," she said. "It would be easy to dismiss this landscape as harsh and unforgiving, but you only have to look a little deeper to appreciate its true beauty."

"Sometimes, I think that's how you see me, too," Rabin said softly as he came to stand next to her.

She exhaled a soft breath as she turned towards him. "It is. You're my secret, and I'm keeping it that way forever."

He gave her a pleased half-smile before they stood together, silently watching the darkening horizon for several minutes. The gentle breeze tugged at her hair and clothing, nipping at her nose and ears.

When the cabin door opened, they turned to find Suria and Dav laden with trays and baskets. They deposited a veritable feast on the small table, including food, wine, fruit, and sweets.

"We hope you'll enjoy this," Suria said. "It's all our best provisions, shipped in from across Rahajhan."

"Thank you," Zarya said. "But this is too much."

"It's not nearly enough," Suria said, her voice thick with

emotion. "Call if you need anything." Then she strode over and threw her arms around Zarya, hugging her tightly and sniffing before she pulled away, wiping her eyes. "*Anything* at all."

"This is perfect."

"Then no one else will disturb you," Dav promised with a bow and his hands pressed together.

After they were gone, Zarya smiled. "Are they always this generous?"

Rabin laughed. "Yes, but I think they went all out for you."

She pressed the corner of her lips together. "I'm glad I could help them."

He walked over and wrapped a hand around the back of her neck.

"I want to help the others, too."

"I knew you would," he said.

"We'd be doing this right under the king's nose. I think Suria is wrong, and his mind can be changed, but I'm also not inclined to wait."

Rabin nodded. "It would mean a breach of his orders, but you don't owe him anything."

Zarya gave him a quizzical look. "But he forbade it. You'd be defying him again."

"I understand. But he's wrong about this, too."

Then he quickly looked away and picked up one of the large mugs from the tray on the table.

"Try this. It's Dav's specialty. Badam milk. Made with almonds, cardamon, and saffron."

Zarya accepted the mug and inhaled the fragrant scent before taking a sip. The creamy liquid slipped through her limbs, warming her insides. "It's delicious."

Rabin then selected a bottle of dark amber liquor on the tray and tipped some into her mug before filling his own. After toasting with a clink, he took her hand and led her back onto the balcony.

They stood at the railing, facing the soaring mountain landscape, staring at the sky now twinkling with a net of stars. Without any cloud cover, they sparkled in rivers against midnight blue. It reminded Zarya of the dream forest and the moment fate brought Rabin into her life.

"What are you thinking about?" he asked.

"I'm thinking about the first time I saw you in the mind plane. Your face wasn't even visible but somehow, I *knew* you'd be important."

That earned her the barest smile. "That night changed my entire life."

He wrapped an arm around her waist and pulled her close, their mouths meeting and tongues sliding, heat rising between them as they luxuriated in each other. He tugged her towards a nest of plush chairs near the fire, settling her onto his lap as they placed their mugs on the table.

Then they kissed and kissed, hands grasping and breaths tangling in puffs of white.

"It's been too long since we've done this," he murmured, sucking on the curve of her throat.

"Far too long," she agreed as her head tipped back to offer him access.

Their wedding night. It felt like a million years ago when they'd sealed their love in that opulent hotel room in the heart of Ishaan.

Then everything had gone to hell, and now they were here in this new place, pretending they didn't mean anything to one another. And then their tainted bonding had cut them completely off from the last thread of their connection. Soon, it might take Rabin away forever.

She did her best to push away those thoughts as she kissed him harder, warmth swirling in the pit of her stomach. They'd fix their bond as soon as Abishek's mystic returned, and nothing would ever come between them.

Maybe one day, they could live together in relative peace. Enjoy their lives and each other without a crisis creeping up their backs. She couldn't wait.

His hand slid up her knee and under her long skirt, finding the cuff of her high wool socks. He teased the edge, his fingers ghosting over her skin and pulling up a shiver. His hand gripped her waist as he shifted her around until her back was against his chest and her legs were spread over his knees.

She melted against him as her arm wrapped around the back of his head, and he continued tracing tiny circles over the skin of her inner thigh. "Rabin," she breathed as his hand drifted higher, finding the dampening seam between her legs.

He cupped her pussy as he kissed her neck. Then he found the band of her underwear before he shoved his hand inside. She moaned as a thick finger found her wet heat, her hips writhing against his hardening cock.

"Remember the alley in Ishaan?" he said as he circled her clit with a gentle touch that was driving her mad. "That rush of maybe getting caught?"

She huffed out a breathless laugh. "Of course."

"We need to do that again," he said, thrusting his finger inside before adding a second, stretching her as he pumped in and out. Her eyelids fluttered, and she whimpered at the coil of fire spiraling in her stomach.

"Gods," she moaned as he teased her, applying varying pressure, featherlight and then rough, as her breath came in tight, gasping pants.

"Maybe in the castle," he mused. "Find a quiet corner where we might get caught."

"I thought we were being discreet," she gasped with a breath that was part moan and part laugh.

She leaned up to kiss him and then flipped around to straddle his hips.

"I want you inside me," she said, grabbing his shoulders

before she leaned in to kiss him hard. He gave her a wicked look, a low, dark chuckle rumbling in his chest.

She felt the swell of his cock against her bared skin and shifted her hips, trying to generate friction. Lifting the hem of his kurta, she exposed the taut lines of his stomach as she traced the curves and planes of muscle. Her hands drifted lower, unbuttoning his pants before reaching in to find his hard cock.

He moaned as she wrapped her hand around it, pumping a few times as he twitched in response to her touch. Then she lifted up, positioning the head at her entrance. She hovered there as she met his gaze.

"Trying to torture me?" he asked with a curl of his lip.

"Is this torturing you?"

"Every moment without my cock filling this sweet cunt is pure fucking torture, Spitfire."

Then he grabbed her hips and *thrust*. They both groaned as he split her wide, the force of his size both decadent and offering just the right amount of pain bordering on pleasure.

A rumble stirred in his chest as he waited for her to adjust to his presence. His hand slipped higher under her skirt, finding her breast and squeezing it before he pinched her nipple hard enough to send a flash of arousal straight to her clit.

She exhaled a strangled breath as he gripped one hip, thrusting up into her with force, over and over, as she felt her release climbing. She was only dimly aware of their surroundings. Of the mountains and the sky. Of the wind gusting over the pristine landscape.

She tipped forward, her forehead touching his as her hips writhed, his thick cock hitting every sensitive spot as she clenched around him. It was hard to believe this could be so hot when they were both fully dressed.

"Zarya," he moaned as he fucked her with abandon, and the cold air chilled their noses and cheeks. She inhaled a deep breath of clean air as he reached down to roughly circle her clit.

She fell into nothing, her release exploding through her limbs. He continued touching her, kissing her, fucking her until a minute later, he let out a deep groan and then came as his hand tightened around her hip, his fingers digging into her flesh to the point of bruising.

When the waves of her orgasm faded out, she collapsed against him. He wrapped his arms around her waist, holding her tight.

"I love you," she said, burying her mouth into the curve of his throat.

"I love you too, Spitfire," he said. "I will protect you with every breath in my body."

She laid her head on his shoulder and blinked, wondering why she detected a thread of uncertainty in those words.

ELEVEN

Two nights later, Zarya had another dream about her mother. She woke up covered in sweat, her breath sawing out of her chest and her heart pounding through her ribs.

She sat up and stared around her dark room, feeling lonely and vulnerable, so she threw off her blanket and crossed the hall, flinging open Rabin's door. He was sitting in bed staring at the fire, a glass of liquor clutched in his hand. At her entrance, he looked over. The last few days, he hadn't been himself. Ever since they'd arrived, he'd been different. He was tense and broody, even more so than usual.

She didn't want to say it out loud, but she worried their tainted Bandhan was already starting to affect him.

"Are you okay?" they both asked together.

"I had a nightmare," she said. "And I needed you."

His eyes brightened as he reached out a hand. She crossed the room and took it, climbing onto the bed before leaning against him.

"Do you want to talk about it?" he asked.

She opened her mouth and closed it before saying, "It's my mother."

He tipped her chin up. "What about her?"

She shared everything about her dream as his expression grew more and more concerned. When she was finished, he wrapped her in his arms and rested his chin on her head.

"I'm sorry," he said. "I can see why that rattled you."

She nodded against his chest as he squeezed her tighter.

"I want to stay with you tonight," she whispered, and she felt him nod. "I know you're worried about the king..."

"Just try to leave me, Spitfire."

She exhaled a sigh of relief and snuggled up against him before falling asleep in his arms.

When Zarya awoke, it was still early, with the sun sitting below the horizon. She decided to return to her room to maintain the facade of their platonic relationship. Rabin still wanted to keep this from Abishek, and she'd respect his wish until he was ready.

Rabin was still asleep, so she leaned over and kissed him softly, noting the dark circles under his eyes. Something was definitely wrong. She stared at him with her heart twisting into knots. What would she do without him?

Finally, she dragged herself out of bed and tiptoed back to her room.

After she'd dressed, Urvi arrived with breakfast and a note from the king.

Kishore had been delayed another two days.

As Zarya stared at the king's writing, she tried not to panic about Rabin or Ishaan. Miraan wouldn't be placated much longer, particularly with reports about the Jadugara snatching up Taara Aazheri and attempting to re-collar them. No one knew if they'd been successful yet, but they were hell-bent on punishing anyone who'd escaped their barbaric enchantments.

Determined to find out how much longer they'd be waiting,

she went to find the king, but his manservant Omar informed her that he wasn't currently available. In a huff of frustration, she returned to Rabin's room, where she found him lying on the sofa, his eyes closed and his skin pale with a sheen of sweat.

She stopped and watched him, another flare of dread swelling in her gut. She walked over and laid a hand on his forehead as his lids fluttered open.

"Are you okay?" she asked, and he nodded.

"I'm fine. What's going on?"

"Kishore's been delayed again."

Rabin met her gaze. "Why?"

"I don't know. I went to find the king, but he's busy."

Rabin's eyes slid closed as he inhaled a short breath to stave off a wave of pain.

"Rabin? What's *wrong*?"

"Nothing," he said, pushing himself up. "Are you heading down to see Dav and Suria soon?"

She nodded as she resisted the urge to argue with him. It was the day she'd agreed to return to free any vanshaj they could gather.

"I'll come with you." He pushed himself up.

"You should rest," she said, and he pinned her with a glare that told her he had no intentions of letting her visit the city alone.

"I'm fine, and I'm coming."

He *wasn't* fine, but she let it lie. He was as stubborn as a mule, but she also suspected he was in denial about his condition.

They entered the city and headed to the inn to find Dav and Suria, who had rounded up several other vanshaj who made up their fledgling resistance.

After Zarya broke their collars, they thanked her profusely, and she urged them to keep it hidden. With Abishek's continued reluctance, she couldn't predict his reaction. There was no doubt that going behind his back would cause more problems than it solved, but she couldn't sit idle if there were vanshaj willing to seek out her help.

The Jadugara did not make a home in Andhera, which meant they wouldn't be subject to their scrutiny. She'd been informed they only visited a few times a year, towing "fresh" vanshaj in their wake and offering them up for sale to the nobility. Those who weren't chosen were simply abandoned here to fend for themselves. The more Zarya heard about the Jadugara, the more she wanted to disembowel every single one personally.

When they were done at Dav and Suria's inn, Zarya and Rabin passed through the city again.

"How are you feeling?" she asked, clinging to his arm.

He shook his head and pinched the bridge of his nose. "I'm... I have a headache."

She peered up at him and pressed her lips together as he pulled his hand away.

"I don't want you to worry," he said. "Kishore will return soon, and we'll fix this."

"I *am* worried. I can't not be worried."

He didn't respond, his jaw hard as he surveyed their surroundings.

"Let's just try and help as many as possible while we're here," he said. "That's better than focusing on something we can't change right now."

She opened her mouth to protest, but he silenced her with a pleading look. Blowing out a breath, she rolled her lips together. She hated this. The uncertainty was already eating her alive. But maybe he was right, and using their time to do something productive made more sense.

But as they passed through the city, even that idea seemed futile given the sheer number of vanshaj everywhere she looked. It reminded her that no matter what happened, she was still vastly unprepared to deal with the scale of this movement.

No matter how fast she worked, it would take years to accomplish complete and total freedom—and that was *if* they received approval from Rahajhan's rulers. Otherwise, it would take decades trying to operate in secret.

As they continued walking, she eyed the grand houses perched on the cliff, wondering if she could appeal to someone else with power and influence.

Again, Rabin rubbed his temple and let out a sigh.

"Why don't you lie down?" she asked.

He looked at her, and she could tell he was about to argue.

"Please?"

He blew out another breath and then nodded before they returned to the castle. Zarya forced him into bed, and it must have been a measure of how he was feeling because he didn't even argue.

Once she was certain he'd stay put, she left him to rest while she headed for the library. After she arrived, she stopped to stare around the room, sensing the king's presence despite his absence. On the days he joined her, they talked about everything—books, music, and history. He had so much to offer, and ever so slowly, she could feel her guard crumbling.

This man was her father. He wasn't perfect, but she could see a future where they might exist as a family. Row would always be her father in a way that Abishek could never claim, but she had more than enough love in her heart for both.

Once upon a time, Zarya believed no one wanted or loved her, but now she was surrounded by people who cared for her. The thought elicited a warm, fuzzy feeling in her chest that she clung to with all of her hopes.

The air was still and quiet, and this place was becoming like a second home. She inhaled the scent of paper and dust as a sense of calm settled into her bones.

After a few hours of reading, a sound drew her attention to the door. Rabin and Ekaja entered. He had a bit more flush to his cheeks, and a tiny knot of relief eased in her chest. Maybe this was nothing, and he was just coming down with something. Except rakshasa immunity was adept at fighting off the sorts of illnesses that plagued humans and even Aazheri from time to time.

"Found anything?" Rabin asked as he dropped into the seat next to her while Ekaja propped her elbow on a nearby shelf.

Zarya had been informed that Ekaja knew about her visions. Apparently, there wasn't much Abishek didn't share with his commander, and she was a bit irritated that the king hadn't asked her permission first. It wasn't that she didn't trust the woman, but she also knew very little about her.

"Not really," Zarya said. "Certainly, lots about past lives and reincarnated souls, but anything I come across doesn't sound right. Mine don't feel like memories in the same way. There's no distance. It feels like those things happened to *me* and not whoever I was before."

Rabin and Ekaja shared concerned looks as Zarya slapped a thick book shut, generating a cloud of dust. Her lungs were probably filled with it at this point. She waved her hand with a cough. Abishek clearly loved his library, but he was selective about who he allowed past the door, including the cleaning staff.

A second later, the door to the library opened again. One of the usual sentries bowed before admitting Urvi. She crossed the room, clutching a note in her hands. "Sorry to interrupt, but the king asked that I give this to you."

She handed the note to Rabin, who opened it, his brows furrowing.

"What is it?" Zarya asked.

"He's throwing a party tonight, and you are the guest of honor."

"Me?" She pressed her mouth together as nervousness churned in her gut. Abishek had made a few passing references about introducing her to Andhera's nobility, but she'd hoped they'd be long gone and on their way to Ishaan before he got around to it. It's not that she didn't want to meet them, but she was apprehensive about how they'd receive her.

Then she recalled those grand houses overlooking the city and wondered if this might be a chance to appeal to someone about the vanshaj.

"He wants to show you off," Ekaja sing-songed.

Zarya threw her a skeptical look.

"A powerful daughter," she continued. "You *are* something to show off."

"I'm not his monkey trained to perform tricks," she snapped, and Ekaja smiled.

Zarya had stepped into the sparring ring with Ekaja only once, and Abishek's commander was as formidable as she looked. But they all *liked* training in that godforsaken Cradle, and Zarya decided her time was better spent on her research.

"You are correct," Ekaja continued. "But the king never expected his line to continue. You were quite the... surprise."

"Okay, so I guess he expects me to attend," she said, taking the note from Rabin and scanning it.

"I think it would be easier to go along with it," Ekaja said.

"I have nothing to wear," Zarya said.

"My lady," Urvi interrupted, still waiting by the door. "The king has already taken care of that."

Zarya stood before the mirror a few hours later, wearing the most stunning lehenga she'd ever seen. A rainbow of soft pearlescent swoops of fabric gathered to form the full skirt while beading in similar hues covered every inch of the choli. Urvi had curled her hair and pinned the top half to her head, adding a pair of dangling golden earrings and a golden hoop to her nose.

Zarya's eyes were ringed in black, and her cheeks and lips were dusted with pink. She looked like a different person dressed like this. Older. Wiser. *Powerful.*

The message was unmistakable. This wasn't just a fancy outfit for a party.

This was how a *princess* dressed.

A knock came at the door, and Urvi opened it to reveal Rabin clad in a simple but well-made black sherwani that fit perfectly to the curves of his frame. Her heart did a little stutter as he stood in the doorway, his gaze assessing her from head to toe.

Urvi excused herself, leaving them alone.

"Spitfire," he said, his voice low and rumbling so deep, she felt it in her very bones.

"Hi," she said, doing a little twirl, "what do you think?"

"I think you're so beautiful you could stop time."

Rabin crossed the room and wrapped his arms around her from behind while she leaned into him.

"Ready?" he asked.

"Have you been to many of these things?"

"A few. They're boring. Full of ancient Aazheri who love the sound of their own voices."

"Oh, good. My favorite."

Rabin brushed a lock of hair from her shoulder and kissed the skin. "They won't know what hit them when you enter the room."

She sighed. "Are Yasen and Miraan coming?"

"I'm not sure. They've received another letter from Ishaan, and I don't think Miraan is willing to wait much longer," Rabin said. "Yasen is trying to calm him down."

Zarya frowned, biting the inside of her cheek.

"Let's go see them."

Rabin nodded and took her hand before heading for

Miraan's room, where they found the pair in the middle of a somewhat heated discussion.

"Zarya," Miraan said as they entered. He strode across the room and wrapped his hands around her shoulders. "I'm sorry, but I can't wait here anymore. My brother sent word that Dishani has been meeting with someone in secret. She's planning to bring in additional forces to quell the riots and root out the resistance."

"Additional forces? Where from?" Rabin asked.

Miraan shook his head. "My brother isn't sure. Dishani held a meeting two days ago, and despite her very delicate condition, she attended alone. A short while later, she announced that more armies would soon join them. They'll slaughter everyone if I don't *do* something."

Miraan released his grip on Zarya and paced away.

"And I'm not sure it's safe," Yasen said.

"I don't care!" Miraan said. "Don't you see? I don't care about *my* safety. If I die, so be it, but I can't sit here idle anymore."

Rabin and Zarya exchanged uncertain looks, while Miraan and Yasen appeared to have a silent conversation.

"Fine," Yasen said after a moment. "If that's what you want."

"You don't have to come with me," Miraan said. "I won't blame you if you want to stay here."

Zarya noted the way Yasen's gaze shifted between her and Miraan. She understood he was being forced to choose between them, but she would never expect that.

"You should go with him," Zarya said, taking the decision out of his hands.

When Yasen opened his mouth to argue, she strode over and grabbed his hand.

"We'll just be a few days behind. Kishore will return soon.

We can deal with the issues with our bond, and then we'll all be back in Ishaan before you know it."

"We said we should stick together," Yasen said almost petulantly.

"I know." Her hand tightened around his. "And after this, we will. But you should go with Miraan. I have Rabin to take care of me."

"I don't know about this," he said. "How long will you stay?"

"Just until we can ensure the bond is stable," she said.

Yasen blew out a breath. "Send us letters every chance you get. Every single day. Or I'll be back here before you can blink."

Zarya folded her arms and grinned. "Are you worried about me?"

"I'm always worried about you, Zee," he answered. He said it so seriously that she felt tears burn in her eyes. "Don't cry."

"I'm not," she answered, wiping the corner of her eye with the back of her hand. They smiled at each other, enjoying their silly game. She threw her arms around him.

"Be careful," she said into his chest.

He smoothed a hand down the back of her head and kissed her temple. "You be careful, too, Swamp Girl."

TWELVE

Miraan wanted to get going as soon as possible. Rabin left his room, heading for Abishek's wing to speak with his people about arranging transport. They burst into a flurry of activity at his command. They were used to figuring things out at a moment's notice.

When he was done, he returned to his wing, where Zarya was helping Yasen and Miraan pack up their things, dressed in her finery. She was like a gorgeous, miraculous butterfly flitting between islands of discarded clothing. The sight amused him so much that he stopped to lean in the doorframe simply to watch her.

Less than an hour later, the carriage was ready.

Zarya and Rabin escorted Yasen and Miraan to the main level of the castle and out through the front doors. Night was falling, and the stars were beginning to appear overhead. Zarya shivered, pulling her sheer dupatta tighter around her shoulders, though the thin material would do nothing to block out the cold.

She hugged Yasen and Miraan goodbye, and they all promised to see each other soon. Rabin hoped that was true, but he couldn't shake the nagging feeling that they shouldn't be separating and that this might be the last time they saw one another.

But he was being maudlin. He'd felt off ever since their arrival. His body ached, and he was exhausted. Even now, his temple throbbed with a sharp pain he couldn't seem to shake. He was rakshasa, and these sorts of minor ailments were incredibly rare amongst his kind unless there was some larger force at play.

Finally, Miraan entered the carriage and waited for Yasen to finish his goodbyes. It wouldn't be as fast as flying, but Abishek's carriage would see them to Ishaan in less than a week. In a few days, Rabin would fly Zarya to Gi'ana, and they'd meet there at almost the same time.

Rabin shook hands with Yasen as he asked in a low voice, "You promise to look out for her?"

Rabin tried not to be offended by the question, even if he understood its intention. No one would look out for her like he would. "With my life."

Yasen paused and then gave him a careful look. "You take care of yourself, too, Commander."

"I will, as long as you promise to do the same," he answered.

Then Yasen spun on his heel and joined Miraan, hopping into the carriage.

Once they were gone, Zarya turned to Rabin.

"So I guess we have some stuffy nobles to meet," she said as she shivered again.

He held out an arm. "Let's get this over with."

Zarya followed Rabin back into the palace and the warmth of its walls before he directed her through the corridors into a large salon. Like most rooms in the castle, it was adorned with colorful tapestries and rugs with massive crystal chandeliers dripping from above. Vanshaj, painted entirely gold from head to toe and wearing gold versions of their palace livery, wove through the crowd, balancing golden trays topped with golden goblets.

Unsurprisingly, the room was filled with Aazheri. Zarya had never been around so many at once, and she could feel the echoes of their power the moment she walked into the room. She stopped, sensing the potent thrum of their magic through her bones.

Suddenly feeling intimidated, a tiny quiver of fear fluttered in her stomach as she clung tighter to Rabin's arm.

"Zarya!" came Abishek's warm voice. "You're finally here!"

He stood in the middle of the room, dashing in a black sherwani embroidered with glossy red thread, and his midnight hair slicked back from his face.

"Come and meet some people," he said, gesturing for her to join him. She looked up at Rabin, her hand tightening on his arm again, seeking reassurance in his gaze. She could feel the weight of everyone's stares and judgment as they progressed into the crowd.

Abishek's smile was wide, and his eyes were uncharacteristically bright with excitement as they approached. "Meet Tanvi and Garu," he said, introducing her to an Aazheri couple dripping with jewels and diamonds. They emanated a fresh, sweet scent that *smelled* rich even from several feet away. She'd never seen skin so lustrous. It was like Tanvi was an actual pearl dug up from the bottom of the sea.

"It's so nice to meet you," Zarya said, dipping her head, refusing to release her tight hold on Rabin.

"Is it true? You are paramadhar and masatara?" Tanvi asked, blinking her big dark eyes framed with the longest, fullest lashes Zarya had ever seen.

"It is," she conceded. "We first met in the mind plane."

"This is remarkable," Garu said. "It seems the old magic is

returning to our world. We must understand why the gods have chosen to bestow us with such wonders."

Zarya remembered Thriti saying something similar when they'd completed the Bandhan. *Why* had they been chosen for this? To free the vanshaj? Or was something else also at play?

"It *is* quite an honor," Zarya said, attempting to keep the worry out of her voice. Rabin dipped his chin though he remained silent, his expression bordering on ferocious. Tanvi and Garu eyed him warily as they turned to Zarya and smiled, obviously pleased with her response.

"The king tells us you've arrived from Ishaan," Garu continued. "Were you caught up in the riots?"

"We were…" she said, wondering how much to reveal. With Abishek's current reluctance to discuss the vanshaj, maybe this was her chance to appeal to a wider, and likely influential, circle.

"It was my magic that broke the collars," she said in a rush as their eyes widened.

"*Your* magic?" Tanvi asked.

Zarya nodded and went on to explain the process using her nightfire, careful to leave out any mentions of the sixth anchor. Her magic was no longer a secret, but she wasn't sure how others would react to the darkness. Did they know the king possessed six anchors? She glanced at Abishek, whose face remained expressionless.

"We must see this," Garu said. "More than one kind of magic is returning. Change is coming to Rahajhan."

He lifted his glass in a toast, and Zarya's chest loosened at his words.

Change *was* coming.

"Yes," Abishek finally said. "Zarya has promised to show me, but I don't believe this is the time or place. We'll invite Kamal and Mohandas to witness her demonstration in a private setting before we share this news more widely. We don't want to repeat the mistakes made in Ishaan."

"Of course," Garu said. "I look forward to it."

They exchanged a few more pleasantries before Abishek excused them to continue mingling.

"When can we arrange for the demonstration?" she asked as they walked.

"Soon," the king assured her. "Let me speak with some of my nobles. It's best to be cautious about who we share this information with."

"Okay," she said, feeling more hopeful than she had in a while.

The king maneuvered their trio around the room, introducing her to dozens of people, each more elegant and refined than the last. They were all fascinated by the Bandhan and the fact they were in the presence of a paramadhar and masatara pairing.

She quickly lost track of the names and faces, hoping no one would notice as she smiled politely and made what she hoped were the appropriate comments for a princess.

She almost laughed the first time someone called her that but managed to restrain herself. The idea was so absurd and far-fetched. She didn't want to rule a realm. She wanted to go to university. She wanted to live with Rabin in a beautiful house in the heart of the city where she could walk to the market whenever she liked. She wanted to be surrounded by friends and family. She wanted the exact opposite of her previous life.

She couldn't wait for a different future. The one she'd imagined so many times in her loneliness.

"Rabin," Abishek finally said after they'd made a complete circuit around the room, and Zarya's head buzzed with dozens of details she would never remember. "Can you see what's keeping Ekaja? I hoped she'd speak with Khari tonight. He has acquired a new weapons stash from across the sea, and you know he'll only deal directly with her."

Rabin bent at the waist and then looked at Zarya. "Will you be okay for a few minutes?"

"Sure," she said. She didn't want him to leave, but it might sound childish if she begged him to stay. What was the worst that could happen within a few minutes?

After Rabin left, Zarya watched the door until he disappeared and returned her attention to Abishek.

"Something to drink?" he asked, and she nodded. He took her arm and led her through the party, finding her a glass of sparkling wine. He tipped his glass against hers with a soft clink. "To our future together, Zarya. I'm so very pleased you're here, and I do hope you'll feel comfortable enough to stay for a long time."

She took a sip as warring emotions twisted in her stomach.

He was planning their futures, and though she also wanted that, she had to leave. Could he understand how important the rebellion was to her? He'd agreed to a wider demonstration, and that had to mean something. Some part of her wondered if Kishore's supposed delays were actually a plot to keep her here longer, but then she felt guilty for thinking it. He *knew* why she had to leave.

"I am, too," she answered as he looked past her.

"Ah! Amir, there you are!"

Zarya turned around to be met by a pair of bright blue eyes and a pretty face with the barest layer of day-old scruff framed by a mane of shaggy black hair.

"Your Majesty," Amir replied smoothly. "It's so kind of you to invite me. My mother sends her regards."

Abishek smiled. "How is the lovely Dipita?" he asked, and Amir grinned.

"Everything ails my mother as usual, but she'll be pleased to know she was referred to as *lovely* outside of her hearing and not just because you were goaded into saying so."

Abishek laughed, but when Zarya looked closer, she noticed how his smile didn't quite reach his eyes and that his voice was a little too bright. It had been the same way the entire night. He was playing a game, and he was playing it beautifully. How much did he owe to these nobles around the room?

She was fascinated by the king's behavior because it was the exact opposite of how he behaved with her. He moved through the crowd with ease, remembering everyone's names and personal details, but she could sense he was also maintaining a careful distance.

In turn, they accepted him with all the politeness due to his station, but there was something reserved in their deference towards him. She remembered what Rabin had told her about enemies on his every side, spreading lies to discredit his position. It was obvious how much of a facade this was, and Zarya didn't think she cared for any of it.

"Please let me introduce you to Zarya," the king said, placing a hand on Zarya's back and gently, if forcefully, moving her closer to Amir.

Amir gave her a bright smile, his gaze traveling up and down as if weighing and assessing the various parts she had to offer.

"So this is the prodigal daughter," he said in an all-knowing tone she also didn't care for.

He took her hand and kissed the back while peering up through thick, dark lashes. Amir wore a green sherwani with expensive-looking gold embroidery around the collar and cuffs. An errant lock of black hair fell out of place, and he pushed it back. "It's a pleasure to meet you, Zarya. The king told me of your beauty, but he was very modest in his assessment."

Zarya frowned. "He did?"

Amir and Abishek both chuckled at her question.

"Zarya, Amir is from the finest noble family in Andhera. You probably noticed their estate overlooking the city. His father was my former commander and spent many years at my side. May the gods preserve his soul."

Zarya looked at Amir. "I'm sorry," she said, but he waved it off.

"I miss him every day, but it was many years ago, and though the loss never entirely goes away, the sting lessens over time."

Amir then gestured to one of the gold-painted servants for a glass of wine. A woman scurried over and dipped into a curtsy as she held up the tray.

"But I lost a father many years ago, and it seems you have found one, Zarya," Amir said. "How remarkable. The king shared some parts of your tale with me. How are you adjusting to this change in... station?"

"It's all been pretty overwhelming," she answered, noting the inflection on the word "station" as though she'd crawled out from a gutter covered in slime. "But I grew up thinking both of my parents were dead, and so it's been a lot to adjust to."

Amir smiled, his blue eyes twinkling. "I can only imagine." He sipped his wine, once again eyeing her, and she couldn't help but feel like he was weighing and cataloging her assets. Or lack thereof.

"Your father tells me you enjoy reading," he continued.

"Zarya has been spending many hours in my library," Abishek said. "She's a very powerful Aazheri. With her lineage, what else could she be?"

"Indeed," Amir said.

"And Amir here," Abishek continued. "He's also a very talented Aazheri."

"That's... lovely," Zarya said, her brow furrowing. Why did it feel like Abishek was trying... to *sell* Amir to her? Was he trying to set them up? Or was she missing some kind of social cue buried in subtext? Abishek hadn't acted this way around anyone else. Did Amir know what was happening? Was she imagining how they were taking their cues from one another?

"I'll leave you to it," Abishek said. "Get to know one another. I'll come and check on you in a bit." And then, before Zarya could say anything else, Abishek turned and walked away, melting into the crowd.

Rabin stormed through the castle, his firm steps punishing the stones underfoot. He remained on edge and hated that he couldn't figure out why. Everything was bothering him lately.

That party. Those people. The king. The way *something* kept nagging in the back of his thoughts.

He'd always had very good instincts and had learned long ago never to ignore that sixth sense until he could determine the source. But he had no clue what this was about.

Plus, he felt like shit.

Turning a corner, he approached the doors to Ekaja's apartments. He wasn't sure why a servant couldn't have managed this errand, but he didn't mind a break from the party. He hated leaving Zarya alone, but she could handle herself for a few minutes. He could see how enamored she was becoming with the king and saw so much of himself in her during his first years living in Andhera.

Ekaja never waited after knocking, and Rabin rarely offered her the courtesy, either. He rapped on the door and flung it open, storming into her room and coming to an abrupt halt. Now he understood the reason for Ekaja's delay.

She was completely naked, her dark hair falling down her back as she straddled the face of another woman, her hips writhing and her back arched as she moaned and gasped. The woman beneath her had her arms wrapped around Ekaja's firm thighs, eating her out with an admirable sort of enthusiasm.

Neither had noticed him yet.

He cleared his throat, but Ekaja continued moaning, her hips shifting back and forth as she ground her pussy into her companion's mouth.

He tried again, louder this time, and then added, "Ekaja!"

Finally, she noticed him. Offering him a sidelong glance, she continued riding the woman's face, keeping up her pace as she licked her lips and tossed him a coy look. He rolled his eyes. He was more than used to her antics.

"What?" she finally asked.

She had never been shy about flaunting her body, no matter the audience, but he always kept his gaze planted firmly above her neck.

"The king wants you at the party."

She returned his eye roll and then resumed fucking the woman's face. "I'm busy."

"Ekaja," he growled, his voice dropping low.

"I'm coming!"

Except she meant that literally. She cried out, her body arching as her movements grew more frantic.

"Fuck, Ekaja. Get your ass down there *now*," he demanded and then turned on his heel and slammed the door behind him to the sounds of Ekaja rocking through what sounded like a pretty fantastic orgasm.

He waited on the other side of the door, pacing, even more irritated than before. He wasn't angry with Ekaja, but *everything* was getting under his skin.

After she finished moaning, he heard them shuffling on the other side of the door, followed by a chorus of laughter and giggling. That was definitely her friend. Ekaja didn't giggle.

Finally, the door swung open, and Ekaja sauntered out with a shit-eating grin. She made a show of slowly wiping her mouth with the back of her hand and then slapped him on the ass before she began stalking down the hall. He barely reacted, a low growl building in his throat.

She looked over her shoulder and called, "Well, are we heading to the party?"

He huffed out a breath and caught up, his long strides matching hers.

"What's in your panties?" she asked.

"Shouldn't I be the one asking you that?"

She snorted. "Just because you're sexually frustrated doesn't mean I have to be."

He grunted. He *was* frustrated.

He *missed* Zarya. Maybe that's what this mood was about, but that didn't seem like him. He'd gone plenty of years without the touch of a woman during the darkest days on the battlefield with only his hand for company. He wasn't ruled by his cock like so many men. But he'd learned enough times that everything he believed about himself went out the window where Zarya was concerned.

Finally, they arrived back at the party and stood in the doorway. Immediately, he caught sight of Zarya with Abishek. They were talking to *Amir*. Or the weasel, as Rabin preferred to call him. He was constantly sniffing around the castle, sucking up to the king, and worming his way into his good graces. Even worse were the whispered rumors that followed the young noble wherever he went—namely, the abuse he'd heaped on a string of female partners, both of a sexual and corporeal nature.

His parents were wealthy enough to ensure the bulk of the accusations were hushed, never to be uttered in polite company, but everyone *knew*.

Amir was also incredibly powerful amongst Aazheri, and that offered a certain type of leverage that not even money could buy. Abishek had even mused once or twice about naming Amir his heir, though Rabin didn't believe he'd ever follow through on such a promise. Abishek believed in blood.

Ekaja currently stood as the Aazheri prepared to inherit Abishek's legacy if he died without naming an heir. She wasn't technically blood, but the king considered her family all the same.

With Zarya in the picture, he couldn't be sure where Abishek's plan lay.

What Rabin wanted to know was why that scum was anywhere near *her*.

He watched as Abishek introduced Zarya and Amir, pressing her a little closer towards him. His eyes narrowed as Amir studied Zarya, his gaze sweeping over her in a way that made Rabin want to walk over and poke his eyes out with the tip of a burning sword. And then step on them to feel the satisfying squelch as they collapsed under his boots.

"Settle down," came a soft voice to his left. Ekaja was also watching the scene, clearly picking up on the same thing he was. Or maybe she was just sensing his mood. "You'll give away your little secret if you can't control yourself."

Rabin growled deep in his chest, his hands curling at his sides. "I'll kill him. He's vile filth."

She barked out a dry laugh. "Absolutely, but go ahead and do it where there aren't a hundred witnesses. You're being so fucking obvious."

"She's mine. In every way."

Ekaja raised an eyebrow. "I've never seen you like this before."

He nodded and then stared back at Zarya, who looked a bit like a rabbit caught in the path of a predator. "There's never been anyone like her before. Nor will there be again."

Ekaja didn't respond. She just tipped her head and scanned the crowd.

"Ah, there's Khari," she said. "I should go talk to him as His Majesty 'suggested.' Don't do anything stupid while I'm gone."

Rabin rolled his neck, attempting to release some of the tension wrenching his muscles tight. "I can't promise that."

She snorted another dry laugh and then melted through the crowd while Rabin kept his gaze focused on Zarya. Abishek had moved on, and now Zarya stood with Amir, obviously trying to make polite conversation.

Rabin watched as Amir inched closer, laying a hand on Zarya's arm. Rabin nearly bit through his tongue, trying to keep himself in check. He knew she wouldn't appreciate him barging in to rescue her, but she also couldn't know what sort of man Amir really was.

He noticed how her shoulders tightened at the contact, and Rabin decided that along with his eyes, he would also rip off Amir's arm and beat him to death with it. However, that seemed too mild a reaction.

When Amir leaned down to whisper something to Zarya, Rabin had enough. He stormed over, practically bowling several party guests out of his way.

"Amir," he said through gritted teeth. "So nice to see you."

It took every ounce of his willpower not to punch his smug face so hard his neck would snap, but Ekaja's warning rang in his ears.

"Rabin!" Amir said in that smooth, oily way that always had Rabin thinking of snakes slithering through poisonous grass. "I didn't realize you were here."

"Well, I am," he nearly snarled as his hand wrapped around Zarya's elbow before he maneuvered them both so Rabin stood between them.

"What were you two talking about?" he asked. He didn't really care if it was rude.

"I was inviting Zarya to my mountain lodge," Amir said as if that were the most obvious thing. "You'll love it. It's very sumptuous. Deep in the Sprucegreen Range with the most breathtaking views you've ever seen. Much better than this." He waved a hand around them as if these majestic soaring mountains were anything to scoff at.

"Oh," Zarya said. "As I was saying, I'd have to consider it. We can't be in Andhera long. We must return to Ishaan soon."

"Ishaan?" Amir asked. "Does your father know of this?"

Rabin felt Zarya go a bit still at the question. "He does. Why do you ask?"

Amir shrugged and took a sip of his wine. "I understood you'd be staying here indefinitely so we could get to know one another better."

Zarya blinked, and Rabin felt a snarl building in his throat.

"Oh, why is that?" she asked, though he could tell she was stalling. She had already put it all together. Abishek was trying to pair her up with this monster. Had the king heard the rumors?

"Oh, well..." Amir said, almost at a loss for words. Did he think Zarya knew and was in on this? What game was Abishek playing?

"We should mingle," Rabin said before Amir could finish his thought. "You haven't met everyone yet."

Rabin glared at Amir and resisted the overwhelming urge to tell him to stay the fuck away from Zarya.

Then, before either could respond, he took Zarya's hand and pulled her away.

THIRTEEN

Yasen and Miraan arrived on the outskirts of Ishaan at the break of dawn. They asked the carriage to drop them off a safe distance from the city walls, using the forest to shield their approach. They planned to sneak in, hoping their arrival would go unnoticed. Picking through the trees, they kept their steps light until Ishaan came into view. They both stopped, listening to the hushed, distant sounds of the morning.

Most people would still be tucked into their beds, but the late-night crowds of Ishaan never slept.

"This is a bad idea," Yasen said.

"Probably," Miraan agreed. "But we have to help."

Yasen sighed and ran a hand along the back of his neck.

Miraan turned to look at him as the first of the day's light gilded the arch of his forehead and nose. He was beautiful—all regal lines and planes with those high cheekbones and that carved jaw. Those dark eyes designed to break his heart into a million pieces once the prince finally realized he was far too good for him.

Yasen had enjoyed his fair share of company throughout his life. But he'd rarely met anyone he wanted to open up with.

He'd lost his family at an age when he'd been too young to remember, and maybe because of that, he'd grown used to this hole in his heart that never seemed to close.

He missed a mother and father he'd never known, and the idea of losing anyone important ever again sat in his stomach like a rock. This gnawing fear had always been his most consistent companion.

Then he'd been adopted into a family where he'd been treated as second best by a man who could have been a father but had chosen the path of his abuser. Sometimes, he wondered if he would have been better off growing up in the streets but then felt guilty for the sentiment when he'd at least always had enough food to eat and a roof over his head.

He'd let Vikram in. The bastard had made it impossible to keep him at a distance. He'd been so eager and happy to have Yasen as a built-in best friend. He'd treated him like a brother from the first day Yasen had stood in the Ravana's great hall while Gopal had looked him over with a critical eye.

Yasen worried about his old friend, who no longer sounded like the man he'd known. He'd never made him feel second best.

And then, despite his best efforts to keep her at arm's length, he'd let Zarya in, too. She'd also made it impossible not to. But she was destined for big things, and all he knew was that he was terrified the world might take her from him, too.

"You okay?" Miraan asked, slicing through his maudlin thoughts.

He tipped a wry grin at the prince, prepared to make a joke. This was his defense. The armor he wore. Always playing the role of the irreverent lest anyone think he felt or cared too much. It helped keep people at a distance, never coming too close.

It took a special person to see past it.

Yasen approached Miraan, wrapping an arm around his waist, deciding to confess the truth instead. They were nearly the same height, though Yasen had an inch or two over him. "I'm... worried," he admitted as he ran his thumb along the line of Miraan's jaw. His rough stubble pricked the tip with a soft rasp.

"I am, too," he replied. "You don't have to come. Return to Zarya if you want."

Yasen blinked, searching for any judgment in that statement, but he found none. All he saw was Miraan's worry and concern.

"You might be safer there," he added after a moment. "It would make me feel better."

Yasen shook his head. "And miss all the fun?"

Miraan gave him a severe look. He was *very* serious all the time. Yasen lived for those tiny moments when he actually loosened up, but this thing between them was so new. Surrounded by the chaos following them across Rahajhan, whatever they were building felt like delicate crystals, ready to shatter at the slightest breath.

"I'm not going anywhere," Yasen said. "Zarya has Rabin to look after her."

"And who'll look after you, Yas?"

"I can take care of myself." At that, he released Miraan and began stomping towards the city, done with this conversation. When Miraan didn't follow, he called over his shoulder. "C'mon. We need you to do your magic thing to get us inside."

After another moment, he heard Miraan following with a huff and mumbling something under his breath that sounded distinctly like "Wish he'd just let me in."

Yasen chose to ignore it as they made their way around the wall, arriving at the same gate they'd entered when Miraan helped bust them out of the royal dungeon. He opened it with a thread of magic, and they slipped through the city's quiet alleys towards Operation Starbreak.

When they arrived at the house, they used their secret

knock and waited, hoping someone was inside. From their exchanges with Vikas, they knew most of the resistance had relocated to a secret spot in the forest.

It took a minute for the door to pop open, revealing Ajay, looking a bit rumpled and bleary-eyed but healthy and whole. His face cracked into a wide, happy smile.

"You're back!" he said, stepping aside to admit them into the house. "We've been so worried." He kept up a stream of chatter, barely pausing as he led them into the kitchen and immediately set some water to boil. "Tell me everything that's been happening."

A moment later, Row appeared in the doorway. He looked terrible, his complexion sallow and dark circles ringing his eyes.

"Yasen," he breathed. "How's Zarya?"

He strode over to the island where they were all seated, his hands clenching into fists.

"She's fine," he assured him. "I promise. Rabin is with her and won't let anything happen to her. Abishek welcomed us with open arms."

Row peered at him with a suspicious look. "You sensed nothing amiss?"

"I don't think so." He shared a look with Miraan, who nodded to confirm the same. "She seems quite comfortable with him, to be honest."

"When is she coming back? *Is* she coming back?"

His expression was so full of tortured hope that even Yasen had to feel bad for him. He explained the issues with their Bandhan and Zarya's sixth anchor and that as soon as they'd met with the king's mystic, they would return to help clean up this mess.

"I've never heard of such a thing," Row said. "But I suppose any lore around the sixth anchor is secretive and rather unknown. I might visit Thriti later to discuss it with her."

"I'm sure Zarya would appreciate that," Yasen said.

"Tell us what's been happening in the city," Miraan asked. "We're here to do what we can."

Ajay and Row shared a careful look.

"None of it's good," Ajay answered. "The Jadugara have been given free rein to arrest anyone they believe is connected to the resistance, and they're hunting down Taara Aazheri left and right. We've heard claims that anyone captured has been subjected to punishments too awful to name." He fell silent. "But let me make us some tea, and then we can discuss everything."

"My sister?" Miraan asked. "Have you heard anything more about her?"

"She's looking for you. And for Zarya. She's making no secret of it. You've both been branded as traitors of Gi'ana, and a steep price for treason is on your heads," Ajay continued.

Miraan pressed his mouth together and nodded. "I figured as much."

"They're saying her injuries are severe. Her healers are doing what they can, but her scars were created by magic fire and thus are much more difficult to cure." He hesitated before adding, "Koura has gone to the palace to offer his services."

"What?" Yasen asked. "I thought he was on our side."

"A Niramaya healer is duty-bound to offer help to anyone who requires it," Row said. "It is a part of his code of honor. He could not live with himself otherwise."

Yasen grumbled at that but had to concede that Koura was more noble than all of them put together.

"As long as he comes back if we need him," Yasen said, and Row almost smiled at that.

"He's still very much on our side."

"What else?" Miraan asked, and then Ajay and Row took turns explaining everything as the sun rose over another bloody day in Ishaan.

FOURTEEN

A few nights after the party, Zarya awoke to the sound of dishes clinking and a pale, cold light. Her head throbbed, almost like she'd drunk too much wine, but she hadn't touched a drop in days. Her first thought was to wonder if the Bandhan was affecting her, too.

After Rabin dragged her out of the room, he refused to say anything. She didn't think she'd ever seen him that angry before.

He'd begged her to spar, and so they'd changed into their training leathers, and he'd dragged her up to that godforsaken mountaintop where they'd fought until they nearly collapsed.

When they'd had enough, they stumbled into his bed, wrapped in each other's arms. Zarya half expected Abishek to storm into the room that very morning and demand to know why they'd left the party, but she hadn't seen him in days.

It seemed he was keeping his distance, and after he'd very obviously tried to set her up with Amir, she didn't mind. But perhaps she wasn't being fair. For all Abishek knew, Zarya was available, and their own deception led him to that conclusion.

She still didn't appreciate being blindsided and wished he'd asked her about it first.

That left them with little to do as they awaited Kishore's return. Zarya had even lost interest in the library after hours of searching had turned up nothing. Her only solace became time spent sparring with Rabin and Ekaja and the afternoons she stole into the city, where she continued breaking the collars of anyone willing.

After the day was done, she'd sit with Dav and Suria, who loved hearing her stories about the Rising Phoenix in Ishaan. In return, she loved hearing them talk about a future that looked very different than the one they had all accepted.

A democracy, they called it. Where representatives from every group had a voice, and the people all had the opportunity to vote on decisions that affected them. It sounded perfect. But it also sounded like a far-off dream.

With each passing day, Zarya slept later and later.

Dreams and nightmares plagued her slumber, interrupted by long bouts of insomnia, during which she stood at the tall, cold windows with her arms folded around her, staring at the still landscape, contemplating a thousand things.

Her thoughts were filled with smoke and fire. Screaming and death. She saw flashes of those demon armies marching over scarred, scorched earth, everything in their path left in smoldering piles of ruin and destruction.

She'd toss and turn until she finally collapsed from exhaustion sometime in the early hours of the morning. Occasionally, she'd cross the hall to find Rabin and take comfort in the warmth of his arms, but other nights, she'd stew in her loneliness, trying not to burden him as he continued to struggle with his health.

This morning, she rubbed her temples as her head throbbed. She sat up and blinked the sleep from her eyes. Urvi stood at the other end of the room, quietly laying food on the small table before the fire.

When she noticed Zarya was awake, she smiled. "I've brought lunch."

"Thank you," Zarya said as she pushed off her blankets. The room was cold despite the fire. The wind howled against the windowpanes, and the snow fell at an angle, swirling in gusts.

"It's a miserable day," Urvi added. "Perfect for curling up by the fire with a good book and some warm chai."

To prove her point, she held up a mug for Zarya, who pulled a thick robe over her pajamas and belted it around her waist before stuffing her feet into a pair of slippers by the bed.

Zarya accepted the tea and sank onto the divan, sipping it as she stared at the crackling logs. She thought of the fireplace back home in the seaside cottage and how they'd rarely ever had the occasion to use it. She smiled as she thought of how much Row had missed the north. She also realized she'd just referred to the cottage as *home* without it calling up a rash of bitter memories. My, how so many things had changed.

She heard Urvi moving about the room as she nursed the warm mug, holding it between her cold hands and again thinking of the other night.

Why had Abishek tried to ambush her with Amir instead of just being upfront? She could have headed off any notions that she was available or was open to having any part of her future decided for her.

When Rabin had intervened, he'd read the situation correctly, and it had probably taken every ounce of his restraint not to pick Amir by the collar and hurl him off one of the castle's high balconies.

He obviously loathed Amir in a way that felt personal, and she wondered if they had any sort of history. When she'd asked, Rabin had clammed up, and she decided not to push it.

It was a little possessive and over-the-top, but Zarya smiled anyway. She'd signed up for this when she'd bound herself to a man like Rabin.

Once Rabin had freed her from Amir's clutches, he'd told her that Amir had been rumored to become Abishek's heir, though he had no idea what the plans were now that Zarya was in the picture. He'd also told her Ekaja was Abishek's stand-in until he made it official.

With no blood heirs—until now—he'd been waiting for the right Aazheri to come along. Ekaja preferred to remain in the role of his commander but had agreed to his request because she refused to let him down.

It didn't matter either way. Zarya needed to return to Ishaan as soon as possible, and she wasn't doing anything with Amir.

She planned to search for Abishek later to clear all of this up. Despite the strides they'd already made, he'd been her father for all of five minutes. He had no right to think he could govern her life or her choices.

"Is everything to your liking?" Urvi asked. "You haven't touched your food."

Zarya looked up, her gaze wandering to the line of stars around Urvi's throat. Zarya also wanted to discuss the promised demonstration as soon as possible. They'd need to organize it quickly so as not to delay their departure any longer.

"Yes, I'm sorry. I'm not hungry." Zarya sat up and gestured to the seat across from her. "Would you like to have a seat?"

"Why?" Urvi asked, confusion denting the space between her brows.

"I know nothing about you. I'd love to chat if you're willing."

The woman looked around the room like someone was about to catch her indulging in an illicit activity, but Zarya tried to affect a reassuring expression. She wanted to test the waters with Urvi but couldn't ask about her collar outright. She also wanted to know more about this woman and what her life in Andhera had been like.

She understood her father was a 'complicated' man. That his relationship with the vanshaj was questionable, and despite his assurances that he respected the mission of the rebellion, he obviously regarded them as little more than furniture.

Urvi looked around the room again and then carefully made her way to the chair opposite Zarya.

"Can you tell me about your life in this castle? How long have you worked here?"

Zarya cringed at the deliberate terminology and the idea that she was a paid worker with the same rights and freedoms as one of Rahajhan's free citizens. "Sorry," Zarya said. "I don't want to dishonor the role you play here. I understand that 'worked' isn't the right way to describe your position in this castle and this kingdom. That you're not here by choice."

Urvi blinked, her expression crumpling with confusion. "Why are you saying such things?"

"Because someone needs to say them."

Zarya schooled her expression into neutrality. She wanted to appear calm and sure of herself so Urvi might feel the same. Urvi watched her for several moments before she finally nodded slowly.

"Yes, I understand what you mean. There's no polite way to describe it."

"No, because this isn't a polite situation. But hearing that makes people uncomfortable. Especially those with the most to lose should things ever change."

"Change?" Urvi asked, her eyes widening. "I hear the rumors. Uprisings in Daragaab and Bhaavana. I've heard..."

She trailed off, her cheeks blushing pink as if she were afraid of even thinking about it.

"What have you heard?" Zarya asked.

"One of the kitchen maids has a cousin who lives in Ishaan.

He sent a letter. That's where you and your companions came from, yes? Lord Ravana? He was there as well?"

Zarya nodded. "Yes. And the stories are true."

She paused, allowing her words to sink in.

Urvi blinked and then blinked again. "They say… they broke their collars."

Zarya nodded. "And they have magic because you are Aazheri. And you always were."

Horror crossed Urvi's expression. "No. That is heresy. We are vanshaj. We have no magic. It is forbidden."

"I know everyone keeps saying that. And I know that's the story that's been fed to everyone for a thousand years, but it isn't true. The truth was stamped out. It was glossed over, and the lie was repeated so many times that everyone believed it. You do have magic, and there isn't any reason you shouldn't have access to it."

She went on to tell the story they'd uncovered about the Jadugara as Urvi's face grew paler and paler.

When she was done, Urvi nodded slowly as if rolling the words around her head for their truth. "And what are they like? Those who've been freed?"

"Like?" Zarya asked. "What do you mean?"

"Are they *different*?"

"They're the same people they always were. But they have more power. More strength. They have their freedom."

"Do they?" Urvi asked. "Does the removal of the collar mean anything? Does it change the laws? Would it free me from this place? Could I marry anyone I choose? Live where I want?"

She swept out her arms to encompass their surroundings and blew out a long breath laden with a lifetime of exhaustion.

Zarya matched her weary sigh. "It's a question I've been asking myself from the very beginning. The collars are only the first step on a long road. But it *is* a start."

Urvi gave her a skeptical look, but Zarya wondered if she spotted the tiniest glimmer of hope in her eyes.

"I could break yours," Zarya said carefully. "If you wanted. My magic was created for this purpose."

Okay, that wasn't really the case. Nightfire existed before the vanshaj if the stories were correct, but the prophecy suggested the magic *had* been given to her for this.

Urvi shook her head. "No. That is... no."

She said it firmly, her eyes glossing over with the threat of tears. She jumped up, her hands balled into the fabric of her skirt. "I must go. I've lingered here long enough."

"Wait," Zarya said. "I'm sorry. I didn't mean to pressure you."

But Urvi wouldn't hear it. She stormed quickly out of the room, slamming the door behind her.

Zarya stared at it, contemplating the endless challenges of this battle they were facing.

All of this would be so much harder than she'd hoped.

FIFTEEN

Zarya had another dream about her mother.

Tonight, it was more vivid—the colors brighter—and she wasn't just observing the scene; she was inside it. She saw herself winding up a narrow stone staircase and opening a door, the hinges creaking ominously against the backdrop of a howling wind.

Asha huddled against the wall, cold and barely dressed, bloody lashes marring her arms, legs, and back. She curled into herself, her head pressed to her knees as she shivered with a helpless whimper.

Zarya slowly entered, her shoes ringing against the hollow wooden floorboards, dust kicking up around her feet. She stretched her arm out, trying to reach Asha, desperately wanting to touch and comfort her.

A flash of golden light flared in her side vision, and she spun around to catch a fleeting glimpse of a golden figure. The same woman she'd seen last time. She stared at the empty space for several seconds before turning towards her mother again.

Asha shuddered, her teeth chattering and her chest rattling with dry breaths.

Zarya took another step, and then the world blinked out.

Her eyes flew open, and she sat up in her bed. It was still dark outside, and the sun was just beginning to lift over the horizon. Her skin was clammy and sweat beaded on her forehead. Her pulse was racing, and her heart thrashed against her ribs.

Why did she keep having that dream? And why now? Who was the golden woman in the corner? And what did she have to do with any of this?

Shoving the covers off, she slid out of bed and padded to the window. Snow fell in soft flakes, covering everything with a pristine blanket of white. She missed the beaches of Daragaab, their warm breezes, and the crash of the sea, but she couldn't deny Andhera's pure tranquility.

Despite her wariness, she realized she was already falling in love with this place. It was as if her consciousness knew this was where she'd always belonged.

Knowing she couldn't sleep anymore, she decided to do some reading.

Tossing on some warm clothes, she made her way through the quiet halls of the castle, her route lit by dim, flickering torchlight.

She stopped before a long stretch of tapestries, carefully studying the buildings and streets of the great city that had once stood nestled in these mountains.

Taaranas.

Through her many hours spent in Abishek's library, she'd learned all about the ancient city where the Ashvin twins had once ruled, their power spreading far and wide over Rahajhan.

She noted the great stepped pyramid of the Temple of Starlight—made entirely of silver bricks—with a massive star hovering at its peak. This had been the twins' fortress where they gathered followers and worshipers, who came bearing gold and gifts to earn the twins' favor.

Zarya noted the hundreds of people woven into the scene.

She wondered who they were, what they'd been thinking. What happened to them when the worst came? She shivered at the thought of these poor families swept away by a tide of nairatta.

A distant noise had her spinning around, her heart thumping in her chest. But the corridor was empty, and she shook it off. She was letting her mind get the best of her. Still, she hurried along, traversing the halls quickly until she spied the familiar entrance to Abishek's library.

She was surprised to find the king seated at a table, reading by the light of a small yellow orb floating next to him. He looked up at her approach, his brow furrowing. "Zarya, what are you doing here at this hour?"

"Where have you been? I've been wanting to speak with you."

"Ah," Abishek said, closing his book and folding his hands over the cover. "I'm very sorry. I've been dealing with some issues at my northern borders. The mountain clans have blocked some critical passes, preventing supply access into the city." He shook his head and pinched the bridge of his nose. "It's all very messy but also very boring and nothing you need to trouble yourself with."

He patted the table. "Come and have a seat and tell me how I can help."

"I was having trouble sleeping," she admitted as she wandered closer, perching on a stool across from him. "Dreams. Nightmares. Visions. I'm having trouble separating it all at this point."

"More of the same? Would you like to talk about it?"

This was one thing she appreciated about him. Despite his never-ending thirst for knowledge, he always offered his undivided attention whenever she spoke. It made her feel important. Maybe even loved.

"It's my mother," she said as she watched his brows climb up his forehead. "I keep seeing her in a room with windows, and the wind howls around us. Someone has hurt her. She's wearing barely any clothing, and she's shivering. She's covered in bruises and marks."

Zarya touched her arm like she could feel her mother's phantom pains.

Abishek was staring at her intently now, something passing behind his eyes. "What happened in the dream?" he asked.

"Not much. I circled up some stairs, came to the top, saw her, and then I woke up."

"That's it?" he asked.

"I almost touched her, and there was a strange flash of light," she said, still feeling the strange chill that had settled over her. "I thought I saw someone else, too. But the dream ended before I could reach her."

Abishek continued to study her carefully. "Who did you see?"

"I'm not sure. It almost looked like a golden woman."

"And what do you think it might mean?"

"I don't know. Maybe it's just my mind playing tricks on me. She's been in my thoughts more than ever."

Abishek nodded. "That makes sense. Perhaps being here, meeting me, and seeing this place stirs up many feelings of family and belonging."

She nodded. That did make sense.

"I just don't understand why my subconscious would be choosing to hurt her."

Abishek seemed to consider that. "Perhaps deep down, you blame her for leaving you. Perhaps you must work through any anger you're holding about being abandoned by the only parent who knew you existed."

Zarya rubbed the tip of her nose, wondering if she sensed a pointedness in his comment. She understood her mother's reasons for keeping her a secret from Abishek, but he probably had a right to feel a touch bitter about the entire situation. Especially since they'd been here for weeks now, and the king hadn't done anything to suggest her fears were accurate.

"Maybe," Zarya replied.

She recalled Dishani's shouted words and Miraan's answer when she'd barely clung to life.

She abandoned us.

She didn't have a choice.

Zarya wasn't the only child she'd left. She wasn't the only one hurt by their mother's disappearance. Maybe with Asha in the picture, things would have turned out differently for all of them. Could she have controlled her daughter? Would her mother have worked *with* the Rising Phoenix or against them?

"How did you meet her?" Zarya asked. "How did you..."

"Come to father you?" he asked with an arched brow.

"Yes."

He leaned back in his chair and crossed his legs. "It's not a particularly interesting story. I was in Ishaan on business, and it's customary for visiting royals to offer lodging to one another." He paused. "She was a fascinating and beautiful woman, and we talked for hours. We had many things in common, and I understood her arrangement with Kabir was only a front." His gaze grew distant. "As one thing led to another, I find you sitting here with me."

He turned to look at her, and she was having trouble reconciling her conflicting emotions.

She tore her gaze from the king's and looked around the room. She didn't want to talk about this anymore. That dream kept polluting her thoughts. Combined with her strange visions, her head was becoming a very dark and tumultuous place.

"Why were you looking for me?" Abishek asked a moment later.

"Hmm?" She returned her focus to the king.

"When you came in, you wondered where I'd been."

"Yes. I wanted to talk to you about Amir."

Abishek arched a brow and gave her a serious look.

"What about him?"

"I hope I'm not overstepping or imagining anything, but I wondered if perhaps..." She stopped and rubbed a hand down her face. Now that she was saying it out loud, she felt silly and wondered if she'd misread the entire situation.

"What is it?" Abishek asked, his tone laced with concern.

"You weren't trying to 'introduce' us?" she finally asked. Abishek appeared confused before his expression cleared.

"Ah, I think I understand," he said. "I simply wanted you to meet him as I did with all the others. I hope... I did nothing wrong?"

Zarya inhaled a breath and smiled. "No. Not at all. I guess I misread things."

Abishek chuckled softly. "Though if you are looking to make a match, you could do worse than..."

She raised a hand. "Thank you. No. That isn't necessary."

"You're sure? You're a young woman, and you'll need to settle down soon enough."

Zarya ignored the chastisement in his tone and sucked in a deep, calming breath.

"I'm positive. There's someone back in... Ishaan."

The lie clogged in her throat, and she wondered how much longer Rabin would insist they maintain this ruse. Surely, with everything Abishek knew, this hardly mattered in the bigger picture.

"I see," Abishek said, and she couldn't determine anything from the tone in his voice. "I should like to meet the lucky Aazheri."

She rubbed the tip of her nose. "What makes you think he's Aazheri?"

Abishek blinked. "No daughter of mine will dilute her bloodline by breeding with anyone but an Aazheri."

Zarya frowned. "Who said anything about *breeding*? And don't you think that's a little... reductive?"

Abishek's gaze darkened. "I have spent my life protecting the power of Aazheri, Zarya, including keeping our bloodline pure. When the time is right, you will marry an Aazheri. One with strong magic. Amir would be the perfect choice."

She stared at the king, every response she could think of withering on her tongue. She had no idea how to respond. Obviously, she would never concede to this demand. So, she brushed past it, eager to change the subject, and asked, "Have you heard from Kishore yet?"

Amir and Abishek's notions of who she should marry would become a distant memory once they met with the mystic and left.

"In fact, I have," Abishek said. "He shall return in two days."

"Two days? For sure this time?" she asked. "Because we've delayed enough."

He nodded. "I understand. If you'll just hang on a little longer. Perhaps I might examine your marking again? I want to ensure the bond hasn't deteriorated any further."

Zarya shifted in her seat, feeling the weight of the dragon tattooed on her shoulder. "You don't need Rabin here for this?"

"It would give me a clearer picture, but I can get a sense with only your tattoo."

"Okay," she said, tugging down the sleeve of her top as Abishek stood and circled behind her. She stared ahead and felt him gently lay a hand on her shoulder, his skin cool and dry. She closed her eyes, concentrating on the dragon, wondering if she could feel it, too. Was there some way to tell if the corruption was growing worse?

She felt nothing. Not the echoing tie that bound her to Rabin like she had two souls living inside her. Their connection was still blocked.

"You still haven't been able to access the mind plane?" he asked as if reading her thoughts.

"No," she answered.

Abishek probed her skin along the lines of the marking for another minute with his clinical touch. She heard him make a soft noise of concern before withdrawing his hand and circling back to take the chair across from her.

"I'm sorry," he said. "It's as I feared. I sense the corruption within the bond is deepening."

Zarya swallowed a knot of anxiousness at that declaration. "Is it much worse?"

Abishek shook his head. "Not so much that the effects are irreversible, but I am growing concerned. You haven't noticed anything amiss with your magic?" He sat forward, bracing his elbows on the table with lines of concern marring his forehead.

"No," she said, shaking her head.

"What about the visions?" he asked. "Have they changed or increased in frequency?"

She nodded. "They come more than ever." She rubbed her arms, suddenly feeling a chill in the air. "You haven't noticed anything unusual within your borders? Creatures that don't belong here?"

Abishek shook his head. "Zarya, the blight isn't returning. I assure you."

Zarya rubbed her nose and sighed.

Surely, you've realized by now that you are responsible for all of this? That the darkness lives in you?

"Zarya," he said after another moment, his tone patient and kind. "Do you *really* think you are responsible for a plague spreading through all of Rahajhan?"

He studied her, worry entering his expression. His look was warm and full of what might be called protection. She shook her head, feeling tears press the backs of her eyes as she let out an amused huff.

"I mean, I don't know. I would have said no if you'd asked me that a year ago. But so much has happened since, and I don't really know anymore. What if I am? What if something inside me is causing all of this?"

She swept her hands over herself, and Abishek considered her with his unflinching gaze. He folded his hands and gave her a serious look.

"I understand why it might feel that way, but these are coincidences. No one person could be responsible for something so devastating. It isn't possible. No matter how strong an Aazheri you may be, not even you could have caused the blight."

She hadn't realized she needed to hear those words so badly. Her shoulders dropped in relief.

"Dhawan was trying to get into your head," he continued. "He was always a master of manipulation—it is the reason I banished him. He was using his 'skills' to turn the nobles' favor against me so he could seize power for himself. It backfired, and when he realized he was no match for me, he tried to worm his way back into my confidence. He was simply trying to coerce you into following him."

"It nearly worked," she admitted. "I almost..."

She stopped and shook her head. She remembered the violent feeling of wanting to embrace her darkness. She'd learned it wasn't the evil entity she'd first thought, but at that moment, she'd *believed* in what it could offer her. And she'd wanted that power for herself.

"Zarya, all will be well," Abishek said. "Kishore may be able to answer some of these questions. Mystics know things about magic that collective memory has forgotten. They know things I only wish I could understand."

"Thank you," Zarya said. "I appreciate this."

Abishek gave her a smile. "Now I'm off to bed, and you should probably do the same."

She nodded and watched as he left before her gaze

wandered to the window and the snow-covered forest. Despite all the king's assurances, there was something she had to see for herself.

A short while later, Zarya found herself traipsing through the snow, her jacket buttoned and her collar pulled up around her cheeks. Her boots crunched on the hardpack, echoing in the stillness of the forest while the moon hung low and bright in a clear velvet sky.

The end of her nose burned with a nip of frost, and she stamped her feet to generate warmth. She wasn't sure exactly what she was looking for, but she wanted to test something out.

She stared up, taking in the constellation of stars and the tall evergreens surrounding her on all sides. She couldn't hear anything save the rush of wind through the branches. The city slept, and the distance drowned out any ambient noise.

Inhaling a deep, cleansing breath, she approached a tree. Everything about her magic seemed to connect to forests and what grew from the earth—including the blight in Daragaab and the trees in Gi'ana. Even Rabin was connected to these trees.

She pulled off her glove and then reached out, wrapping her hand around a prickly branch. The soft needles poked at her skin while she filtered out a thread of her sixth anchor.

The dark ribbon of black magic swirled around her, forming clouds of billowing shadows. A moment later, flashes snapped across her vision—the same as always—a wasteland of nothing. Screams and fires. Demon armies marching over scorched earth, their dulled weapons glinting under a weak sun.

The man's voice, speaking in that language she didn't understand, but it felt almost like it was within reach today. Something shifted, and she saw him peering at a mirror, studying his reflection. But no, that wasn't it.

The reflection moved independently, walking in the opposite direction. Not a reflection. It was two different men. *Twins.* They spoke rapidly, their hands flying and their eyes alight with manic light.

And that's when she recognized their location. The silver Temple of Starlight stood behind them, stretching to the sky. The twins turned to face a crowd reaching up to them, their cries beseeching as they reached for the Ashvins.

Taaranas.

The lost ancient city.

Her gaze swept up the stepped temple and to the massive star hanging above it, slowly spinning on an axis. Her breath caught. This is what she'd been witnessing all along. She'd been right when she'd asked Abishek about the Hanera Wars.

She was seeing the start. The days before the world fell into ruin.

Zarya gasped and pulled her hand away, stumbling back and falling into the snow. She looked around her, feeling tears press the back of her throat.

The trees surrounding her were dead now.

Everything charred black and rotten, forming a wide, accusing circle.

She had done this.

She had been responsible for everything.

No matter what Abishek claimed, she knew he was wrong.

Surely, you've realized by now that you are responsible for all of this?

There was no denying it anymore.

The darkness was following her.

SIXTEEN

"Zarya," came a rough voice. She spun around to find Rabin standing in the trees. "What happened?"

They both scanned the ruined clearing before their gazes met.

"What are you doing out here?" she asked.

"I saw you leave the castle, and I was worried." He took a step towards her, holding out his hand. "Are you okay?"

"It happened again," she said. "The visions... they're growing stronger, and I saw something else. I think I just figured something out."

"What?" He searched her face, his brow furrowed with worry.

"I've always thought it was one man I was seeing," she said. "It was always the same face."

She looked up at him as nervousness swelled up her throat.

"Zarya, what is it?"

"There are two men. Twins."

She paused as those words settled around them.

"Twins?" He blinked.

She swallowed hard as she scanned the quiet forest. An owl hooted in the distance, echoing against the still night.

"I recognized the Temple of Starlight and the ancient lost city of Taaranas. There was no mistaking it." She clutched her heart as it hammered in her chest.

"Zarya, what is it?"

"I don't think they're actually visions," she said, her voice hollow.

"What do you mean?"

"I can't explain it," she replied as she bent over, suddenly feeling like she was having a heart attack as her ribs constricted. "It's not something I'm witnessing. It's something I've experienced. I was *there*. These aren't... recollections or the echoes of past lives. These are... *my* memories."

Rabin circled his arms around her waist as her knees buckled, her weight falling against him.

"What does that mean?" he asked as he slowly led her towards a rock where she collapsed. He sat beside her as she spread her knees and dropped her head between them, trying to catch her breath. The snowy ground spun, twisting the edges of her tilting vision.

"I don't know," she said. "Is it possible..." She looked up to find him watching her with a concerned expression. "Is it possible that I *was*... the Ashvins?"

Rabin frowned. "I don't think it works like that. You can't be two different people."

"Maybe it's different with twins? Maybe they share a spirit or something?"

Rabin huffed out a short breath. "I suppose it's possible."

She shook her head and scrubbed her cheek with the back of her hand, catching an errant tear. "When it first happened, it felt like I was bearing witness to it, but this time I was *there*. I felt their passion and their anger. Their desire to seize power and conquer everything in their path."

"Wouldn't you understand their language, then?"

She shrugged. "It's been a thousand years. Maybe I forgot."

They shared another look before they both fell silent. The wind softly rustled the leaves, and the screech of a bird echoed in the distance.

"What will you do? Talk to the king?" he asked. She noticed the lines around his mouth tighten at the question.

She shook her head. "He doesn't seem to think any of this is a problem. He thinks I'm just imagining it, or it's all in my head."

Rabin took her hand and squeezed it. "We'll figure out what this is."

She chewed on her bottom lip. "What if Dhawan was right?"

Rabin's brow creased. "You are *not* the darkness, Zarya. You are the very definition of light."

She gestured around them and the damning evidence of what she'd done. Her gaze skirted over the dead trees. "How can you say that? You remember what happened to your flowers. *Something* isn't right."

His jaw turned hard as he surveyed their surroundings before he shook his head. "There is some explanation for this. Some other one."

"What if there isn't?" she asked. "What if I did cause it, and what if it's returning? What if something evil lives inside of me?"

"Zarya—"

"No, don't deny it. Answer me. What if this is real?"

Rabin reached out to tuck a lock of hair behind her ear. "Why are you asking me this?"

"Because I'm afraid. Because I might be a monster, and you are bound to me. I should have told you about the visions before I let you perform the Bandhan."

He studied her with his intense gaze. "Zarya. What if this

were the other way around? What if the darkness lived in me? What would you say?"

She swallowed. "I'd tell you that we'd find a way to fix it, or we'd both die trying."

He huffed out a small laugh. "Zarya, don't you think that I feel the same? I promised you that I would protect you no matter what. Whatever the fates throw our way, I will be there for you. If this is something we must deal with. If evil lives inside you, I will also stand by your side for as long as it takes."

Zarya's mouth pressed together as tears filled her eyes. One slipped down her cheek, and she said, "I love you. I know we had a rocky start, but I love you, and I'm so lucky the fates chose you to be my paramadhar."

He offered her a tipped smile. "They chose well. I can't imagine being bound to anyone else."

Then he leaned in to kiss her and she sensed he was trying to offer a message of his truth and his commitment. That he was trying to prove the sincerity of his words. She would do the same for him. Of course she would.

He pulled away and touched his forehead to hers.

"I love you, too," he whispered as they sat quietly holding one another, surrounded by the ruin of all her secrets.

Rabin held Zarya tightly as she continued to shake. The look on her face was unbearable when she asked him if he would stand beside her. He understood why she needed to voice the question. He understood what it felt like to worry that the ones you loved might walk away.

After a few minutes, she pulled away and wiped her eyes with the back of her hand.

"It's freezing out here," she whispered. "We should probably go back."

She looked around the withered clearing, blinking as if wishing she could make it disappear. "Can you... fix this?"

Her wary look was so full of apprehension that he immediately nodded. "I can."

He stood up and took a moment to circle the clearing while calling on his magic. Swirls of coppery light floated from his fingers, touching the trees and curling around their trunks and branches.

He watched as his magic took hold, restoring the plants to their former state. When he'd finished, he turned to find Zarya watching him with a sparkling sort of wonder.

"You're amazing," she said, eliciting a warm twist in his heart.

He approached and held out a hand, drawing her up.

"Do you want to go back to bed, or are you open to seeing something special I've been saving?"

She offered him a small smile. "What is it?"

"It's a surprise. But I promise it will take your mind off all this for a little while."

"Then I'm in."

He leaned in to kiss her cheek, her skin icy against his lips. Then he took her hand and tugged her through the trees, away from the castle and the city. The sky was dark, with only the moon providing light, but he had no trouble navigating the terrain with his enhanced sight.

"Where are we going?" Zarya asked, and he was relieved to hear the excitement in her voice. Whatever this thing was, they'd figure it out. He knew she wasn't evil.

"Almost there," he promised.

They twisted down the path and broke through the trees.

"Oh," Zarya breathed as she took in the steaming hot springs spreading before them. Dozens of bright blue pools nestled amongst the rocks, connected with tiny waterfalls, stone bridges, and ladders carved into the sides.

"Okay, this was worth the wait," she said, grinning as he dragged her closer.

"Care for a swim?" he asked, arching a brow.

She nodded eagerly. "Absolutely."

"Then strip," he growled, and she was already tugging off her clothes and folding them on top of a large rock. Once Zarya was naked, she tiptoed over to the water and immediately sunk in, exhaling a sigh.

"Gods, that feels amazing," she groaned. She dunked her head, soaking her hair, and popped up before looking to where he stood watching her.

"You coming?" she asked, tipping her head and giving him a coy look that made his dick stir. Still wearing his pants, he nodded with his hand on the laces. The cold dragged goosebumps across his skin, but he wanted to watch her enjoy this for a moment.

She pushed off the wall, swimming back, giving him a wicked grin.

"Rabin," she whispered. "Get in here now."

He smirked and finally shucked off his pants and boots, settling everything on the same rock to keep everything dry. Then he stood at the edge, peering down.

Zarya's eyes wandered over his body, her gaze tracing the curves of his shoulders and the planes of his chest. He felt that look as it traveled lower and to his cock, which already stood hard and swollen, ready for her.

Zarya floated closer, folding her arms on the ledge. "Do you need some help with that?"

Her eyes dipped to his hips, and she licked her lips before peering up with an innocent smile.

The corner of his mouth curled in response before he strode over and leaped into the water. Zarya screamed as he splashed her, and before she could recover, he snaked an arm around her waist, dragging her back to his chest.

She pretended to fight him as she laughed, and he buried his nose into the curve of her throat. He dragged her deeper, moving between the rocks until they entered a deep pool lit from within by bioluminescent plants. This was his favorite spot.

They stopped in the center, and he wrapped a hand under her chin and tipped her face up to reveal the sky sparkling with a million stars. Soft moonlight beamed down, making the air foggy and soft. It was easier to forget your troubles in this place. It made his heart slow and his mind go quiet.

Zarya spun around in his arms, flattening her body to his. She was warm and soft, and he pulled her closer, his hand pressing against the small of her back.

She gasped as his erection pressed between her thighs, and she wrapped her legs around his hips, writhing against him, sliding herself along his cock as her head tipped back. He admired the glint of moonlight highlighting her throat, noting the pulsing vein tracing down its length.

His mouth watered for a taste as he cupped her head and drew her in closer. Positioning the head of his cock at her entrance, he slowly arched his hips and lowered his head to suck on her throat.

He groaned as he entered her, the walls of her heat clenching around him. She gasped his name as her legs cinched tighter, and he gripped her hips as he pumped into her.

She looped her arms around his neck as he moved them across the water, pressing her against a wall for leverage. Once she was secured, he tipped her chin up so he could lick up her neck.

"Yes," she whispered. "Please. Do it."

Gods, how could he resist when she begged for it? He whipped his hips back and then thrust into her again, bottoming out as his teeth sank into her skin. Warmth filled his mouth, her blood sparking through all his senses.

He would never get over how she tasted so alive and electric. Like storm clouds and sunrays, all twisting together. As he drank, he continued fucking her, thrusting his hips over and over.

She gripped his shoulders as she met him, her hips slamming against his.

He could feel her nearing the edge. Her breath fluttered out in tight gasps. His release tightened, a tingle running across his back as he pulled his teeth out and slanted his mouth to hers.

She'd taste her blood on his tongue, and he wanted her to experience this singular flavor. She moaned into his mouth as he thrust again, and then she cried out as he felt her tighten around him.

The pressure was insane, his brain whiting out as he continued pumping into her, and then a moment later, his release broke out of him in a shudder. They kissed under the moonlight as they slowly caught their breaths.

Then he pulled away and stared into her eyes. She'd been terrified that he'd leave her an hour ago. He knew she wasn't evil. He knew that she would never do anything like the Ashvins.

Everyone was tested sometimes, but Zarya would never fall.

"Thank you," she whispered, and he sensed so many things buried in those words. He didn't need thanking. He should be the one on his knees.

He looked down and smiled at her. He was worried about her visions, too.

Something was happening that neither of them could explain, but they'd have to tear him apart piece by piece before he'd ever walk away.

SEVENTEEN

Yasen and Miraan followed Ajay and Row through the streets of Ishaan, passing through the chaos churning around every corner. Miraan wore a scarf over his mouth, nose, and hair, leaving only his eyes uncovered, hoping to avoid recognition.

Posters hung all over the city, hammered with purpose by the royal guards in their crisp, emerald sherwanis. One half featured the likeness of Miraan's serious face, and the other half bore Zarya's.

The words TRAITORS WANTED FOR TREASON were printed across them in bright red ink.

These were no hazy illustrations. They had every detail of Zarya's face accurate down to the last freckle.

Yasen worried that if she set a toe over the borders of Gi'ana, Dishani would drop shrieking out of the sky. He did think "traitors wanted for treason" sounded a little redundant, though. Who was editing these things back in the palace?

Yasen also wore a hood to obscure his features, namely his bright silver hair. Despite his role in rescuing Zarya and the prince from Dishani's clutches, it didn't appear he'd made the priority list of traitors for now.

He was trying not to be offended.

Miraan stared at a poster, his dark eyes shining with the threat of tears before he turned and walked away, leaving Yasen to catch up. They passed through the wreckage of Ishaan: the burned-out buildings, the broken-down carts and fruit stands, the crying women and children.

Had they made everything worse in the name of progress?

Could anyone stand here and say they were better off?

After arriving in Ishaan last night, they'd all chatted for a while before Ajay and Row promised to take them to their new hiding place.

They turned a corner, passing through a square where a giant jade astrolabe dominated the center, surrounded by flower boxes that a few weeks ago had been bursting with the last of summer's blooms.

Ajay then ducked down a dark alley, and they walked in single file until they came to a gate set into the city wall. He used a bit of magic to unlock it, and they found themselves in a dense section of forest.

Without saying a word, they continued through the trees as the sun rose overhead. Yasen lost track of time but estimated it was about an hour before Ajay said, "We're nearly there."

Finally, they emerged to find an encampment swarming with people. Makeshift tents had been erected while dozens of bedrolls lay lined up in neat rows on the ground.

"You did this all in such a short time?" Miraan asked, his voice hushed to a whisper.

"We had no choice," Ajay answered. "The Jadugara were coming for them."

"This way," Ajay said, leading them deeper into the trees until they came upon a clearing where hundreds of people had gathered.

Someone had erected a few wooden crates in the center where Vikas, Farida, and Rania stood, looking over the crowd.

Yasen also spotted Suvanna and Apsara on the fringes, stalking back and forth to help keep order.

"The Jadugara are hunting us!" Vikas was shouting to the crowd.

With Farida's recovery, they had become co-leaders. Row had informed them that Farida and Vikas became friends almost immediately and were working together as one.

"You must protect yourselves. We're doing everything we can to get your friends and family out of the city, but the palace has increased patrols, and it's becoming harder and harder to hide."

Farida stood next to him, nodding and agreeing. Shortly after their attempted coup, she discovered she had four anchors and was learning how to use them.

"What happened to the ones they've captured?" someone shouted, and Farida shook her head.

"We've been told they are attempting to re-collar them. Jadugara from other realms have been sending their stockpiled ink back to Ishaan," she said, her voice soft but with the strength to carry over the clearing. "Our informants claim they've been unsuccessful so far. Something about the procedure is preventing the magic from taking hold again."

"With the manor no longer useable, we'll continue with Operation Starbreak in the forest," Vikas said. "I'm urging everyone to line up and have your collars removed. Once you're free, they can't take you again."

An anxious murmur rippled through the crowd. "Some are still unsure about Aazheri magic," Row whispered under his breath. "I can't blame them."

Yasen nodded as Farida began speaking again. "We will resume training for the Army of Ashes imminently," she said. "We must protect ourselves. We can't hide out here forever. We have people scouting the city to collect whatever weapons were left behind. Once they're gathered, I urge you to train during every spare moment. You will also continue to receive lessons from the Aazheri who have joined our cause."

Last night, Row and Ajay claimed the Rising Phoenix hoped to approach the palace again, but they disagreed on whether another attempted coup was the answer or whether they should approach things with more diplomacy.

Either way, they had to prepare themselves.

The royals weren't currently fighting back, and it was their one advantage. With Dishani indisposed and Miraan out of the picture, the prince suspected they were retreating into the safety of the palace walls to lick their wounds and hide behind the Jadugara as they'd done for so many years.

He'd explained that the king consort, Kabir, had always been a figurehead. He'd rarely been included in important state affairs or politics when Asha had been queen.

When they'd first married, he'd bristled against it, but ultimately, his wife had no interest in including him in these matters.

She was the queen, and her word was final.

Eventually, he gave up and decided to enjoy his life of luxury without responsibility by drinking and sleeping around. It was the arrangement Miraan's parents had made many years before his birth, and they both seemed happy enough with it.

When Asha disappeared, Dishani had already been acting as her mother's right hand for many years. She stepped directly into the role, once again leaving Kabir to tend to himself.

That left Miraan's two youngest siblings, who'd also been sidelined from making any important decisions. Dishani had spent her entire life shutting people out, terrified someone would try to take her power. She'd allowed Miraan to assist her only out of necessity and only because she refused to trust anyone who wasn't blood.

Not that any of that had worked in her favor, either.

"We must come together for our freedom!" Vikas was

shouting now. "We can only survive if we learn to trust each other and those who've come to support our cause. I understand why you are wary, but change is here, and there is no stopping it anymore."

Yasen moved along the crowd's edge, studying their faces and bared necks. The temporary tattoos were gone, and there was no need for pretenses out here.

Vikas and Farida took another few minutes to address everyone's concerns before they broke apart and returned to their tasks and training.

Vikas, Farida, and Rania jumped down from their perch and quickly headed over at the sight of Miraan.

"You're back!" Vikas said, throwing his arms around Yasen. "We were so worried about you."

Apsara and Suvanna joined their huddle a moment later.

"Where have you been?" Rania asked.

Yasen and Miraan filled them in on everything they'd experienced in Andhera.

"When is Zarya coming back?" Farida asked.

"Soon," Yasen said, though his words sounded more confident than he felt. He hated leaving her behind. Despite Rabin's assurances, he was worried. "But in the meantime, we're here to help however we can."

"You could help Apsara and Suvanna train the army," Farida suggested.

"Consider it done," Yasen said.

He was done with fighting, but for this, he would return to that life one more time. They'd need to assess their weapons stock and create some kind of order within their ranks. Then write up ledgers with names so they could keep an eye on their numbers.

"What are you planning to do about the Jadugara?" Miraan asked.

"We're deflecting them as much as possible," Rania

answered. "Sending them on wild goose chases. Their power is slipping away, and they're lashing out."

"We've also been keeping an eye on them," Suvanna said, gesturing to Apsara. "Intervening whenever they try to harass anyone. A few tried to arrest us." She barked out a wicked laugh. "They're all dead now."

Vikas blew out a breath and ran a hand down his face. "We've been trying to quell the riots amongst those who remain in the city, but it's been impossible so far."

Yasen had been impressed with Vikas from the day he'd met him. When he'd saved him in that gambling den, he'd shown no fear. When Zarya had freed him, he'd accepted the change in his destiny with stoicism. When he'd been made the leader of an entire rebel movement, he'd stepped into the role like he'd been born into it.

And now, when everything had gone to shit, he was bearing the weight of it all in a way that would have seen most people crumble.

Everyone fell into silence as they watched the area slowly empty.

"We proceed with our plans," Farida said. "We resume Operation Starbreak and do whatever else we can to dissuade the rioters. We understand why they're angry, and though I'd prefer to channel my rage in other ways, we also can't deny this to those who need it as an outlet.

"But we also need to keep moving forward. We try again. We learn from our mistakes, and we take the palace down. Nothing changes if we can't convince those in power to amend the laws, no matter how many collars we break."

Everyone around the circle nodded.

"I think I need to talk to her," Miraan said. Yasen gave him a sidelong look, but he didn't object. At least not externally. Internally, the idea of Miraan going anywhere near his batshit crazy sister made his stomach twist. He didn't like that he cared this much about the prince, but there it was. Eventually, he'd have to detangle himself from these feelings, but that was a problem for another day.

"She'll arrest you immediately," Row said. "You've seen the price she's put on your head."

"I have to try," Miraan said. "I will send a note seeking amnesty so that we may discuss these matters. My sister is many things, but she is a woman who takes pride in her honor. I believe any promise she makes not to harm me."

Everyone shared skeptical looks around the circle. Yasen's mouth pressed tight, holding in the tirade he wanted to unleash on Miraan.

The prince then turned to Vikas and Farida and bent at the waist. "If you'll allow it, I would like to act as the liaison between the resistance and the Madans. We all know that change must come from the top for it to be permanent, and I am best positioned of anyone here to make that happen."

Vikas and Farida traded another look before she nodded. "I do think that makes sense. But we don't want to put you in danger."

Miraan shook his head. "I accepted the risks the first time I sent money to the Rising Phoenix. At that moment, I committed myself to the very end. I cannot stand idle and allow this to continue while I have the power to do something."

He inhaled a deep breath.

"My sister has ruled with fear and abuse for long enough. It's time for me to do what I should have done from the very start and either convince her to see the error of her ways or, finally, take her down."

EIGHTEEN

Zarya held another party invitation in her hand. She sighed before pinching the bridge of her nose as pain throbbed behind her eye. Despite Abishek's promise, Kishore had been delayed yet again, and she'd spent almost every evening since entertaining at Abishek's side while she answered a million questions about the Bandhan with Rabin.

But she hadn't minded it all completely.

Abishek spoke of her with such pride and joy, and it touched the piece of her heart that had always craved this. He was constantly looking out for her, ensuring she was comfortable, and included her in every conversation. And when the night was over, he'd tell her how much he appreciated her presence and valued her place in his life. It also helped that every event came with the gift of a new dress to rival the previous one. She stared at the sparkling fabrics hanging in her closet, already lamenting that she'd probably have to leave most of these behind.

He was also warming up to her requests about the vanshaj. He'd spoken with several higher-ranking nobles to discuss the issue. Not surprisingly, some were reluctant, but several had agreed to attend a demonstration of the removal. The king planned to gather everyone before they left for Ishaan. Hopefully, soon.

She was growing weary of life at Abishek's court. They were all fake, constantly posturing and maneuvering, brokering alliances and breaking them when something suited them better. Abishek had made it clear he hoped Zarya would accept the role as his heir, and she wanted to please him, but she also didn't see herself spending her life amongst these people.

Now the last thing she wanted was to attend another party, but the king had promised Kishore would return to Andhera tomorrow, and she wanted to get this over with. She could suffer through one more event. Rabin's condition was deteriorating before her eyes, though he was doing his best to pretend he was fine. She knew him too well to believe it.

She'd had more dreams about her mother and the Ashvins every night, and her exhaustion was dragging her down. She reached for her mother's necklace, her eyes closing in frustration when her fingers met with her bare throat. She'd do anything to get it back.

Yasen had written to tell her that he was assisting with training the Army of Ashes and that Miraan had contacted his sister hoping to appeal to her better nature. Zarya wasn't sure if Dishani had one or how smart this was, but she trusted they were all considering the possible pitfalls and consequences of their actions.

With Row and the others around, they would have plenty of solid advice and guidance at their disposal. She whispered a prayer for her friends and hoped she'd see them again soon.

Standing before the mirror, wearing only her underwear, she studied her reflection, searching for evidence of the evil living in her soul. She closed her eyes and tried to reach for Rabin inside the mind plane, but the way remained frustratingly blocked. She screamed for him inside her head but was rewarded with nothing—just silence and emptiness, along with the echo of her thoughts.

She twisted her torso, studying the tattoo on the back of her shoulder and searching for evidence of the taint. If Kishore *still* hadn't arrived tomorrow, maybe it was time to return to Ishaan and talk to Thriti instead. Maybe she would know how to fix this.

A knock came at her door, and Urvi entered, her eyes down as she crossed the room. Ever since Zarya had offered to remove her tattoo, she'd avoided eye contact, speaking to her only when necessary.

"Urvi," Zarya said as she pulled her robe on and tied it around her waist. "I want to apologize for the other day. I should never have put you in that position. I'm very sorry."

Urvi stopped what she was doing at Zarya's dressing table, her spine straightening before she peered over her shoulder.

"It's okay," she said softly before nodding and resuming her work. A moment later, she gestured for Zarya to sit so she could start her hair and makeup.

Zarya slipped onto the bench while they both maintained an awkward silence. Urvi started with her makeup, then brushed her hair while Zarya watched her in the mirror. Urvi was still carefully avoiding meeting her gaze, and Zarya dropped her eyes, trying not to make her uncomfortable.

A moment later, a soft, whispered voice said, "It's not that I don't want to be free."

Zarya looked up, but Urvi was again focused on Zarya's hair as though she hadn't said a word.

Zarya nodded. "I understand," she whispered. "If and when you're ready and want to talk about it, please let me know. I won't ask again unless you bring it up."

Urvi continued brushing her hair with long, careful strokes. If Zarya didn't know any better, she might believe Urvi hadn't heard her, but the slightest flicker in her eyes acknowledged Zarya's promise.

Urvi spent a few minutes curling her hair and pinning half of it up in a few intricate twists. Then she met Zarya's gaze in the mirror and smiled brightly. "Now, let's get this dress on, shall we?"

Abishek had sent her another gift: a stunning lehenga made from the deepest crimson silk, embroidered with intricate red beading and layered with an overskirt of delicate lace.

She helped Zarya into it and tied the ribbons that ran up the back of the choli. When she was done, Zarya couldn't help but admire herself in the mirror. It was a beautiful gift, and she appreciated the king's effort. He was trying very hard to make her his princess.

But Abishek expected her to marry an Aazheri. Row had been right when he'd warned her. She'd thought he was being overly cautious, but it was clear Abishek took this issue seriously.

He loved Rabin like a son, and surely he wouldn't feel that way once he knew about their marriage. Regardless, if Abishek truly wanted to take on a father-figure role in her life, he'd have to accept her husband. If he genuinely wanted Zarya as his heir, then Rabin would become the king consort of Andhera.

She kind of liked the thought of that.

He'd look very handsome and powerful sitting on a throne.

They had to tell him. Tonight, she'd convince Rabin they couldn't keep this secret any longer.

A knock at the door drew her out of her reverie.

"Come in," she called as she adjusted a wayward curl.

Rabin opened the door, and she caught his approving look.

"Hi," she said as Urvi excused herself from the room. Rabin closed the door and immediately strode over, wrapping his big hands around her waist as he came to stand behind her.

"You look..." He shook his head. "You look like a fucking goddess."

She smiled at his reflection. "How are you feeling?" she asked as his arms banded around her, drawing her against him.

"I'm fine," he said, repeating his usual mantra.

"I was thinking if Kishore still doesn't return tomorrow, we should head for Ishaan and see if Thriti can help us instead. I'm worried about you."

Rabin nodded. "The king won't like it, but I agree. We've lingered here long enough."

He dropped his chin into the curve of her neck before he kissed her.

"Gods, I miss the taste of you," he rumbled.

"Perhaps we should pay another visit to the hot springs?" she joked. His answer was a feral smile.

"Don't tempt me. A few more days, and we'll be on our way."

"I think we should tell him about us before we leave," she said carefully, gauging his reaction. "I'm trying to build a relationship with him, and you're maintaining one. We shouldn't keep lying about this."

She watched as Rabin chewed the inside of his cheek and then pressed a kiss to her shoulder. "You're right. Tomorrow, we'll tell him."

"Okay," she said. "We should probably go. Don't leave my side, okay? I don't want to have to fend off Amir."

Despite Abishek's assurances, Amir had attended a handful of the king's parties while continuing to draw Zarya into conversation. He made her skin crawl. She was tempted to tell him to back off in a less polite way, but she didn't want to embarrass Abishek in front of his nobles.

Rabin growled low in his throat. "If Amir wants to keep his dick attached, he should learn to stay as far away from you as possible."

Zarya smiled. "I love it when you sweet-talk me."

Another low growl rumbled in his chest before he took her hand and tugged her towards the door. Opening it, he gestured for her to proceed, and they walked side by side.

Dinner was held in an opulent dining room, which, like all the parts of the castle, was magnificent. It had gleaming black floors and chandeliers made from black crystal. A long table ran the length of the room, with high-backed chairs framing each side. The room's edges were lined with dozens of small plush booths, where silver trays of pakoras, papadums, and samosas with a variety of chutneys sat on small round tables.

At each end stood a long bar tended by about two dozen colorful fairies. They poured drinks, dressed in scant clothing, showing off their toned bodies and perfect features. Zarya had never seen any outside of Daragaab before.

"You're here!" came a voice, and she turned to find Abishek walking towards them. He stopped and swept his gaze over her with appreciation. "You wore my gift."

She looked down at herself and then up. "Another beautiful dress. Thank you."

"It suits you well. A fitting dress for a princess."

He smiled so warmly that she felt a twist of guilt for planning to leave. He seemed to love having her here, and she appreciated his attention, but she couldn't stay here attending parties when Ishaan and the Phoenix needed her.

"Shall we get a drink?" he asked, directing them to the nearest bar, which was entirely made of glass and lined with colorful lights.

"Where did they come from?" Rabin asked. His brow furrowed as he watched the fairies.

"They were a surprise from Amir," Abishek said. "He had them brought in specially for tonight."

As if the sound of his name was a summons, the man in question suddenly materialized out of the crowd.

"Zarya," Amir said, taking her hand and kissing the back. "You are radiant."

She sensed Rabin behind her, inches from ripping his head off. She cast a glance over her shoulder with a brow raised and a look that she hoped said *Don't kill him*.

"Thank you," she replied. "This is very... grand." She waved a hand at the bar. She wasn't entirely sure how she felt about it. Had he pulled these fairies out of their environment and forced them into this harsh climate? Could they survive here?

"Nothing but the best for the king," he said in a kiss-ass voice that nearly made Zarya roll her eyes. "What are you having?"

"I'm not sure." Zarya turned to watch a bartender execute several fancy flips, tossing colorful glass bottles of liquor. He crafted a gorgeous cocktail by pouring the contents into a few light blue glasses and then garnished each with a sugar snowflake. When he was done, he slid them over.

"I hope you enjoy it," he said with a wink.

She accepted a cocktail, as did Abishek and Amir, while Rabin nodded a "no thank you."

"Rabin," Abishek said a moment later. "Khadi is here. Ekaja warmed him up the last time he deigned to join us, but he's still holding out on us and needs a nudge."

Rabin looked at Zarya and opened his mouth, about to protest.

"Go on," she said. "Do what you need to. I'll be okay."

He pressed his mouth together as a muscle in his jaw ticked. "You're sure?"

"I think I can handle it," she said, and he huffed. She'd use the opportunity to tell Amir that she wasn't on the market in no uncertain terms. The last thing she needed was for Rabin to escalate the situation.

Though Abishek hadn't been trying to set them up, Amir

was clearly interested. Hopefully, he wouldn't make the scene she'd feared, but enough was enough.

"I'll be back in a minute," Rabin said.

She nodded and watched him cross the room with Abishek as they approached a group of men, who all stood to shake their hands.

When she turned around, Amir was standing so close she nearly jumped.

"How are you enjoying your time in Andhera?" he asked. "It must be wonderful getting to know your father. He's truly such a great man. Brilliant. Powerful. Generous."

Zarya didn't answer as Amir waxed on about the king for another minute while she did her best to appear interested. It was becoming exceedingly clear that Amir wasn't after *her* but instead wanted an in with the king. He was interested in a crown and Abishek's influence.

Thus, Zarya felt no guilt for tuning him out as her gaze wandered to the center of the room, where several fairies had gathered. A group of musicians in the corner shifted their tempo as the music turned from upbeat to sultry.

Zarya recalled the party in the Jai Palace the night she'd first kissed Rabin. The air had been charged with sex and the heat and scent of bodies, and maybe that had been part of the reason she'd caved to his 'request' to give him another chance.

As the fairies moved together, their bodies slithering and undulating, their hips circling and their backs arching, Rabin looked over, his gaze meeting hers with fire.

She suspected he was thinking about the same night, and Zarya took a sip of her drink to cover her smile. Mercifully, Amir had stopped chattering thanks to the fairies. In fact, everyone had abandoned their conversations, jaws hanging slack around the room.

Two females were writhing together, their breasts crushed and their hips grinding. Zarya noted Ekaja watching them with a flush on her cheeks and a knowing smirk that suggested she intended to devour every inch of these two later.

As they continued dancing, Zarya's gaze wandered back to Rabin, where she found him staring with that intensity that always did its best to undo her. They stared at one another while he licked the tip of his sharp canine. Gods, that always had her stomach dropping and her thighs clenching.

She wasn't sure how much longer she could hold out.

The room held suspended in fascinated stasis for several more minutes as the fairies continued dancing while Zarya's neck flushed and heat climbed over her scalp. She could feel Rabin's eyes on her but avoided his gaze, knowing that she was about one second away from crossing the room, taking his hand, and dragging him out of here, consequences be damned.

Finally, the music stopped, and it took several prolonged seconds for everyone to stir out of the fairies' spell before a chorus of polite applause circled the room.

"Dinner is ready!" Abishek said after a moment, and Zarya watched as he attempted to steer Rabin away from her. She was sure she wasn't imagining it. Her eyes narrowed as the bitter taste of worry twisted in the back of her throat. Did he already know? Or at least suspect?

She could tell Abishek favored Amir and what he could offer, but once they told him about their marriage, he'd have no choice but to let this go.

Two servants directed Zarya and Amir to a pair of seats near the end of the table while she kept her eye on Rabin. He made his way over, planting himself on Zarya's other side.

Thus, she found herself between Rabin, Amir, and their glares.

A moment later, Abishek settled into his seat at the head of the table, his gaze finding hers and then jumping between the two men flanking each side.

She rolled her eyes and picked up her wine, taking a long

sip and deciding she would probably need several of these to get through the night.

NINETEEN

Dinner was a drawn-out affair. Abishek dominated most of the conversation, chatting with his higher-ranking nobles while Amir listened, and Zarya and Rabin sat mostly silent. As usual, Abishek tried to include her in the conversation, but she wasn't in the mood tonight.

She was worried about Rabin. About their bond. About the resistance and the fact that they'd lingered here for too long.

The king caught her eye, his gaze brimming with concern, and she shook her head slightly to indicate that she was fine.

He took the hint and left her to her thoughts. She marveled at how well he could read her. Amir was happy to take her place, injecting himself into the conversation until Rabin started interrupting him every time he spoke, forcing him to give up. He sneered at Rabin, his expression petulant as he sat back and folded his arms.

When Abishek's friends began asking Zarya and Rabin about the paramadhar bond, it was Amir's turn to interfere until Rabin threw him a glare so withering that he finally shut up.

Zarya politely answered their queries while Rabin simply nodded, his shoulders tense and his jaw hard.

As the conversation continued, the fairies resumed their entertainment, moving through the crowd and offering favors to interested guests.

Zarya had difficulty taking her eyes off them as heat swirled below her navel. Rabin was conversing with a man across the table, asking about the process of the Bandhan and the procedure they'd undergone with Thriti.

Well, conversing might have been too strong a word. The man kept asking questions, and Rabin kept returning a series of short grunts resembling affirmative or negative answers.

What he needed was something to take his mind off things.

Her gaze once again slid to the fairies and their sensual dance before her hand landed on his knee. She felt him tense, his breath hitching as she walked her fingers up the inside of his thigh.

"And what words did the mystic recite?" the Aazheri asked. "Was it a song or a poem, perhaps?"

"Words?" Rabin asked, his voice dipping noticeably as her hand traveled higher, her fingertips gently brushing the bulge between his legs.

He cleared his throat as the Aazheri repeated his question while she made small circles, her fingers inching closer. Rabin shifted, his shoulders rolling. She clamped down on her grin, delighted at how this was throwing him off.

"Yes?" the Aazheri asked. "What did the magic look like? How did it feel?"

"Feel?" Rabin asked as his gaze slid to her for the briefest of seconds, where she detected a hint of *What are you doing?* in his expression.

"Yes," the Aazheri asked. "Are you quite all right?"

"I..." Rabin shook his head.

"My honored friends!" Abishek said, standing up, clapping his hands, and rescuing Rabin from further interrogation. "That concludes dinner. We'll continue with the entertainment if you all take your seats on the other side of the room. You've had a small taste of our special guests"—he nodded towards the fairies huddled behind the bars—"and they have so much more to offer."

He clapped sharply again, ushering in a string of vanshaj servants, all bearing a silver tray covered with dozens of glasses, each one steaming with frothing clouds of white smoke.

"I've also procured some bottles of mist wine that I hope you'll share with me."

An excited murmur circled the room, followed by the scrape of chairs as everyone stood to snatch a glass. They shuffled to the far end, gathering around the low tables to continue chatting.

"Zarya, are you all right?" Abishek asked, approaching her. "You've been quiet this evening."

"I'm fine, just a bit tired. Go and enjoy yourself. If it's okay with you, I might head to bed early tonight."

"Of course," he answered with a tip of his head. "But have some wine before you leave. You'll like it very much."

"Sure," she said. "Now, enjoy yourself, and don't worry about me."

Abishek smiled and grabbed her shoulders before kissing her on each cheek, pulling back, and staring at her. "You've made me so happy, my daughter."

Her heart leaped in her chest every time he said those words, thumping with the force of all the wishes she'd carried for so long.

"Me too," she answered before Abishek clapped Rabin on the shoulder and then crossed the room to join his guests.

Zarya watched the servants passing glasses of mist wine around the room, noting how the translucent smoke filled the air around them. "What's mist wine?"

"A mild hallucinogen," Rabin said. "Very difficult to find. They skim water from the surface of the hot springs when the moon is full and the stars are aligned just right." He snorted. "Or it's all bullshit, and someone just told a very good story, adds some drugs to basic spirits, and charges a fortune for it."

Zarya turned around to notice Amir hovering in her periphery. Oh, for fuck's sake. Couldn't he take a hint? Hoping to discourage any further interaction, she turned the other way. Unfortunately, it didn't work.

"Zarya," came his clipped voice a moment later. "I hoped you would join me for a walk in the gardens."

She willed patience and slowly turned around. "Gardens? It's a little cold for that, isn't it?"

"Not at all; it's quite beautiful when the ice forms."

Zarya affected a tight smile. "As flattered as I am, I must decline your invitation. And any others," she added. "I am not available or interested in anything beyond a friendly acquaintance."

"I beg your pardon," he asked, his brow furrowing. "Your father..."

"My father?"

"He suggested we meet," Amir said, and Zarya wasn't entirely sure what that meant. Had Abishek *lied* to her?

"Regardless, he doesn't decide these things for me," she finished. "Thank you. It was nice meeting you, but we'll be leaving Andhera soon, anyway."

She was about to turn away when Zarya saw it all happen in a flash.

Amir reached for her, his clawed fingers nearly wrapping around her arm until another hand stopped him. Rabin stood with his large fist, crushing Amir's fingers with such force that Zarya was surprised they weren't already broken.

"Do not touch her," he snarled in a low voice rippling with bottomless menace.

Zarya's gaze darted quickly around the room. No one else appeared to notice the exchange, too occupied with their drinks and conversation. "If you even think about touching her again, I will shatter every bone in your miserable fucking body."

Amir's nostrils flared, his eyes darkening. She saw a flicker of *something*. Rabin squeezed his hand, and even over the din of the room, Zarya heard the sick crunch of bone before Amir went pale.

"Get out of here and don't bother her again," Rabin whispered before Amir slowly nodded. Rabin released his hand, and without saying another word, Amir quickly turned and left.

When he was gone, Rabin sank into his chair, his eyes burning and his jaw hard enough to crack diamonds.

"What was all that about?" she asked. "I had it under control."

He looked up at her, but she couldn't understand the expression on his face. She dropped in her chair and laid a hand on his arm. "Rabin, what is it?"

"He's a monster, Zarya. He abuses women. Locks them up and chains them down. Beats them and burns them and does all kinds of sick fucking things for his pleasure."

The words were hollow, his gaze trained on the far wall as if he couldn't meet her eyes.

Zarya frowned. "Amir? How do you know that?"

"Everyone knows that."

He paused another beat before his gaze finally slid to hers.

"Including the king?" she asked, something bitter twisting in her chest.

"I don't know."

Zarya chewed on her lip as she glanced at the corner where Abishek convened with his nobles. They were all sipping their mist wine, nearly obscured by the fog drifting through the room.

"Why didn't you tell me?"

"You told me he wasn't trying to set you up, so I didn't think it mattered. But I can see he'd prefer someone like Amir for you, and I thought it would hurt knowing your father would ever consider a man like that."

"It has to be a mistake," she said. "He can't have known. This is all because we haven't told him about us."

Rabin's jaw clenched. "Tomorrow. Like I promised."

Together, they sat in silence while the fairies danced in the center of the room, still weaving their spell over the crowd. She picked up her glass of mist wine and sniffed it. The scent was sweet, with hints of bitterness buried underneath. As she looked about the room, she could tell its effects were already taking hold.

The laughter swelled, and the chatter rose as she watched several people wavering in their seats. The fairies continued dancing, weaving their spell.

She noted Ekaja in the corner, sandwiched between the two female fairies she'd been eyeing earlier. The commander caught Zarya's eye and winked, causing some of the tension to drain from her body.

Everyone was enjoying themselves, so why shouldn't they also indulge?

But she didn't want the drink. What she wanted was the man who made her blood hot without anything but a look. She waved a hand as mist swirled around them, tiny droplets condensing on her cheeks and clothing.

She watched the king speaking intently with someone while someone else tried to get his attention. He was completely occupied and seemed to have forgotten all about Zarya, Rabin, and even Amir for the night. She was confused and angry about the Amir situation, but she refused to let it ruin the rest of the evening.

Zarya's gaze slid to Rabin, who turned to face the table, one hand on the surface, his frame coiled with tension, obviously still angry about Amir. His long black hair hung loose tonight, and his black jacket hugged his broad chest like it worshiped him. Gods, how she missed him.

She scooted her chair a bit closer.

Rabin gave her a side-eyed look.

Again, she gently placed her hand on his thigh and then dragged it up.

"Spitfire," he growled in a low voice. "What are you doing?"

"Nothing," she said innocently as she tiptoed another step, her finger brushing the swell between his thighs. He made that low rumble in his throat that always made her stomach clench.

His golden-flecked gaze twitched, a midnight eyebrow raising a fraction. She smiled and leaned forward, bracing an elbow on the table while her hand continued trailing along the inside of his thigh and then between his legs.

She felt him *trying* not to react as his fist clenched on the table. When she gently applied pressure, he stiffened under her hand. "If you don't stop that, I'm going to drag you out of here and fuck you in the first dark corner I find," he said in a raw voice.

With a sweet smile, she looked up. "Is that supposed to deter me?" She rubbed him harder, and despite his protests, he spread his legs a little wider. She bit her lower lip as their eyes locked, and the room's noise faded behind them.

"Someone might see you," he said, his voice low.

"So let them see," she said as her hand slid higher. She didn't care anymore. He was hers, and she wanted everyone to know it. She gripped his cock, and he grunted as it grew thicker and harder under her attention. "We're telling him tomorrow, anyway."

Rabin gave her another side-eyed look.

"This is ridiculous," she said. "We're adults. We're *married*."

She glanced at Abishek holding court in the corner of the room through the hazy mist.

She returned her attention to Rabin. "Don't you agree?"

Rabin nodded. "He won't be happy I defied him."

Zarya blew out a breath when she caught the expression on his face. "We don't have to if you don't want to."

"No, I do," he said. "I owe your father so much, but I don't owe him *this*. I don't owe him *you*. You and I are a done deal."

He stared into her eyes and then offered her the barest hint of a reassuring smile.

"Okay, good," she said. "Then where were we?"

"Fuck," Rabin said, his voice rough. "You need to stop that, or I'm going to lose my mind."

Her smile turned wolfish, and she pulled her hand away. "Fine." Hands pressing against the table, she stood and walked away, feeling Rabin's eyes burn into her back.

On quick feet, she headed towards her room. She was about halfway there when she heard him. Arms circled her waist, and she squealed as he lifted her up and carried her the rest of the way before throwing open her door and locking it behind him.

"I need you," she breathed as he set her down and flattened her to the wall with his body. "I miss you."

He dragged up her skirt and cupped her between her thighs before he yanked her panties aside. "Spitfire, if I can't fuck this pussy tonight, I'll lose my damn mind."

Then he crushed himself to her again as his finger thrust into her already wet core. He sucked on her throat as her hips arched with a moan. He fingered her roughly for a few strokes, plunging deep as she whimpered.

Then he stepped back and raked his gaze over her body.

"Take off your clothes," he ordered in that bossy way that always made her a little breathless and totally helpless. She began undoing the ties on the beautiful red skirt before stepping out of it and pulled off her top. A low growl emanated from his throat.

"Back to the wall," he said, stepping closer. "Hands over your head."

Fire pooled in her stomach as she did what he asked, stretching up and causing her breasts to peak. He licked his lips, his nose flaring before he curled a fist. She watched green vines grow from the walls, snaking around her wrists and pinning her arms in place.

He smirked as he took her in, his tactile gaze wandering over her, and he then approached, running a warm hand over her ribcage and down her hip. He unbuttoned his jacket and removed his pants, his eyes never leaving hers.

When he was naked, she took a moment to appreciate him as she studied the hard lines and planes of his chest and stomach, along with the tattoos that ran down his arms and the dragon stretching over his ribs.

Her heart beat faster, fluttering against her ribs as he moved closer. She was so fucking in love with him, and he took her breath away every time.

"You were very naughty tonight, Spitfire," he said, his body so close but not quite touching. It was driving her crazy.

"Is there a problem, Commander?"

He smirked. "Only if you stop," he said and ran a finger down her throat, slowly dragging it down between her breasts and her stomach, stopping below her navel, where he traced a lazy circle.

She grunted in protest, struggling against the vines holding her in place, and he let out a low, wicked laugh.

"What do you want, Zarya?"

"Touch me."

"I am touching you." He stepped closer, his body pressing against hers, hard and smooth and hot. She shivered from her toes to the roots of her hair.

"Touch me where I need you."

His mouth met hers as his hand slid lower, finding her wet center.

"Gods," she said, her head falling back against the wall as he circled his thumb over her clit.

His mouth traveled down the side of her throat and to her breast, where he took a nipple in his mouth and bit gently as he slipped a finger inside her. Her back curved as his other hand grabbed her ass and squeezed.

He slid lower as he fell to his knees and looked up, their gazes locking. "You are so beautiful, Spitfire," he whispered. A hand hooked under the back of her thigh, and he propped her knee over his shoulder.

Without pausing, he swept his tongue over her pussy, and she cried out. Her hips arched forward, attempting to seek more friction, but he kept his touch light, driving her wild. How she longed to grab his head and move him where she wanted, but his magic kept her dangling on the edge of madness.

Hips writhing, she squirmed as he ran a rough tongue over her clit and then finally increased the pressure with his hands pressed into her backside as she rode against his face.

He slid two fingers inside her, and an ache ripped through her very bones. Curling his fingers, he tugged on her clit with his teeth, and she burst apart as she came in a shower of sparks. Waves crested, crashing against each other, and her knees almost gave out, but for the vines still holding her in place.

A moment later, his magic snapped away, and she collapsed. He caught her in his arms and kissed her, his mouth hungry and devouring.

"My turn," she whispered, and he lifted a brow.

"Your turn to what?"

She offered him a feral smile as she filtered out a thread of dense shadows. His answer was a smirk as she placed a hand on his chest and backed him up until he fell onto the bed.

"What are you doing, Spitfire? I'm the one in charge here."

She snorted a small laugh. "Not this time."

Then she pulled on a thread of her shadows and circled his

wrists before binding them to the bedposts. It was time to return the favor. He studied the swirl of her smoky magic as he turned those golden-flecked eyes her way. She loved watching the way they sparked and danced when he was happy or angry, or horny.

Or really, any time he was feeling something.

Then she dragged out another tendril of magic and used it to tease her way down his torso, circling his nipples and tickling the trail of hair that led under his navel and to his cock bobbing against his stomach. She licked her lips as she contemplated the dusky head and the veins running over its thick length.

"Zarya," Rabin growled as he tugged on his restraints to no avail. She ignored him as she directed the thread of her shadow magic lower and then circled his cock, pulling her magic tight. He made a sound resembling something between a gasp and part choking on his tongue.

"How does that feel?" she asked softly while he met her with his burning gaze.

"Like I'm being turned inside out in the best possible fucking way."

She smiled and then approached, using her magic to drag up and down his length. He pulled against his restraints, and his head tipped back. She watched a sheen of sweat surface on his skin while she pumped him with the thread of her shadows.

She wanted to touch him but was also enjoying watching this too much. She continued working his cock as the tendons in his neck stood out, and then she slowly moved closer, straddling one knee over his hips and then the other.

"Who's in charge this time?" she asked, and he smirked as she tugged out another shuddering moan.

"I think it might be you," he gasped, and she couldn't help but laugh.

Then she positioned herself over his erection, taking him in her hand while her shadows swirled. She positioned him at her entrance and then slowly lowered herself. She gasped as it all came together. His wide cock and her spinning magic filled her up, touching her in every secret place that had her knees turning weak and her fingers tingling.

"Fuck, that's so tight," he whimpered. "What are you doing to me?"

"I'm not even sure," she answered truthfully. She'd wanted to see what it would feel like, and the combination was mind-numbing and earth-shattering at the same time. She could feel her release cresting again.

"Can I have my hands back?" he begged, and she freed him immediately before they came to her hips, his fingers digging into her skin. He thrust up into her as they moved together, and her shadows spun around them, adding just the right amount of pressure.

She tipped her head against his, and then they both seized as one, coming together in a bright flash that left her breathless and her head spinning. She rode him as he thrust his hips until they both stopped panting.

"Fuck," he said before he kissed her. "We are doing *that* again."

"Now?" she asked, laughing.

"In just a minute," he said. "Let me catch my breath."

Then he smirked. "I told you the darkness was nothing to fear."

TWENTY

Yasen and Miraan stood at the palace gates, staring up at the sky-blue walls and darkened windows. Dozens of soldiers manned the ramparts, crossbows aimed at their hearts. Ash hung in the sky like shadows, obscuring the sun into a burning red orb bleeding across the horizon.

Miraan pushed his hood back and ran a hand through his hair. As promised, he'd sent his sister a letter, and they'd agreed to a temporary truce.

Yasen didn't trust it or *her*. He'd tried to talk Miraan out of this, but the prince wouldn't be deterred. The longer the riots continued, the more he internalized everything as his fault. Never mind that Dishani, Gi'ana, and a thousand years of oppressive rulers had brought this misery upon themselves.

"We can still turn back," Yasen said as he stared at the guards who flanked the entrance. Despite the crossbows trained on their movements, their welcome was more subdued than he'd expected. He'd been prepared for a hundred armed soldiers waiting to escort them into the palace, maybe in cuffs or chains.

Instead, they'd entered the empty courtyard where the

massive astronomical clock dominating one wall stood silent. Yasen couldn't help but compare it to a ribcage with its heart ripped out. Their footsteps echoed against the quiet while he noted the piles of wet, crumpled paper crowded into the corners. The notes that Yasen and Rabin had dropped over the city, sharing the truth about the Jadugara.

"We're going in," Miraan said, and Yasen nodded. Initially, Miraan planned to go alone, but Yasen had threatened to tie him up and toss him in a pit if he attempted to visit Dishani without him.

Eventually, Miraan conceded so they could at least walk into their deaths together.

"Let's go," Miraan said, and they approached the door. As they drew closer, guards shuffled into their path while more appeared behind them. It took a moment for another figure to appear—Talin, the youngest of the Madan siblings.

The guards parted to allow him past.

"Talin," Miraan said, obvious relief in his tone. "How are you?"

Talin shook his head and ran a hand through his hair in a gesture so similar to his brother's that something twisted in Yasen's chest.

"Not great," Talin said.

The younger Madan brother looked entirely different than when Yasen had seen him last. He'd been full of life and exuberance, but now he appeared on the verge of falling apart. Dark circles ringed his eyes, and he wore rumpled clothing. The effect was compounded by the shadow growing on his chin. "Why did you do it?"

Miraan opened his mouth and then closed it while considering how to respond. "I had to," he said. "I couldn't sit idle anymore. You know I'm right."

Talin stared at his brother, his expression blank, before he blew out a long sigh. Yasen couldn't decide what he read in the younger prince's demeanor. Confusion perhaps. A touch of betrayal. But also grim resignation.

"I'm to retrieve your amulet." He said the words carefully as if he wasn't sure how Miraan would react.

Miraan nodded, reached into his kurta, and revealed the token dangling from a chain around his neck.

"I'm sorry," Talin said. "She insists."

"I can't say I'm surprised," Miraan said as he pulled the chain over his head and handed it to his brother. "Though, I'd rather hoped she'd demonstrate *some* goodwill by allowing me to keep it."

Yasen didn't know much about how it all worked, but he did know the palace's blue stone suppressed magic. Only members of the immediate royal family and those they deemed worthy possessed an amulet to nullify the effects. Without Miraan's magic, they were truly entering defenseless.

"You know how she can be," Talin said as his curious gaze fell on Yasen.

"This is Lieutenant Yasen Varghese of Daragaab," Miraan said. "My... friend."

Yasen's gaze slid to Miraan, unsure what to make of his hesitation.

"Weren't you in our dungeons?" Talin asked, narrowing his eyes.

"I was," Yasen said. "It was an honor to experience the famous Madan hospitality."

Miraan shot him an exasperated look, but Yasen only grinned.

Talin pressed his hands together and bowed. "Welcome back, I suppose."

"Thanks," Yasen said. "I'm here to watch his back in case your charming sister decides to stick a knife in it."

Talin arched a brow. Yasen knew it was impertinent, perhaps even bordering on treasonous, to speak of the princess this way, but he'd never cared much about rules or decorum. He often woke up wondering how he'd managed to escape the end of a noose or a blade, but he'd enjoy his days while he had them.

"Fair enough," Talin said, tipping his chin before spinning on his heel. "You'd better come with me, then. She's waiting for you."

Miraan and Yasen exchanged wary looks while the guards surrounded them. They had been allowed to keep their weapons, but it was only for show. Without Miraan's magic, they were vastly outnumbered.

As they walked, Talin snuck anxious glances over his shoulder, and Yasen suspected he was uncomfortable treating his brother like a criminal. Miraan had only spoken briefly about his relationship with his family, but Yasen knew that despite the brothers being very different, they were also close friends.

Perhaps Talin was hurt that Miraan had never confided in him about the Rising Phoenix, but he had to understand why his brother had to keep his actions a secret, even from those closest to him. Yasen looked at Miraan, who met his gaze. He tried to offer a reassuring smile, but Miraan's expression remained stoic.

"Is she really bringing in another army?" Miraan asked.

Talin shook his head. "Someone arrived, cloaked and hooded, to meet with her."

"Who was it?"

"No one knows but her," Talin said. "Only two blindfolded healers were allowed to accompany her to the meeting."

Yasen's brow furrowed. Who would be acting with such secrecy?

"But yes," Talin continued. "I believe she intends to invite them into Ishaan."

"It will be a massacre," Miraan said softly.

Talin pressed his mouth together. "Possibly."

They turned a corner and approached a massive set of wide

doors painted white and gilded with flowers. Four guards flanked the entrance, also wearing white uniforms trimmed in silver. The queensguard.

Yasen wondered how long their mother's body had been cold—metaphorically speaking—before Dishani had claimed these quarters that didn't technically belong to her.

Talin came to a stop and turned to address them. "I'll warn you. She's in very bad shape. Try not to react. It makes her... angry. Pretend nothing is amiss, and you might leave here with your heads."

Yasen snorted. "I wasn't that attached to it, anyway."

Talin cocked his head in a gesture that seemed to say *Fair enough* before they entered a palatial suite with windows running the entire length of one wall. The curtains were drawn closed, admitting only narrow slivers of light and casting the space into shadows.

Dozens of people filled the room, speaking in low, hushed voices. Miraan and Yasen exchanged another wary look as their shoulders brushed, almost as if Miraan was seeking reassurance in Yasen's presence. He wished he could offer something to make this easier.

"Dishani," Talin said softly. "He's here."

They moved deeper into the room and towards the sunken area in the center, where several curved divans lined the perimeter. At least a dozen healers surrounded her.

A moment later, Yasen spied a familiar figure.

Koura turned to look over his shoulder from his position kneeling before a divan. He nodded to Yasen and then stood, bowing to the princes before he moved away to reveal a shrouded figure lying on her back with several cushions propped under her head. Yasen inhaled a deep breath, suddenly nervous. He could feel the tension radiating off Miraan.

Talin looked over his shoulder yet again, then kneeled before Dishani. She wore a long, soft white dress and a white veil over her face. Through the light fabric, Yasen caught the barest shine of her eyes.

"Dishani," Miraan whispered.

She lay entirely still, studying her brother.

Yasen could make out the inflamed skin on the right side of her face before his gaze wandered to her right arm, where her sleeveless dress exposed a rash of angry red blisters, glistening with a sheen of ointment.

Yasen had been a soldier for decades. He'd seen every injury under the sun, and it had never bothered him, but something about this room and its shadows sent a chill skating down his back. The healers, the pulled curtains, the hushed voices made it feel like they were standing inside a tomb.

He'd witnessed the moment when Rabin attacked with that blue fire, not caring who he hit. Yasen understood. He would have done the same, but he knew Zarya would carry this guilt with her forever.

Despite how Dishani had treated her, Zarya would always look for the good in people and situations. It's why they were friends. Things would have gone as usual if she'd given up on him the way most people did. He knew he had no one to blame but himself for that, but trusting people was difficult.

"Dishani," Miraan said again. "How are you?"

She remained still for several long seconds as the tension in the room stretched. Yasen wondered if she *could* speak.

"You come to ask after my welfare?" came her words a moment later. They were barely whispered, dragged over charred vocal cords. Yasen could distinguish them easily with his rakshasa hearing, but everyone else leaned forward.

"I'm sorry for what happened," Miraan said. "This is never how I wanted things to turn out."

Dishani went silent as if gathering her strength to answer.

"And yet... here we are."

Again, she whispered the words like they caused her immense pain.

"Dishani, I'd like to talk about what happened," Miraan said. "Perhaps when you're feeling a bit... more yourself. We need to discuss the resistance. They have demands, and we must hear them out."

Yasen tensed. He wasn't exactly the most diplomatic in most situations, but even he was cringing at Miraan's directness. Dishani was a wreck, and they were arriving to call for reform. It needed to be done, but this room and these people were seriously creeping him out.

"The resistance..." Dishani said after another long pause, "... will be crushed."

Yasen felt the weight of those words hang in the room. The princess had been bent but not broken. At least not yet.

"Dishani, you can't mean to keep this up," Miraan said. "Let's negotiate with them. Let's meet them where they are and find something that works for everyone. They know what's possible now. The collars will continue to come off, and they cannot be caged again. Disband the Jadugara and strip them of their power. The vanshaj are no longer defenseless. If you continue clinging to the old ways, you risk losing everything."

As Miraan finished speaking, the room fell into absolute silence. Everyone was staring at him with a mixture of respect and fear. Several vanshaj stood around the room, and Yasen noticed a few absentmindedly touching their throats.

Sweat gathered on Miraan's temples as he stared at Dishani, willing her to listen. To see reason.

"The city is in shambles," he continued. "You have lost control. Soon enough, they will organize themselves again and storm this palace. Now their secrets are out, and they have no reason to hold back. You have already lost. Show them what kind of queen you can be. It's not too late to *fix* this."

Yasen bounced on the ball of one foot and then the other as

everyone awaited her response. He was nervous. More nervous than he could remember being in a long time. He noted the queensguard stationed around the room with their hands all carefully cradling the hilts of their swords. Yasen wondered what their orders were. Hear them out and then attack? Or allow Miraan to walk out of here?

Yasen moved an inch closer to the prince, gripping his sword. A few noted the shift but displayed no outward signs of aggression.

Yasen's attention returned to Dishani, who was struggling to sit up. A vanshaj attendant rushed to help using her good arm. She drew in deep, rattling breaths as she carefully placed her feet on the ground. She must be in immense pain despite whatever relief Koura had been able to offer.

Once seated, she reached for the edge of her veil and slowly lifted it.

Yasen had seen it all. Bodies blown apart. Men hacked to pieces. But he swallowed thickly at the sight of her ruined face. Charred skin and red oozing welts covered one half, her right eye was gone, and her lips were a twisted mass of cartilage.

"This is what they did to me," she said. Her voice was weak but fueled with so much rage and anger that it practically vibrated in the air. "I will not rest until every single one of them suffers like I have."

Miraan had gone as white as a sheet. "Dishani," he whispered, his voice on the edge of cracking. "I'm so sorry it came to this. I never wanted anything like this to happen."

"You did this," she replied. "You are responsible for all of this."

Miraan dropped his head, his dark hair falling around his face and his shoulders shaking. It took every ounce of self-restraint not to rush over and comfort him.

Yasen wasn't really the comforting sort, but he had to admit that Miraan had found some secret place he hadn't known was there.

"Dishani—"

"Get out," she said with a bit more force this time. "I allowed you to come here only because we share blood, but after you leave today, you are dead to me. A price is on your head, and should you come anywhere near the palace again, my guards have orders to kill you on the spot."

"Dishani!" exclaimed Talin from the corner. "You can't mean that! He wasn't the one who hurt you."

Dishani ignored him as she dropped her veil and then leaned back, once again moving with great difficulty. Her servants swarmed around her, helping her get comfortable.

"Dishani—" Miraan pleaded as he stood. A moment later, the queensguard surrounded him with their blades pointed at him and Yasen.

"You've been granted leave to exit the palace," one said. "Once you cross the threshold, all royal protections shall be removed. You have two minutes."

Miraan opened and then closed his mouth as he glanced at his sister, clearly trying to understand how she could mean any of this.

"I think we'd better go," Yasen said gently, and Miraan blinked before he turned, tears forming in his eyes. He looked at his brother and then back at Dishani. Finally, he raised his hands in a gesture of surrender.

"Very well," he whispered before the pair were escorted out of the palace and all but shoved out the exit. The door thudded behind them with a resounding boom, and Miraan spun around, staring back as if he couldn't believe he'd just been tossed from his home.

Yasen noted the guards manning the walls with their crossbows cocked.

"Okay," Yasen said as he wrapped a hand around Miraan's

arm and tugged him through the plaza, "let's get the fuck out of here before one of those bolts makes a home in your chest."

Miraan didn't have another chance to protest as Yasen practically dragged him into the roiling streets of Ishaan.

Well, that went as poorly as it possibly could have.

Time to consider a plan B.

Whatever that was.

TWENTY-ONE

"Bad news," Abishek told Rabin and Zarya the following day over breakfast. He held a note that had just been delivered by his manservant, Omar.

Rabin sipped his coffee, trying to keep from wincing. His body ached from head to toe, and he was feeling more and more lethargic with each passing day. It had taken all his willpower to maintain a healthy facade last night.

As usual, they ate in the king's solarium, the windows filtering soft light across the flowers and trees. Last night, it had snowed, dusting everything with a fresh blanket of pristine white.

Despite whatever drug-induced haze Abishek had lost himself in at the party, the invite had found them in her room first thing this morning.

"Kishore has been delayed yet again. He'll be here in a few days," Abishek went on.

Rabin glanced at Zarya. He was growing increasingly suspicious. Kishore was never away from Andhera this long, and Rabin was beginning to wonder if Abishek was purposely trying to keep them here. The generous reason would be that he wanted to spend more time with Zarya.

"I see," Zarya said, her voice tight. "In that case, we'll be returning to Gi'ana today. We can consult the mystic who performed our Bandhan instead."

"How can you trust her after she already made such an error?" Abishek asked, his tone sharp.

"She didn't know about my sixth anchor," Zarya protested.

"She should have asked," Abishek said. "Any qualified mystic would have known to confirm it first."

She opened her mouth and then closed it, glancing over at Rabin.

Perhaps the king had a point.

"Just a few more days," he added. "I swear to you. We must ensure this is done right for both of you."

"It's been just a few more days for weeks now," Zarya said. Rabin could tell she was attempting to stay calm and affect a diplomatic tone, but her frustration was obvious. "When will he be back?"

"Have you been able to enter the mind plane yet?" Abishek asked, the question pointed as he regarded both Zarya and Rabin.

They hadn't. Neither of them had been able to for weeks, and Rabin was ready to tear his hair out. He'd combed through the paramadhar primer cover to cover, looking for an explanation. The book never mentioned a thing about the sixth anchor, but it was written shortly after the Hanera Wars, and any reference to the darkness would have been expressly forbidden and suppressed.

He thought of the Jai Palace Library and wondered if another book might answer this question. There was no chance of writing to Vik to ask. He'd burn up his letters and scatter the ashes to the wind.

"No," Zarya finally confessed a moment later. "We haven't been able to enter the mind plane."

Abishek nodded and sat back, steepling his fingers as his knowing gaze swept over them.

"Then you must wait for Kishore. This mystic of yours can no longer be trusted."

Rabin reached out and wrapped a hand around Zarya's wrist. Abishek blinked, noting the gesture, his gaze zeroing in on it. It was an involuntary movement. One he couldn't help. He nearly snatched his hand away, but they'd agreed to come clean with the king this morning, and there wasn't any need to continue hiding this.

They were currently working their way up to the topic.

Zarya nodded as her gaze slid to Rabin with a look that suggested they'd discuss this later. "Very well," she said, and then they exchanged another look. It was time to reveal their relationship to the king.

"We have something we must share with you," Rabin blurted. It wasn't a particularly elegant segue, but he wanted to get this over with. "Something we haven't been entirely forth-right about."

Suddenly, he was nervous. When Abishek had first forbidden their relationship, he'd thrown caution to the wind. No one would tell him who he couldn't be with. His feelings for Zarya were too strong to ignore.

Abishek cocked his head, studying Rabin while waiting for him to continue.

"When I left Andhera to seek Zarya out in Ishaan, you asked that I sever any romantic ties with her." Rabin paused as he folded his hands together on the table.

"I believe I forbade it," Abishek said, his eyes narrowing. "Quite clearly and explicitly."

Rabin nodded as he cleared his throat. It was Zarya's turn to grab his hand. They'd agreed he'd be the one to share the news, as Rabin felt it was his responsibility. Again, Abishek's gaze narrowed on their contact.

"And you've defied my order," the king said as his eyes lifted. "I was wondering when you'd finally admit it."

Rabin inhaled a sharp breath. Of course Abishek had known. They'd been fooling no one, and this was just another test. Abishek had only wanted to gauge how long they would keep lying to him.

Rabin nodded. "I'm sorry, but my feelings for your daughter could not be cast aside."

"Nor mine," Zarya said. "Rabin shared your... concerns, but we made this decision together. This was inevitable."

Rabin's heart squeezed at those words. She'd tried so hard to fight him and hearing her say this with such conviction felt like winning a battle.

"Inevitable?" Abishek said, arching a brow.

"Yes," Zarya said.

The silence in the room stretched. Rabin hoped the king didn't really care that much about what they did, but he *would* care that Rabin had disobeyed a direct order.

"And I'm sorry, but this isn't your call," Zarya said. "We are both adults and free to do what we want." She sucked in a sharp breath. "As I've already explained, your efforts with Amir are wasted. Besides, it surprises me that you'd consider a man with such a reputation as a suitable partner for your own daughter."

She said the words pointedly as Rabin judged Abishek's reaction.

Abishek's brows pinched together. "You understand I've named you my heir. Whoever you marry will effectively become the ruler of Andhera."

Rabin felt how she tensed at that statement.

"If I'm to be your heir and take over in your stead, then *I* will rule, not who I *marry*."

She issued the words with a challenge.

"Of course," Abishek said. "I only meant that you are inexperienced in the ways of my court and would perhaps like to have some guidance from someone familiar with Andhera and its dealings."

"We're married," Rabin said a moment later. He couldn't keep this in any longer. "You might as well know that in naming Zarya your heir, I will stand beside her. I understand Andhera and its dealings and would be happy to offer anything she needs."

Rabin watched something pass over the king's face. Something like rage and disappointment. It was there for a flash and then gone, but maybe a part of him had always known this would be his reaction. When he examined the root of his feelings, maybe Rabin also wanted to hide this because he already knew Abishek might have cared for and even loved him. But in the end, Rabin wasn't Aazheri and would never be good enough for his daughter.

"Married?" he asked, turning to Zarya. "Is this true?"

"It is," she confirmed. "We were married in Ishaan shortly before we left."

Zarya's chin lifted as if bracing for his wrath.

The king's gaze fell on Rabin again, another flash of judgment passing over his expression. "I gave you a direct order," he said.

"You did," he replied. They held each other's gazes while Abishek's jaw hardened and his eyes turned dark. What was going through his head?

"I know you wanted me to marry an Aazheri," Zarya said, and Rabin felt the sting of those words cut straight to the bone. "But that was never a consideration for me."

Abishek remained still for another moment before he finally nodded. "I suppose... you are right, and this is not a decision I get to make."

Rabin's shoulders eased a fraction. He wasn't entirely sure

what he'd feared. A withdrawal of Abishek's approval? His anger? His hate? Disappointing him in all the same ways that he'd disappointed his biological father? But he already had. He recognized that familiar spark in the king's eyes. It was the same one he'd witnessed in his father so many times.

"Okay, well, that's settled, then," Zarya said. "We're sorry for keeping it from you, but we worried about what you might say. But this is done, and it cannot be undone. We have pledged ourselves to one another in all the ways that connect us, and we will honor that until the end of our days."

Abishek's gaze swept over her. "I understand," he said.

"We have some decisions to make about our plans," Zarya said. "I need to check on Row and Yasen and the others, and we must return to Ishaan soon. Before we leave, I'd like to perform the demonstration the nobles asked for—when can we arrange that?"

"We've been trying to find a time that will suit everyone," he said. "But I'll let them know it's become more urgent."

"Great," Zarya said as she stood up from the table while Abishek watched them both. Rabin threaded his fingers through hers as the king's attention moved between them, lingering on Rabin for several prolonged seconds.

As they turned to leave, Abishek called out, "Rabindranath, may I speak with you alone for a moment?"

Rabin tensed and turned around before checking with Zarya. "Give me a minute."

She nodded and slipped out of the room before Rabin approached the king.

"Will you sit?" Abishek asked, gesturing to the chair across from him.

Rabin slid into it and sat forward, prepared for anything. A verbal lashing. The king's disappointment. Whatever it was, he would endure it.

"You've been quiet since you returned," Abishek said. "I've seen very little of you."

Rabin exhaled a short breath. "I think... I've been avoiding you."

Abishek arched a dark brow. "Because you knew I'd be displeased. I can become rather unpleasant when my orders are dismissed."

Rabin dipped his chin. "I grappled with the decision. But I had to do what was best for me and Zarya."

Abishek's mouth pressed together, his chest expanding with a deep breath. He appeared calm, but the king was skilled at masking his emotions.

"I am angry," he said. "I won't deny it. Disappointed. But... you did bring my daughter home, and I haven't thanked you for that."

"I'm sorry," Rabin said. "I hope you can forgive me."

Abishek offered a considering tip of his head. "How are you feeling? Is the Bandhan affecting you?"

Rabin nodded. "I think it is. I don't feel quite myself. Another reason I've been quiet."

"I do wish you'd stay," he said next. "Besides what Kishore can do for you, I enjoy having her here. I enjoy having you both here. The castle isn't the same without you."

Rabin's shoulders finally eased at the warmth in the king's tone. Despite his insubordination, perhaps he'd survive Abishek's wrath.

"Zarya is worried about the resistance."

"Yes," Abishek said with a smile. "Happy wife, happy life, yes?"

Rabin exhaled an amused snort at that. "Yes. Something like that."

"I understand," Abishek said. "Go forth with my blessing, and please tell me if you need anything."

"Thank you." Rabin dropped his head in a gesture of respect. "I'm sorry again. We never meant to deceive you."

"Love makes one do impulsive, sometimes reckless things, doesn't it? You've always been that way. I shouldn't be surprised."

Rabin frowned. He didn't really think that was a fair assessment of his character, but he let the comment go. He was just grateful Abishek wasn't angrier.

"Thank you again," Rabin said, pushing up from his seat. "Where *is* Kishore, anyway? It's unlike him to be away for so long."

Abishek sighed and wrapped his hands around his armrests in a gesture of weariness. "Initially, I sent him to speak with the mountain clan leaders. They're still causing me problems, and they've always been more amenable to speaking with the mystics. I was hoping they might be persuaded to open some key mountain passes."

"And?"

"And it's ongoing," he said. "After I wrote to him about your Bandhan, he said he'd need some specific ingredients to rectify the issue. Since he was already near the source, he thought it made more sense to gather everything before returning home."

"Why didn't you tell us this?" Rabin asked.

Abishek shook his head. "Sometimes, I forget I don't have to keep everything close to my chest. Old habits die hard."

"I see."

After a short bow, Rabin again turned to leave.

As he crossed the room, Abishek called out to him one more time, "Rabindranath, should you ever defy a direct order from me again, understand there will be consequences."

Rabin came to a stop and peered over his shoulder. The king watched him unblinking as Rabin dipped his chin.

"Yes, Your Majesty," he said before striding from the room,

trying to ignore the apprehensive shiver crawling down his spine.

TWENTY-TWO

Zarya paced across her room. Her conscience floated lighter, though now she worried about what the king wanted from Rabin. Hopefully, he just needed a chance to talk things out privately. They were close, and their relationship had taken a blow.

The door opened, and Rabin entered before closing it behind him.

"Are you okay?" she asked. "Is everything all right?"

Something about the look on his face had her guard up.

"Yeah," he answered. "I'm fine. I really thought he'd be angrier, to be honest."

"Well, he had no right to be," she answered. "He should never have given that order in the first place. It was overstepping."

Rabin huffed out a scoff. "As if being right matters to him."

She noted the bite in his tone. He'd been the one who'd convinced her to come here, extolling the king's virtues, but ever since they'd touched down on the roof, he'd been behaving very differently.

"Is there something you're not sharing?" she asked.

"You're... I'm not sure how to put this, but you told me what a great guy my father is, but now that we're here, you seem kind of suspicious?"

Rabin shook his head and ran a hand down his face. "I'm sorry. You're right. I did tell you all that, and none of that has changed..."

"But?" she asked, sensing the hesitation in his words.

"I can't explain it. Ever since we arrived, I have this sixth sense that something is *off*."

She stared at him, waiting for him to elaborate.

He shook his head again. "I'm sure it's nothing. I'm just intent on protecting you and jumping at the slightest sounds."

"Is it the Bandhan?" she asked. "I know you're pretending to feel better than you do."

He sighed and rubbed the back of his neck. "I'm fine."

"You're *not* fine."

When he didn't answer, she dropped her shoulders, crossing the room to wrap her arms around his waist. Pressing her cheek to his chest, she listened to the steady beat of his heart.

"I'm glad we told him," she said. "That it's finally in the open."

"I am, too," he said, murmuring into her hair. "I don't want to hide the way I feel for you from anyone."

She peered up at him, searching his face for signs of the sickness he refused to name.

He leaned down to kiss her, his hand sliding up the side of her jaw and then to the nape of her neck. He tipped her head as his tongue probed the seam of her lips, and her mouth opened to welcome him while his hands slid up her back.

When he pulled away a second later, he pressed his forehead to hers. "When we return to Ishaan, do you think we could get another night in that honeymoon suite?"

She laughed. "Perhaps Miraan can swing us another favor."

His expression turned serious. "Zarya, do you think we should return to Ishaan at all? I fear what we might be walking into. The city is a mess, and your sister wants you dead. There will be no safe place for you there."

Zarya nodded. "I know. But Yasen confirmed that she can barely move. I don't wish that pain on her, but it is also our chance to make things right. We started this... *I* started this, and I can't abandon them."

He nodded. "I know, and I'm not asking you to, but I wish there were a way to do that without putting you so close to your sister."

"I don't see how. This started in Gi'ana, and it will likely finish there, too."

She pinched the bridge of her nose and exhaled a heavy sigh. "You should know that Yasen's last letter said he and the other rebels were considering appealing to Daragaab for support."

Rabin cocked his head and studied her. "To Vik?"

"Yes. Since Dishani is still unwilling to hear out the Rising Phoenix, they wonder if they might convince another realm to amend their laws. The hope is that if one goes first, the others might eventually follow. Abishek is warming up to the idea, but I think it's best we work every angle we can."

"Why Daragaab?" Rabin asked.

"I think Yasen is hoping Vik will listen to him."

Rabin considered that. "If there's anyone he might hear out, it's Yas."

"I think so, too. Other news is that Kindle is making strides in Bhaavana with their rebellion, and Apsara is in touch with friends in Vayuu. Koura is working with people in Svaasthy who say their queen may be amenable. It's happening. Slowly but surely, things are changing. And Daragaab is the largest region in Rahajhan. They're hoping it would send a message."

Rabin blew out a sharp breath. "It's a good point. Maybe it could work."

"Hopefully, Yasen can make him see the truth. What possible reason could he have for wanting to keep the vanshaj bound? I know we had our issues, but deep down, I have to believe there's something good in there."

"Vik has never been malicious."

"I'm not sure how eager Yasen is to return to Dharati," she said. "But he's willing to try."

"What do you want to do next?" Rabin asked.

"Are you okay to travel?"

"I'm fine, Zarya. We'll see Thriti to fix this. I'm sure it just didn't occur to her to ask about the sixth anchor."

"Maybe," Zarya said. "But what if the king has a point?"

"He wants us to stay. He told me he likes having us here."

She nodded and bit the corner of her lip. She didn't want to disappoint her father. She wanted to know more about him. "If things were less volatile, I'd want to stay, too."

"If Thriti isn't able to fix this, we can come back when Kishore returns," he promised. "For your demonstration, too."

"Okay," she replied. "Then let's go. I just want to check on everyone."

Rabin ran a hand down his face and through his hair. "We'll figure this all out. There *is* light at the end of this."

Zarya nodded. "I truly hope so."

A few hours later, they'd sent word to the king of their plans and packed up their things, preparing to leave. Zarya was buttoning up her coat when a knock came at the door. She opened it to find Omar waiting on the other side. He handed her a note, and she unfolded it, immediately recognizing the king's handwriting thanks to all the hours she'd spent in his library.

Zarya, good news. Kishore has returned early. I hope you'll consider delaying your trip and come to see me at once.

She frowned. For weeks, Abishek had been promising Kishore would return, and now, just as they were leaving, he suddenly appeared?

"Thank you," Zarya said to Omar. "Tell him..."

She cut off when she saw Rabin stalking down the hallway with a note also clutched in his hand.

"Tell him we'll be there in a minute," he said.

Omar dipped at the waist. "Don't keep him waiting." Then he turned and stalked off.

"It's weird, right?" Rabin asked, holding up the note.

"Or just a lucky coincidence?"

"Maybe."

She pressed her mouth together and nodded. "Well, since we're here, should we see what he has to say?"

He shrugged. "I suppose we've waited this long."

Zarya removed her coat and tossed it into her room before reaching out to take his hand. He threaded his warm fingers with hers; it felt good to have this out in the open. They made their way through the castle and to Abishek's wing, where they were immediately admitted.

Upon entering his study, they found Ekaja waiting with Abishek and a third person, whom she presumed must be the famous Kishore. For some reason, she'd been expecting an old man. But the mystic was as young and handsome as Thriti had been beautiful, though his eyes suggested the same agelessness. He had the same deep brown skin and silver hair hanging to his shoulders. Zarya wondered if the hair was a common marker for a mystic.

"Zarya," Abishek said as he approached. "The fates must truly be smiling on us." He held out an arm and beckoned her forward. "Meet Kishore. A fortuitous turn of events has found him here earlier than we expected."

"That's very lucky," she said, smiling and nodding hello.

"Kishore," Rabin said, reaching out to shake the mystic's hand. "What timing you have. We were nearly out the door."

Kishore gave him a tight smile that didn't reach his eyes. "Yes, well. The gods look favorably on us when it is most prudent."

"Sure," Rabin said as he offered a short nod to Ekaja.

"Can you help us with our Bandhan?" Zarya asked. "We haven't been able to enter the mind plane for weeks now."

Kishore's dark eyebrows drew together. "Not at *all*?"

"No," she said. "It's pretty worrisome."

"It's more than that," he said but didn't elaborate as he gestured to them both. "I'll need to see your binding markings."

Rabin and Zarya exchanged a look.

"Come now. I can't help you otherwise."

Reluctantly, Rabin lifted his tunic, and Zarya shrugged off the sleeve of her shirt.

Kishore then laid a cool hand on her shoulder while goosebumps prickled her skin. The mystic inhaled deeply with a gusty sound, his eyes fluttering closed.

"This was well done," he said. "*Nearly* as good as my own work."

There was something needling in the sentiment, and Zarya controlled the curl of her lip. He was trying to help.

"Your father tells me you bear the darkness," Kishore said, his penetrating gaze meeting hers with such intensity that it felt like he was trying to see straight into her. The sensation was so unsettling that she almost backed away.

"He told you correctly."

"And nightfire? The queen's prophecy has finally come true?"

"It has," she whispered, her voice suddenly too tight to speak. A strange wave of melancholy hit her then. She kept missing a woman she'd never met. She wanted guidance and someone to confide in the way only a mother could offer. She had no idea what kind of mother Asha would have been, but in her daydreams, she pictured someone kind and loving and supportive.

Kishore gave her a scrutinizing look before also laying a hand on Rabin's tattoo, but not before admiring it with a gleam in his eyes. He took another deep breath, and Zarya watched the mystic as silver bands of magic swirled around him.

She felt a tug deep inside her shoulder, almost as if he were pulling at the Bandhan from under her skin. She winced as he tugged harder. It didn't hurt exactly, but the sensation felt awkward and intrusive.

Her gaze met Rabin's, and she noted the hardness of his jaw. They all stood in silence as more of Kishore's magic swirled around the room in glittering trails of silver.

After several minutes, they faded away, and Kishore opened his eyes, a frown denting the space between his brows. He turned and addressed Abishek.

"It is exactly as you feared. The mark was applied incorrectly and has been corrupted. They should have waited for me."

He said it in a chastising tone, and though he wasn't speaking directly to Zarya, she felt she was being scolded like a small child. How were they to have known any of this?

"Is there anything you can do?" Abishek asked, his voice grave with concern. "How far gone is it?"

"It's not good," Kishore answered. "If they'd come to me immediately, we would have had a better chance at saving them."

Zarya opened her mouth, about to protest that they'd been waiting on *him* for weeks, but Abishek was already speaking.

"And what should we do now?" he asked.

"We must fix the Bandhan as soon as possible. We'll detoxify the existing markings, strip out their magic, and redo the binding. It's a difficult process, but I am obviously more than capable."

Zarya resisted the urge to roll her eyes. What was it with these self-satisfied men who hung around her father?

"When can we do it?" Zarya asked, dread pooling in her gut. Rabin had already been affected. How long until it resulted in something more permanent?

At that, Kishore whirled around to face her.

"You would rush this?" he said, his tone sharp. "I've just explained that you are corrupted by the very magic running in your veins. Your Bandhan is tarnished. Toxic. It will eat at you from the inside if you do not address this. You think you can hurry this along?"

"I was merely wondering how long it might be," she asked, gritting her teeth. "I'm worried."

Kishore folded his hands at his waist and gave Zarya a smug smile. "It will take a few days to prepare the necessary ingredients. We'll strip the markings first, which will be quite painful. Then you may need a day or two to recover before we reapply the Bandhan. Is that a sufficient enough answer for you?"

Zarya hardened her jaw—another few days at best.

"And then we'll be able to enter the mind plane again?" she asked as he dipped his head.

"Then your connection should return."

"Okay," Zarya said. "We appreciate your help."

"I will summon you when I'm ready," Kishore said.

"Thank you."

She looked at Rabin, and his expression suggested that he didn't like it, but he understood they had no choice.

TWENTY-THREE

With their relationship out in the open, there was no further need to maintain pretenses. Thus, Zarya moved her things into Rabin's room.

They shared a quiet dinner by the fire as the weather turned, a blizzard sweeping over the mountains with driving gusts of snow and howling winds.

"Maybe it was a good thing we didn't try to fly in this," Zarya said, gesturing outside.

"Hmm," Rabin responded as he stared out the window. He'd been even more quiet since their meeting with Kishore.

"You okay?" she asked and turned towards him.

"I'm fine," he said again before sitting forward with his elbows on his knees. "It's killing me to know that this incredible thing that brought us together is tainted. It's my fault—I'm the one who insisted we do this."

"No," Zarya said, shaking her head. "We aren't doing that. The resistance needed us, and I wanted it, too. This was a decision we made together. You didn't force me into anything." She reached out a hand and squeezed his wrist. "It's only the magic. Nothing between us has changed."

He cocked a small smile, his gaze raking over her. "I just can't shake the feeling Kishore isn't being completely honest with us."

"He does seem rather weaselly," she remarked. "Do you know him well?"

"Not especially. He's always been around, but he mostly sticks with Abishek. I get the sense that he thinks he's too good for everyone else. He has his own workshop in another part of the castle where he spends most of his time."

"Has he ever given you a reason to distrust him?"

"No," Rabin said. "He's the one who did this." He gestured towards the dragon under his kurta.

"And you trust my father?"

Rabin stared at her for several long seconds. "I do. He's grown fond of you and wouldn't let anything happen to you."

She smiled. "Then let's take care of this, and we'll be on our way."

After dinner, they prepared for bed. She stripped out of her dress and stood before the mirror, turning to examine her inked dragon, its sheen of iridescence barely visible in the falling light.

Rabin came up behind her, also bare down to his underwear. He wrapped an arm around her waist and pulled her towards him before brushing aside her hair to expose her shoulder.

He leaned down to kiss the dragon on her skin.

"Rabin," she said. "Do you feel it? The taint? Be honest with me."

He was silent for several moments, his expression suggesting he'd gone into himself. Then he shook his head. "Sometimes, I think I feel it. Like an echo that wasn't there before. But then I wonder if I'm imagining it."

"It's changed, though," she said. "I don't feel anything in the marking itself, but our connection *is* different."

He sighed. "It is. I suppose that must be what we're feeling."

"I don't like it. I want to head back to Ishaan, but I also want this fixed."

"We'll fix it," he said as he turned her to face him. His hand swept over her hip and settled on her lower back. "This is nothing we can't handle. We'll allow Kishore to work his magic, and everything will be fine."

"I'm worried about you."

He smirked. "I've been through a lot worse, Spitfire. It'll take a lot more than that to kill me."

She sighed as he leaned in to suck on the curve of her neck, then he took her hand and tugged her towards the bed. "Now we don't have to hide this anymore, and I'm about to have my way with you in *my* bed."

She giggled as he tossed her down and then landed on top of her before they lost themselves in each other.

That night, Zarya dreamed of her mother again.

Only it was different. She was wandering the corridors of a dark castle that felt familiar, though she couldn't pinpoint why. She traversed a narrow hall of dark stones lined with faded tapestries, their threads nearly leached of color.

A sound echoed in the distance, but she couldn't determine its source. It was both soft and sharp, like a hammer striking nails against the backdrop of leaves whispering in the wind.

She noticed the cold stones beneath her feet and the air chilling her skin, sending a shiver skating down her back. In the dream, she was propelled forward. Even when she stopped walking, the scene continued to move, finding her at the bottom of a winding staircase spiraling up into the darkness.

She saw her hand grip the railing, the metal cold as ice, and then she ascended smoothly, almost like she was floating. As she wound higher, the air grew colder, freezing in her lungs, nipping the tips of her ears and nose with the sharp, burning sensation of frostbite.

She reached the door she'd come to recognize, and without pausing, she pushed it open to reveal the same circular room and her mother huddled in the corner, shivering violently. Zarya choked on a sob as she tried to reach for Asha, but the closer she moved, the further the scene retreated.

Zarya stopped and stared at her mother's huddling form. At the bruises and lacerations marring her skin. She couldn't look away from her hair hanging knotted and lined with strands of white, nor her threadbare clothing or dirty bare feet with their jagged, torn nails.

"Mother," Zarya tried to call, but nothing came out. She felt herself say it, but she couldn't *hear* it. She wanted to scream in frustration, stomp on the floor, and pound on the walls until this entire room collapsed.

A movement caught her eye, and she turned towards the corner as a new sense of premonition climbed up the back of her scalp.

There were windows in this tower.

Though her subconscious had always known this, she'd never paid attention until now. She approached the nearest one with her heart wedged in her throat until she peered over the edge, taking in the sight before her.

Mountains and snow. Pine trees and endless grey rocks. She *knew* this view. She'd looked upon it every night before she'd gone to sleep, ever since the day they'd landed on a high tower painted with a dragon in Andhera.

Her stomach dropped as she stumbled towards the wall and then blinked.

Her eyes flew open, and she sat straight up in bed with a gasp. She was covered in sweat, her pulse racing.

"Zarya," came Rabin's deep voice. "What's wrong?"

She shook her head as she tried to catch her breath.

"Zarya? Are you okay?" He placed a hand on her back. "What's going on?"

"I... had another dream. About my mother."

He watched her, clearly sensing there was more.

"It was different," she said. "I saw more of it. I was in a castle, and it seemed familiar. I still couldn't reach her, but I looked out the window."

"The window?" he asked.

"Snow. I saw snow and mountains."

"Zarya, what are you saying?"

Her mouth opened, and she huffed out a sharp breath. "I don't know. I think... she was here. I think he *put* her in that tower."

"Zarya, it's just a dream. Of course you'd see this place. This is where you've been living for weeks."

She shook her head and clutched her throat.

"I don't think it was just a dream," she said. "It felt... like something else."

He shifted closer, leaning in as he grabbed her chin between his fingers. "Zarya, what are you saying?"

She looked up at him and blinked. "I'm saying that either he locked her in that tower at some point... or... she's still there."

TWENTY-FOUR

Zarya couldn't get the image of her mother out of her head. She was convinced it hadn't been a dream. But what could she do with this information? Was this something that had happened a long time ago? Or was it *still* happening?

Her mother had *disappeared* shortly after her birth. No one knew where she'd gone. What if Zarya had uncovered a buried truth?

What if Asha was still alive?

"There was a hallway with black stones and worn tapestries," she was telling Rabin the next morning. He remained skeptical it had been anything but her mind playing tricks, but he was also humoring her for now.

"I don't know of any place like that," he said. "Why would he have worn tapestries in the castle? He's meticulous about making sure everything is perfect."

She blew out a frustrated breath as she paced back and forth. "Then we need to search the towers. She's in a tower."

"Is she?" he asked, seated on the divan with one arm propped on his elbow. "Zarya, I know it felt real, but is she *really* here?"

She rubbed a hand down her face. "I don't know. Maybe. Or she was here, and now she's gone. In that case, we have to find out why. And, more importantly, what happened to her."

She stopped pacing and then turned to him as tears pressed the backs of her eyes. "What if she's *alive* somewhere? What if... he's hurting her?"

Rabin pushed himself up from the divan and wrapped his arms around her. "Why would he do that? What would be gained by locking her up?"

"I have no idea, but I know what I saw. I need to search the towers."

"There are probably a hundred in this castle," he said.

"Then I'll search a hundred. I have time. We're stuck here until Kishore can fix this." She gestured to her shoulder. "If you don't want to help me—"

"No," he interrupted. "That's not what I'm saying. I would help you if there were a million towers, but I don't want you to get your hopes up."

She blew out a sigh. "I won't."

"Zarya, they're already up."

She huffed. "Fine. I will *try* to temper my expectations and delusions, okay?"

He shook his head. "Then where do we start?"

Rabin trailed Zarya as they combed through the castle for the next two days, searching through long corridors and winding halls, up spiraling staircases leading to countless towers. Some ended in opulent rooms offering sweeping views of the endless landscape, while others ended in small, empty spaces covered with cobwebs.

What they didn't find was a prison keeping the queen of Gi'ana.

Zarya was convinced she was here, but it seemed impossible.

He hoped. That same itching worry pricked at the back of his scalp that something wasn't right.

On their second day, the king invited them to dine with Kishore, but Zarya claimed she wasn't feeling well, so Rabin went in her stead while she used the opportunity to continue searching the castle. He didn't want to let her out of his sight but told himself he was being foolish. She was perfectly safe here. He was the one who'd promised her that. So why couldn't he shake this?

As they continued hunting, he watched her frustration grow with each dead end. He understood how much she wanted this to be real.

At night, he lay awake listening to her whisper in her sleep, begging for her mother, pleading for her to be somewhere she could find her. It cracked a fissure in his heart. He wanted this for her, too—not whatever Abishek had done, but for Asha to be alive.

If Zarya's visions were, in fact, visions, then what she'd described was horrific. If Abishek had locked Asha away, why would he treat her in such a brutal manner?

Rabin feared that troubling feeling in the back of his head was worming its way into the cracks of his faith in his mentor. He'd based the last twenty years of his life on his belief in the king of Andhera. On the man who had rescued him from the brink of death. Had he not found him on that ice where Rabin lay dying, he wouldn't be here now.

But something had shifted in the past months.

It started when he'd forbidden him from having a relationship with Zarya, and doubt started working its way in. That feeling that had been dogging him since they'd arrived wouldn't go away, and he was almost ready to say fuck it and fly her out of here once and for all.

Forget Ishaan. Forget Dharati. Forget Andhera. He'd fly them over the sea and find somewhere far from here where no one could ever hurt her. They'd find someone else to fix their bond.

Except Rabin himself had revealed Zarya to Abishek, and if the king had sinister intentions, he already knew there would be nowhere they could hide. If Rabin was wrong about all of this, he'd never forgive himself.

"Rabin?" she asked as she turned another corner. "You okay?"

"I'm fine," he answered. It felt like he was saying that a lot lately. He wasn't fine. His body ached. His mind was clouded. He'd never experienced anything like this before. It almost felt like he was dying.

They stood in yet another castle corridor lined with the usual bright, vibrant tapestries, none faded or worn as she'd described.

Another round staircase led them up another tower.

Zarya flung open the door, exhaling a sound of frustration at finding yet another room that clearly hadn't been used in a while. The bed had been stripped of a mattress and sheets, and dust covered the wooden furniture.

She stomped over to the window, gripped the ledge, and pressed her forehead to the glass. He gave her a moment to gather herself.

Slowly, he approached from behind, keeping his eyes on the horizon.

"Where is she?" Zarya whispered. "Why can't we find her?"

"Zarya..." He stopped himself from saying anything that might hurt.

Asha probably *wasn't* here. If she'd *ever* been here, then it was more than likely that she was already dead. But he couldn't voice that out loud. Zarya wasn't a fool. She already knew it, but her single-minded sense of hope kept her moving forward.

"When did you arrive here?" Zarya asked a moment later, her gaze sweeping over the snow and mountains.

"About twenty years ago," he said. "But you know that."

"But when exactly?"

"Just shy of that. Almost nineteen years ago."

She paused. "So, after I was born."

A beat of silence passed between them. "Yes, I suppose. Why?"

"And *after* she disappeared."

Again, Rabin hesitated, wondering where she was headed with this line of questioning.

"I'm not exactly sure when she disappeared, but yes, it likely happened before I arrived."

She didn't answer as she continued looking out the window.

"Zarya, why would he do this?"

She huffed out a sharp breath before she pushed away from the window.

"I don't know," she answered. "Let's keep looking."

Then she stalked out of the room.

TWENTY-FIVE

Yasen stood with an elbow propped up on the mantel of some snooty noble's home. With the manor compromised, Miraan had appealed to a friend for shelter and a place to hide from Dishani's wrath.

Rudra seemed nice enough, but Yasen was wary of trusting him to keep their presence a secret. Miraan had contacted more of his rich friends and invited them to discuss the rebellion. Now the seven men sat facing each other, talking and arguing.

"Miraan, this is madness," one of them said. Yasen thought his name was Pransh. "Your family will kill you."

"I don't care," Miraan said, and Yasen did his best to restrain a loud sigh. Miraan kept saying he didn't care about his life or his safety. But Yasen cared. Maybe a little too much.

"Where are the vanshaj now?" Rudra asked. "How are they faring?"

"Hiding in the forest," Miraan said. "I will not reveal their location. But they are gathering weapons and training in combat and their new magic. They will attempt another coup if my sister won't listen to reason."

"And what of those left in the city?" Pransh asked.

"They're trying to get everyone out. It must be done slowly and cautiously, lest they draw the attention of the Jadugara," Miraan said.

Yasen listened as they all discussed strategies and ideas, weighing the pros and cons, some more willing than others to throw their lot in with Miraan.

"Do you know anything of this army my sister is bringing in?" Miraan asked.

"I don't," Rudra answered. "At first, I assumed it must be the Kiraaye Ka, but I've spoken with their captain, and he confirms he hasn't been in contact with the princess."

Yasen raised an eyebrow, wondering why this fancy noble was in communication with the mercenary leader from Bhaavana.

"Then who?" Pransh asked.

"I don't know," Miraan answered.

They resumed their conversation for a while longer until they agreed to meet again tomorrow. They hadn't come to any definite conclusions, but Yasen was relieved that some were willing to help.

After the door closed on the last visitor, Rudra excused himself, stating he had business to attend. When they were alone, Yasen said, "I need to get going. Row is taking me to Dharati soon."

"I still don't know about this plan," Miraan said.

"Dharati is my home. And I'll be with Row. He's a badass who no one would cross."

Miraan's mouth pressed together. "I'll still worry."

"I'm worried about you, too. What are you planning next?" Yasen asked.

"I still want to get through to my family," Miraan said. "I refuse to believe they don't want to find a way to fix this."

"You can't return to the palace."

Miraan ran a hand through his hair, his gaze unfocused.

"No, but Rudra said he's willing to meet with Dishani on my behalf."

He stopped talking, and Yasen sensed something he wasn't saying.

"What?" Yasen asked, his awareness prickling with worry.

Miraan's gaze pinged to him. "I wonder if we can appeal to my father. Technically, he is in charge until Dishani's coronation and his orders would supersede hers. Just because he's never done so and has always defaulted to my sister doesn't mean it's the only way."

"Sure, piss her off a little more. She'll love that."

"She's leaving me no choice," he answered, his voice full of buried emotion.

"Then what's your plan?"

"To invite them to a mutual safe space—I trust that neither my father nor Talin would betray me. I think they're too scared to do anything independently, but I'm not afraid of Dishani."

Yasen stared at the prince and the determination in his eyes. He didn't want to admit to himself that he was falling for this man. There was something enduring and noble in how he bore everything with grace and calm. He was beautiful on the inside and out. Despite his stern exterior, Miraan had a heart that bled gold.

Miraan looked at Yasen, and their gazes met. He didn't understand what he read in the prince's expression. He didn't know what to expect or even what he wanted. He was a prince, and if things continued, perhaps he was destined to become a king.

The female line had always ruled Gi'ana, but he was confident Zarya didn't want the job, and as he'd said, just because something had always been done a certain way, it didn't mean it always had to be so.

"What are you thinking?" Miraan asked, stirring Yasen out of his thoughts.

He blinked and sighed. "That... I'm wondering where this leads." He gestured between them, and Miraan strode over instantly, cupping Yasen's face in his hands before his lips crashed into his. Miraan kissed him deeply, his mouth hot and his tongue probing.

Yasen clung on, almost like he was drowning. And maybe he was. Sinking into the soft, dark eyes and the stoic expression of a prince with so much riding on his shoulders.

They pulled apart, their foreheads touching.

"Be careful," Miraan said.

"You, too."

Then Yasen pulled away and turned to leave, trying not to think of everything he stood to lose.

A few hours later, Yasen and Row left for Dharati. They arrived inside the haveli, away from the scrutiny of prying eyes. As Row's magic dissipated around them, Yasen blinked several times to shake off his dizziness, stumbling as he reached for a table to steady himself.

"Sorry," Row said. "It isn't the most pleasant way to travel. I actually avoid it as much as possible, to be honest."

"Oh, it's no problem," Yasen said. "I love having my eyes squeezed to the point of bursting."

He shook his head, blinking heavily several times, casting away the last of his disorientation before inhaling a deep breath.

He'd been nervous about returning to Dharati for a variety of reasons. While his departure had been justified—or at least he'd done an adequate job of convincing himself of that—he couldn't shake the guilt that had followed him for months.

Vikram needed him, and Yasen had run as far away as possible. But he'd spent most of his life being there for Vikram, and while he'd never expected anything in return, it had also been time to look out for himself.

"You ready?" Row asked as he crossed the living room with a purposeful stride.

"We're going now?" Yasen asked.

"No time like the present, is there?"

Yasen pushed himself from the wall. "I suppose not."

They exited the haveli and crossed the plaza towards the Jai Palace. Yasen had always loved the sight of those sky-blue gates and the flowering canopy casting its shadow over the city. It had always felt like protection, and though he'd never admit it out loud, it also felt like a warm hug.

His gaze scanned the plaza full of people holding signs with messages about freeing the vanshaj, chanting and shouting at everyone who passed. Row's and Yasen's gazes met before proceeding through the crowd.

They drew up to the gates, studying the guards who were monitoring the protestors with a wary eye.

"Aren't you worried about being arrested?" Yasen asked, referring to the near miss in the library with Zarya and Rabin a few weeks ago.

"Not particularly," Row answered. Perhaps it made sense. Row was pretty ancient and probably had seen some shit. He could handle a few measly palace guards. "You're the one arriving with me," he continued. "Maybe you should be worried."

"Already ahead of you," Yasen grumbled. A few soldiers recognized Row immediately, their eyes narrowing with suspicion. He raised his hands in a placating gesture.

"I need to speak with the steward," Row said.

"You are under arrest," a guard replied.

"I understand Vikram is unhappy with me, but if you'd just tell him I need to speak with him, I will enter your dungeons without a fuss."

Yasen offered Row a curious, side-eyed look, but Row's expression suggested he was being entirely sincere.

"If he won't see Row, tell Vik that his best friend is here," Yasen said. The guards noticed him then, and they immediately straightened. Lazy bastards.

"Commander," the head guard said. "I'm... I'm... sorry... I..."

"It's fine," he replied with a wave of his hand. "But must we stand out here any longer?"

"Of course not," the guard said with a bow. "The steward is currently with the queen. Follow me."

Then he spun on his heel, leaving Row and Yasen to follow.

"Probably should have started with that," Row said, and Yasen snorted.

"Probably."

They entered the tall doors admitting them into Amrita's throne room. Yasen took in the sight of the shiny black and white tiles and the metallic flowers in pink, blue, and green. He scanned the high dome overhead, noting the leaf-covered ceilings and walls, and couldn't help but feel like something was *off*.

The air was heavy and cloying, and he wondered if he smelled the barest hint of rot. He shook his head as they approached. Amrita looked different, too. Instead of her usual nut browns and fresh greens, her bark had turned nearly black and her leaves into midnight emeralds.

Yasen swallowed at the sight of the baby hovering in her stomach. The clear seed allowed one to view the twisted tangle of roots and leaves within. It shone with an inner light, casting a gentle glow over the room. He stared at it for several long seconds as he straddled a line between horrified and fascinated.

Finally, he turned his attention towards Vikram, who stood by Amrita, watching them both. He looked different, too—thinner, tired, with dark circles under his eyes. He was dressed casually in a cotton kurta with the top buttons undone, the fabric a bit wrinkled. His hair, always neatly trimmed and styled, hung in his eyes in desperate need of a cut.

Yasen blinked as guilt flared in his gut. He had no idea

Vikram had been under so much stress. Their letters had been sporadic at best, while Yasen had attempted to leave his past behind. But seeing his oldest friend like this churned up a rush of ashamed feelings.

"Vik," he breathed as he crossed the room and threw his arms around him. Vikram took a few seconds to respond, his arms slowly circling Yasen. They stood there together for several long moments before they pulled apart.

"Are you okay?" Yasen asked. "You don't look great."

Vikram stared distantly, almost as if he didn't recognize him before his gaze cleared.

"Yasen, it's so good to see you. I'm fine. Just tired with the baby coming and everything..." He waved a hand as he trailed off. Yasen narrowed his eyes as Vikram turned towards Amrita and stared up at her with a blank expression. When he said nothing else, Yasen exchanged an uncomfortable glance with Row.

"Vik?" Yasen asked.

Vikram turned and blinked like he was surprised to find them standing there.

"You should join me for dinner," Vikram said. "How long are you staying?"

Again, Yasen and Row looked at one another.

"We were hoping to talk to you about the vanshaj," Row said carefully. "The rebellions in the north are growing, and we need support. The Madans refuse to hear reason, and we thought Dharati might be interested in leading the charge and defending what is right."

"The vanshaj," Vikram said. "Yes..."

"Vik," Yasen said. "Are you okay? You don't seem like yourself."

Vikram brought a hand to his forehead and rubbed it. "I'm fine." He took a few steps towards Amrita, laying his hand against her to communicate in their silent way. Yasen's gaze drifted around the room, wandering over the abundance of leaves and flowers when it snagged on a chilling sight.

A dark spot.

He squinted, trying to determine if it was simply a trick of the light, but he was sure his eyes weren't deceiving him. He continued searching, studying every leaf and petal, finally noticing the barest outline of black along the edges.

His stomach dropped as he noticed more tiny pinpoints peppering the leaves and vines. They blended into the surroundings so well that they were nearly undetectable, but surely *someone* had noticed this?

"Vik, why does Amrita look so different?" Yasen asked.

Vikram blinked heavily. "We believe it's a side effect of the pregnancy."

"You believe? You don't know for sure?"

Vikram shook his head. "I just assumed. I hadn't really thought about it."

Row was now giving Yasen a quizzical look.

How many others had recently seen the queen?

"When did the change start happening?" Yasen asked. "Before or after Koura left?"

Vikram's brows drew together as though he was having trouble recalling. "After. Definitely after."

"So, he hasn't seen this?"

Yasen took a step closer, placing one foot on the dais and approaching the baby. He waited to see if Vikram would stop him, but he allowed Yasen to move closer. He peered into the clear seed, attempting to parse out the various parts of the child growing within, searching for further evidence of the rot.

A moment later, Row came up behind him.

"What's going on?" he asked in a low voice.

"Look around you," Yasen said. "Do you notice it?"

Row followed the line where Yasen was pointing before he paused, and then his eyes widened the barest fraction.

"What..." he said before he trailed off, and a look of dread passed between them.

Vikram was watching them both now, and then Yasen noticed something very strange. Vikram's emerald green eyes were darker than usual. At first, Yasen had played it off as a trick of the light, but there was no mistaking it now.

What was happening?

"Vik," Yasen asked. "Have you seen any more demons in Dharati?"

"No," he replied almost immediately. "We got rid of them all. Don't you remember? The darkness is gone."

But it wasn't. Yasen didn't have magic and didn't know much about it, but he'd talked enough with Zarya to know it *wasn't* gone. They had simply beaten it back. Her magic, Vikas's magic, were proof of that.

"Have you noticed those?" Yasen asked, pointing to one of the black spots on the roof. Vikram *should* be able to see it clearly, but he squinted and then scratched his nose.

"Oh yes. I've been wondering about those."

"How long have they been there?" Row asked.

Vikram shook his head. "Not long. A few weeks?" He rubbed his chest, and the pit in Yasen's stomach grew.

"Let's check her roots," Row said. "I... think we should go below."

Yasen nodded as he stared up again. When the blight had broken through decades ago, it hadn't touched the queen. What did this mean?

"We're going to look around," Yasen said, addressing Vikram. "Okay?"

"Of course. You'll join me for dinner after you get some rest?"

"Sure," Yasen said, and then they veritably stumbled out of the Jai Tree and into the courtyard. Again, Yasen scanned overhead, searching for signs of the rot.

"Do you see anything?" Row asked before Yasen pointed.

There it was again—the faintest black outline around the shimmering flower petals.

"What does it mean?" Yasen asked. "We're sure this didn't happen last time?"

Row shook his head. "I'd stake my life on it," he answered.

"Let's go down."

A row of soldiers approached, clearly intent on arresting Row as promised.

"The steward pardoned him," Yasen said quickly. They really didn't have time for this nonsense.

The soldier in front opened his mouth, but Yasen waved him off. "Go and ask him yourself. Until then, we have more important things to worry about."

Then they brushed past, entered the palace, and approached one of the staircases leading to Amrita's roots. Yasen held his breath as they circled down the tight spiral to be greeted by a terrifying sight.

The blight had found its way back into Dharati.

Blackened roots spread before them, everything covered in the rot that had plagued Daragaab for years.

Yasen exhaled a shocked breath as his heart beat against his ribs.

The darkness.

It had returned.

TWENTY-SIX

It took two more days for Kishore to summon Zarya and Rabin for the rebinding of their Bandhan. He'd asked them to wear something to give him free access to their backs, chests, and shoulders, so they'd opted for robes layered over their undergarments.

"Ready?" Zarya asked as she tied up her hair to get it out of the way.

"The sooner we get this done, the sooner we can get out of here," Rabin answered. She watched him pull his robe over his shoulders and tie it loosely at his waist.

"Rabin…"

He furrowed his brows, obviously predicting what she'd say next.

They'd had this argument several times already.

Zarya wanted to return to Ishaan but was desperate to find the tower from her dream. The longer their search went on, the more skeptical Rabin became. She couldn't blame him, but *something* told her it was real.

A knock came at the door, and Urvi slipped inside with fresh towels for the bathroom.

"Describe it one more time," Rabin said, definitely humoring her at this point. She did it, anyway, crossing the room to retrieve the notebook where she'd started recording everything. Her mind had become a muddled wash with all her strange visions and dreams.

Images of her mother contrasted with flashes of a war-torn Rahajhan and the sparkling city of Taaranas. It was becoming harder and harder to separate them, and she'd taken to writing everything down.

She read out her list while Rabin listened intently. She appreciated that he was still trying despite the fact he didn't quite believe this.

"Excuse me," came a soft voice after she'd recited her list from top to bottom. Urvi stood in the bathroom doorway, wringing her hands. "I think I might know the place you're describing."

Zarya nearly dropped her notepad. "You do?"

"I believe it's in the vanshaj wing of the castle."

Zarya clutched the notebook to her chest. They hadn't searched there yet.

"It is?"

"I believe so," she answered. "It reminds me of a spot I've passed a few times. It isn't a place anyone goes to often."

Zarya's heart began thumping harder at those words.

"Do you think it would be okay to take us there?"

Urvi shook her head. "No, I couldn't. It's haunted."

When Zarya was about to press, she added, "But I can tell you where it is."

"Yes," she breathed. "Please."

"Zarya," came Rabin's stern voice. "I don't know about this."

"Please, let's just look. I promise to drop it if we don't find her there."

Rabin's jaw firmed before he dipped his chin. "Fine."

"What do you mean, it's haunted?" Zarya asked a moment later, curious about the second half of Urvi's comment.

She shook her head. "Sometimes, noises come from the corridor. Wailing. Crying. It sounds like ghosts. It's why so few are willing to pass anywhere near there."

"But you do?"

"I have no choice when my duties take me that way, but I avoid it as much as possible." Urvi visibly shivered.

Ghosts. Crying and wailing.

Or maybe just a woman in pain?

"Okay, please tell me where to find it?"

Urvi drew a picture with arrows, pointing to the spot, and Zarya studied it.

"Let's go right now," she said to Rabin.

"We're supposed to meet the king."

"Right." She turned to Urvi. "Would you let His Majesty know that we got held up for a few minutes, but we're on our way?"

"Of course," Urvi said. "But... be careful."

"Thank you," Zarya answered. "Please don't tell him where we are."

Urvi opened her mouth and then closed it. "I'm not sure I can lie to His Majesty." Her gaze slid to Rabin and back to Zarya.

"It's okay," Zarya said. "This is a safe space. You can be honest with us. We would never do anything to get you in trouble."

"His Majesty has a way of finding out the truth. All the servants agree. Any time they've tried to lie about something, he *knows*."

Zarya huffed out a breath. She wasn't all that surprised to hear it.

"Okay, just do your best, and we'll be as quick as possible."

"We could do it after," Rabin said, and she shook her head.

"I can't. I need to see now."

"Okay," he replied, probably knowing that would be her answer. "Then let's go."

They headed for the vanshaj wing, using Urvi's drawing as a guide through the twisting, narrow corridors. Her map wasn't quite to scale, and the wing was much larger than Zarya had initially imagined.

She kept getting lost and having to double back while Rabin quietly followed her.

She stopped in the middle of a hall and turned around as he approached her. "I'm worried about Urvi," she said. "What if he catches her in a lie? You saw how scared she was."

"We should go," he said, a warm hand settling on her lower back.

"I want to keep looking for a little longer. Would you go and check on her?"

His mouth firmed into a hard line.

"I'll be fine," she promised. "Please? It would make me feel better."

"I'd prefer not to leave you."

She laid a hand on his bicep and squeezed. "I'll look for exactly ten more minutes, and if I don't find anything else, I'll come back, okay? I don't want her getting in trouble because of us."

His gaze narrowed before he shook his head. "Ten minutes. You swear?"

She held up a hand in a promise. "I swear."

He looked around the hall, peering left and right. "Okay," he said. "I'll see you soon."

He leaned down to peck her on the cheek, then turned to walk away. Zarya watched until he rounded a corner and then resumed her search.

.   .   .

He didn't like it, but Rabin headed towards Abishek's library. He trusted Zarya would keep her word, but this mystery was consuming her, and he worried that she'd do something reckless.

But they couldn't abandon Urvi to the king for the sake of their lies.

He strode through the halls, passing tall arched windows opening to the sky. The blizzard continued, dusting the world with ice and driving snow. He was more than ready to leave. It was strange how quickly Ishaan had started feeling like home when for so long he'd felt sure his place was in Andhera. Maybe it was Zarya. Or maybe it was the resistance and fighting for something he'd always believed in. Likely a little of both.

He turned into the hall leading towards Abishek's study and strode down its length. The sentries bowed as he entered. Inside, he found Abishek and Kishore conferring in low voices at the worktable. At his entrance, they both looked up.

"Where's Zarya?" Abishek asked.

"She's on her way," he answered. Rabin scanned the room for Urvi. "Someone should have told you."

Abishek nodded. "Yes. I was informed."

His gaze slid to the corner, where Urvi sat crouched against the wall with her arms wrapped around her legs and tears staining her cheeks. She looked at Rabin with a worried expression in her glassy gaze.

Rabin turned to the king with his senses firing in warning. "What's going on?"

The king faced him and approached on slow steps, his gaze raking Rabin from head to toe.

"What is she looking for, Rabindranath?" Abishek asked, his voice dropping to a menacing whisper. "What does she seek in the vanshaj wing? *What* has she been looking for the last few days?"

Rabin shook his head, trying to think of a lie.

Abishek watched him with a calm expression, and it was

then Rabin knew Zarya hadn't been dreaming at all. Asha *was* in the castle, and if Abishek didn't already know Zarya had learned his secret, he was about to find out.

"Nothing," Rabin said. "She hasn't been looking for anything. She only went to speak with some vanshaj interested in hearing more about the Rising Phoenix."

Abishek chuckled with a dry, cold sound. "The resistance. Yes, my noble daughter and her *precious* vanshaj."

Rabin didn't care for the mocking tone in his words nor what he was implying about Zarya, but he bit his tongue because something was very, very wrong. "Why are you acting so strangely? She'll be here in a moment, and we can finish this thing and be on our way."

The king's expression turned hard. "Yes, you're both so eager to escape me, aren't you?"

Rabin shook his head. "That's not..."

"I took you in, rescued you from death, nursed you back to health, and gave you everything."

Rabin shook his head again. "I don't..."

The king took another step towards him. "And then you defied me. Not only bonding to but *marrying* my daughter after I expressly forbade it. You've ruined everything."

Cold fire entered the king's eyes as Rabin took a step back. He'd arrived without weapons or armor—just as he'd been asked.

"It wasn't your decision to make," Rabin said. "She's a grown woman, and I love her."

"Did you think I'd approve of my own flesh and blood mating with a *rakshasa*?"

Rabin's blood turned sluggish at the venom in the king's words.

"It was *her* decision," he finally answered, hating the uncertainty in his voice.

Abishek shook his head with a dark laugh. "Rabindranath, I

have only one heir, and I would rather die than see anyone but an Aazheri on my throne."

Those words hurt. The king had always been protective of Aazheri magic, but he'd claimed so many times that he loved Rabin like a son.

"Oh," the king said, perhaps reading his expression. "You're wondering why you aren't an exception? You thought you were *family*?"

Rabin took a step back. "Aren't I?"

Abishek clasped his hands behind his back. "I can see why you think so," he said. "But I needed to earn your loyalty, didn't I?"

Rabin backed up another step. "I don't understand."

"No, I don't suppose you would. I did my job well."

"What... job?"

Abishek said nothing as the door to the study opened, and a flood of soldiers filed into the room. The world around him slowed as Rabin took in his surroundings. He studied the guards. The men and women he'd trained with and fought alongside over the years. They stood in a line looking straight through him.

A moment later, Ekaja entered, her long legs carrying her with purpose.

He stared at her. At the blank expression on her face. It took her a moment to meet his eyes. When she finally did, all he saw was darkness. All he saw was the cold certainty of her duty.

"She's somewhere in the vanshaj wing," Abishek told Ekaja. "*Find* her."

"What's going on?" Rabin snarled. "If you touch her..."

Abishek chuckled as he shook his head. "He warned you, didn't he? Row didn't have the exact flavor of it right, but he did have the meat of it. And you all dismissed him."

Rabin's blood ran cold, and his limbs began to tremble as the reality of his situation slowly sunk in.

"What are you planning?" Rabin demanded.

Abishek ignored the question and gestured to Ekaja, who rattled off a set of orders to her guards to search the castle for Zarya.

"*Kaj*," Rabin said. "How could you do this to me?"

He noticed her shoulders stiffen as she slowly turned to face him.

"He is my king. He gave me my life, too." A small breath blew past her lips. "Unlike you, I do as he orders."

Her voice was flat and devoid of emotion.

"Ekaja," he whispered as his heart cracked with a betrayal he'd never expected.

The soldiers he'd trusted—ones he called friends—circled closer as a noose tightened around him. He couldn't seem to move. He was paralyzed, stuck in the churning darkness of his mistakes.

He'd trained his entire life and never frozen in the face of a battle. He knew he should be doing something, but his brain wouldn't catch up with his limbs.

The guards closed in, and all he could hear was white noise. His gaze jumped from Abishek to Ekaja and back again. He'd trusted them. He'd put his faith in them. He'd brought Zarya here, sure that she would be safe.

What was happening? Why couldn't he say or do anything?

"Tie him up," he heard Abishek say. "As soon as we find the girl, we can begin."

TWENTY-SEVEN

Zarya continued wandering through the vanshaj wing, consulting Urvi's map. It had been almost ten minutes, and it was nearly time to return to Rabin. She'd just explore a little further and turn back.

She rounded another corner, and her breath caught. Her vision tilted, and her blood chilled as she stared down the length of a hall. Lightheaded, she clutched the wall for balance at the disorienting sensation of déjà vu.

This was it. She was sure of it. Her gaze traveled over the pale stones and the tapestries hanging on the wall—threadbare and faded, worn by time and neglect.

She took a tentative step as if knowing she was crossing a threshold into a place from which she could never return. Whatever lay at the end of this hall might change everything. The hairs on the back of her neck rose, warning her to be cautious, but she couldn't stop. She had to see what lay beyond.

With one hand still pressed to the wall, she slowly made her way down the abandoned corridor. One foot in front of the other. Her hand brushed a tapestry, churning up a cloud of dust as the delicate, rotted threads crumbled under her touch.

She rubbed the dry fibers between her fingers.

They felt like an omen, a sign that everything was about to fall apart.

She stared down the hall again. With every step, it felt like the light was growing darker. Her knees were weak and her throat dry, and she swallowed hard as she limped along the corridor.

At the end stood a thin wooden door with a rusted handle. She reached for it slowly, both eager and dreading what she might find on the other side. Her emotions wobbled between fear and anticipation when it clicked softly under her touch.

She flattened a hand to the surface and pushed, revealing a stone staircase spiraling up into yet another tower. She'd done this dozens of times over the past few days, ending in only disappointment.

But as she placed her foot on the bottom step, something told her this time would be different.

She looked back. It had now been longer than the promised ten minutes, and she expected Rabin to appear around the corner at any moment. She should turn back, but curiosity was eating her alive.

She closed her eyes and conjured the dream of her mother, reliving the fear and the terror. The loneliness of that place. It couldn't be real. She looked up the stairs.

But what if it was?

Zarya took another step, breaking through the last of her hesitations. She spiraled up, winding along the narrow column as the air grew crisp and her breath condensed in soft puffs.

Finally, she reached a landing and another door, this one made of heavy iron, banded with more iron, and secured with heavy bolts.

Her heart climbed into her throat.

She crossed the landing slowly, the floor cold under her slippered feet. She tried the handle, not surprised when it offered no give. Swallowing her nerves, she filtered out a thread of air magic into the lock, prodding the mechanism until it clicked with an echo that seemed to ricochet throughout the entire castle.

Then she reached for the handle and turned.

The door swung open on oiled hinges, suggesting they were the only thing cared for in this neglected tower. That overwhelming sense of déjà vu hit her again as it revealed a round room with windows overlooking a snowy landscape.

And in the corner...

A woman.

Zarya blinked as her heart beat with such force that her vision swam. She clung to the door for support, sure her knees were about to melt out from under her.

She inhaled several deep breaths through her nose, willing her pulse to settle. Bile crept up the back of her throat, and her limbs trembled.

Finally, she managed to take a step and then another before she crossed the room and fell to her knees. The woman huddled against the wall, hugging her legs to her chest. She was whispering something over and over that Zarya couldn't make out.

She wore only a threadbare shift and was so thin that bones jutted from her joints at alarming angles. A tray sat beside her with a bowl of congealing rice swarming with a cloud of fruit flies.

The woman didn't move except for the barest flutter of her rattling breath and her lips chanting something in a ragged whisper.

Zarya lifted a hand to reach her and then stopped.

She didn't want to frighten Asha. Did she know Zarya was here?

"Hello?" she whispered softly. "Are you okay?"

As soon as the question left her mouth, Zarya cursed. Obviously, she wasn't okay. Obviously, she'd been locked in here and forgotten, left to starve in the cold.

Zarya swallowed down the acid in her throat as she crawled around the woman to get a better look at her face.

She'd already known what she would find. The dreams had already told her.

But there was no mistaking this was the same woman she'd seen in the drawing in Row's study. She really did look just like Zarya, down to that line between her eyebrows that always appeared when she was worried.

Zarya exhaled a choked breath. She'd hoped she'd just been dreaming. She'd hoped this wasn't real. But what did any of this mean?

"Mother," Zarya whispered, and the word seemed to hang in the air, suspended between them like something plucked from the threads of fate. "What has he done to you?"

Because she knew this was him. *Abishek.* Row's warnings came rushing back. All this time, he'd been right. Anyone who could do something like this was evil. What could her mother possibly have done to warrant such naked cruelty?

"Mother?" she asked, suddenly feeling like a small child as tears pressed into her throat. She'd spent every single day of her life wishing for a mother. For a family to call her own. Her mother was dead. She'd lived her entire life shaped by that truth, but now here she was, returned from the grave.

But only barely.

How was she even alive at all?

Asha stopped whispering and looked up at Zarya, distant recognition reflecting in the depths of her eyes.

"Mother," Zarya said. "It's me, Zarya. I don't know what's happened or why you're here, but I will get you out."

She wasn't sure why or how she believed that, but at that moment, it suddenly seemed more important than anything.

Asha blinked again, her brow furrowing. Zarya stared at

her. Her eyes were brown with flecks of green, just like Zarya's. There was something so infinitely sad buried in their depths that she felt her heart crack and leak between her ribs. She wanted to hug her. Wrap her in her arms and protect her until the end of her days.

"Row," Asha whispered. "Row."

That's when Zarya realized that's what she'd been repeating.

Row.

Gods, her heart hurt so much it felt like it would burst. Had Asha been trapped here for decades, missing him? She wanted to tell her that Row still loved her. That he searched every corner of Rahajhan trying to find her, refusing to believe she was gone.

How would Row react when he learned the truth?

"Mother," she whispered, her voice cracking. It was the only thing she could manage. "Mother."

She was here. She was alive. How would they get her out? Abishek had clearly locked her up here for twenty years for a reason. But *why*?

That's when a noise drew Zarya's attention. Someone was coming up the stairs. At first, she thought it must be Rabin returning to find her, but the echo of dozens of footsteps floated up the tower as a shiver crept down her spine.

Slowly, she stood, gathering her magic, her anchors spinning in her heart. She stepped in front of her mother, shielding her. She would never let anyone hurt this woman again. She didn't care what she'd done. She didn't care what had happened. She would do everything in her power to bring her home.

Dark shadows swirled at her fingertips, prepared to strike as the footsteps drew nearer and nearer.

Zarya inhaled a sharp breath as Abishek, Kishore, and about two dozen of his royal guards appeared on the landing.

"Zarya," Abishek said. "What are you doing here?" He stepped into the room while the others hung back. She held onto her magic, assessing the situation. She was devoid of weapons, and this was her only defense.

"Where's Rabin?" she asked.

"He's waiting for you in my study," Abishek said. "Why don't you come with me, and we can go and see him?"

His voice was light, but she was sure she caught a flash of mania in his eyes. Something was up beyond the secret she'd just uncovered in this room.

"Why do you have her locked up in here?" Zarya asked, her voice barely a whisper. "Why have you treated her this way?"

Abishek sighed. "I didn't want you to learn the truth like this."

She frowned as her fingers clawed in, clinging to her magic.

"What *truth*?"

Abishek took another step, and Zarya looked down at Asha lying by her feet. She stared at Abishek with horror in her eyes, her face turning even paler.

"Oh, Zarya," he said. "I knew."

He took another step as Zarya's chest grew tight. She shook her head.

"I don't understand," she whispered.

He took another step until he was nearly upon her. She couldn't move or think.

Her breath stuck in her chest like wet sand.

"Knew what?"

"That you existed from the very beginning."

And then, he lifted a hand.

Zarya flung out her magic, but it was already too late.

Smoke filled her eyes and lungs and mouth, and then everything went black.

TWENTY-EIGHT

Yasen and Row explored the twisting vines and corridors of Amrita's roots, assessing how deep the darkness had penetrated. They'd been down here for hours, searching the vast organic network, coming up on more bad news at every turn.

"We're sure this didn't happen last time?" Yasen asked as they crossed into a cavern where black rot crept up from the floor, stretching towards the ceiling. He spun around and shook his head. He couldn't shake the feeling that a thousand invisible eyes were following them.

"I'm sure," Row said. "Rani Vasvi's roots were examined regularly. We would have noticed this."

"Yeah," Yasen said. "We did, too." They crossed down another path to find more rot spreading in every direction. "Unless it was too insignificant to notice."

"I suppose that's possible," Row said. "But the blight existed for decades. This started weeks ago. Even if we'd seen this last time, the rate of growth is alarming. Why is it moving so quickly?"

Yasen blew out a heavy breath. "Because something even worse is happening?"

Row exhaled a wry huff. "It does seem that way, doesn't it?"

"Do you think the swamp returned to the surface?" Yasen asked.

They rounded a corner, and Yasen nearly wept to find a patch of clear roots, pristine and nearly white, glowing with the pearlescent sheen.

He crossed the cavern, laying his hand on the line where the rot gave way to healthy roots. He'd never had rakshasa magic, but he still had the same connection to the earth's plants and flowers. Though most people didn't feel it, they gave off an energy specific to their strength and vitality.

Yasen felt it. The frequency telling him that Amrita was suffering. Maybe even dying.

"What will happen to the baby?" Yasen asked.

Row shook his head, pressing his mouth in a thin line. "We might need to call for Koura. But first, I think we should check the swamps."

Yasen studied the ceiling, twisting with a network of roots and vines. "Do you think Vik knows about this?"

Their gazes met, neither wanting to voice their thoughts out loud.

It seemed impossible that Vikram could have missed this, but he wasn't himself.

"Only one way to find out," Row answered, his expression dark with worry.

When they entered the throne room, they discovered Vikram had returned to his apartments to lie down since he felt ill. He'd left behind a circle of armed guards, who stood watch over Amrita and her baby. They let Row and Yasen know that Vikram had invited them for supper later and that Row had indeed been pardoned from his transgression in the library.

Row pressed his hand together in thanks at that news, but

Yasen was fairly certain he'd never intended to cooperate with his arrest.

Once they accepted Vik's invitation, they prepared to visit the shoreline. Row held out his hand while Yasen wrinkled his nose. "Not this again."

"You can stay here and do nothing if you prefer," Row said rather pointedly.

He wasn't a dick. In fact, he was a pretty decent guy, especially once you got to know him, but he also didn't suffer fools.

"Fine," Yasen said. He gripped Row's hand, and a second later, it felt like someone was ripping out his spleen while also squeezing his organs to the point of rupture. Though Row claimed it took only seconds, it felt infinitely longer before they found themselves standing on the beach where Zarya had once lived.

Yasen inhaled a sharp breath at the sight, strangely moved to be standing here.

He'd heard Zarya talk about this place so many times but seeing it in person felt like glimpsing a piece of her soul. It felt especially strange to be here without her.

He stared out at the sea he knew she loved so much and the house where she'd felt like she was living in a cage. It was pleasant here. Pretty and calm. The breeze was fresh, and the greenery was lush, but it was lonely. He could understand why she'd hated it so much.

She wanted to be around people. She wanted to feel life. She wanted to feel *everything*.

"So, this is where you kept her, hey?" Yasen drawled.

"Don't start with me," Row grumbled as he turned and stalked towards the cottage.

"Weren't you supposed to burn it down?" Yasen continued, but Row ignored the question as he passed the house and crossed into the trees.

"Rude," Yasen said.

He studied the garden, the pergola Zarya had described, and the stretch of beach where she'd fallen asleep that last night before escaping to freedom. He felt weirdly proud of her at that moment. After living in this sheltered spot her entire life, setting out alone must have been terrifying.

Yasen turned to follow Row, passing a line of healthy trees and crossing into the ruined forest where the swamp had once existed. Immediately, Yasen could sense how different it felt from before. With his rakshasa connection to the earth, he'd always recognized the sinister energy that had permeated the dying plants and flowers.

But now he felt nothing. The magic was gone, and the only thing left was the dead forest that had yet to regrow. Perhaps Rabin would return someday to work his power over this land, but for now, it lay dormant.

Row stood at the swamp's edge, peering into the water as Yasen stopped beside him.

"There's nothing here," Yasen said as Row nodded.

"You're right. The blight hasn't returned. This is just dead."

"So, what does this mean?"

"I'm truly not sure."

Yasen exhaled a long breath as he scanned their surroundings. Row then returned to the cottage, and Yasen followed again. They entered the small house, and Row immediately went for a cupboard, producing a bottle of dark liquor and a couple of glasses.

"Want one?" he asked as he poured himself a healthy measure.

"Sure," Yasen answered. He accepted the glass before sitting at the table to sip quietly while Row stared out the window. Yasen sensed that he needed a moment.

"You okay?" he said after a minute, his question hesitant.

Row sighed and braced his hands on the counter before he dropped his head.

"Being here stirs up a lot of things," he said and once again fell silent.

"You want to talk about it?"

Row looked up and turned around. He picked up his glass and took a long drink.

"I feel so much guilt for how I raised her," he said. "I shouldn't have locked her away. I should have hunted Abishek down and shoved a sword through his heart to protect her. I thought about doing it so many times, but I was too afraid."

Yasen arched a brow at the coldness in Row's voice.

"Then he probably would have killed you, and Zarya would have had no one. According to Rabin, none of this was really his fault, anyway."

Row stared straight ahead and took another sip.

"Then whose fault is it?" he asked. "Someone was lying. Or mistaken. Someone told me to take that little girl and hide her away so she would be safe. But what was I really protecting her from? Was I wrong about everything?" He inhaled a sharp breath. "Did Asha lie to me? Or was she deceived, too? Have I spent the last two decades pining for a woman who used me for some reason I might never understand?"

Yasen watched Row as he blinked heavily, his chest expanding with deep breaths. He had no idea how to answer those questions. Row had loved Asha. *Still* loved, if this reaction was anything to go by, and Yasen couldn't begin to understand the depth of Row's sorrow.

"She doesn't blame you," Yasen said. "Zarya, I mean. She understands why you had to do it."

Row shook his head and downed the rest of his drink. "I don't deserve her forgiveness. And that still doesn't make it right."

"Maybe," Yasen said. "But we do our best with the hand we're dealt. You wanted to protect her, and you did. She grew up to be a strong, capable woman, and you were part of that. She loves you, Row. I know she does."

Row exhaled a wry laugh, finally meeting Yasen's gaze. "Thank you for that. I had no idea you could be so insightful, Varghese. I actually feel a bit better."

Yasen winked and took a sip of his drink. "Any time. Just don't tell anyone about this, okay? I have a reputation to maintain."

That earned him a warm smile. "Your secret is safe with me."

A short while later, they returned to Dharati, where protestors continued chanting at the palace gates. Yasen wanted to tell everyone that the resistance was doing everything it could to help the vanshaj, but he knew they still had a long way to go.

With a few hours until dinner, Yasen couldn't get comfortable in his opulent guestroom. It was unsettling to be treated like a visitor, considering he'd lived here his entire life.

He decided to visit his old room in the army barracks. Though he hadn't planned on a reunion, he ran into a few familiar faces who were all happy to see him. He ended up having a few drinks before he practically had to peel himself away for dinner.

When he finally returned to the palace, he found Row in the dining room adjacent to Vikram's suite. Yasen ground to a stop at the sight of another glowering face.

Gopal Ravana paused mid-sip to eye Yasen up and down.

"Nice of you to join us," he said with a curl of his lip. This had been one of Yasen's chief reasons to escape Dharati, and maybe he'd convinced himself he wouldn't have to face this monster again. Gopal's sneering face made him want to curl into a ball and hide in the corner.

Even with his pulse racing, he shrugged, adopting the

casual air of someone who didn't care too much. It was his armor. His defense. "I was having a drink in the barracks. I can't help it if I'm a beloved figure around these parts."

Gopal glared as Yasen dropped into a chair before a servant hurried forward to fill his wine glass. He exchanged a look with Row, who offered him a nod that suggested he fully agreed with Yasen's thoughts on Gopal Ravana.

"Where's Vik?" Yasen asked Row.

"I'm not sure."

Yasen wasn't in the mood for conversation with Gopal staring him down, so they all sat in awkward silence while Row's gaze jumped between them. Once or twice, he opened his mouth as if planning to start a conversation but then snapped it shut when he clearly thought better of it.

"So, where have you been?" Gopal asked Yasen.

He arched a brow. "Why do you care?"

"I don't. But I do want to know what you're both doing here."

"We're here to speak with the steward."

"About the vanshaj," Gopal said. "I know your agenda, and this will not stand in Daragaab."

Yasen's pulse kicked up, anger swirling in his chest. He leaned forward. "That's *really* none of your fucking business," he hissed.

Gopal's eyebrows hitched the barest fraction. Yasen had never stood up to him before, and he wanted to enjoy it, except for the sick feeling in his stomach that made him want to throw up.

"How dare—" Gopal seethed, his green eyes burning.

Yasen was saved from a tirade when the door finally opened to reveal Vikram.

"I'm so sorry to keep you waiting," he said. "I got held up."

The tension in the room eased a fraction while Yasen studied his friend and the alarming changes he witnessed earlier. The limp hair and the dull eyes. The way his clothes were still slightly rumpled.

"It's no problem," Row said, probably thrilled about the interruption.

Vikram took his seat and gestured for the food to arrive. A flurry of servants entered with silver dishes laden with delicacies, but Yasen had no appetite. Gopal's presence always left a bitter taste in his mouth.

While they were eating, Row attempted to broach the topic of what they'd seen earlier.

"You're aware of what's been happening to Amrita?" Row asked carefully, including Gopal in the conversation while he watched with a sullen expression.

Vikram blew out a breath. "I am."

"And what have you done about it?"

He shook his head with a blank look. "What should I do about it? Nothing can stop this now."

"You should have called for me. Or one of the other Chiranjivi. We could have tried to help. Have you spoken with Tarin?"

Vikram waved him off at the mention of Amrita's former steward. "No. There's nothing to be done. She is dying."

He said the words so matter-of-factly that Yasen choked on his wine. He met Row's worried look while Vikram continued eating like he hadn't just dropped a bombshell.

"She'll hold out long enough for the baby to be born."

Vikram focused on his dinner, still oblivious to their shock.

"Vik, what's going on? What aren't you telling us?" Yasen asked.

"What if this hurts the baby?" Row asked as Vikram's brow furrowed.

"The baby isn't your concern," Gopal said coldly. "When she is born, she will be placed under my care and grow up within my household so that I may protect her."

Yasen and Row stared at him as Gopal simply picked up his

drink and gulped it down in one long swallow. Gopal would keep the child under his thumb as he had with Amrita, ensuring his control over Daragaab. This was why he'd forced Vik to become her steward.

Yasen's stomach churned with his hatred for this man.

After a moment, he directed his gaze to Vikram, wondering about his reaction to his father's decision. He couldn't interpret what he read in the dull reflection of his eyes. He'd changed so much.

Vikram blinked, and then his eyes spread wide. He started coughing violently, and his utensils clattered to the table.

Yasen was up immediately, striding over before dropping to a knee.

"Vik!" He thumped Vikram on the back. Vikram slid off his chair, clutching his stomach.

"The medic," Gopal said. He pointed to a servant in the corner. "Get the medic!"

Vikram's attendants had already begun scrambling, passing messages to the guards at the door. It felt like a coordinated dance. Like something that had happened before.

A moment later, a palace healer entered the room carrying a bag, his long robes swishing around his ankles. He dropped down next to Vikram and rolled him onto his back.

Yasen's blood turned to ice as he looked into Vikram's eyes. They'd turned completely black, and he was shaking and gasping for breath. The healer grasped Vikram's collar and tore open the buttons.

Black lines ran all over Vikram's body like tree branches. Bile climbed up Yasen's throat as he crawled closer, noticing they weren't vines but rather his veins filled with some kind of black substance creeping over his chest and stomach and neck.

"What is this?" Yasen whispered. "What's happening to him?"

"We aren't sure," the healer said. "It started a few weeks ago."

The healer reached into a bag as Vikram convulsed, his back arching as he made a low keening sound. His limbs shook as he writhed on the floor.

Yasen leaned over and framed his face with his hands. "Vik!" he called. "Can you hear me?"

"He won't answer," the healer said. "This is the only thing that helps."

Then he jabbed Vikram's pectoral with a long needle and depressed the plunger. Yasen watched the clear liquid drain into his friend before Vikram finally went limp. His body relaxed, and the blackness in his veins slowly faded but failed to disappear completely.

He looked over at Row, who stood with his hands braced on his knees, shock and surprise in his face.

Whatever was going on, this was so much worse than any of them had feared.

TWENTY-NINE

Rabin opened his eyes to the blur of a ceiling above him. He blinked, attempting to clear the pounding in his head. When he tried to sit up, he discovered he was held in place, his wrists and ankles strapped to a surface where he was lying.

He tugged on his bindings to no avail as the previous events came flooding back.

Abishek. Ekaja. They'd betrayed him. Done something to him.

But what and why?

He lifted his head——to discover he was naked except for his underwear. What the fuck was happening?

He looked to his right and began thrashing harder against his restraints. Zarya lay on another table, similarly trussed, wearing only a bra and panties, her eyes closed and her dark hair spilling over the edge.

"Zarya," he called, but she didn't move. Her chest rose and fell in a slow rhythmic pattern, suggesting she was asleep or passed out. He thrashed again, but the cuffs offered no give. He couldn't feel his magic, either—Abishek had blocked it.

Forcing himself to calm down, he took stock of his surroundings. He was in Abishek's wing of the castle. He recognized this room as the formal entertaining salon he used only occasionally for private meetings.

It was decorated luxuriously with velvet furniture in maroon and hunter green. The rugs were thick brown fur, and a large fireplace crackled at each end. Vaulted windows overlooked the snow, hung with heavy dark drapes that were currently drawn closed.

A chandelier dangled in his vision, rendered from deer antlers hunted in these very mountains. He inhaled deeply, trying to calm his breath and think.

Abishek had been lying to him. *What* had he been lying about? What was Rabin doing here, and why had Ekaja betrayed him?

The king's treachery stung but didn't cut to the bone. Maybe deep down, he'd always understood he was living on borrowed time with the ruthless king of Andhera. Perhaps he'd convinced himself of what he'd wanted to see and, in doing so, had disregarded the warnings that had been there all along.

But *Ekaja*.

He truly thought she had been his friend. He'd trusted her wholly. They'd been drunk together. Trained together. Complained about the king to one another. And she'd walked into the study and looked at him without emotion. Like she hadn't cared at all. Like he meant nothing.

And now, he lay on this table, having no idea what would come next. And worse, Zarya lay next to him, knocked out and subjected to the gods only knew what. He was responsible for all of this. He had spent months convincing her it was safe. Months convincing her that her father only wanted to know her.

Gods, what a fucking fool he was. He'd been so desperate for approval. So desperate for a place to call home that he'd endangered the most important person in his life.

Zarya groaned, and her head swung to the side.

"Zarya," he said in a low voice. He had no idea where the king and the others had gone, but given their position and the crackling fires, he could only assume they would be returning soon.

She groaned again, the sound desperate and lonely.

"Mother," she whispered, her voice raw and broken. "Mother, I'll get you out."

Rabin swallowed the thick knot in his throat. Was she dreaming again, or had she found her? Was that why they were lying here now?

"Zarya," he called a bit louder, his voice cracking.

Finally, her head rocked towards him, and her eyes slowly peeled open. She blinked, clearing her vision as her gaze traveled over him, and tears gathered in her eyes.

"Rabin," she whispered. "What happened?"

"He lied to us. To me. I'm so sorry."

"I saw her," she said. "She's here. He's been hurting her."

A tear leaked from the corner of her eye and slipped to the table.

"You saw her?" He still couldn't believe it. All this time, the queen of Gi'ana had been right *here*?

"Why are we tied up?" she asked as she yanked on her restraints, her voice rising to panic. "What's going on?"

"Spitfire," he said in a low voice. "Try to stay calm."

She shook her head, squeezing her eyes and pinching her mouth together. "He's planning to take my magic and then kill us, isn't he? Row was right all along."

"I don't know," he answered. "But we can't panic. We will figure this out."

She exhaled a shuddering sigh and stared up at the ceiling, her head arching back as she willed her tears down.

Then she looked at him. "What happened? How did he get you?"

Rabin inhaled a deep breath and explained how he'd been overwhelmed.

When he was finished, her jaw was hard. "She betrayed you. I'll kill her. I'll kill them both."

"Zarya, can you feel your magic?" he asked.

She blinked as if it had just occurred to her and shook her head. "I can't. Did he take it away?"

They watched each other over the narrow space that felt like an ocean keeping them apart.

"He said Row was right," he confessed as his heart twisted in his chest.

She yanked again, making a sound of frustration before she gave up and stared up at the ceiling.

"Zarya," he said, after a minute of silence. "I'm sorry. This is all my fault." He turned to find her facing him. "I brought us here. I was so fucking sure everything would be fine."

"It's not your fault," she said. "Something tells me he planned this all along. When he found me with my mother, he said he knew who I was from the very start. He would have found me no matter what."

His brow furrowed at the despondency in her voice. He opened his mouth, about to say something else when the door to the room opened.

Zarya's head whipped over at the sound, her entire body tensing. A shiver traveled over her arms and legs, both from fear and the air chilling her exposed skin. First, Abishek appeared. He paused and stared at her, their eyes meeting. Following him were Kishore and then Ekaja.

That bitch. She couldn't believe she'd betrayed them. She'd pretended to be Rabin's friend, and now she was standing with Abishek like his obedient pet. Kishore had given her the creeps from the moment she'd met him. She wasn't at all surprised by his lies.

And Abishek... maybe a part of her had known they'd end up here all along. Maybe part of her had run towards him to get it over with. Without this confrontation, she would have lived her entire life with one eye peering over her shoulder, and that would never have been a life.

Maybe a part of her had always known it would be her or him.

Abishek stopped at their feet and looked down, waiting. She refused to give him the satisfaction of lifting her head. It was a pointless defiance, but it was literally the only thing she had.

Rabin's anger rumbled in his chest, the sound echoing through the room as Abishek regarded them both.

"You're probably wondering what's happening," the king said. He moved between them, and Zarya shivered as the fabric of his cloak brushed her hand. "I'll tell you the story, shall I? My dearest Zarya, I knew you existed from the beginning."

She blinked, trying not to react. She wouldn't give him this satisfaction, either.

"Your mother had a special gift of her own."

He paused, and she couldn't help but frown.

"Everyone believed that an oracle shared the prophecy of your birth, and she spent her life convincing everyone else of that, going so far as to leave you a message telling you the same, isn't that right? She couldn't risk anyone knowing the truth; even her precious Row didn't know the full story."

Zarya's hands and feet were turning numb despite the roaring fires. From the corner of her eye, she noted Kishore and Ekaja watching silently. Ekaja with a dispassionate expression, and Kishore wearing a smile of smug satisfaction.

"She was a powerful nali. An incredibly rare gift amongst Aazheri."

Nali. Zarya shook her head to indicate she didn't understand.

"A nali is a conduit between our world and the heavens. They can speak with the gods. She concocted the lie about the Oracle as nalis have a violent history in our world. They were often captured and forced to offer predictions for those who sought to control them.

"Though some nalis can see the future as it relates to those around them, some are limited to something specific. Asha only saw the future as it related to herself and her offspring. Or, more specifically, one offspring in particular—a daughter yet to be born."

Zarya's jaw tightened.

"I've never fully understood her reasons for revealing the information about your nightfire. I suspect it was to bolster her position. During the Khetara Wars, she lost favor after so many setbacks at Daragaab's hand." He gestured casually to Rabin. "I believe she did it to make herself appear more powerful and that she was here to deliver her people to salvation.

"But as the years waned, she gave birth to four children, all without the gift she had promised."

Abishek turned and walked around them, stopping on Zarya's other side.

"When I first heard the prophecy, I was intrigued. *Nightfire.*" He said the word like he was tasting it. "I had been seeking it out for so many years and hadn't heard that word beyond these walls in centuries. Then suddenly, a queen claimed she would bear a child who could wield it. That's when I took a very specific interest in the queen of Gi'ana.

"When the promised child failed to appear, I grew tired of waiting, so I traveled to Ishaan on the pretense of some diplomatic matter I've long since forgotten. It was obvious she was growing increasingly worried that you would never appear. Some called her a liar, claiming she had used the prophecy to bolster her image. Grumblings of dissension had started within the nobility, many of whom planned to withdraw their support and back her eldest daughter, who was already quietly maneuvering to take her mother's crown."

Zarya's mouth pressed together at that information. Dishani truly was the worst.

Abishek sighed. "And in me, she found a sympathetic ear." He stared at Zarya with a curious tip of his head.

She felt sick, on the verge of fainting. She wanted to cry and scream, though she was already sure she hadn't heard the worst of what was coming.

"We became lovers, though I knew she didn't entirely trust me. But we grew close enough that I could execute my plans. When she fell pregnant, I sensed it immediately. But she kept the news from me, and that's when I suspected treachery."

Zarya swallowed hard as his casual tone turned cold.

"She disappeared for several months, and when she resurfaced, there was no child. When I demanded answers, she denied everything, but I knew she was keeping things from me. So, I took her. I kept her locked up, and that, dear Zarya, was when she was forced to reveal everything."

He offered her a bland smile.

"I tortured her. She confessed it all. After her first children were born, the gods revealed that *I* was to be the father of the prophesized child, and when I showed up, I played right into her hands. She enjoyed sharing that she felt sick at the idea of fucking me, but she needed you desperately. So, in a way, we played each other. Only, I got the last word, didn't I?"

Abishek rolled his neck as he started walking around her table. She kept him in her view as she slowly rotated her head.

"Asha blocked your magic, and you were useless to me until you came of age. So I let you live peacefully with Row while I got to work on my other plans."

At that, his gaze fell to Rabin.

"Asha had visions about Zarya and... the man who would become her paramadhar. The very same man who was the reason for her loss of favor. Such a twist of irony. She saw him lying in a cell, abused at his father's hand. He needed help. He needed a way to escape. He needed a *reason* to live."

Zarya met Rabin's wide-eyed gaze, dread pooling in her stomach.

Abishek stared down at Rabin. "It was nothing to find you over the miles and offer you some encouragement. You didn't even notice me entering your thoughts, giving you a little nudge to free yourself from your prison and then guide you... north. Guide you to me, where I then nursed you back to health and you *everything* you wanted to hear."

He blew out a resigned sigh, almost as if he felt sorry for what he'd done.

"And then, I convinced you to get a tattoo that would mean something to you, yes, but would also be infused with a special type of magic to ensure you sought out your masatara in your dreams when the time was right."

He inhaled a deep breath. "Somehow, Dhawan found out about all of this and hunted you down so that he might win my approval again. I understand he tried to entrap Asha before you were even born. The fool. As if I didn't know already. As if I didn't already have a plan. At least it kept him busy. In the end, he got everything he deserved."

"No," Zarya said, the word rushing out as Abishek offered her a cold smile. She couldn't hold it in any longer, and a tear slipped from the corner of her eye. All those deaths in Dharati had been for nothing. Rani Vasvi might still be alive if Dhawan hadn't interfered.

And Rabin and Zarya—they had both been played from the very start.

"Row warned you. He told you to stay away from me, yet

you ran here, anyway." He laid a hand on Rabin's shoulder. "And I have you to thank for it."

"You want my magic?" she asked. "He was right?"

"In a manner of speaking," he answered. "I *do* need your magic, but not for myself. At least not right away."

She shook her head. "I don't understand."

His mouth turned up into a patient sort of smile. "Your visions, Zarya. They've puzzled you for months. The darkness. You wondered why it was following you."

Her blood turned to ice. "You said it wasn't," she whispered.

"Zarya. You're smarter than that."

She gave him a hard glare as he continued.

"Nightfire. It hadn't been seen in a thousand years. The last Aazheri to possess this gift were the Ashvins. What your mother and what no one understood is that when it returned, it would also signal *their* return to our world."

He paused, and Zarya shook her head. "What does that mean?"

"It means they live inside you, my *daughter*. They have waited patiently over a millennium to gather their strength and find the right... vessel. It means the seal behind where they were trapped by the kings and queens of Rahajhan a thousand years ago is weakening. It is time to break them out once and for all, free the darkness, and take back the power that we lost."

The king's face stretched into a slow, pleased smile.

"And you, my dear—my *child*—will help me achieve all my wildest dreams."

THIRTY

"What!" Zarya shouted. "No!" She fought uselessly against her bonds. "They're not *inside* me. You're insane!"

Abishek's smile turned remorseful. "Why do you think you keep experiencing their life? Dhawan wasn't wrong when he said the blight started with you. The seal has been slowly leaking for centuries, but it needs a little *push*."

A shiver climbed over her scalp, spreading over her skin. No one was *inside* her. She suddenly couldn't breathe. She thrashed against her restraints, desperate to hide. To curl into a ball and pretend none of this was real.

"And then what," Rabin asked, his voice a low, menacing growl. "What happens when you free them?"

Abishek clasped his hands. "Once Zarya breaks the seal, two things will happen. It will unleash the nairatta trapped with the twins, and they've all been left starving for so *very* long."

"And the second?" Rabin asked. Zarya listened, relieved he was staying calm because she couldn't seem to form a single coherent thought.

"The Ashvins will eventually regain their full strength but will still require a vessel to exist on this plane."

"Let me guess," Rabin said as Abishek smiled.

"Their power will become mine. I will take control of the nairatta, and finally, the Aazheri will rule over the continent as it was always meant to be."

"No!" Zarya screamed. "No, I won't help you. I will never help you. I'm not breaking anything! You'll have to kill me first!"

Abishek tutted. "Yes, I assumed that's what you'd say. I only let you remain in my home as guests for as long as I did because I had hoped you'd cooperate. We could have done this together —we'd be so much stronger—but I see that was never meant to be."

"Together?" she snarled. "*Never*."

"You're sure? I'll give you one more chance to change your mind. Break the seal, give up the Ashvins willingly, and I'll allow you to live. I might still claim you as my heir, though I expect you to marry an Aazheri—Amir, of course." Abishek flicked his fingers at Rabin. "Which means we must deal with him after I get what I want."

"No!" Zarya screamed, fighting and bucking against her bonds. "If you *touch* him, I will destroy you!" She couldn't move. She couldn't *breathe*. She screamed in frustration.

When she was done, she lay panting on the table, sweat pooling in her collarbones.

"Look at you," Abishek said. "So utterly useless."

"*Everything* was a lie," Rabin said, his voice deadly calm, storm clouds swirling in his eyes.

"It was," Abishek answered rather matter-of-factly. "Don't feel bad. I planned it very well, and I am rather good at this. Anyone would have fallen for it."

Rabin snarled while Abishek turned away and gestured for Kishore.

"Our first step is fixing your Bandhan," Abishek said.

"That part was true?" Zarya asked.

"It was, but not in the way you think. We can't break the existing one, so we'll apply a new one so I may use it to use *you*."

"So there was no issue with our bond?" Zarya demanded. "Where has Kishore really been?"

"Exactly where I said," the king replied. "But I couldn't let you leave until he'd gathered the necessary supplies and prepared the new ink. A bit of magic to block you from the mind plane and a bit of poison in Rabin's food to make him think he was dying—and you were both convinced it was true."

"You monster!" Zarya screamed, choking on a sob.

Abishek continued as if she hadn't spoken. "I admit, I never thought you'd do such a thing without my input, Rabindranath. You surprised me."

Rabin glared, a muscle in his jaw feathering.

The king's gaze swung to Zarya. "You still insist on remaining tethered to him?"

She narrowed her gaze. "Absolutely."

Abishek shrugged and sighed. "We could have ruled Rahajhan, but a rakshasa will sit as king consort to Andhera over my dead body."

"Fuck you," Zarya said, and Abishek raised a brow.

Then he gestured to Kishore, who appeared over Zarya. Her lip curled as he gave her a bland smile. She wanted to spit in his face. Twist his balls so hard his ancestors would feel it.

He laid a cold hand on her shoulder, making her skin crawl. She attempted to shake it off, but he only pressed down harder.

"Get your hands off my *wife*," Rabin snarled.

Zarya watched Abishek's eyes darken at the reminder of what they were to one another.

Kishore ignored him entirely, and another tear slipped from Zarya's eye. They were trapped. Their magic was blocked, and they were at the king's mercy.

The mystic walked away, and Zarya could only move her

head enough to see him approach a table a few paces away, where he began doing something with his back to them.

She looked at Rabin. Zarya wanted to sob. Her heart squeezed, and her ribs compressed. How could they have been so stupid?

Kishore then turned around and held up a needle, the sharp tip glinting in the light. In his other hand, he held a small stone vessel.

"Ekaja, if you'd be so kind," he said, gesturing to a nearby torch suspended in a set of brackets. She paused momentarily, her jaw clenching before she stalked over and pulled out a tendril of fire, using it to light the torch.

It flared to life, the flames burning orange and red before slowly transforming into inky black. Zarya stared at it, noting the brushes of purple and blue reflecting in its depths. Holding it with only his bare hands, the mystic walked over and held the bowl up to the fire as it began to glow hot.

When he appeared satisfied, he removed it from the fire and then stalked towards Zarya.

"A dragon," he mused, staring at the spot where the wings Thriti had drawn curved over her shoulder. "It's like you knew all along."

"What does that mean?" she demanded at his smug look.

He ignored her as he lifted the needle and brought it down over her heart. She jerked.

"What are you doing?"

Kishore sighed. "One of your errors was placing this in the wrong spot. Now we're fixing it."

Again, he lowered the needle. She writhed under him until she felt invisible bands cinch around her arms, legs, and throat, pinning her in place so tightly she could barely breathe. Abishek appeared over her.

"Hold still, and I'll let up on your windpipe, or you can stay like this while he works."

She met his gaze, tears pressing the back of her eyes. Her father. She'd spent her entire life wishing for a family, but they'd been a disappointment in every direction she turned. He gave her a hard look as her head swam. He would follow through on this. He couldn't kill her yet, but he could leave her in enough discomfort to make her suffer for hours.

She blinked, attempting to acknowledge his threat. He must have read it because the pressure on her throat eased a moment later. She sucked in a deep breath but still couldn't move a single muscle other than to blink and swallow.

"Proceed," Abishek said.

Kishore once again placed the needle over her heart, and she whimpered at the first prick. She wished she could at least see Rabin. What was he thinking on the other side of Kishore? They'd blocked her view of him on purpose.

Tears slipped down her face as Kishore worked methodically, covering her in a new marking that would do... what? Bind her to Rabin but in a different way? What did this have to do with freeing the Ashvins?

She shivered again, thinking about his words and his threat. The Ashvins were *inside* her? Suddenly, it felt like they were crawling under her skin, and she itched like a thousand bugs were slithering over her. She cried harder, wishing she was strong enough to keep her fear and emotions contained. How had she come from that quiet life by the sea to *this*?

But that had all been an illusion. Abishek had known where she'd been the entire time. Row had never been protecting her from anything despite what he'd believed. And her mother had been locked up here since she'd been born, unable to warn them while Abishek had left her to waste away. If Zarya got out of this alive, she would make this man suffer.

She allowed her mind to drift inwards as she attempted to block out the pain of Kishore's needle, wishing she were anywhere else.

With Rabin on a quiet beach, the water crashing on the shore. With Yasen in a seedy tavern, daring each other to take another shot while he drank her under the table. With Row sitting comfortably by the fire as he read one of his boring books while she read one of her smutty novels.

Gods, what she wouldn't give to go back.

She'd spent so long craving more but look where that had gotten her.

As pain wracked through her body, she clung to the ephemeral possibility of this *other* existence. She couldn't wait to get her hands on it.

The room was quiet while Kishore worked, the wind muffled by the dark curtains, with only the crackle of the fires filling the silence. Ekaja hovered on the edges, her hand on her sword, where Zarya could just make her out with the corner of her eye.

After what felt like hours, Kishore stood back, admiring his handiwork. Abishek appeared above her, a satisfied smile curling on his lips.

"It is complete?" he asked.

"Enough to serve your purpose," Kishore answered. "Thankfully, his is already prepared."

Abishek had encouraged Rabin to get the dragon inked onto his skin. He really had been planning this all along.

"Now what?" Abishek asked.

"Now we complete the Bandhan."

He placed the needle and bowl on the table, and the binding air around Zarya released. She breathed out a sigh of relief. Looking down, she gasped at the sight of the silver dragon now tattooed over her heart. She had a thousand questions she knew would go unanswered.

Finally, she willed herself to meet Rabin's gaze. He was already looking at her, fire and rage burning in the depths of his dark eyes. She had so many things to say, but they all went unspoken, searing the tip of her tongue.

"Zarya," he whispered, and she shook her head.

"I love you," she whispered back.

A moment later, her view was blocked again as Kishore moved between them. He then circled a cold hand around her wrist and squeezed.

She watched as bands of silvery light filtered out around them. After a few seconds, the silver began to twine with red and black, like blood and darkness, all three meeting to create something that felt distantly ominous.

Then came the pain. It burned in her chest, searing her from the inside out like she'd been dipped in liquid iron. She screamed as she attempted to bow off the table, but she was trapped. She was desperate to move her legs and arms. Desperate to clutch at herself. This was nothing like it had been last time when she'd clung to Rabin. When she'd felt herself grow stronger in that moment. More complete. This felt like a piece of her was being stolen, stripped away, and ground to dust.

"Rab—" she tried to gasp. She reached for him, her fingers stretching uselessly against her restraints.

"Zarya!" he called, and a sob cracked out of her chest. How could any of this be happening?

Another twist of pain had her screaming, tears spilling from her eyes, sweat breaking out on her forehead, and her breath seizing in her lungs. Her chest burned. Her skin burned. Her bones ached.

Finally, after several long, agonizing minutes, the pain eased. She lay panting on the table, her limbs shaking as sweat cooled on her body. She listened to the crackle of the fire and the shuffle of Kishore walking away.

A moment later, Abishek appeared over her again. He gave

her a soft look, and something exchanged between them that she couldn't interpret.

"This could have been different," he said. "We could have been something great."

She sensed a strange sorrow in his words and felt strangely sad.

Like she'd given up something she'd never even wanted.

"Now what?" she gasped. "Is it over?"

He tipped his head, his mouth pressing at the corners.

"That was only the beginning."

He laid a hand on her forehead and closed his eyes before he opened them again.

"Now... the real work begins."

THIRTY-ONE

"What's happening to him?" Yasen demanded as he paced along the foot of Vikram's bed. "Why is he like that?"

After Vikram had passed out during dinner, Row returned immediately to Ishaan to retrieve Koura. Now the healer sat at Vikram's bedside, examining the black veins running over his chest, arms, and shoulders. They'd faded somewhat, but he still hadn't woken up.

"I'm not sure," Row answered. "I've never seen anything like this."

Gopal also stood in the room, his arms folded and his brow creased, observing the scene. Yasen wanted to wrap his hands around his neck and *squeeze.*

"This happened before?" Yasen demanded, no longer caring what Gopal Ravana might do to him. "How are you helping him?"

Gopal sneered. "How should I *help* him? He's infected." The nawab shook his head and glared at his younger son like he'd brought this on himself. The rage in Yasen's chest swelled to dangerous proportions. He teetered on the very edge of pulling out a sword and lopping off this bastard's head.

Row snatched him around the arm and pulled him back. "He's not worth it," Row said in a low voice. "Don't let him get to you."

Yasen inhaled deeply, trying to calm his temper. Row was right, and Gopal Ravana deserved nothing from him. One day, he'd make him pay for allowing Vikram to waste away. And for so many other things.

"Let's focus on Vikram," Row said softly. "He needs you right now."

Yasen nodded and turned to watch Koura run gentle fingers over Vikram's arms, chest, and throat, tracing the ominous black lines. Koura closed his eyes as soft yellow light filtered out from his palms and hummed softly as he swayed over Vikram's lifeless body.

Row and Yasen exchanged worried looks while waiting for answers to this mystery.

A minute later, Koura opened his eyes. "I agree that he appears to be infected with a virus or a plague of some kind."

"Infected with what?" Yasen asked.

Koura shook his head. "I'm not entirely sure, but it isn't something of this plane."

When his eyes met Yasen's, he read the wariness in their golden depths and the things he couldn't bring himself to say.

"What do you mean, not of this plane?" Yasen croaked.

Koura shook his head and ran a hand over his tense jaw. "I've lived many centuries on this continent and have always believed the darkness was banished. Then the blight proved me wrong." He stopped and inhaled a deep breath. "In Ishaan, I was proven wrong, yet again when Zarya and the Taara Aazheri revealed their nature. The darkness was never truly banished, and it's clear now that after a thousand years, it is returning. Or rather, it has *already* returned."

Yasen felt his stomach drop to his feet.

"Vikram is infected with the darkness," Yasen said, his voice hollow.

"As is Amrita," he added. "Whatever plagues her, affects her steward as well."

"Did this happen to Tarin?" Yasen asked. "Can we talk to him?"

"It didn't," Row said. "He researched ways to stop the blight many times. He would have said something."

"We should still talk to him," Yasen said.

"I think we need to speak with Amrita," Koura said. "I suspect only she can tell us more about what is happening to both of them."

"Or Vikram when he wakes up, right?" Yasen said.

"Possibly," Koura said. "Based on what I've learned from his caregivers, he is no longer of sound mind. It's possible that whatever he tells us is the truth, but it may also be a fabrication."

Yasen blew out a breath. "Can we find Tarin?"

"I know where he is," Row said. "I will send a message."

Yasen nodded, his jaw firm. He started pacing again and ran a hand through his hair. He stopped and stared at Row and Koura. "What are we going to tell everyone? What are we going to do?"

When neither one could answer, he began pacing again. Yasen was no stranger to feeling helpless. He understood the emotions that came with utter despair and the sense that nothing would be the same ever again.

But as he stared at his friend and the fine dark lines creeping over his skin, Yasen had never felt more helpless in his life.

Koura hadn't been wrong about Vikram. When he awoke, he

couldn't remember anything. He was disoriented and babbling about things that had never happened.

When Yasen pressed him about speaking with Amrita, he recited a string of banal sentiments about taxation bills, land claims, and pointless things that meant nothing. The darkness was eating him alive.

When Row asked him to speak with Amrita about her rotting roots, Vikram gave him a bemused look and told him there was nothing to worry about.

As they waited for Tarin, Vikram went about his days. Yasen couldn't stop staring at those black veins reaching above his collar. On more than one occasion, he would stop and give Yasen a quizzical look and ask, "What?"

Yasen would shake his head and mumble, "Nothing."

Vikram didn't seem to understand anything was happening, and maybe that was the most terrifying thing of all.

A few days later, Tarin arrived. He moved as slowly as ever, shuffling into the throne room, where Yasen waited with Row, Koura, and an increasingly confused Vikram. Gopal Ravana had also arrived, claiming he had a right to know about the state of his son.

"Since when do you care what happens to him?" Yasen asked, and the heat in Gopal's gaze could have melted iron from the center of a mine. He turned his back to the nawab and vowed to forget his existence.

Yasen had to resist bombarding Tarin with a thousand questions. He could have kissed the old tree. Thankfully, Row walked over, holding out his hand.

"Tarin," Row said with a breath of relief. "Thank goodness you've come."

Tarin dipped his head, leaning on his cane as he slowly approached Amrita. "Tell me what's been happening," he said, his low voice rolling like tumbling stones across the chamber.

They quickly filled him in while he listened with a curious expression.

"You've freed the vanshaj," he said with a touch of awe in his voice. "I never thought I'd live to see it."

"Zarya figured it out," Row said.

Tarin dipped his chin, a small smile stretching over his gnarled lips. "I remember the day she arrived in Dharati, a ball of energy ready to burst. I smelled destiny on her, and I'm pleased to hear I was right."

Then he turned to Vikram and assessed him up and down.

Vikram watched warily as Tarin approached. "How's Amrita?" he asked.

"She's... well?" Vikram said.

Tarin cocked his head and studied him with calm scrutiny. "With your permission, I should like to speak with her."

"Can you do that?" Yasen asked.

Tarin raised a hand. "With the steward's blessing, yes."

Tarin returned his attention to Vikram and waited.

"Vik," Yasen urged, and again, Tarin silenced him with a wave.

"Do not rush him. The relationship between a steward and his queen is extremely personal. It is difficult to consider, and it would be natural to refuse my request. I never once allowed it in my many years at Rani Vasvi's side."

Yasen pressed his mouth together but stepped back, giving Vikram space to decide. He shared a look with Row and Koura, who wore their worry in their expressions.

After a moment, Vikram dipped his chin. "I suppose that would be fine."

"You're sure?" Tarin asked, and when Vikram hesitated, Yasen wanted to scream.

"I'm... sure."

"Excellent."

Tarin turned to face Amrita, slowly shuffling towards her. He briefly regarded the baby stirring in her mother's womb before looking up. Then he went still, and Yasen could only presume he was speaking with the queen.

Yasen started pacing. Again.

He stopped and rolled his neck, wishing they could speed this process along. He wanted to return to Ishaan and Miraan but couldn't leave Vikram. When had he suddenly become responsible for so many lives? He'd always tried to avoid this shit as much as possible.

He huffed and started pacing again as they all stewed in silence.

Finally, after what felt like three days, Tarin turned around to face them. The expression on his face didn't invite the warm fuzzies.

"What is it?" Row asked as Tarin shook his head.

"It is as we feared, and the darkness is returning as the seal grows weaker than ever. It started here twenty years ago when the Ashvins returned to this plane. The Chiranjivi managed to subdue it for a time, but as you can see, those efforts were only temporary."

He swept a hand over the room, highlighting the rot creeping through the throne room and the queen.

"What do you mean, the Ashvins *returned*?" Row asked. "They're still trapped in their prison."

Tarin's gaze shifted as though he was wary to reveal the rest.

"What is it?" Row demanded.

"While their corporeal forms remain locked away, their spirits escaped. They found a vessel to carry them, and as a result, the tether keeping them bound is weakening."

"The Ashvins," Row echoed hollowly. "The Ashvins caused the blight."

Tarin nodded. "In a manner of speaking."

"I don't understand," Yasen said. "What does that mean?"

"Zarya," Tarin breathed. "It started with her."

"Zarya? What do you mean?"

Tarin lifted a hand. "I do not fully understand it, but Amrita is now certain the blight that started on the shore began because of the twins and somehow ties to Zarya."

That news dropped between them with a solid thump.

"I don't get it," Row said.

"Nor do I," Tarin admitted.

"Is she okay?" Yasen demanded.

Tarin shook his head. "I cannot answer that."

"What do we do?" Yasen asked.

"What else did you learn?" Row asked Tarin. "Is the seal in danger of failing completely?"

Right. Good question.

"Amrita has confirmed something feels different. She only realized it recently, but whatever she protects is... escaping, leaking, and poisoning her roots, her steward, and soon, her child."

"So, what do we do?" Yasen asked. "How do we stop this?"

"Zarya is the key, but I don't know what that means, nor does Amrita."

"How do we close the seal?" Row asked. "Can Amrita do it?"

Tarin shook his head. "I do not believe so. The Jai Tree was planted to seal in the darkness, but it also keeps so much more contained."

"As in the Ashvins?"

"Yes."

"So we search in her roots or something?" Yasen asked, and Tarin shook his head.

"No, what you need is lower. Deeper."

"I'm not following," Row said.

Tarin exhaled a long breath. "The Ashvins once ruled over the ancient city of Taaranas. When the kings and queens of

Rahajhan banished the twins, they were trapped inside their home—the one they destroyed in their hubris. That is where you must go. That is where you will find a way to close up the seal."

Yasen's mouth opened and then closed. "We have to find Taaranas? The mythical city?"

"It was never mythical," Tarin answered. "It was real."

"How?" Koura asked when Yasen couldn't reply.

Tarin clamped his hands at the top of his cane. "That is all she could tell me. But I do think you will need help."

"You *think*?" Row asked.

"You must gather the Chiranjivi," he said. "If the seal is broken, you can only close it by harnessing the same power the kings and queens of Rahajhan used all those centuries ago. Perhaps you will need more."

"More?" Koura asked. "How?"

Tarin shrugged his broad shoulders. "I wish I could tell you that."

Yasen turned to look at Row and Koura, who both wore equally puzzled expressions.

"We'll return to Ishaan," Row said. "Find Apsara and Suvanna. Zarya must have returned by now, and we'll send word to Kindle. Tarin, can you find out *how* we might enter Taaranas?"

He nodded. "I shall access the library."

"Good," Row said, and Yasen blew out a breath of... something. Not of relief, but at least someone was taking charge.

"What about Vikram?" Yasen asked, watching his friend quietly observing their entire exchange.

"I will keep an eye on him," Tarin said. "But I do fear that if you cannot keep the Ashvins contained, then both the steward and the queen may be in danger."

"I should remain here with the baby," Koura said.

"You are needed with the others," Tarin said. "Can you

send for someone to watch over her in your stead? Someone you trust?"

Koura nodded. "I will write home immediately."

"Good," Tarin said. "You must not delay. I sense time is of the utmost essence, or we are all doomed to lose ourselves to the darkness forever."

THIRTY-TWO

After Kishore completed their new Bandhan, Zarya and Rabin were left alone in the study for several hours while they recovered. Her tattoo throbbed—the pain so much worse than when she'd accepted Thriti's marking, hinting at its darker sort of magic.

Finally, Abishek's manservant Omar appeared with Urvi in tow. They released Zarya and Rabin's bindings and offered them food and clothing. Zarya rubbed her tender wrists and stared suspiciously around the study. Why were they being released without anyone to watch them?

She had access to her magic again—she could feel it sparkling in her chest—but she would never use it against either Omar or Urvi. Perhaps Abishek was counting on that.

Urvi remained silent as she helped Zarya dress in fur-lined leather pants, a fitted cotton shirt, a thick sweater, and wool socks. Then she gestured for them to eat the soup and drink the water they'd brought.

Zarya and Rabin sat across from one another, passing wary looks. She stared at the food as her stomach twisted in knots. She had no appetite.

After several minutes, the door opened, and Abishek appeared with Kishore and Ekaja on his heels.

Everyone remained silent as they entered, sizing one another up.

"Where are you taking us?" Rabin demanded, also ignoring his food.

"All in due time," Abishek said, his tone casual, like he wasn't the least bit concerned about what was coming. It felt like an obvious tactic to get under their skin. Rabin's jaw ticked with murderous anger as he glared at the king.

"What will happen to my mother?" Zarya asked. She couldn't stop seeing the battered, broken woman in that tower. Asha had brought Zarya into the world to save her crown, but Zarya couldn't find it in her heart to be angry about that.

Abishek paused and turned to face her. "I suppose she's finally reached the end of her usefulness, though perhaps I'll keep her alive a bit longer on the off chance I need her again. Your story may not be entirely finished." Zarya's blood ran cold at the detachment in his voice. "After this is over, I'll be rid of her once and for all."

"Did you ever care for her?" Zarya asked, her voice barely a whisper. She didn't know why it mattered. It *didn't* matter, but in her daydreams about the family she'd never met, she'd always fantasized about a mother and father who'd been deeply in love when they'd brought her into this world. Discovering she'd been created to fulfill the ambition of a power-hungry king made her feel like she should never have been born.

Abishek tipped his head and studied her as if he could read everything she was thinking.

"Zarya, don't be a ridiculous girl. I didn't love or care for her. She was a beautiful woman, and I didn't mind sharing her bed, but don't harbor any delusions about your place in this world. You were made to be used by me."

Zarya swallowed the burning knot in her throat, attempting

to keep her expression neutral as acid burned through her heart. She couldn't let the king see how much those words affected her.

"Eat up," Abishek said. "You'll want to keep up your strength. We have a long journey ahead of us."

Then he turned and walked away while Zarya stared at his back. She could feel Rabin's eyes on her, but she couldn't bring herself to look at him. She couldn't stomach the pity she might find in his expression.

After a minute, she inhaled a shaky breath and then forced her gaze towards him. But she didn't see pity. What she saw was fire and rage and the promise that he would do everything in his power to destroy Abishek while screaming her name.

She dipped her chin before focusing on the fare before her. They both picked at their food in silence while Abishek, Ekaja, and Kishore conferred in hushed voices on the other side of the room. Could Zarya and Rabin fight all three off? Why had they been left unbound and allowed access to their magic at all?

The food tasted like ash in her mouth, and the new tattoo on her chest ached every time she swallowed. She tried reaching out to Rabin with her mind, attempting to force through that wall of blackness keeping her blocked. Her eyes fluttered closed as she concentrated with all her strength.

There. She noticed something. The dark surrounded the faintest glimmer, crushed in from all sides by a barrier of blackness. But it was him.

She reached for it, exhaling a small huff.

A second later, it slipped away. When she tried again, she hit another blank wall. She reined in her frustration. Had she just imagined it? Or was she breaking through?

She looked up to find Rabin watching her. Had he felt it? She didn't want to give any advantage they had away. They'd have to settle for exchanging looks and the occasional whispered words if they wanted to communicate.

After they had eaten, Urvi brought in fur-lined boots, mitts, coats, and hats to complete their attire. Zarya donned it all with a kind of guarded caution, wondering what all these layers meant.

"It's time to leave," Kishore said. "When I redid your markings, I infused them with an enchantment that altered their properties. Should you try to use your magic, you'll discover there will be consequences."

Zarya's mouth opened and then closed. "Consequences?"

"If you'd like a demonstration, I'm happy to offer one," Kishore said. "It will be quite painful for him."

"Him?"

His face stretched into a smug smile. "Your Bandhan now ensures that when either of you use your magic, you will cause excruciating pain to the other."

"You're lying," Zarya said, but there was no conviction in it. The tattoo on her chest throbbed with a deep ache, almost as if trying to confirm his words.

"Would you like a demonstration?"

"No!" Zarya said as he lifted a hand. "No. Stop. I believe you."

"Then we're understood," Kishore said. "Come."

He spun on his heels and strode for the door without looking back. Rabin stood from the table, his eyes on Ekaja as they regarded one another with cold looks.

"How could you do this to me?" he asked.

"If it hadn't been me, he would have found someone else." Though her expression remained stony, Zarya thought she caught the slightest dip in her voice.

"That makes it okay?"

"Don't do this," Ekaja said. "It doesn't become either of us."

She gestured to the guards, who moved in closer. "We're leaving now," she said. "Don't make this harder than it needs to be."

Then she turned, and the guards ushered Zarya and Rabin out. She watched Rabin staring at Ekaja's stiff back with an ocean of hurt in his eyes.

They wound through the castle and to the front entrance, where they were met with a line of iron carriages pulled by teams of massive black horses. Zarya, Rabin, and several of their guards were shoved into separate carriages. The doors were then slammed and locked before the carriages lurched to life.

Zarya slid over to the window, peering out as they marched through the streets of Andhera. A few people stopped to look as they passed, but most were oblivious to their presence while they hurried about their busy days.

"Help!" she screamed, but the carriages must have been soundproofed because no one even blinked. Even if they could hear, what could any of them do?

"Shut up," one of the guards snarled. "Or we'll get the mystic."

She glowered and returned her focus to the window as they exited the city and entered the forest, traversing an icy road bordered by snow-dusted pine trees and the endless forest.

She tried to snatch a glimpse of Rabin's carriage, but the angle was wrong.

Eventually, she resigned herself to whatever waited at the end of this journey, sitting back while she scowled at her guards, and they returned the favor for the next several hours.

Rabin watched the landscape pass, his gaze fixed on the horizon as day shifted into early evening. He'd tried to catch a glimpse of Zarya in the carriage behind him, but all he saw was the trotting horses and dark windows, and it tested every single one of his reserves not to smash through every one.

Gods, he'd fucked up worse than he'd ever fucked up in his entire life.

Abishek had known from the very beginning and had manipulated him into seeking refuge in his arms. And then tricked him into finding Zarya, all while worming into his subconscious. Rabin had fallen for it like a fucking fool.

And now they were tethered by Kishore's sick magic and headed to the gods only knew where for some nefarious reason. His teeth ground so hard it was a wonder they hadn't turned to dust.

They hit a bump, and the carriage lurched as the terrain became rockier. He had already surmised they were heading for the mountains, but he had so many questions.

Impotent rage churned through his gut, making him nauseous.

Ekaja sat across from him, her posture stiff, studiously avoiding his gaze. They'd stewed in this awkward silence for hours, pretending the other didn't exist. He still couldn't believe she'd done this.

He glanced over, watching as she stared out the window, but he *knew* she could sense his scrutiny.

"You have nothing to say for yourself?" he asked, unable to contain himself a moment longer.

Ekaja blinked. It was the barest show of emotion. She always kept her feelings close to her chest. Most people found her difficult to read, but they'd spent years together, and he wasn't most people.

After a beat of silence, she slowly turned her head to meet his accusing stare. "What should I say?"

"Anything? An explanation for why you'd betray me like this? Give me some clue about where we're going? Why are *you* in here? You can barely stand to look at me."

Again, she blinked, her dark eyes brimming with something he couldn't name. "He insisted."

Then she returned her gaze to the window without another word.

The king. He'd forced her to join him. But why? To punish Rabin further? To punish *her*?

"Give me something," Rabin said. "Some clue about where we're headed. I don't care about myself, but I must protect Zarya."

With her gaze still focused on the landscape, her lips parted gently on the softest breath. "I don't know," she said. "If I knew anything, I would tell you."

"Why should I believe that?"

Her head shook ever so slightly. "He'll use the bond against you. He will free the darkness. He will gain the power he's sought for centuries, and you and your bride will help him."

"That tells me nothing. I already know all that."

Again, she blinked before inhaling another deep breath. "You'll see soon enough."

Rabin glared, studying her profile. He watched as the last of the sun sank beneath the horizon and the first stars illuminated the sky. When it was apparent no other answers would come, he sat back, staring out his window, wishing he could see Zarya.

They rolled through the foothills as the terrain became even more rocky. The carriage tilted as it bumped up a curving mountain path, and Rabin clung to his seat to maintain his balance. The moon sat high, the sky inky black, and the wind had picked up, rattling gusts of snow against the windows.

They climbed for a short while before the carriage leveled off and then came to a stop.

Rabin sat up straighter in his seat, trying to peer out. All he saw was snowy mountains and nothing else. His stomach rumbled, reminding him it had been hours since they'd left the city. Gods, he wished they'd departed for Ishaan just one day earlier. They would have been fine—the Bandhan had never been tainted, and Rabin would have recovered once he was no longer subjected to the king's poison.

But Abishek never intended for them to leave.

They would have been trapped here regardless.

He would have found them no matter where they ran.

A moment later, the carriage door swung open, and Ekaja immediately leaped out to confer with her guards.

"Come," she said to Rabin, holding the door and waiting for him to descend.

His feet hit the hard-packed snow, and his chest expanded with relief when Zarya exited her carriage a few feet away. Immediately, her gaze found his. She gave him a quick tip of her chin to indicate she was okay.

He thought about what Kishore had promised regarding their magic and wondered if it was true. But how could they prove it? When they got the chance, he'd convince her to try it, just a bit to be sure he hadn't lied.

Rabin scanned their surroundings. They stood inside a sheltered plateau bordered by mountains. On the far side, a narrow path led up a steep incline. Two massive men flanked the entrance, wearing furs from head to toe and clutching spears nearly twice their height.

Rabin recognized them as members of the clans who inhabited these mountains. Abishek strode over to confer with the one on the left, their heads tipping together. He could only presume Abishek had hired them as guides.

Once the king appeared satisfied, he peered over at Rabin, their gazes locking momentarily before Abishek arched a brow.

"We go on foot from here," he announced.

The first mountain man turned and began easily making his way up the tricky path. The guards flanking Zarya urged her forward while Ekaja gestured for Rabin to follow.

He placed one hand on the wall as he took the first step, peering up. Zarya looked back before she turned and began the ascent.

He searched the heavens, seeking strength in the stars and the moon, nearly blocked by the soaring snowy peaks, and wondered if they'd ever see the sun rise again.

THIRTY-THREE

Zarya stamped her boots, doing everything she could to keep herself from falling apart. Night had come, and they'd been walking for hours. Her toes and fingers were numb, her cheeks frostbitten, and her ears chilled from the falling snow.

She could sense Rabin's presence as he marched closely behind, catching her when she stumbled. Every once in a while, she looked over her shoulder to ensure he was still there. It might have been silly, but she couldn't shake the feeling that he'd disappear at any moment.

Then she'd return her focus ahead and stare at the back of Raja Abishek, wishing she could burn him to ashes with the heat of her glare. Ahead of him tromped the mountain man. She'd heard Abishek call him Catana. She remembered the king saying Kishore was meeting with the clans. Was this the reason? What had they been promised in exchange for their help?

She peered up at the night sky and swirling gusts of snow. She could just make out the stars and the glowing moon. On either side, the mountains stretched so high the peaks were lost to her sight.

She tried reaching Rabin as they walked, forcing her mind

towards his. She'd glimpsed that tiny shimmer earlier. She was more sure than ever that she hadn't imagined it. So, while she was forced on this trek, she tried to use her time towards something useful. With her teeth gritted against the cold, she folded her mind inwards, searching for him in the layers of her subconscious.

There, she spotted something again. The faintest sparkle, like a firefly trapped in wax. She tried to reach for it and snag it with her mind, but it slipped away, and she was once again left with nothing. She looked over her shoulder again, meeting Rabin's gaze. His brow was furrowed, and she wondered if he'd felt it.

Finally, the path leveled off, and they found themselves atop a small plateau with an opening on the far side. Catana led them towards it, ducking his head as they passed out of the wind into a dark tunnel.

Zarya could have wept with relief when the howling cut off. There was the sound of a click and the strike of a flint, and then, a moment later, Catana held up a lantern. He hung it on a hook jutting from the wall.

"Ekaja will handle the rest," Abishek said, gesturing behind him and waiting for her to march along the line and reach the front. She disappeared into the darkness, and another hanging lantern flared to life a moment later.

They continued winding deeper into the tunnel as the sound of the wind faded and the temperature grew a few degrees warmer. After walking for another minute, they entered a tall, wide cavern with a dark firepit in the center.

Ekaja sent out a tendril of fire, and they all watched it catch the logs as the heat of the flames immediately warmed the air.

"We'll rest here for the night," Abishek said. "And continue our journey tomorrow."

"To where?" Rabin asked, but the king turned on his heel and stalked towards the tunnel.

"Ekaja, Kishore," he said. "With me."

Zarya watched them leave as the second mountain man entered and crossed the room. He crouched next to his companion, and they began speaking in low voices in their own language.

Zarya stumbled over to Rabin, who opened his arms and wrapped her in his embrace. She held onto him tightly, wishing she could just let go and cry until she had no more tears left.

But they might not get a chance alone like this again.

"Did you learn anything from Ekaja during the ride?" she asked.

"Nothing Abishek hadn't already said."

She stared about the space and the darkened tunnel where the king had disappeared a moment ago.

"They're not even worried about us escaping," she said.

"Where would we run?"

"You could shift?"

"That's magic, Zarya," he said. "If what Kishore claimed was true..."

"How bad could it be?" she asked, already knowing it was stupid even to hope.

"Zarya, we are not testing it on you."

"Fuck!" she hissed. "They have us completely trapped. With just a few ominous words, we have no idea what might happen."

Rabin's mouth flattened into a line. "I mean... I think that's the point."

She huffed. "Clearly." She clutched the fabric of his coat. "What are we going to do?"

"Look for an opening," he said. "They'll make a mistake at some point. That will be our opportunity."

"That's not much of a plan," she said. "Especially since we can't communicate in the mind plane."

"I'm aware," he answered dryly.

"Did you feel it earlier?" she asked. "I was trying to reach you. I think I might be able to break through his magic."

His brow furrowed. "While we were walking?"

"Yes! You felt something?"

He nodded slowly. "I think so."

She almost squealed with joy. "Maybe you need to reciprocate—"

Just then, footsteps sounded down the tunnel, and she cut off. Ekaja appeared in the doorway. Zarya and Rabin slowly pulled apart as she scanned them up and down, her expression giving away nothing.

Had she heard them talking?

A moment later, more footsteps preceded the entrance of Abishek and Kishore. The king didn't seem bothered by the tension in the room as he swept towards the center, swinging his cloak and planting himself in front of the fire.

He rubbed his hands and held them to the heat. "Well, come and get warm," he said. "We'll sleep for a few hours and then continue our trek. I don't wish to delay for long."

Kishore moved into the circle, and then slowly, Zarya, Rabin, and Ekaja followed.

Zarya sat across from the king, her gaze never leaving him. When he glanced up, he noted her stare, returning it as they beheld one another.

"Don't look at me like that," he said. "All you had to do was cooperate."

"Why are you doing this?"

He peered at her, his brow furrowing. "You are young and don't yet understand the importance of one's legacy. The Aazheri are dying out. Thousands once roamed this continent, and barely hundreds remain. If this keeps up, then we will soon be gone forever."

Zarya blinked. "There *are* thousands of Aazheri in Rahajhan," she bit out. "The vanshaj. You could get what you want *without* bloodshed."

Abishek's assessing gaze traveled over her face. "Vanshaj," he sneered, his voice dripping with disdain. "This is your solution?"

"Why not?"

He shook his head. "You were working behind my back," he snarled. "Breaking collars in the city, believing you were *hiding* it from me?"

Her breath caught.

"I know all about their little 'resistance.' I only allow them to exist to give them hope. They think they're defying me, but I know every move they make."

She didn't know what to say.

"I'll deal with every single one after we're done here. End them for good."

"You said you believed in their cause," she whispered. Gods, she'd been so stupid. She'd wanted to believe him so much.

Abishek shook his head. "I truly didn't think my own flesh and blood could be this dense. I don't want the *vanshaj*. I want *real* Aazheri."

She thought about the story Yasen had told her about the king of Andhera killing thousands of vanshaj and Rabin claiming it had been a lie. But it was just another falsehood the king had used to earn his trust.

She opened her mouth with a small breath. This was no use. This argument wouldn't get them anywhere. What she needed was to understand his plans. She had to survive whatever was coming. She had to protect the vanshaj from his cruelty.

The mountain men rose from the corner where they'd been preparing food, both bearing wooden plates. They handed them out and passed around warm drinks while everyone fell silent, stewing in their thoughts.

"*Where* are you taking us?" Rabin finally asked after they'd been quiet for several minutes. "Surely you can tell us now."

Abishek gave him a piercing look and then set his plate on the ground by his feet. Wiping his mouth, he sat forward with his elbows braced on his knees.

"I'm sending you to the lost city of Taaranas," he said. "To find the seal that will release the darkness."

"Taaranas?" Rabin echoed, his voice hollow and full of dread. "But it was razed to the ground a thousand years ago."

Zarya remembered the name. It was the same city she'd seen in her visions. The one depicted in the tapestries lining Abishek's castle. The place where the Ashvins had once lived and ruled.

"Yes and no," Abishek said. "When the seven original rulers sealed the twins and the darkness away, they sequestered the brothers *and* the city in another plane. There was no one left alive in Taaranas by then. Then they planted the Jai Tree to seal them off. The roots grow for thousands of miles throughout Rahajhan, creating a wall between our worlds."

Zarya blinked, trying to absorb the scale of this information.

"A city? In another dimension?" Rabin asked.

Abishek sat straighter and accepted another mug of chai from Catana. He sipped it and stared into it before he finally looked up. "We are heading for a bridge that marks the entry point into Taaranas. There, we will send you inside to seek out a fortress. Beyond its gates, you will find the trigger to open the seal. Only nightfire can accomplish this, and once you do, you will free the Ashvins, their darkness, and the nairatta again."

He fell silent as his words echoed around the cavern, and Zarya's blood ran icy cold.

"That's what you needed my nightfire for," Zarya said as so many things fell into place.

Abishek tipped his head. "Row wasn't entirely wrong, you see? While magic *can* be taken, unfortunately, my research suggests that nightfire is the exception to this rule. So, I had to go about it another way. Besides, what I'm asking you to do accomplishes *so* much more than simply gaining new power for myself. *This* will change the world."

"We're *not* doing that," Zarya said. "You can't make us do that."

Abishek turned to her with a cold smile. "No, *you're* doing it. It's your magic I need."

His gaze flicked to Rabin as if he wasn't quite finished yet.

"And Rabin? Why is he coming with me? And what did any of this have to do with our Bandhan?" she asked.

At that, the corner of Abishek's mouth twisted into a cold smile.

"He's my insurance that once you're out of my sight, you will be motivated to *cooperate*."

THIRTY-FOUR

The city was quiet when Yasen, Row, and Koura returned to Ishaan. They prowled through darkened streets, passing burned-out buildings and piles of rubble, exchanging wary looks.

"Why is it so quiet?" Yasen asked.

Row shook his head. "Let's head to the manor to ensure everything is fine."

"I want to see Miraan first," Yasen said, and Row and Koura nodded. "Then I'll join you."

"And I must return to the palace to check on the princess," Koura said.

"Do you, though?" Yasen asked, earning him a raised eyebrow.

"I don't think I'll dignify that with a response," Koura responded before he bowed. "I'll see you soon."

Once he was gone, Row turned to Yasen. "Meet me in the forest when you're done. I'll head there now to explain what we've learned."

They parted ways, and Yasen turned down a side street that would take him past Rudra's manor.

He knocked on the door and was admitted into the salon by a servant.

"Yas!" Miraan said as soon as he entered. "You're back!"

He scanned the room, finding Rudra and Miraan's other friends.

"How did it go in Dharati?" Miraan crossed the floor, throwing his arms around Yasen. "I was worried about you."

"I'm fine," Yasen said, returning his embrace before they pulled apart. "Things are bad, though."

"Tell us everything," he said, indicating a spot for Yasen to sit.

He ran through the events in the Jai Palace. When he was done, every man in the room was silent, the shock in their expressions clear.

"The seal is weakening," Rudra said. "How do we stop this?"

"Rani Vasvi's former steward is looking for answers in the library, but I'm not holding out much hope," Yasen said.

Everyone started talking, speaking over one another as they offered up various theories and ideas to solve this mystery.

Eventually, Miraan interrupted and raised his hands. "I'm not sure this is productive," he said. "We need to focus on issues we *can* influence."

The room fell silent as he continued. "As we've discussed, I cannot approach the palace, so I'm asking you to be the voice of reason. If Dishani will no longer listen to me, she might consider the request from one of you."

"We could threaten to withdraw support and back you as king," Rudra said carefully as every man in the room shared wary looks.

Yasen watched Miraan for his reaction as several emotions crossed the prince's face.

"I have never desired my sister's crown, but if that's what it takes to end this, then there may be no choice."

A tense silence circled around the group. What they were discussing was treason. But Miraan had already set that cart in motion the first time he'd sent money to the Rising Phoenix.

"Then we shall state our case," Rudra answered. "Are you all with me?"

His gaze fell on the five other men who wielded influence in this queendom. One by one, they nodded until every man had agreed.

"Then let's hope we don't lose our heads," Rudra said, lifting his glass in a toast. "To King Miraan. The future of Gi'ana."

Every other man in the room raised their glasses, murmuring their support.

Yasen watched the entire thing, wondering if this would work.

Miraan, a king. It made sense.

As if feeling Yasen's eyes on him, Miraan looked over, his jaw hard and his eyes brimming with the weight of the choice he was making.

And the consequences and possibilities of what came next.

After they finished their discussion and Rudra and the others had made plans to visit the palace, Yasen and Miraan headed for the rebellion's hideout in the forest.

When they arrived, they were surprised to find how much had changed in their absence. Their numbers had swelled as more vanshaj were secreted out of the city. Dozens of makeshift homes spread through the trees and well into the distance. Yasen could see where Apsara and Suvanna were busy training their army in a large open field.

He spotted Row chatting with Ajay, Vikas, Farida, and Rania and made his way over with Miraan. As they approached, they all stopped talking.

"I can tell from your expressions that Row has told you everything," Yasen said, and they all nodded.

"Any progress on your side?" Vikas asked Miraan.

He filled him in on everything while Yasen scanned the forest. When Miraan was done, Yasen asked, "Where's Zarya?"

"She isn't here," Ajay said.

"We haven't heard from her at all," Farida added.

Yasen's eyes narrowed as wary premonition crept up the back of his scalp. "She hasn't sent any letters. None at all?"

"Sorry, no," Ajay answered.

Yasen's jaw clenched, his teeth grinding together. She *promised* she'd write every day. That's when his gaze met Row's.

"Do you think they're okay?" Yasen asked, and Row shook his head.

"If she isn't sending letters..."

"Something could be wrong."

Everyone was silent for a moment before Row said, "I'm planning to see the mystic who performed their Bandhan. I've been meaning to do so for a while. Perhaps something has happened with their bond."

"I'm coming, too," Yasen said, and Row dipped his chin.

"Then let's go."

It took a short while to arrive at the mystic's door, where they were greeted by a striking woman with deep brown skin and silver hair hanging down either side of her face. She wore a deep blue dress with long wide sleeves and embroidered with metallic threads along the hem of her skirt.

"Hi," Yasen said. "We're sorry to disturb you, but you performed a Bandhan for our friends not long ago, and we have a few questions. They might be in danger."

She blinked, her expression curious, and then opened the door wider. "Come inside."

They entered the small shop, lined with shelves and hundreds of ingredients. Their fragrance combined to give the place an unusual scent.

"What is this about?" the mystic asked as she closed the door behind them. She folded her hands in front of her and waited.

Yasen deferred to Row, who understood more about this magic stuff.

"When you performed the Bandhan for Zarya and Rabin, did you sense anything amiss with the bond?" Row asked.

"Amiss?" Thriti asked. "I'm not sure I understand."

"Zarya didn't tell you she has unique magic, did she?"

Thriti's head tipped as she stared at Row. "Unique?"

"She has six anchors," he said and paused.

Yasen almost rolled his eyes—it was a bit exhausting how dramatic they all were about this.

Thriti considered that answer. "I see. That's rather unusual, I suppose, but not unheard of."

"You've met others with the sixth anchor?" Row asked.

Thriti folded her arms and nodded. When it was clear she didn't care to elaborate, Row continued.

"How would the presence of a sixth anchor affect the Bandhan? If Zarya failed to disclose it, what precautions could you take now to rectify it?"

Thriti's dark eyebrows drew together. "What are you talking about?"

"We've been told the sixth anchor taints the Bandhan, and theirs has been affected. They were blocked from entering the mind plane, and Rabin is quite ill. I'm worried Zarya will soon be, too."

"No," she said, shaking her head. "The sixth anchor has no

effect on their bonding. A Bandhan cannot be broken by anything but the paramadhar or masatara's death."

The blood in Yasen's veins turned to ice at those words. "You're sure," he asked. "It's not just something you're unaware of?"

She tossed him a cold look. "What do you take me for? Of course I'm sure. Who told you such nonsense?"

Row and Yasen looked at one another.

"He lied to them," Yasen said. "He's keeping them there for a reason."

"Who?" Thriti asked.

"Raja Abishek," Row said as Thriti's lips parted.

"Ah," she said as though that made everything clear.

"What?" Yasen asked. "What is it?"

"When they arrived, they chose a dragon as the symbol to bind them," she said. "Rabin already had a tattoo used to aid in his transformation."

"Right?" Row asked, his shoulders curving with tension.

"I thought I sensed something else buried in its magic."

"What?" Yasen asked.

She shook her head. "I wasn't entirely sure. I almost thought I imagined it. However, if Kishore is the mystic who applied it, I'm slightly more confident it was layered with a form of controlling magic."

"And you didn't say anything?" Row asked.

She raised her hands in defense. "That was not my place. People choose to mark their bodies with many kinds of magic. Besides, I wasn't even sure I was right."

They all fell silent as Yasen's heart pounded in his chest.

"Fuck!" he said a moment later. "He's done something to her. To both of them. That's why she hasn't sent a letter! He lied to them."

His gaze met Row's, who looked at him with worry and fear in his dark eyes.

"We have to find them."

THIRTY-FIVE

Rabin wrapped his arms tighter around a shivering Zarya, trying to offer some warmth. The fire burned in the center of the cavern, casting just enough heat to ensure they didn't freeze to death but not much else.

They lay on a thin pallet, covered by a thin blanket, with their teeth chattering. Abishek, Kishore, and Ekaja had their magic to keep them warm, and the mountain men were accustomed to these harsh elements.

"Use just a bit of air," he whispered into her ear. "Whatever happens to me, I'll handle it. You're freezing. Warm us up."

"Absolutely not." She said it so softly that only he could hear it, but he felt the bite in her words. "We have no idea how it might affect you. Until we understand what Kishore meant, I'm not using my magic." She buried closer to him. "We'll be fine. At least we have each other."

Rabin didn't respond. Abishek hadn't tied them up or set a watch, which meant he truly believed there was nowhere for them to escape. Where would they run in these unforgiving mountain passes? He'd hired Catana and his companion to guide them for a reason. Not even Abishek knew how to navigate this remote part of his kingdom.

Rabin could have easily flown them out, but he wouldn't risk his magic, either. Not if shifting might hurt Zarya. His teeth ground together in frustration. Everything Abishek had told them made their situation sound worse and worse. He had no idea how they would get out of this, nor what he'd meant in saying Rabin was his insurance.

Zarya shivered again, her teeth clacking together.

A moment later, he felt a breath of warm air settle around them, covering them more effectively than any blanket. He looked up to find Ekaja staring from across the cavern, the firelight reflecting in the darkness of her gaze.

His eyes narrowed as he stared back. She'd used her magic to help them. Was this some kind of peace offering? Was he supposed to forgive her now?

Zarya noticed the direction of his stare and watched Ekaja before she turned her focus on him.

"Ignore her," he said before they lay back down, but Ekaja's magic held. He considered telling her to knock it off and that he didn't need her help, but the color was returning to Zarya's lips. He'd endure his ex-friend's brand of misguided support for her sake.

Zarya crooked a finger, gesturing for him to lean in.

"I want to try entering the mind plane again," she whispered in his ear. "Concentrate on reaching me."

He nodded and watched as her eyes slid closed. He did the same, searching in the layers of his mind for that spot where she lingered. He'd felt it earlier when she'd tried to reach him, but could they fight through the king's magic?

He saw the faintest glimmer deep in his mind's eye and stretched towards it, reaching for her. The glimmer grew brighter and flared momentarily before it stuttered away, his mind turning everything black once again.

He opened his eyes to find her looking at him. She peered over at Abishek and gave her a bemused look before she reached up to speak directly into his ear.

"I was worried pressing against his magic might alert him, but it doesn't seem so. At least not so far."

Then she smiled, her eyes lighting up. "Something happened there."

"It did."

"It wasn't much."

"No, but it was something."

She huffed out a breath. "Okay, we'll keep trying. It feels like we're close."

He nodded. "But first, get some sleep. We have no idea what's ahead of us."

She pressed her mouth together and looked up into his eyes.

"I'm scared," she whispered.

"I know. But we're in this together until the end."

She laid a hand against his heart. "Until my very last breath."

When Zarya opened her eyes, it felt like she'd been asleep for only minutes. Her entire body ached from stress and worry and the fact that she had no idea what awaited them.

The others were already stirring, sitting down to breakfast with mugs of tea steaming in the crisp morning air. Ekaja had kept them warm last night, and though she didn't deserve it, Zarya tipped the slightest nod of thanks in her direction.

Slowly, she made her way over to the fire and warmed her hands. Abishek watched while she glared at him. His expression was impossible to read. Did he feel any remorse for what he had done? About what he still planned to do? It was one thing to seek out world domination, but to use your own child to do it?

She supposed she didn't mean anything to him. That she had never meant anything to him. She'd fooled herself into believing he'd cared about her. She longed for Row and the comfort of his steady presence—if she survived this, she'd never take him for granted again. She'd beg his forgiveness for dismissing his warnings. He'd been right all along.

She reached for her necklace, still lamenting its absence. A tear slipped down her cheek as she saw her mother huddled in the corner of the tower. Finally, unable to stand looking at the king a moment longer, she tore her gaze away. They ate in silence until it was time to pack up and continue moving.

They exited the cavern and traipsed down the tunnel to find the glaring morning sun. Zarya lifted a hand to shield her eyes from the brightness against the sparkling blanket of snow. A fresh layer covered everything, rendering the world into soft, puffy clouds. At least the wind had died down a little.

They wasted no time, making their way up another mountain pass, carving higher and higher into the soaring peaks. The air grew thinner, the wind more biting, and Zarya's sense of foreboding thrummed to the backs of her teeth.

She pulled her coat tighter as she stumbled over a chunk of ice, nearly losing her balance. Rabin was behind her immediately, an arm banding around her waist.

"Got you," he rumbled as she resisted the urge to turn to him and cry.

She wanted to know what lay at the end of this. The anticipation was almost the worst part.

She lost track of the minutes and hours as the sun climbed overhead. Finally, they reached the end of the path, exiting onto a cliff overlooking a sprawling mountain valley.

Hundreds of snowy peaks stretched in every direction. The damp air fogged around them, creating tiny particles of ice that clung to their hair and eyelashes. They had nearly reached the clouds. Zarya exchanged a look with Rabin, and then she followed Abishek and Catana across a cliff where, inexplicably, a narrow rope bridge ran out from the edge.

She stared at it, swinging in the wind, the far end obscured by the mist.

"This is it," Abishek said, turning to face her. "The entrance to Taaranas."

Zarya folded her arms tighter as the tears she'd been clinging to pressed the backs of her eyes. He expected them to walk out onto that? It looked like it would snap under the weight of a ghost.

"I won't do it," Zarya said. "You can force me in there, but I won't free the Ashvins and will never give you access to the darkness."

Abishek offered what she could only describe as a disappointed smile. "When I first learned I was a father, I had such high hopes," he said. "I thought you would be someone in my image. Someone who understood everything I did. I thought all my dreams would fall into place when you came to me."

Slowly, he approached her, his feet crunching over the snow. They stood somewhat sheltered from the wind, but it was just as cold as ever. He reached out to run a finger down her jaw. She jerked back, her skin crawling at his touch.

"I see now it was a mistake to allow Row to raise you. I should have done it myself. I should have overseen your education. You would have turned out the way I wanted. Instead, you are a *rebel* and a dissident. You *married* a rakshasa."

He spat the last word out like it was a filthy thing, and her anger twisted in her chest.

"But before I send you to your grave, you will, at the very least, be useful to me."

"I won't do it!" she screamed.

Abishek laughed, the sound cold and dead.

"I think you will." He turned to the mystic. "Kishore! It's time."

The mystic stepped forward and raised his hands before his silver bands of magic began twirling around him. He shifted his focus before they surrounded Zarya and Rabin.

"What's going on?" Rabin demanded as the magic spiraled tighter. Zarya suddenly couldn't breathe.

A moment later, the tattoo on her chest burned. She winced as the pressure squeezed her heart, exhaling a choked gasp. She clutched herself, and Rabin bent over, holding his side.

"When I recalibrated the Bandhan, I made a few tweaks," Kishore said. "As well as binding you together, it is also a leash. In a manner of speaking."

"What?" Rabin asked through gritted teeth.

"You'll see in a moment."

Kishore's smile was cold as Rabin cried out, his knees buckling as he sank to the snow.

"What's wrong!" Zarya screamed as black smoke began swirling around him.

"I'd back up if I were you," Kishore said.

Rabin kept dissolving, his screams echoing off the high peaks. That's when Zarya realized Kishore was forcing him to shift.

She'd seen him change enough times to know that if she stood too close, she'd be trampled underfoot. Quickly, she retreated as he thrashed against the change.

Her knees buckled as pain lashed through her limbs and bones—searing, burning, twisting. *His magic.*

Kishore had been telling the truth. It turned her inside out, her throat raw from screaming as she waited for his shift to stop. She collapsed on the snow, panting and writhing until, finally, his dragon emerged, rock shattering in every direction to accommodate his size.

Zarya covered her head, waiting for the dust to settle and the pain scraping her limbs to cease.

She felt the blast of wind as his wings flapped, and slowly, she pushed herself onto her knees. Her hands were ice, her skin raw. She stared at Rabin as he struggled against some kind of invisible hold, his head whipping left and right.

Kishore remained focused on Rabin with his hands out as more silver magic swirled through the air. She watched as his magic cinched around Rabin and then lifted him up.

Rabin roared, his body twisting in the cage of Kishore's power.

"Leave him alone!" she screamed.

Kishore lifted his arms higher, directing Rabin into the sky before he threw them up and freed Rabin from his tether. Rabin flipped in the air and then recovered, his wings flapping as he circled across the horizon with a bellowing roar.

Zarya watched him, noting that his eyes were red instead of blue. They glowed with inner fire, and she *felt* the moment he saw her. With his teeth bared, he *dove*, streaking towards her. She would have sworn on her life that Rabin would never hurt her, but there was no mistaking the murderous intent in that crimson glow.

She screamed as he swooped, missing her by only a few inches, and then he came to an abrupt halt. Again, he struggled against Kishore's invisible bonds as he was shoved into the sky again.

"He is now trapped in this form," Abishek said. "The bond has also been reversed so that instead of protecting you, he will now be intent on killing you. When you find yourselves in Taaranas, the only way to save yourself will be to find the seal, open it, and release the nairatta. Once that's done, the seal will nullify all magic within Taaranas for a few minutes until the darkness can escape. Luckily for you, it will cause my enchantment on your dragon to break."

Zarya watched in horror while Kishore continued to hold a fighting Rabin back from trying to... *kill* her.

"And if you think you can use your magic to protect yourself, nothing has changed in that regard," Abishek added. "You felt what happened when he shifted—and that was only a fraction of his power."

Cold dread pooled in her stomach as she realized she was trapped. She had no choice unless she let Rabin kill her. And if she died, he might be locked in this form forever.

Abishek turned to Kishore, and the mystic flung his arms, seizing Rabin again. He screeched and thrashed, trying to break from Kishore's hold.

Then Kishore tossed Rabin towards the mist at the end of the swinging bridge.

Zarya screamed as Rabin disappeared in a bright flash.

"Rabin!" The sound echoed off every surface as his name repeated into infinity.

"Your turn, my dear," Abishek said.

She looked at the king and swallowed the thick knot in her throat. Her hands clenched into fists, and the icy sting of the wind numbed her skin where tears tracked down her cheeks.

She stared at the end of the bridge. She had no choice. She had to find him. She would find some way to bring them out and keep Abishek from getting what he sought.

She took a step. It felt like the hardest one of her life.

Then another as she drew towards the edge.

Abishek and Kishore parted to allow her through.

Ekaja stood at the entrance to the bridge, watching her.

Zarya looked at her. "I hope you understand what you've done," she whispered.

"I'll live with it every day of my life," she answered softly.

Then Zarya nodded, placing one foot on the first plank to test her weight. When it held, she took another step and then another. The bridge swung in the gusting wind, and she whimpered as she clung to the rope.

She willed herself not to look down.

Another step and then another. All she could do was move forward and hope for an escape.

She didn't look back.

She couldn't bear looking at the man who'd tricked and fooled her.

Even when she'd been warned.

She couldn't bear to look at the sum of her mistakes.

She inhaled a deep breath and peered down at the endless valley disappearing into the mists.

Looking back up, she stared at the nothingness before her.

Another step, and then... the mist swallowed her up.

THIRTY-SIX

Zarya braced herself, expecting a plummet or something equally harrowing, but a moment later, the mist cleared, leaving her standing alone in the center of the lost city of Taaranas.

It looked just like the tapestries she'd studied in Abishek's castle, except that everything had been leached of color and now stood pale and lifeless, almost like it had been carved from chalk.

Whisps of dark smoke curled around the corners, drifting like spirits.

Taaranas.

A ghost city. A dead city.

A mysterious light illuminated the entire space revealing ornate buildings and homes, wide boulevards, and shops that must have once been vibrant with life. She could make out mosaic tiles and stone pillars. Domed roofs with jewels embedded into the surface. Large round windows framed with intricate carvings.

But it was all blank. Whatever colors once decorated this place had been wiped away.

To her right was a castle. It was small compared to those

she'd seen over the last few months but was still magnificent with its soaring towers and intricate carvings etched into every surface. This must have been the Ashvins' home.

Finally, she looked left, and her breath hitched in her chest.

The star temple stood at the far end of the boulevard, stretching into the sky.

Absent of the sparkle or shine she'd seen in her visions, it, too, was drained of life, color, and spirit.

Finally, her gaze swept up to the unbelievable sight stretching high overhead.

Roots. Thousands of twisting roots curved against a ceiling, shimmering in soft white and punctuated with patches of black rot.

Amrita.

The Jai Tree.

It had always been connected to the darkness and her nightfire.

This was why Zarya's magic was always linked to forests.

But the magic was killing Amrita, crawling over her roots, attempting to reach the surface.

Zarya spun around and around, searching for answers, half expecting to find her walking down the boulevard. But she was immobile, trapped in her body a thousand miles away.

Finally, Zarya understood that *this* was what the Jai Tree had been guarding.

She swallowed thickly, wondering where Rabin had ended up.

She heard nothing. Not the sound of wind or the distant echo of water. The air was so still and dry that her ears popped from the absence of sound.

She wondered how she would find sustenance in this sterile environment, but would she be here long enough for it to matter?

She inhaled a deep breath, considering her next move.

She had to find the fortress and the trigger that would open the seal. Abishek had given her nothing to work with, but she guessed it was because he didn't know where it was, either. What she needed to find was a way to thwart his plans and ensure no one could ever open the seal again.

But she couldn't even begin to understand how she might accomplish that.

If the seal remained closed, would Rabin be trapped in Kishore's enchantment forever? Would she be trapped here, too?

She stood rooted to the spot, paralyzed by fear.

But she couldn't just stand here.

Inhaling another breath to quell the trembling in her limbs, she willed one foot forward, expecting to kick up a cloud of dust, but there was nothing. Just this smooth, dead material for which she had no name.

Something told her the key to this riddle was inside the temple.

This was where the Ashvins had once lived and worked, where they plotted, schemed, and gathered their disciples. Surely, this was where they'd opened the door to another world to invite the nairatta in.

As she walked, the dragon on her chest throbbed, pain radiating out to her arms and legs. She ignored it as the call of the temple drew her closer. On the lightest of steps, she approached. The only sound was her heavy breaths and the gentle tap of her boots against the ground.

She grew warmer, sweat gathering at her hairline. These heavy furs were too much without the snow and wind of the mountains. She unbuttoned her coat and let it slip from her shoulders, where it fell with a soft thump, almost as if in slow motion.

She studied the ceiling, tracing the lines of Amrita's roots.

Was the key buried somewhere in there? She wondered again where Rabin was. Had he arrived in the same place?

She considered calling his name but then remembered those murderous red eyes and how he'd *lunged* for her. A tear slipped down her cheek. Not only had Abishek betrayed them both, but he'd also turned Rabin against her. And now he was trapped in his dragon form, bent on hunting her down.

Rabin.

She didn't say his name or even whisper it. She only made the shape of it with her lips. He'd find her soon enough if what Kishore claimed was true. In the meantime, she'd use her time to learn something about this place.

Shucking off more layers as she walked, she approached the temple. She wished she had something other than these heavy boots, but the only alternative was going about in her socks or bare feet.

When she reached the temple, she stared at the star hovering over the top.

Nightfire.

She could only guess how the twins had created this to honor their unique power.

Zarya stared at her hands, feeling the strangest sense of belonging. Her magic connected her to this place. Her fingers curled, nails digging into her palms as she looked back up. She placed a foot on the first step and then the next, drawn towards the temple. Almost as if it was calling to her.

The tall doors stood open, admitting her into a large square room that must have been beautiful at some point. Every wall and window was decorated with swirling curls carved into the stone. The floor was made of thousands of tiny white tiles that must have once been a multi-hued mosaic.

She stepped carefully into the space as light from some unknown source filtered beams across the floor. Not a speck of dust floated in the air.

The room was mostly empty, except for a pool in the center. The water was the same white, chalky material, and the sight worried her again about how she would survive without food or water.

A set of stairs led to the pool. She climbed to the top and stared down before crouching on her haunches. Reaching for the solidified surface, she nearly tumbled back when it moved at her touch.

Rippling, the pool transformed into clear blue water. She blinked in shock before crawling around the perimeter. With each touch of her hands, the chalky white stones transformed into shimmering silver.

What did this mean? If the twins lived inside her, maybe she could manipulate Taaranas in a way no one else could. She continued around the circle, transforming the entire area around the well.

She peered into the pool, wondering about the source of light. After waiting for the surface to calm, she could see straight to the bottom, where she could make out something written on the stones.

Should she jump in? That might leave her vulnerable. She was far too aware of an enchanted, feral Rabin trapped somewhere inside this dimension. Plus, what other creatures might call this place home?

A noise drew her attention to a window set high in the wall.

She knew that sound. The snap of wings. The thump of leathery membranes hitting the air.

"Shit," she whispered, and a moment later, Rabin crashed through the ceiling with a roar.

THIRTY-SEVEN

Zarya leaped up and ran, her legs pumping as she hightailed it out of the temple. Rabin screeched so loud she winced as she pounded down the steps and onto the chalky white street.

She looked back to discover that the top half of the temple had collapsed under his weight. The star remained suspended in mid-air, overlooking the city. She heard Rabin thrashing inside, and then, a moment later, he appeared, hovering above the rubble, his wings flapping slowly.

His red eyes found her immediately, and she started running.

She wove back and forth as flames of red fire struck the ground, nearly singeing her hair and clothing. Rabin screeched again, and she looked back as the toe of her heavy boot caught the ground.

She landed on her hands and knees, her skin scraping open against the hard surface as it transformed beneath her, shifting into grey stone and the street it was a thousand years ago. She had a brief moment to note that nothing marred the strange material. Not even the scorch of Rabin's fire.

Rabin advanced, and without thinking, she held out a hand,

blasting a shield of air to hold him back. As soon as the magic left her fingertips, Rabin shrieked, rearing up, his entire body writhing mid-air, trapped in the throes of agony.

She screamed and pulled her magic back. She'd forgotten she couldn't use it. A choked sob escaped her throat as she flipped over and used this moment to get a head start. She ducked around a corner, sliding between some narrow buildings.

Keeping her head low, she snaked through the tight alleys once home to these lost people. She heard the flap of Rabin's wings and then the crunch of stone as he alighted atop a building. He perched on the roof, scanning below, waiting for her. *Hunting* her.

She wondered what he was thinking. Did he have any sense of what was happening? Could she reach him through his mind?

Slowly, she crept forward, keeping low. Even the slightest sound or movement would attract him inside this dead zone. She stepped slowly and carefully, maneuvering herself to the end of a passage where she could see him.

She closed her eyes and felt through the layers of her mind, hunting for the glowing spot that signaled his presence. After a minute, she sensed him and reached for it, forcing herself towards it. She'd been desperate before, but this had become a matter of life and death.

She dove deeper into their connection, shouting at him through her mind.

Rabin! Can you hear me? This isn't you!

She watched as he shook his massive head, his red eyes blinking. Everything went dark again a moment later, and she wanted to scream. But he was there. She'd just have to work on it.

She searched her surroundings for a place to hide. Her hand brushed the wall, and the building immediately rippled. She gasped as the surface shifted from the strange white material into grey bricks. She snatched her hand away, but the damage was done.

Rabin roared and lifted off his perch, hovering mid-air.

She started running as he dove, blasts of fire chasing her heels as he smashed through buildings like they were made of twigs. He hunted her around corners and through alleyways. She had to find cover. She was too visible out here. She threw open a door and hurled herself inside a small house. Then she stopped and listened for the sound of flapping wings.

When she was sure he was making a wide loop, she dashed to the next house, hoping he wouldn't notice. He roared as he circled again, so she continued in the same vein until it seemed he'd lost her.

She stood in the middle of a house, as far from every window as possible, holding perfectly still as she listened for him outside. Again, he made another pass. She could hear the sound of his wings as he continually moved further and then closer.

She wasn't sure how long she stood there, her muscles seizing as she tried not to move or break down into sobs. She was terrified. Scared of being ripped to shreds by the most important person in her life.

Sweat beaded on her brow as she held still, waiting for him to take another circle. He was having trouble finding her. She'd escaped, for now, but she already knew she couldn't wait forever.

She stood for so long that her arms and legs began to shake. Sweat dripped into her eyes and slid down her throat. But she still didn't move as his shadow darkened the window again.

Finally, after what seemed like forever, he stopped. The sound of his wings went silent, and she listened intently, wondering where he'd gone. After waiting in stillness for several more minutes, she slowly sank to her knees when she couldn't stand another moment longer. Hopefully, he'd grown tired of chasing her for now.

As her hands touched the floor, it rippled and transformed, giving way to a small patch of tiny, colorful tiles. She inhaled a sharp breath. She'd have to be careful.

She paused, then slowly crawled across the floor, which changed beneath her with each step. She moved towards the kitchen, nearing a small table surrounded by four chairs and a long counter covered with boxes and jars.

When she reached the counter, she flipped around, leaning against the surface as she caught her breath. She was exhausted. The night in the mountain cave felt like a lifetime ago, though it couldn't have been more than a day. She'd barely slept since Abishek had caught her in her mother's tower.

Her stomach groaned softly, and it was becoming obvious that her vitals would need addressing soon. She closed her eyes and inhaled several deep breaths, listening for any hint of Rabin searching again. When everything remained quiet, she pulled herself up to study her options.

She spied bread, fruit, and several other items on the counter. Everything was made of that same chalky material, but she hoped this strange reaction to her touch would become her savior. Reaching out, she closed her hand around a banana and nearly cried when it immediately shimmered and turned into what appeared to be an edible piece of fruit.

She did it again, transforming the bread and a jug of water. She devoured it all without hesitation. If it were poisoned or toxic, then it wouldn't matter either way. She was dead without this. Thankfully, it settled into her stomach and only made her feel better.

When she'd had her fill, she slowly moved through the house, finding a room where she transformed the bed into a soft surface. She needed to lie down for just a moment. Her body ached, and her head throbbed. Her heels were rubbed raw from the climb up the mountain. Moving as quietly as she could, she slipped off her boots and stretched her toes.

She'd have to return to the temple and get a better look at what was written at the bottom of the pool. It was the only clue she'd seen that might lead her to the fortress. She wasn't sure what she'd do if she found it. If she refused to break the seal, Rabin would be trapped in this state, and Zarya would probably never see the light of day again.

But she couldn't release an army of demons into Rahajhan, and she couldn't choose herself over everyone else.

Her face dropped into her hands as she choked on a silent sob.

Quietly, she cried, wishing Rabin were here. Together, nothing could stop them, but Abishek had known that. He'd found a way to use their love against them.

She was *afraid* of Rabin. This was so unfair. So monstrous.

She'd have to figure this out on her own. She'd find a way to get through to Rabin and find a way to break the enchantment that had corrupted their connection. She would *fix* this.

After some rest, she'd return to the temple and figure out what to do next. Tucking herself under the covers, she wondered if she could even sleep, but exhaustion weighed heavily, towing her under.

Her dreams took her to another place. She was lying on the ground, bathed in warm, glowing light. Slowly, she pushed herself up to find someone watching her from a few feet away.

She looked like a statue. Her skin was pure gold, and her hair fell in midnight waves to her knees. She wore an elaborate gold sari, sparkling with so many beads and crystals that it was nearly blinding.

"Who are you?" Zarya whispered as she got to her feet. "I... remember you..."

She'd glimpsed this woman in the tower with her mother.

"I am Loka, the God of the People," the figure answered.

Zarya's blood turned sluggish at those words.

"A god? The one my mother saw?"

Loka dipped her chin. "It was my duty to bring the visions that foretold of your coming. To share that you would be the one to bear the power that would free the vanshaj."

Loka gestured to Zarya's hands and the magic contained within them.

"I've been doing it," she said. "Or I was. I was breaking their collars, but now I'm trapped here."

Loka nodded. "The gods have noted your actions and commend your efforts." She fell silent, eyeing Zarya up and down.

"But?" she asked, sensing Loka had more to say.

"But that was not what we meant when we said you'd free them. While your magic does break the collars, you have already surmised the problem with your plan many times."

Zarya exhaled a long breath. "There are too many of them. I can't do it fast enough to stop this once and for all."

"Exactly," Loka responded. "When I spoke with your mother, I told her about you. The gods granted you a para-madhar to aid you in this quest. Never has there been anyone who needed a protector more."

Tears filled Zarya's eyes. "But Abishek turned him against me. He... broke us."

"He's in there," Loka said. "You will reach him, and you *will* need him at the end. You will need everyone."

"At the end of what?"

"The seal must be opened," Loka said. "Only your magic can do it, and that, my dear child, will free every vanshaj from their chains. It will break the enchantment on every Aazheri who was unjustly caged. It will also lift the curse we placed on the Aazheri that nullified their children's magic when they bred from outside their line."

Zarya blinked heavily at those words. "That was a curse?"

Loka nodded.

"You mean I could have a child with magic? With Rabin?"

"Perhaps," Loka answered. "It was the only way we could stop the Ashvins and their followers from spreading their evil any further."

"But if I open the seal, it will *free* the nairatta."

Loka dipped her head. "It will."

"But isn't that trading one set of problems for another?"

"You can defeat the nairatta by ending the Ashvins once and for all. The Chiranjivi will have the power working together. The twins' death will break the ties between the demons' world and ours. It will purify the magic they once tainted and send them back to the realm of shadows where they belong."

The tattoo on Zarya's chest throbbed as Loka spoke.

"But the Ashvins live inside me," she whispered.

Loka nodded. "So they do."

She didn't finish her sentence, and Zarya couldn't bring herself to ask, but the pitying look in her eyes told her everything she needed to know.

The only way to free them was for Zarya to die.

She felt a tear slip down her cheek as she mourned so many things. Her life with Rabin and Yasen and Row and all the other friends she'd made.

The future she'd never have.

The life she couldn't wait to find.

But she had committed herself to this.

She'd sworn to free the vanshaj no matter what it took.

She rubbed her shoulder and the dragon tattoo, thinking of Rabin. Always him.

Loka watched her quietly, and Zarya swallowed. "I understand."

"May luck find you. We are all praying for your success."

Then Loka disappeared in a bright flash of golden light, and

Zarya found herself lying in bed in the strange house in Taaranas.

She sat up, running a hand down her face as she looked towards the window. That same strange light filtered through the thin curtains.

She had to return to the temple. She had to open the seal and free the vanshaj and, in turn, the nairatta. Then she had to find the Chiranjivi and ask them to kill her.

She reached for her mother's necklace, her hand flattening against her chest as tears slipped down her cheeks. She would have done anything to hear her mother's words right now.

She will be the one to free them all.

She thought back to that night on Ranpur Island when those words had shifted her entire course.

She thought of the cottage and the seaside where she'd spent most of her life, wishing for a purpose. Wishing for something bigger than this life.

She never imagined where those wishes would find her.

She dropped her head, inhaling a deep breath.

She had to do this.

If she had to pay with her life, then that's what she would do.

There was no other choice.

THIRTY-EIGHT

Yasen and Row arrived in Andhera at night with the wind howling off the peaks. Their surroundings desolate and ominous.

The city was quiet, with everyone hunkered down in their homes to escape the raging storm. Yasen stared up at the sky, finding only a blanket of grey, and something about that made him nervous.

What would happen when they knocked on the king's door?

More importantly, what happened to Zarya and Rabin?

They entered the city and traversed the quiet streets, approaching the castle, where, despite the weather, numerous guards flanked the entrance.

"We come to see Raja Abishek," Row said with a bow. An older guard recognized him instantly, pressing his fist to his heart.

"Rajguru," he said with reverence before they opened the door. "It has been many years. Welcome back."

"What did they call you?" Yasen asked.

"It was the title I once carried," Row said after they passed through the entrance and into the soaring front hall of the castle. "The king's keeper of magic before he replaced me with that so-called mystic."

Sharp footsteps drew their attention to Omar, Abishek's manservant.

"Omar. Is that you?" Row asked. "It's good to see you."

He pressed his hands together and offered the man a bow.

"Rajguru," Omar said, again using the same title. "I hadn't expected to ever see you again."

"We've arrived on a matter of some importance. I'm here to see the king."

Yasen watched Omar's gaze shift imperceptibly.

"The king is not here," he said. "Nor do I know when he'll return."

"Where did he go?" Yasen asked.

Omar blinked a set of owlish eyes. "I am not at liberty to disclose that information."

"Omar, please," Row said. "It's a matter of life and death."

Omar's gaze returned to Row, and the man scanned him up and down. Then he shook his head. "I truly don't know where he went."

Yasen was inclined to believe him.

"Where are Zarya and Rabin?" he asked. "We'll see them."

Omar shook his head, and a band tightened around Yasen's ribs.

"I'm sorry, but they have also departed. They returned to Ishaan."

Now Yasen knew something was very wrong.

"What about Ekaja?"

"She is also... away."

Yasen was about to launch into a list of accusations, but Row laid a hand on his arm, his expression suggesting Yasen should cool it.

"Then, if you'd be so kind as to set us up with rooms for

tonight," Row said, addressing Omar. "We'll be on our way first thing. It seems we've wasted a trip."

Omar watched Row, his gaze sliding to Yasen before he slowly tipped his chin. "Of course. I wouldn't expect anyone to travel in this storm."

"Thank you," Row said. They followed Omar through the castle. Yasen was set up in the same room as his last visit while Row was placed across the hall. Immediately, they went to Rabin and Zarya's rooms.

They rooted through their belongings, and it was painfully obvious they hadn't left for Ishaan, but their search turned up nothing that might suggest where they'd gone.

"I don't suppose we can break into the king's room?" Yasen asked, running a hand through his hair.

Row snorted. "We'd sooner all turn into dragons, like Rabin."

"That's what I thought."

Yasen paced back and forth.

"Where can he have taken them? And why?" he asked while they discussed what to do, coming up with various theories and then dismissing them. Nothing felt right, and if they couldn't access the king's study, how could they prove any of this?

It took Yasen a moment to notice someone hovering in the doorway. He remembered her as the vanshaj woman who'd been tending to Zarya.

When Yasen met her gaze, her face crumpled into a worried expression.

"Do you know what happened?" Yasen asked, immediately crossing the room. "Please come in."

He gestured towards the divans around the fire, but the woman shook her head.

"Urvi, isn't it?" Yasen asked. He noticed Row perk up, watching them both carefully.

"Yes," she whispered.

"Urvi," Yasen said, his hand pressed to his heart. "Did you see what happened to Zarya and Rabin? Please, this is very important."

Urvi's eyes filled with tears as she nodded and then recounted the tale of Zarya searching for something in the vanshaj wing.

"Do you know what?" Row asked.

Urvi nodded. "Something about her mother."

"Her mother?" Row asked sharply. "What about her?"

"I'm not sure," Urvi said. "Her Highness was trying to find her."

Yasen looked over to note the shocked look on Row's face. "Did she?" he asked in almost a whisper.

"I don't know... I was still in the library when Lord Ravana returned," she said. "The king said he intended to reverse their Bandhan to break the seal on the darkness." She nearly choked on the last words as her hand wrapped around her throat. "Could that happen?" she asked. "The darkness is wicked. It cannot be released."

Row still appeared to be in shock, but he shook it off. "We're not sure," he said. "Did you hear anything else?"

Urvi nodded. "The mystic used his magic, and they both fainted. Then they were taken into the king's private study. That's the last I saw of them for a few days." She bit her bottom lip as a tear slipped down her cheek. "She offered to free me. She wanted to help."

Her gaze met Yasen's, and he nodded as he put the pieces together. Zarya had offered to remove her star collar, but Urvi still wore it, meaning she had refused. But the gesture had been appreciated.

"I heard screaming," she said. "And a lot of talking. I could only make out some of it. The king said they'd be helping him and that Master Ravana would be used in some way."

"For what?" Row asked, his voice low and deadly.

Urvi shook her head. "I don't know." She squared her shoulders as if gathering her courage. "Then they were taken out of the castle and put into carriages before heading for the mountains."

Yasen blinked, sorting through these various bits of information.

"The mountains," Yasen said, and Urvi nodded. "And you can't remember anything else? Any detail that might tell us where they've gone?"

She clasped her hands to her stomach. "I heard the king say something about meeting up with the mountain men when they arrived," she said. "Something about the Ashvins and the city they once ruled."

Row exhaled a sharp breath as his gaze met Yasen's. They both immediately understood. Abishek had sent them to the seal. To the place Tarin had mentioned.

"The entrance to Taaranas," Yasen said. "He knows where it is."

Row nodded. "So it would seem."

Yasen then turned to Urvi. "Thank you. You've been so much help."

Urvi's eyes filled with tears. "If there's anything I can do..."

"Keep yourself safe," Yasen said. "I have no idea what's coming."

Urvi nodded, her eyes brimming with fear.

After she left, Yasen and Row looked at one another before their gazes wandered to the window and the snow-swept peaks stretching across the horizon.

Yasen ran a hand down his face. "I guess we're going hiking."

THIRTY-NINE

Once Zarya had rested and filled her stomach, she carefully approached the window. It had been quiet for hours. Rabin could likely see everything from above, including how far the city stretched, giving him a distinct advantage.

She had to get to the temple, and the only way to do so was to venture out. She pushed every thought out of her mind except Rabin and the seal. She'd deal with the consequences of what came next later.

Steeling herself, she stepped out onto the street and peered left and right past the chalky-white buildings. She took a step, grateful when the material absorbed her footfalls rather than echoing them. Maybe if she was quiet enough, she could do this. She ventured towards the temple and surveyed the collapsed roof, praying a pile of debris hadn't blocked the pool.

Her heart thudded painfully as she scrambled up the steps and quickly ducked inside. Light flooded in from the roof's missing section, but thankfully, the glowing pool remained accessible.

Still keeping her movements quiet, she prowled over the wreckage and peered into the water. The surface was still, giving her a view of the bottom. She leaned over and squinted, but it was too far away to read clearly.

She had no choice but to swim. After slipping off her boots and socks, she placed them on the edge. Next came her sweater, leaving her only in a black top and fur-lined leathers. None of it was ideal.

She scanned the temple one more time before sinking her hand into the water's surface. It was icy cold, but she inhaled a deep breath before dipping her feet, the chill instantly creeping up her limbs.

She scooted off the edge and plunged, sinking under the water, willing her arms and legs to move. With her eyes open, she flipped over and fluttered towards the bottom. All those years living by the sea were proving useful.

She kicked as hard as she could, consciously aware of the depleting oxygen in her lungs. Thankfully, it took less time than she expected before she touched the floor. It turned out to be a map.

Tracing the lines, she tried to memorize every detail—a tunnel led from this building into mountains, twisting to the left and right before it opened to a valley, a fortress, and then a door.

She counted the turns in her head—left, left, right, left, right... 1, 2, 3. Her fingers caught on something sticking out of the bottom. A small bump on the surface. Instinctively, she pressed it, and she almost blew out the last of her air when the water started churning.

Swept up in the current, she kicked for the surface. The pool continued twisting as she kicked harder and harder. When she finally emerged into the crisp air, she realized it was draining out, and she was about to be left trapped at the bottom.

She grabbed the wall, clinging to the rocks and trying to haul herself up. The force battered against her, shoving her to the side as she attempted to cling on.

Finally, the water level dropped past her, and she dug in

with wet toes and fingers until it completely drained away. She blinked, staring down.

Realizing she would have to climb, she jammed her toes into the shallow holds and slowly inched herself up one hand over the other while her muscles quivered with effort. As she ascended, she repeated the instructions on the map to herself over and over. Maybe she could find something to write them down. Her lips moved as she whispered to herself and made her slow ascent.

Sweat dripped into her eyes from the effort, and the rough stone scraped the tips of her fingers and toes raw. She inched slowly up, and it felt like it was taking forever. Just as she was about to reach the edge, a shadow darkened the room.

She gasped as it swept past, and the telltale flap of Rabin's wings beat against the soundless atmosphere. Had he seen her, or was he only searching? She debated on her next move. Try to climb out and run? Or fall to the bottom where she'd be trapped? Could he reach her?

She heaved again, trying not to moan or grunt despite the ache in every bone of her body. Finally, she snagged the ledge and almost sobbed in relief. Slowly, she eased herself up, and just as she was about to pull herself over, the shadow returned.

She watched in horror as Rabin dropped through the ceiling, landing on the floor with a heavy thump. His red eyes glowed as he stared at her, unblinking.

"Rabin," she whispered, and his lips pulled back to reveal his sharp, deadly teeth. "Rabin! Can you hear me? It's me! Zarya! It's your wife!"

Even as she screamed, her words felt dull and muted. They *should* have echoed off the temple's high corners, but they dissipated into nothing. She'd never get through to him like this.

"Rabin, please!" she shouted, tears streaming down her cheeks. "Please hear me!"

She choked as he took a slow step and then another. His red eyes brightened, his mouth opening wider. This wasn't working.

She looked down at the pool, her gaze skirting over the map before noticing a dark sliver in the side of the wall. An opening? Was *that* the tunnel? The water had to go somewhere.

When she turned back to face Rabin, his feral expression was wholly focused, still in the hold of Kishore's twisted magic.

So, she made a decision.

With one hand, she knocked her boots over the ledge. As they thunked to the bottom, it seemed to awaken something in Rabin. He roared and *lunged*, snapping his teeth, barely missing her shoulder as she dropped off the ledge. She felt the heat of his breath and the pressure as it tugged her hair. She tumbled to the bottom, landing in a crouch and then rolling, ignoring the pain shooting up her legs.

Rabin roared as he thrust his massive head into the pool. Rocks and stone sheared from the edges, crashing down. He snapped, just barely missing her again. She scrambled to the wall and pressed her back against it, inching along the edge as Rabin tried to root her out.

Thankfully, the space was too tight for him to turn or get much leverage. He snapped again, the edge of a tooth grazing her arm and tearing a long, bloody gash. She choked on a sob and then nearly collapsed in relief as he pulled out of the well.

She lunged for her boots and dashed for the tunnel.

As she reached it, she turned for one last look at the map.

A second later, Rabin attacked again, his jaws spread wide. She leaped into the tunnel, crashing to the floor as his entire jaw smashed into the bottom of the pool, destroying the map.

She lay on the ground, breathing heavily as she watched him continue to sniff around, searching her out. His large nostrils flared. He could smell her, but he couldn't reach her. At least for now.

But she'd finally caught a lucky break. She stood on shaky legs and tugged on her socks and boots.

Rabin retreated and smashed into the floor again, aiming for the tunnel. Rocks fell around her as she tried to keep her balance. He couldn't fit down here, but given enough time, he might find a way through.

She had to keep moving and find the seal.

Rabin snarled and let out a roar that shook everything around her.

Gods, how she wished she could reach him.

She wiped at the tears coating her cheeks and blew him a kiss.

She knew he wouldn't understand, and maybe he would never know.

"I love you," she whispered. "I'm sorry we might never get to say goodbye."

Then she turned around and ran.

FORTY

After Row and Yasen acquired clothing and provisions, it didn't take long before they found themselves at the base of the mountains. Yasen scanned the peaks dusted with white as a shiver skated down his back.

"This way," Row said as they trudged down a path, their boots crunching in the snow.

Row hadn't said much since they'd left the castle. He'd asked Urvi more about Asha, and she'd led him to the spot where she'd directed Zarya days earlier.

But the tower had been empty. Asha was gone. Yasen had watched Row's face and the conflict in his eyes as he wrestled between tearing down the castle brick by brick to search for her or going after Zarya.

"You're sure about this?" Yasen asked over the howling wind.

In the end, Row opted for Zarya. He hadn't shared his reasons, but Yasen knew it hadn't been an easy choice.

Row claimed he once had contact with the mountain clans and hoped they would remember him. He also hoped they could tell him where Abishek had taken Rabin and Zarya.

"Pretty sure," Row shouted back. Then he muttered under his breath, "It's been decades, of course, but hopefully, they're still around."

They continued walking for hours as the sun disappeared and the temperature dropped. Yasen couldn't feel his fingers or toes, and the wind's incessant screams howling in his ears were enough to drive even the sanest man to the edge of reason.

Just when he didn't think he could take another step, a light appeared through the curtain of snow.

"This way!" Row shouted, the relief in his voice unmistakable. They approached a tall, wide cave, passing into what must have served as an antechamber. A large fire crackled in the center, and Yasen immediately strode over to warm his hands.

It took less than a minute before a line of men dressed in furs and leather filed out from a branching tunnel. They all held spears and swords aimed at Yasen and Row, each one turning up a vicious snarl.

Yasen and Row shared a cautious look as they slowly raised their hands to indicate they meant no harm.

"I'm here to see Catana," Row said. "We were friends a long time ago."

The mountain men regarded Row with a skeptical eye before he said something in a language that Yasen had never heard before. A moment later, their weapons lowered.

The man in front approached Row, and they spoke for another moment before he turned around and disappeared the way they'd come. The others remained, still watching but with less open hostility.

"What happened?" Yasen asked.

Row kept his focus on the men. "They're bringing Catana and believed what I told them."

"What did you tell them?"

"We're looking for the king of Andhera so I can kill him."

A beat of silence filled the cavern.

"You okay, Row?"

He turned around to face Yasen, his mouth set in a firm line. "Many years ago, I left this place because I could not support the lengths Raja Abishek would go to protect his power. He was becoming a tyrant, blind to his own ambition. And I didn't even know the half of it. He never told me he had six anchors, and I can't begin to imagine what else he was hiding.

"I could have let it go. I did—I gave him little thought for many years. I moved on with my life and found other ways to occupy my time. Sometimes, I missed this place, but it was for the best."

He paused as he looked around the cavern and the shadows dancing along the surface.

"But then overnight, I became a father and swore to protect a little girl with my life. I spent so many years living in fear for her safety. She hated me for it. She hated being caged to that shoreline, and who could blame her? She wanted to live. She wanted to see the world and all it had to offer. And all I *could* offer her were her beloved books. But it wasn't enough. Sometimes, I wondered if reading about everything she was missing only made it worse.

"But then, one day, I couldn't contain her any longer. The time had come. I had known it from the very beginning. I couldn't keep her there forever. I didn't know the rest of the prophecy, but I already knew that if she were indeed the bearer of this rare gift, then there was little chance our quiet life by the sea was all that awaited her."

He stared into the fire, his expression pensive.

"But now he's taken her, and I don't know why exactly, but I will find out, and then I will do what I should have done all those years ago. I will repay him for everything she missed and for what he did to the woman I love."

Row fell silent, a grim set to his features. A movement at the cavern's edge drew their attention to a mountain man wearing even more furs and leather than the others.

"Catana," Row said, striding over and bowing at the waist. "I'm sorry to barge in on you like this, but I need your help."

"I heard everything," Catana said, raising a hand. "I know where they are."

FORTY-ONE

Zarya barreled down the tunnel lined with burning torches. Anytime her hand touched the chalky white surface, it transformed into grey stone. She left herself a trail of breadcrumbs on the off chance she might find her way back.

If there was such a thing as *back* from whatever awaited her at the end. She continued repeating the memorized instructions, winding through the pathways and taking a left and a right at each fork, but she was scared and tired and hungry, and the directions jumbled in her head. As she ran, Rabin's ferocious roars shook the ground as he fought against the stone, desperately trying to reach her.

She stopped and looked back, wondering if she was on the right path.

Was that supposed to be left at the last fork? Or right? Her stomach grumbled, reminding her that a clock was ticking over her head. She needed water.

She stumbled as the ground shook again, using her hands to catch herself. Her palms scraped open with a wince. The floor transformed under her, revealing a patch of mosaic tiles carefully laid out in intricate patterns. She frowned as she realized this tunnel had been man-made. Was this a clue? She crawled on her hands and knees, watching the ground shift.

When she reached a fork with several tunnels branching off in various directions, she headed left and watched as the floor turned to stone. She stopped and backed up, turning in another direction. Again, she was met with blank stone.

Another try; she chose the tunnel on the far right. This path shifted into another field of colorful mosaic tiles. She made a noise of surprise. This had to be a sign. This had to be right.

She leaped up and headed down the tunnel, periodically reaching down to touch the floor to ensure she was still on the right path. Every so often, she'd stumble when the mountain shook with the force of Rabin's roars filtering through layers of stone.

She wanted to scream and cry. She wanted to reach him so badly. She'd give anything to break through the enchantment.

Another fork had her turning left as she revealed more of the tiled floor.

Finally, she entered a massive round room with a dozen arches leading in different directions. The ceiling reached high overhead, where small openings cut into the surface, let in beams of that mysterious light, and offered a view of Amrita's roots.

She pressed a hand to her chest to settle the thrashing of her heart and her panicked breaths. She remembered this room from the map. At least she was headed in the right direction.

Her memory suggested the path continued somewhere on the other side of the chamber, so she crossed the floor, keeping light on her feet.

It didn't take long before a shadow swept over the room. Rabin had seen her. Should she stop or run? What would draw his attention?

Another pass of shadow had her stalling in her tracks. He

flew away, and she tracked his movements using only the sound of his wings.

Then she started running.

With her legs and arms pumping, she barreled across the chamber. She was about halfway to the end when a roar came from above, and Rabin crashed through the ceiling in a shower of stones and bricks. She screamed and covered her head, weaving back and forth. When she felt the warmth of his moist breath on her neck, she nearly tripped.

She swerved as a giant boulder dropped in her path and she went flying, arcing through the air for several feet. She landed, skidding against the floor as it tore at her knees and elbows.

All she could focus on was the sound of Rabin's snarls and the crush of falling stone. She looked up as a giant chunk plummeted from above. She screamed again, rolling over as it landed inches from her head.

She lay on the ground with her heart nearly pumping through her chest. But she couldn't stop.

Pushing up, she raced for a tunnel as her foot caught on a piece of debris. She tripped and stumbled, losing her momentum. After recovering, she started running as Rabin roared again. Then came the swipe of his claws tearing across her back. It *burned*. She screamed. The sound filled with agony.

She stumbled again, crashing into a fallen piece of the roof before recovering and doing her best to ignore the pain ripping through her body. Weaving back and forth to avoid the obstacles in her path, she finally reached a tunnel where she collapsed to her hands and knees and watched as the floor turned into... stone.

Fuck. She'd chosen the wrong one.

Her vision blurred, her head spun, and she stared between her hands for several seconds trying to orient herself. It felt like she was going to pass out. Then a crash roused her back into the moment.

Rallying her strength, she stood and dashed for the next tunnel. Rabin was fighting through the rubble, trying to reach her, and he lunged, snapping his massive jaw. She flattened herself to the wall, screaming as his teeth came so close she could see the tiny imperfections marring their surface.

When he reared back to take another bite, she ducked and collapsed into the next tunnel. As her hands pressed to the floor, it transformed into more mosaic tiles, and she almost fainted again. This time with relief.

The cavern shook as Rabin slammed into the wall, causing her surroundings to shake and more rocks and debris to fall. If she wasn't careful, he might trap her inside.

She sucked in three deep breaths. Her back felt like it was on fire, and the pain was making the edges of her vision blur.

But she gathered her flagging strength, pushing up on her feet. With each movement, she could feel the gush of her blood soaking her shirt and pants.

Rabin crashed into the wall again as the doorway began to crumble.

Limping away, she wove through the dark tunnels while his roars grew more and more distant. Occasionally, she reached down as her back screamed with agony to ensure she was still heading in the right direction. When the sound of Rabin's roars dissipated, she allowed herself to slow down.

Winding deeper and deeper into the tunnel, she came upon a soaring underground cavern. In the center was a large, crystal-blue pool, reaching to the edges save the small rocky beach where she stood.

Coming to a stop, she planted her hands on her knees and inhaled ragged breaths, wondering if it was safe to drink.

Her stomach rumbled as she realized how many hours it had been since she'd eaten. Slowly, she approached and touched the surface. It rippled softly, making barely a sound. At the far end of the cavern, she could see where the path continued. Approaching the shallow edge, she crouched down with a groan and pressed her hand to the bottom of the pool.

She was only partially surprised when the floor transformed into the same field of colorful tiles that had become her signpost. Exhaling a weary breath, she dropped her head and willed her pulse to settle.

Her entire back was both throbbing and numb. She peered over her shoulder, trying to gauge the damage Rabin had caused. All she could tell was that it fucking hurt. She needed bandages, and she needed to clean herself up.

Tentatively and with great difficulty, she stripped out of her clothing. Every moment ached, sending fire across her back. Teeth gritted, she dipped a toe into the pool. Creeping forward, she scooped up a handful of water and sipped it up.

It slipped down her throat, and she drank her fill before slowly submerging herself beneath the surface. She couldn't help squeaking when her wounds hit the water as another wave of intense agony pulsated over her skin. Hissing through her teeth, she swished back and forth, attempting to clean off the blood and dirt.

Once done, she did her best to wash her clothing before laying it all out to dry. As she exited the pool, gooseflesh rose on her skin. She rubbed her arms, her teeth chattering. She'd give anything for a warm blanket right now.

Instead, she found a soft patch of moss that would have to suffice. She dropped to her knees and crawled over it, lying on her stomach to give her back a chance to breathe.

Exhaustion quickly overcame her, and she drifted off into a troubled sleep.

FORTY-TWO

Rabin's mind was a sinking cavern of dark halls and corners. He couldn't seem to focus. All he could see was red. Rage and hate and anger. He wanted to kill and rip and shred.

He wanted *her*.

He wanted to sink his teeth into her flesh and taste her blood. He wanted to tear her apart piece by piece and then *crunch* through her bones.

Her.

He *knew* her. He knew he was supposed to protect her and that something tied them together. He recognized her voice and the way she smelled. He could sense her buried somewhere in the depths of his subconscious. He knew something was off.

He was supposed to *protect* her, guard her with his life.

But he wanted death.

His mind was tormented by dark shadows and screaming voices.

She was the object of his rage, and the only way to end it would be to end himself. Somewhere in the spiral of his tumbling thoughts, he knew this.

Rabin bellowed out a roar so raw it made his throat hurt.

He'd lost her. He'd battered himself bloody trying to break into the tunnel, but it was too much. She'd escaped, and deep down, that made him feel something almost like relief.

But he would hunt her again.

He'd resist it. He'd tried to resist the *urge* to go after her. He'd thrown himself against the cavern walls for hours, attempting to snap himself out of his crippling *rage*, but it was no use. Something kept him tied to her. Something kept calling her. To seek her out. To bite and tear and shred.

Exhausted from hunting, he flopped onto the ground, his head lying between his claws. He inhaled deeply, his hot breath kicking up a cloud of dust with every powerful gust.

The warring thoughts in his mind made his head hurt and his vision blur. His eyes drifted shut as he tried to find peace. He saw something in the layers of his mind—something bright and shiny—something he knew he should want but couldn't reach.

He shifted as he tried to get closer, reaching for it.

Her.

He knew it was her. He didn't know how, but he was sure she was calling to him. Why would she call to him when he'd tried to hurt her? Not tried. He *had* hurt her. He noted the blood on his claws, congealed with bits of flesh and clothing.

Slowly, he dragged his arm closer before his forked tongue lashed out, licking the tips of his talons.

The taste filled his head, and a memory returned—an electric flavor layered with shadows, light, and *happiness*. That was the only way he could describe it, whatever this was.

Whoever she was—she was happiness.

But he wanted her dead.

Why?

Why couldn't he remember?

FORTY-THREE

Catana led Yasen and Row up the winding mountain through the snow and wind and cold. Yasen hated every minute of it. He wanted to be back in Ishaan with Miraan, waking up in bed with sunlight on their skin.

He wanted to bask in a spring breeze and inhale the scent of fresh leaves and flowers. Instead, he was cold and shivering, and his toes were seconds from snapping off.

But this was for Zarya. He'd promised to follow her anywhere, and no one was more surprised than him to discover he'd truly meant it from the bottom of his skeptical heart.

Finally, after climbing for what felt like forever, they found themselves on a level path and a plateau surrounded by soaring peaks. Ahead was a bridge disappearing into nothing. Yasen blinked as dread pooled in his gut. Was this where they were headed, and what the fuck was that?

To their left sat a cave opening.

Catana ducked inside while Row and Yasen studied the bridge swinging in the wind.

"Is that where we're going?" Yasen asked.

Row huffed out a breath. "I think so."

Then he turned and also entered the cave.

Yasen followed him a moment later to find Catana starting a fire. The space was tiny, barely large enough to accommodate the three of them.

Once the fire was crackling, Yasen squatted before it, holding out his hands for warmth. Row stood at the doorway, quietly conferring with Catana before the mountain man shook his hand, clapped him on the back, and then disappeared, presumably to return home.

"What now?" Yasen asked. "How much of a lead do they have?"

"A day at most, according to Catana."

"Why did he help Abishek? I thought the clans didn't trust him."

Row shook his head. "Abishek and the mountain clans have never seen eye to eye on much. Riches are buried in these mountains, and it's always been a sore spot for the king. Many years ago, he sent his army to destroy the clans so that he might have free access to the minerals and jewels. It was a massacre. I tried to talk him out of it, but he wouldn't be swayed.

"Eventually, I trekked out to meet with the clans myself. Catana and I talked for hours, and I returned to Abishek with an offer of truce. They'd stay out of each other's way, and the clans would pay a tax for the use of Abishek's resources."

Row stared at the fire as some long-buried memory passed behind his eyes. "I should have left him right then, but I foolishly believed I could keep him in check." He looked up at Yasen. "Abishek threatened to break the peace of their accord and finish the mountain clans off for good if they wouldn't lead him to this spot."

Yasen blew out a long breath as he ran his hand through his hair. "Well, I guess I can't blame them for that."

Row shook his head.

"So, what happened when they got here?" Yasen asked.

"Catana remained behind to watch," Row said before sharing a story about Abishek and his mystic forcing Rabin into his dragon form while telling Zarya she had to find and open the seal as Yasen listened in horror.

Once Row was done speaking, they both fell silent.

"So, we're crossing a bridge hanging in the middle of nothing to enter some ancient city full of evil magic?"

Row nodded. "So it would seem."

"Fabulous."

"I can only presume Abishek followed Zarya and Rabin once he assumed she was close to what he wanted."

"Fucker," Yasen grumbled under his breath as Row made a sound of agreement. "So, we're going in," he added. "To help Rabin and Zarya and then close up the seal once and for all."

"I don't think we have any other choice," Row answered. "We have to get to Zarya."

The fire crackled, and the wind howled outside as they stared at the flames, lost in their thoughts.

"You don't have to come," Row said a moment later, and Yasen looked up. "I'll go after her. You can return to Ishaan."

Yasen shook his head. "Absolutely not. You need my help."

Row nodded, and Yasen wondered if he caught a hint of respect in the depths of the old warrior's eyes.

"Very well. Then I don't think we should waste any time. Eat something, and we'll get moving."

Once they were done, they packed up their belongings and headed back into the snow. Row and Yasen stared at the bridge, swinging in the wind.

"Ready?" Row asked, and Yasen nodded.

With a swallow, he approached the bridge and laid a tentative foot on the planks. It felt like it would collapse with a breath, but Zarya had managed it. And he would, too.

He stepped onto the bridge, clinging to the rope as it swung under his weight—another step and then another as he neared the end.

"I'm coming, Zee," he whispered. "I'm bringing you home."

And then... the magic swallowed him up.

FORTY-FOUR

Zarya drifted in and out of a troubled sleep as she shivered in the cold cavern. Her back ached, and her nightmares plagued her dreams. She saw her mother huddled in the corner of her tower while Loka stood over her, giving Zarya a sad smile.

She saw the Ashvins and Taaranas as it once stood in all its glory. She saw their temple and the people who worshiped them, offering benedictions as they fell to their knees.

She saw their magic—glittering stars against black night. A door opening high in the mountains. The demons entered, and shadows and darkness swept over the land.

She moaned as she shifted against the moss. Part of her wanted to wake up, but part of her wanted to remain inside the cocoon of her dreams forever.

A rush of warm air coasted over her chilled skin as she exhaled a sigh of relief.

It pulled her eyes open to reveal a violet sky strewn with a river of stars so thick, it felt like she could scoop them up and tuck them into her pocket.

Her mouth parted on a surprised exhale as a tear slipped down her cheek.

The forest.

She pushed herself up into a seated position as the wounds on her back pulled, causing her to wince. At least she'd stopped shivering, but she couldn't say much else for her state. The moon hung low and large, and the leafy trees waved softly in the breeze.

With some difficulty, she forced her aching body to her feet. Still naked, the grass tickled her soles. She slowly spun in a circle, seeking out the dark corners, with her breath held in anticipation.

Was he here, too? Had the enchantment finally broken?

Everything remained still and silent for several long minutes, but she wouldn't give up hope. She called for him in her mind, trying to reach for him. He had to be close. Why else would she be here?

When she noticed a shift deep in the shadows, her breath hitched.

A moment later, moonlight revealed a sliver of a face she knew and loved with every piece of her heart.

Rabin emerged from the darkness, also naked, his brown skin gleaming in the starlight. He kept his head down as she watched him approach, her gaze sliding over the contours of his shoulders and chest and stomach and then to his erect cock, bobbing as he walked, the tip shining with the hint of his arousal.

As he drew closer, he lifted his face, and she inhaled sharply at the sight of his glowing red eyes.

He was here physically, but where was he in his mind?

"Rabin," she whispered. "Are you there?"

He blinked, watching her carefully, like a predator assessing a weaker opponent. She studied him with her breath held, wondering if she should run. Wondering if there was anywhere she *could* run.

A growl rumbled in his chest before he prowled towards her

on sure steps. His pace never slowed, and she found herself retreating, having no idea what to expect. Her breath squeaked when she came into contact with the trunk of a wide tree, the wounds in her back causing her to whimper.

He stopped at the sound, his gaze assessing and his head cocking with a feline sort of grace. Wincing at the ache, she clung to the bark as he drew closer, looming over her and planting his hands on either side of her head.

"Rabin?" she whispered as he stared down, his eyes glowing brightly as he perused her from head to toe. She felt that look as it touched her face and her throat. Her breasts and her stomach, then dragging lower as a growl rumbled in his chest.

Without warning, he reached out to grip her arm and flipped her around so her stomach was against the tree. He pressed himself against her, and she sighed at the familiar warmth of his big body. Gods, how she'd missed him.

He gathered her hair in his hand and pushed it over her shoulder, exposing her back.

She tried to contain her agonized moans as his hand drifted over her shoulder and then ghosted over her wounds. She gritted her teeth as her skin burned from his touch before he placed his hand flat against her back. She gasped as a tear escaped her eye, and then *heat* seared her skin, almost too hot to bear.

Relief came next as she felt the wounds begin to knit together.

The Bandhan.

Kishore couldn't break their bond. Their connection had been the will of the gods. No mere mystic could shatter destiny.

She felt the dragon on her shoulder pulse as Rabin healed her wounds. Her skin flushed hot, and the cuts sealed up until the pain melted away. She tasted the salt of her tears on her lips as her head tipped against the tree while she sobbed from relief.

Rabin moved, crushing his body against hers. He folded

himself so that he was covering every inch of her skin before his nose buried into the curve of her throat, and he took a long, shuddering breath.

"Rabin?" she whispered. "Are you there?"

She kept trying to reach him. Kept trying to call to him in her mind.

He flipped her around so she faced him again.

She couldn't help the way her thighs flexed as he licked his lips, his fiery gaze hungry with desire. He lifted a hand as smoke swirled around his fingers, weaving back and forth. A moment later, they transformed into a set of sharp dragon claws.

His gaze met hers, and she exhaled a short gasp. What was happening?

Slowly, he reached out, the tip of a claw touching her cheek and then carefully dragging lower. Her breath pushed out in tight gulps as he trailed his nail over her throat and collarbone and down one breast.

She whimpered as he scraped over a nipple, his talons coming together to gently pinch it with just enough sharpness to send a straight shot of heat between her thighs.

He drifted lower over her stomach and stopped right below her navel. She looked down, her gaze snagging on his bobbing cock covered in veins—the tip swollen and purple, begging for release.

"Rabin," she said again, her voice barely a whisper as he dragged his hand lower. He knocked her ankle with his foot, forcing her to spread her legs. His burning red gaze found hers again, but she wasn't afraid. He was there, buried somewhere inside the enchantment.

She let out a sharp breath as his hand moved lower, the pointed tip of his nail grazing her clit. She gasped and her stomach clenched when he did it again. The touch was feather-erlight, yet it felt like she was being turned inside out.

Slowly, he continued exploring her body, using his sharp

talons as he scraped her breasts and stomach, leaving red streaks that didn't break the skin. She pressed against the tree, no longer in pain—all she could feel was the hollow ache between her legs.

He snarled, his lip curling up as he gripped the tree behind her head. Then, without warning, he wrapped his other hand around her leg and hoisted her up. He thrust against her, his hard cock rubbing her clit to the point of bruising. She clung to his shoulders as he rutted against her, and then, without warning, he slammed in.

Her back arched as she cried out, waves of pleasure rolling through her limbs. He fucked her with abandon, their flesh slapping and their moans and growls tangling in the clearing.

He filled her up, stretching her, hitting so deep that she whimpered with every thrust.

"Rabin," she practically sobbed. "I feel you. I see you."

She clung to him as he continued pounding into her. His dragon claws melted away as he grabbed her breast, pinching her nipple, and then dipped his head and sunk his teeth into her throat. She cried out as the magic of his bite filtered into her blood, her release tightening in her stomach.

He churned his hips over and over as sweat coated their bodies, and her cries grew more frantic. He squeezed her ass as he thrust again, then they both came together in a flash of bright blinding light and sparks.

Her nails dug into his shoulders as her release crashed over her, twisting her from the inside, sending waves of tingling sensation straight to the tips of her fingers and toes.

He continued pumping, wringing out his release as she felt his warmth spill between them. With a growling shudder, he pulled up to meet her gaze.

She recognized him buried in the depths of his glowing red eyes.

"Come back to me," she whispered.

. . .

Zarya's eyes opened a moment later, and she found herself lying on her stomach in the chalky white cavern. She shivered from the cold air and wondered if it had all been a vivid dream.

She rolled over to notice a throbbing ache between her legs along with the faint red marks Rabin had left on her skin.

Not a dream.

She'd nearly reached him there. She'd nearly found him.

That had been real, and maybe that meant something.

Yasen and Row entered Taaranas to an eerie silence. They shared a worried look. A chill skated down Yasen's back as he took in the strange white buildings and the complete stillness.

"Is this it?" he asked as he turned around slowly, searching for threats or clues.

"It looks like the city I've seen in drawings," Row answered. "But this..."

"Is dead," Yasen finished.

Row nodded as they turned to face the massive temple standing at the end of the road with a glittering star hovering over it. It had obviously stretched to the sky until something had destroyed the roof.

"I suppose that's probably where we're headed," Yasen said.

Row grunted something that sounded like agreement as they searched their surroundings again. Looking up, Yasen noted thousands of shimmering white roots clamoring across the ceiling peppered with tiny black marks of rot. He looked back at the city and the wisps of black smoke curling around the windows and buildings.

"What do you think happened there?" Yasen asked, pointing towards the street where a patch of grey stone had broken up the endless stretch of white.

Row shook his head. "Maybe it has something to do with Zarya."

The way he said it didn't make it sound like a good thing.

After drawing their weapons, they marched towards the temple, up the steps, and through the high doorway. Inside, they found a mess. Large stones covered the floor, and dust hung in the air.

They approached the largest pile sitting in the center.

Yasen climbed on top to find himself looking down into an empty well.

"It looks like this was a pool," he said. "And someone cleared this all away to enter."

Row nodded as he ascended the rubble. "This must be the way they went."

Yasen peered down. "Only one way to find out."

He scrambled down the wreckage and peered into the well. Broken stone filled the hollow, and someone had cleared it to reveal a narrow path.

Yasen took a step and lightly dropped to the bottom in a crouch.

With any luck, they'd catch up to Zarya soon.

And with even more luck, maybe they'd bring her home.

FORTY-FIVE

When Zarya awoke again, it was to the sound of banging. Her eyes fluttered open as she blinked away the haze of sleep. The cavern was... vibrating?

She shook her head, trying to clear her mind as she thought of Rabin and the forest. She twisted her shoulders, relieved to find she could move without pain. She stretched her hand across her skin, feeling the ridges of remaining scar tissue.

He'd *healed* her. He'd overcome whatever Kishore had done to the bond and helped her so she could carry on. Another thumping crash sounded in the distance, rousing her from the floor. She checked on her clothing to find it was still damp, but it would have to do.

Another crash and bang echoed in the silence, and she cocked her head, listening.

Despite what they'd shared last night, Rabin was still trying to get to her.

She folded up her clothing with her boots, tucking everything into a bundle, and entered the pool. Holding the ball over her head, she did her best to kick across the water, attempting to keep everything as dry as possible.

Thankfully, the water was shallow enough to touch the bottom with her tiptoes most of the way. By the time she reached the other side, her shoulders and back were screaming. She would probably have died in this cold cavern without Rabin's help.

She heaved her bundle onto the bank and climbed onto the ledge. Throughout it, she could hear crashes in the distance.

She shook off the water and struggled into her damp clothing. Thankfully, her boots were dry, which would make running easier. If her memory of the map was correct, she would soon arrive at the fortress guarding the trigger that would open the seal.

She tried not to think too hard about what lay ahead.

She only wished she could warn everyone about the horror coming their way.

Suddenly, her chest constricted with the knowledge that once she was done here, she'd find the Chiranjivi and convince them to kill her. When she died, Rabin would, too. This is what she'd been afraid of. This is what he'd been so certain he could handle.

He would try to talk her out of it—not for his life, but for hers. She already knew that. He would beg her not to do it, but how could they fight off an army of demons on their own? What choice did she have?

Maybe the bond could save them... he'd brought her back from near death once.

She shook the thought aside because near death wouldn't be enough.

Could their bond overcome a *true* death?

It seemed impossible.

But for Rabin to even try, he'd first have to break out of Kishore's curse.

She touched the ground and watched the surface ripple to reveal the colorful tiles.

A deep sense of premonition told her this was the end.

She felt it calling to her. Reaching out and begging her to find it.

Another rumble shook the cavern, and she focused ahead, picking up her pace as she ran through the tunnel.

Knowing it was close, she wanted to... get this over with. Waiting would only delay the inevitable.

The temperature began to climb as the path sloped up. She slowed as sweat dripped down her forehead and into her eyes. After wiping it away with the back of her arm, she noticed a bright glow at the end of the tunnel.

Slowly, she approached, one hand pressed against the wall as chalky white turned to grey stone. At the end of the tunnel, she found a road leading her into another high cavern. In the distance, a massive fortress stood surrounded by a high fence.

Everything was made of the same white material, and more of Amrita's roots crowned the roof soaring above her shimmering with a riot of rainbow colors, as if her magic were struggling to contain the evil trying to escape.

This was it.

On careful steps, she walked down the road, one foot in front of the other, while the never-ending silence sent a chill down her back.

She approached a tall gate standing many stories over her head. She looked up to another star—this one rendered into glittering black—hovering over the fortress, spinning slowly in the air. She swallowed thickly.

Crouching down, she placed her hand on the ground and watched as white gave way to more colorful tiles, only this time, the transformation didn't stop. It rippled, spreading out and climbing across the floor, up the gates, and over the fortress.

A minute later, she stood before silver gates and black stone looming over her like a demon.

Licking her dry lips, she pressed a hand to the gate. It gave under her touch, opening on silent hinges. She inhaled a fortifying breath and then *pushed*. A stone path led to the entrance, and it took all her willpower to keep moving.

The air echoed with each step as she slowly approached.

Tall open arches framed the entrance, and she passed into a hollow space of rough black stone. The walls stretched for what felt like miles, and her breath condensed in soft puffs of white.

A pillar stretching to the ceiling stood at the far end surrounded by swirls of black smoke.

The seal.

And the magic leaking out.

As she moved closer, her mouth parted with a small gasp. She could feel the power shimmering from the seal, the darkness pressing in on her from every side, and that same voice calling her.

She remembered this feeling. In the swamps when the darkness had spoken to her. When Dhawan had nearly convinced her to embrace it. She'd rejected the sinister side of darkness then, and she would do it again. There would be no glory in accepting this fate. There would only be death and destruction. There would be only the loss of herself and everything she stood for. She'd rather be dead.

The darkness wasn't inherently evil, but the Ashvins and the nairatta had poisoned it.

She didn't realize she was crying until she touched her cheek to find the tips of her fingers were wet.

Continuing her journey across the cavernous space on careful steps, she became lightheaded from holding her breath. Finally, she stood before the seal. The material was smooth and featureless, except for an etched image of a flower with six petals, each decorated with the essence of the six anchors.

Just like the one Rabin wore on his back.

Abishek must have shown it to him, and Rabin had wanted to honor his mentor.

She stared at it, contemplating so many things.

Her father's lies. The mistakes she'd made.

But this moment had been inevitable. The king didn't know that breaking the seal would free the vanshaj *and* break the curse on the Aazheri. This would give every side something while taking so much away.

She heard Loka telling her this was her only choice. She heard her mother's voice floating from the stone the night her entire course changed.

She will be the one to free them all.

She reached for the pillar, her hand hovering an inch away.

Her heart thundered in her chest, and her body trembled.

Could she do this? Could she unleash a scourge upon everyone?

A shadow swept over the room, and a heavy thump shook the ground.

She spun around to find Rabin standing in the archway, staring at her with his glowing red eyes.

They narrowed on her as he took a step, huffing as he approached.

"Rabin," she whispered. "You'll soon be free of this. I hope."

Then she turned around, inhaled deeply, and slammed her hand against the pillar, calling on her nightfire. Her anchors spun, gathering in the center before a thick ribbon of magic blasted from her hand, channeling into the pillar in waves of power.

Magic as dark as night, sparkling with a million stars.

Tears ran down her cheek as the stone absorbed her nightfire bit by bit. She held on, waiting for some kind of signal. The pillar began to glow around the edges with silver light.

Slowly, it grew brighter and brighter until her magic cut off. This was it. Kishore had said all magic in Taaranas would stop when the seal was opening. It would free the vanshaj, break the mystic's enchantment on Rabin, and...

She took a step back as the pillar became a beacon of glowing white light. Widening her stance, preparing for what came next, she felt the hairs on her head rising from static energy as the air around her vibrated.

A high-pitched noise filled her ears, and then... the seal shattered, exploding in a shower of silver radiance. The floor opened up, revealing a dark hole. She heard voices. Chanting. The sound of iron and boots striking the earth.

With a gasp, she stumbled back, barely catching herself as clouds of black smoke billowed up from another world.

She'd known it was coming, but nothing could prepare her for the horror of watching swirls of shadow transform into the demon army that had lived in her dreams for months. They screamed and wailed, the sound inhuman as they flowed from the seal in a rush of fire and fury.

She watched hundreds of them—thousands of them— emerge and enter a shimmering portal that opened in the wall as they approached. They were headed for Rahajhan. She stared up, imagining everyone at home, hoping this had worked. That the vanshaj were free and that everyone could hold on long enough for her to finish the rest.

As more and more demons flowed out of the seal and entered the portal, she felt her heart crack beneath her ribs.

It was then she remembered Rabin.

She spun around to check that he'd returned to his rakshasa form but instead of Rabin, she was greeted with three familiar figures standing in the doorway.

Her father stood flanked by Kishore and Ekaja while Rabin lay in a crumpled heap on the floor.

Abishek lifted a hand and blasted out a beam of fire, striking her in the chest before she went flying, and everything went dark.

FORTY-SIX

"No, you fucking don't!" Yasen screamed as he ran for Abishek, his sword already drawn.

They'd caught Zarya's trail, picking up the evidence of her route, assuming she was responsible for those patches of colorful tile. Yasen and Row had run as fast as they could, trying to catch up.

Abishek had followed her, too.

They entered the fortress just as Zarya broke the seal, and they watched as thousands of nairatta flowed from the earth and entered a shimmering portal.

Something told Yasen they were headed for Rahajhan. The demons had returned to sweep over the land like they'd done a thousand years ago. Why had she done it? She must have a good reason, but what?

Then she'd turned around, and Yasen's heart stopped when Abishek hit her with a blast of fire. She flew several feet, landing on the stones, her body going limp.

Yasen was going to kill him.

Except Row obviously had the same idea.

He rushed past Yasen with a snarl and barreled for Abishek,

knocking him in the back with his shoulder. The king went flying, landing on his hands and knees with a surprised cry.

Yasen took the opportunity to seize the mystic, wrapping an arm across his chest and pressing a dagger to his throat. He was much smaller than Yasen, fine-boned, and more of a thinker than a fighter.

"Don't fucking move, or you're dead," Yasen hissed in his ear, causing the mystic to fall still. "I'll snap your neck before you can blink."

That left only the army commander to deal with. She could probably take them all one-handed, but the uncertainty in her expression had Yasen wondering which side she was actually on. Her gaze kept finding Rabin, who lay passed out on the floor, his chest rising and falling.

When their gazes caught, she raised her hands in a gesture of surrender while training a watchful eye on the king. Row now stood over a prostrate Abishek, his sword in one hand and his eyes brimming with fire.

"Turn over," Row ordered, pressing the tip of his blade into the back of the king's skull. As he began to roll, Row stamped his foot into Abishek's ribs and *shoved* him onto his back. "What have you done!"

With the mystic in his hold, Yasen watched Zarya, who lay crumpled in a heap, her dark hair covering her face. Was she breathing? Gods, why was he stuck holding onto this windbag?

"Unhand me!" the mystic declared, trying to sound authoritative, but it only came out petulant.

Yasen considered his options. Zarya needed him, and he had no obligation to play the good guy in this situation. These assholes had started this. So, he grabbed the mystic's chin in one hand and the top of his head in the other and neatly snapped the mystic's neck with a crack. He dropped to Yasen's feet, sinking in a heap.

Yasen blew out a breath and studied the mystic's limp body

before looking up to meet Ekaja's slack-jawed expression. A moment later, her mouth snapped shut, and she nodded.

Yasen wasted no more time, crossing the cavern to reach Zarya. He rolled her over to feel for her pulse. When he detected nothing, he immediately laid her down and began chest compressions while blowing air into her mouth. From the corner of his eye, he watched Row keep his blade pointed at the king while he struggled to his feet.

"Zee! Don't you dare fucking die on me!" Yasen snarled as he tried to get her heart started. Sweat dripped down his forehead as he worked, and he was trying very hard not to cry. Zarya would mock him until the end of time.

No one was taking her away.

Suddenly, a hand landed on his shoulder and shoved him aside.

"Move," Rabin snarled. "I'll take care of this."

He looked like hell. He was all scraped up, his clothes ragged, his hair a mess, and dark circles ringed his eyes. What the fuck had happened to them?

Rabin sank to his knees and stretched across Zarya, burying his face in the curve of her throat. Yasen was about to protest so he could continue first aid, but Zarya began to glow, her skin shimmering as coppery beams of magic swirled around them both.

He remembered Zarya explaining that Rabin could bring her back to life as her paramadhar. Rabin pulled up, kissing Zarya's slack mouth and eyelids, whispering as he clutched her hand and ordered her to wake up.

Row and Abishek were now circling one another, firing magic around the room.

"You think you can stop me?" Abishek hissed. They both reacted, attacking with blasts of fire. They ducked, missing each other's strikes before they collided with opposite walls, sending a shower of stones raining down.

They kept trading blows as magic ricocheted off the corners, and Yasen moved in front of Zarya and Rabin, hoping to protect them from an errant blast of magic.

Ekaja watched Row and the king before her gaze again met Yasen's. Another blast of magic struck high on the wall, sending more stones showering to the floor.

She quickly made her way around the perimeter and waved her hand. Yasen could now see the faintest outline of a barrier surrounding them. Rabin was still holding Zarya, whispering to her.

Row's cold laugh drew Yasen's attention back to where Row and Abishek were still trying to kill each other. "Where is your sixth anchor?" he demanded. "Why aren't you fighting harder?" He flung out a hand, striking Abishek in the shoulder.

The king retaliated with an arrow of fire, but Row ducked at the last moment.

"You were lying, weren't you?" Row accused. "To Rabin? To Zarya? To make yourself seem more powerful so they wouldn't suspect what you wanted?"

Yasen watched Abishek's face pale as he took another step and flung out another flare of magic. He noticed the king limping and favoring his right arm.

"I knew it," Row shouted. "You've never been able to touch the darkness. I would have *known*."

Abishek scowled, shuffling back as Row advanced with his sword aimed at his heart.

"I should have been the strongest!" Abishek shouted, his voice cracking. "I was born for this."

"I knew Asha was right!" Row screamed. "I knew she didn't lie to me. You *were* the strongest. You've extracted astonishing feats from your power. Things people could only dream of. You are talented by all measures, but it was never enough. All of this because you've always been so fucking insecure!"

They continued circling while Yasen kept one eye on Zarya

and Rabin. Whatever he was doing was working because her chest was rising, and he heard her groan.

"That's it," Yasen whispered in encouragement while Rabin focused on Zarya, his attention never wavering. As Zarya's chest rose and fell in a steady rhythm, Yasen's own heart began to beat normally again.

While the fight continued, Ekaja stood over them, her fists bunched as she looked between Rabin and her king. It seemed like she couldn't decide whether to intervene or stay out of it.

Row and Abishek were arguing, blaming one another for a litany of hurts and mistakes they shared over the years. Row's eyes burned with anger and fire as they traded blows, both vying for an upper hand.

Abishek only had five anchors, and Row was one of the Chiranjivi, a role chosen by the gods. With Yasen's limited knowledge of magic, he wasn't sure who had the advantage, but he was praying it was Row.

A blast of air had Row flying back, tumbling end over end before he crashed into the wall with a thump. Yasen tensed, wondering if he should help, but something told him this was a fight that had been brewing for a very long time.

Row coughed as he tried to catch his breath, rolling over to face the king. Abishek's manic grin sent a chill skating down Yasen's back. He strode over with his hand outstretched, magic flashing at his fingertips.

The king raised an arm as a ball of fire formed in his palm. He hurled it, but Row flung out a bolt of shadow, striking Abishek in the stomach. The king was knocked off his feet as Row stood up, a hint of bewilderment in his eyes.

Yasen blinked. Had Row just used the sixth anchor? It looked just like Zarya's magic.

"Why?" Row shouted, recovering from his shock. "Why would you kill her? All she ever wanted was a family that wasn't me. I *know* that's why she came to you. She would have *loved* you."

"To free the Ashvins!" Abishek screamed as he struggled to a knee. They were both bleeding from several wounds and slowing down. "I wanted to spare her. I thought she would cooperate. It didn't have to be this way!"

Abishek fired another shot of magic, striking Row in the shoulder. He stumbled, hunching over.

"You created a child only to use her," Row said. "You manipulated the woman I loved, and I *know* you are responsible for her disappearance." Row advanced a step, fury rolling off him in waves. "She was right all along. You wanted to hurt Zarya. I never wanted to believe it, but I did everything I could to protect her."

Row advanced another step, and Yasen saw something falter in Abishek's expression for the first time. Yasen wasn't one for mushy stuff, but it was obvious Abishek was fighting with hate, but Row... was fighting for *love*.

For Zarya and Asha, and maybe *that* made him stronger.

"The day Zarya was born, I became a father," Row said as he limped across the floor. "I never expected it, and gods know I made so many mistakes along the way, but I loved her like she was my own. I only ever wanted to protect her."

Yasen noticed Zarya stirring as Row took another step. Rabin rolled off her, and somehow, he looked even worse. His pallor had turned to ash, and he panted with labored breaths, staring at the ceiling.

Yasen helped her sit up. She blinked heavily, noting Row and Abishek in the center and Rabin lying beside her. She fell on top of him, sobbing as she whispered, "You're back" over and over.

The sound of shattering stone had them both looking up as Row and Abishek continued battling, magic flying in every direction.

"When I left Andhera, I did so out of disgust and a loss of faith in you," Row shouted. "You had lost your way. You wanted to free the darkness, but you also wanted so much worse. You want to destroy everything in the name of restoring Aazheri power."

He pushed a sweaty lock of hair from his eyes as Abishek stalked towards him. They fired again, their magic clashing in a bright flash.

"I should have stopped you then, but I was a fool," Row said as he retreated. He was breathing heavily, his forehead shiny with perspiration. "Instead, I ran away and found a different purpose. Raising a little girl into the remarkable woman she has become, and when she came to you, looking for a father, *this* is what you did!"

Abishek blinked, and Yasen wondered if the barest flash of guilt passed over his expression.

"The mistake I made was not hunting you down and killing you," Row continued, his voice filled with icy rage. "The mistake I made was allowing you to live; instead, I kept her hidden where she was forced to live a half-life."

Whatever remorse Yasen saw in Abishek's face cleared as he snarled and ran for Row, shoving him in the chest until he was backed against the wall. The king's hand wrapped around Row's throat.

"You dare speak to me this way?" Abishek hissed. "I am your king!"

"You... are... not..." Row gasped as Abishek squeezed.

The king laughed. "Oh, Row. Noble Row. You've made a commendable effort, but you cannot beat me." He pulled Row from the wall, shaking him like a rag doll, and forced him to his knees, caging him in bands of magic.

Row looked up, his long, dark hair hanging limp in his eyes. Yasen slowly stood as he scanned the room, trying to figure out a plan to get them all the fuck out of here.

"I wish I'd ended your miserable existence," Row snarled, and the king laughed.

"You've lost. First, I will end *you*, and then Rabindranath and my embarrassment of a child are next."

It was at that moment that several things happened at once.

Abishek lifted an arm, magic swirling at his fingertips.

Ekaja shouted, "You will not touch him!" and lifted her hand.

Yasen leaped for Row, preparing to throw himself at the king.

But Ekaja's magic struck Abishek in the chest, knocking him down and releasing his hold on Row.

He might have been nearly beaten, but Row didn't miss a beat.

It was then that Yasen saw the warrior Row had been centuries before he'd ever been born.

Row crossed the room and stomped on Abishek's throat with his boot, murder in his eyes. The king gasped and choked, flailing as he fought for air.

"This ends now," Row hissed. "And you will *never* touch my daughter again."

Row blasted out a thick beam of pure fire. Yasen could feel its heat from where he stood. It climbed over Abishek, igniting his hair and clothing as he screamed.

It was an inhuman sound. An unholy wail that echoed into every corner of Taaranas.

Row didn't blink. He didn't shake. He didn't move.

He just fried the fucker to a crisp.

Yasen wanted to cheer, but he held it in, thinking it might be inappropriate.

When Row was done, when nothing of Abishek was left, he dropped his hand and sunk to the floor, his head bowing as his knees landed amongst the ashes of his former king.

FORTY-SEVEN

"Row?" Zarya whispered, her throat aching from screaming.

He looked over, instantly jumping to his feet. Striding across the cavern, he collapsed and drew her into an embrace.

"Gods," he whispered as she sobbed into his chest. "I thought..."

"I'm fine," she said. "I'm fine. Rabin saved me."

Rabin and Yasen hugged her from each side as she was wrapped in the comfort of her husband, father, and best friend.

"What happened?" Zarya asked. "How are you here?"

Row and Yasen filled her in on everything before her gaze fell on the crumbling ashes of Raja Abishek.

"He tried to kill me," she said. "He said he would... but..." She turned to Row. "I'm so sorry I didn't listen to you. You warned us, and I thought I knew better."

"It's not your fault, my girl," he said, brushing a lock of hair off her face. "He's always been very good at manipulating everyone to get what he wants."

Zarya," Rabin said. "I'll never forgive myself for this."

"Don't," she said, squeezing his hand. "It isn't your fault, either. I wanted to come. I don't think anything could have stopped me. From the moment I learned of his existence, I already knew I'd meet him, no matter what anyone said."

His gaze darkened. "What did I do when I was enchanted? I can only remember flashes and..."

"I'm fine," she said, pressing a finger to his lips. "You weren't in control, but you healed me when it mattered."

He stared at her but obviously wasn't convinced.

"It's okay," she whispered. "I know that wasn't you."

"I almost got you killed," he said, his voice dark with menace. "I'll never forgive myself."

He shook his head before she leaned in and pressed a kiss to his cheek. "Do you remember the forest?" she asked softly in his ear. "You helped me. You were in there, even when it seemed like Kishore had taken you away."

He blinked, shaking his head. "I think I remember," he said. "I... we..."

She gave him a small smirk. "We sure did."

He reached over to cup the back of her head and pulled her closer. "No. I will make this up to you. I'll spend the rest of my days fixing this."

He leaned down to kiss her deeply until Yasen pointedly cleared his throat.

Zarya pulled away and grabbed his hand. "Yas, you came for me."

"I told you I always would, Zee. I'm just glad you're okay."

"I can't believe you're all here," she said, choking on a sob. "I thought I'd never see any of you again."

"When we knew you were in danger, we didn't hesitate," Row answered.

"The demons are free," she said.

"Zarya, why?"

"I had no choice."

She then explained her dreams and what Loka had told her.

"And now?" Rabin asked. "How do we deal with an army of demons?"

"We reunite with the rest of the Chiranjivi."

"Why?"

She took Rabin's hand and kissed the back. She had to tell him because no matter what happened, this would mean the end for him, too.

"Because Abishek was telling the truth when he said the Ashvins were living inside me."

Everyone watched as she took a deep breath. "The only way to stop the nairatta is to kill the twins." She paused as the words clogged her throat. "And the only way to do that... is to kill me."

Rabin stared at Zarya as panic swirled in his gut. His entire body ached, and the remnants of Kishore's enchantment clouded his head. He could still see the burning red haze taking over his vision. Taste the rage in his mouth. Feel the twitch in his bones when he'd wanted nothing more than to find Zarya and tear her apart.

Gods, he would hear her panicked screams and see the terror in her eyes for the rest of his life. How could he have let himself be so used?

And now she was sitting here calmly telling them they would have to *kill* her?

He'd never forgive himself for any of this. He'd fallen for Abishek's lies and then ushered Zarya straight into his arms. What a fucking fool.

"No," Rabin said. "Absolutely not."

She laid a hand on his arm. "We'll discuss it when we're all together."

"Zarya."

"I know, but we should get out of here first."

He wanted to protest, but she gave him a pleading look that silenced him. For now.

She was terrified, even if she was putting on a good show.

Finally, they all remembered Ekaja. Rabin looked over to find her staring at him. She stood awkwardly, her hands balled into fists as if afraid of getting too close.

He turned away as Row and Yasen helped them to their feet. Zarya leaned against him, and he wrapped an arm around her shoulders before placing a kiss on her temple. He would never let her go again.

"I'm... sorry," Ekaja said in a small, unsure voice that was nothing like her at all. "I had no choice."

Rabin scanned her from head to toe and huffed.

"I don't want to hear it right now. I don't even want to look at you."

He turned to face Row and Yasen and heard her shuffle as she moved closer.

"I deserve that," she said to his back. "But let me help you fix this."

Rabin peered over his shoulder. Two people he'd trusted most in the world had betrayed him this week. He'd truly thought Andhera was his home, but all of it had been a lie.

He looked at Zarya, who was watching them both and raised an eyebrow in question.

"It's up to you," she said. "We could probably use all the help we can get."

He grunted and then eyed Ekaja up and down. "If you follow, I won't stop you."

They all headed towards the softly glowing portal.

"This is the way back?" Yasen asked, eyeing it dubiously.

"Let's hope," Zarya said, dropping her hold on Rabin and then stepping forward, pausing for a moment before entering the glowing door. She disappeared into the light a moment later.

Rabin followed her immediately. He stepped through the

opening and found himself at the top of a mountain, wind and snow battering him from every side.

Zarya shivered with her arms wrapped around herself.

"Where are we?" she shouted into the wind as Rabin spun around and took stock of their surroundings. A moment later, Row, Ekaja, and Yasen all appeared. Row slid off his coat and draped it over Zarya's shoulders.

"Can you get us out of here?" Yasen asked, and Rabin nodded.

"Give me some space."

They all shuffled back, and Rabin transformed, his magic suspending inside nothing as he dissolved into his dragon. Once he was finished, he was warmer, his hide protecting him from the harsh elements. He lowered himself so everyone could scramble on, then took a few steps and launched himself into the air.

They swooped into the watery blue sky in a wide arc. He saw the sea to the north and the mountains stretching towards the south covered in snow... and thousands of demons.

Armies of the nairatta marched along the terrain in neat lines, snaking over the pristine snow, calling out to one another as they chanted and pounded their weapons against the earth.

They spread out in every direction. Some headed east, and some west, but all of them drifted south and towards every corner of Rahajhan.

They were moving inhumanly fast.

Rabin swooped back and over the mountains, heading in the same direction.

They had to stop these monsters before they destroyed everything.

FORTY-EIGHT

Zarya watched the nairatta march over the landscape with her heart wedged in her throat. She had no doubt about where they were headed. They carpeted the mountains in a blanket of darkness, feeding off everything in their wake.

Trails of lifeless trees and grass followed their path as everything died underfoot. Andhera would be the first kingdom to feel their wrath.

Rabin must have sensed it, too, because he dipped south and towards the city. Despite everything that had happened, this had been his home. These people were innocent of Abishek's deception. Zarya thought of everyone she'd met during her short visit. Urvi, who had helped her, and Dav and Suria, who'd been so hopeful about the future.

She thought of her mother. Was she still trapped in the tower? Abishek claimed he might keep her alive longer if she proved useful. If she was still there, Zarya *couldn't* let the nairatta consume the city.

A phalanx of demons was already nearing the walls. Zarya screamed into the wind, but the effort felt futile. She glanced over her shoulder to notice Ekaja staring down with a blank expression. This was her home, and it was about to be devoured.

Rabin streaked across the sky, coasting over a row of demons who barely registered his presence. He dipped his head and blasted out a stream of wild blue fire, torching through their line.

The nairatta screamed, the sound otherworldly, as he fried them all to dust. But more replaced them as they careened over the landscape. Rabin blasted out ribbons of fire while Zarya, Ekaja, and Row used their magic to attack from the sky.

Rabin swooped, pulling ahead of the horde and nearing the city walls.

"Let us off!" Zarya yelled. Rabin briefly touched the ground, and they all scrambled off before he looped into the air and continued mowing through great swaths of demons. He then glided over the city, bellowing out a battle cry in warning.

Zarya heard the shouts from the city's soldiers registering the threat.

Then Zarya stood with Yasen, Row, and Ekaja as they turned to face the approaching line. She drew on her nightfire, cautious about what it might do. Would it hurt the demons? How was her magic related to theirs?

She shook out her arms and then her shoulders. Only one way to find out.

Placing one hand on top of the other, she stretched them out and called on all six of her anchors, drawing them in before they collided in the center of her heart. Pure sparkling nightfire burst from her palms, sweeping out in a wall of dark magic flecked with light.

It crashed into the line of nairatta like a hammer. They screamed and wailed as her magic tore through them, shredding them apart like shattering glass. She watched in fascinated horror as they exploded, black blood spraying across pristine white snow to the sound of their dying screams.

She blinked, staring at what she had done.

"Zarya!" Row called. "Again! That worked!"

His voice dragged her out of shock, and she nodded.

Ekaja used blasts of fire, wind, and earth to crush the demons while Row drew on dark veins of shadow. The darkness had been freed, and he could finally access it. Yasen cut them down with his sword while Rabin continued circling the sky, taking out pockets of demons with his deadly blue fire.

She had only a moment to wonder why Andhera's army hadn't joined them before she focused on the horde and began stalking towards them. Pressing her hands together, she channeled another wall of nightfire, blowing the nairatta apart to the unholy sounds of bodies exploding and blood spattering across the air.

She felt possessed. For the first time in this long and bloody battle, she felt like she had a voice. She screamed as she aimed at another line, tearing through them like a knife through paper.

Through the red haze of her anger, she dimly registered the presence of Andhera's soldiers filing out of the city. About a dozen Aazheri made up their first defense. They each set to work destroying the monsters—Zarya noticed one filtering out black ribbons of smoke, and her chest tightened at the sight.

But where were the rest?

Hours passed as the sun drifted over the sky, and the demons attacked over and over. This was only a small group compared to their army; the others were already receding into the distance, heading for the other realms.

They had to warn everyone.

Finally, the line of advancing nairatta dissipated as Zarya and the others dealt the final blows of death.

When they were gone, an eerie silence fell over the landscape as she stared into the distance. The wind tugged at her hair as tears slipped down her cheeks.

This wasn't a victory. There was nothing to celebrate.

This was not an ending. It was only the beginning.

She inhaled a deep breath and pressed her hand to her chest as her gaze met Row's and then Yasen's, reading the truth in their faces.

Again, they turned to watch the nairatta snaking over the landscape, crawling over Rahajhan like a plague.

Soon, everyone would feel their wrath.

Rabin dropped into the trees and shifted into his rakshasa form.

He jogged through the trampled snow, leaping over bodies. Zarya turned at his approach as she inhaled a shaky breath. Black smoke swirled around her, and black lightning flashed across the sky.

His attention fell on Andhera's army—or what was left of it. Why were there so few?

"Where are your soldiers?" he asked Ekaja.

She shook her head. "The king... needed them."

"For what?" he asked as he stalked towards her.

"He asked me to gather my best generals and prepare them to march for Gi'ana."

"Gi'ana?" Zarya asked. "Why?"

Ekaja pressed her mouth together as she glanced at her soldiers.

"To help quell the resistance."

Rabin blinked. *This* was Dishani's mercenary army? He couldn't believe she would do this.

"Is there no level to which you won't sink?" he asked, and her face turned pale.

"I tried to stop him," she said softly.

He scoffed and turned to Zarya.

"We have to warn the others about the nairatta," she whispered. "They'll hit Gi'ana next."

He studied her face, trying to detect her reaction to yet another of Abishek's betrayals, but she gave nothing away.

"Just give me a moment to catch my breath," Rabin said, his chest heaving in and out. "We can get ahead of them."

"You're exhausted," Ekaja said. "Stay for tonight and leave in the morning. You need food and rest, all of you."

The corner of Rabin's mouth curled up. "*Now* you're concerned about us?"

She flinched like he'd slapped her.

"I'm sorry," Ekaja said. "He promised that no real harm would come to you..." She chewed her lip. "And I believed him. I *wanted* to believe him."

"Did you know?" Rabin asked. "Who I was all along? Who Zarya was? Did you know he was manipulating me from the moment I arrived?"

She shook her head as her expression crumpled. "I swear to you that I didn't. Kishore was the only one he took into his confidence. Had I known..."

"What?" Rabin asked. "Had you known, would you have warned me?"

Ekaja blinked. "I'm... not sure."

Rabin exhaled a derisive sound that burned the back of his throat. "I'm the fool," he answered. "I was a fool ever to trust any of you."

"Rabin—"

"I don't want to hear it right now," he said with a wave of his hand.

"He gave me my life when no one else would!" she shouted. "You *know* what that's like. You know how he is. He would have tossed me out!"

He heard the plea in her voice. He heard that little girl who had been half-starving in the streets when Abishek found her and then molded her into his personal soldier.

"I do know," Rabin said softly. "But I would have chosen

you. You're the only real friend I've ever had, and I would have chosen *you*."

Her expression twisted into shame and guilt, but he refused to feel sorry for her.

Forcing himself to turn away, he addressed Zarya and the others.

"We must leave. Gather some food for the journey, and we'll be on our way."

"I'll come with you," Ekaja shouted at his back. "Let me help you."

He peered over his shoulder. "You have no army. The king left the city vulnerable when he *knew* what was coming. You are all Andhera has left. Stay here and protect the city. There's no reason these people should suffer for your mistakes."

Ekaja nodded, her mouth pressing together, her eyes shining with the threat of tears. He'd never seen her cry before. She gestured to one of her guards and whispered a few words before he ran to do her bidding.

"I shall see that you have proper clothing and food for the rest of your journey."

Rabin said nothing. He glared at Ekaja as they all took a moment to rest in the snow. When he didn't answer, she turned and began shouting further orders to the few soldiers she had left, arranging them around the walls to ensure the city's protection.

Zarya walked over and sank onto the snow next to Rabin as Row joined them, followed by Yasen.

"I have to tell you something," Zarya said to Row, swallowing thickly. "Asha is alive. Or at least she was before we left for Taaranas."

Row exhaled a shaky breath. "Urvi told us you were looking for her."

She shook her head. "He was keeping her there because she was a nali, and the same god who found me also spoke to her.

He was torturing her for information about me, all in service to this plan."

Rabin studied Row's face, his skin pale and his lower lip trembling.

His gaze met Zarya's as the depths of haunting loss reflected in his dark eyes. "We went to look for her," Row said. "Urvi helped us."

Zarya inhaled a sharp breath, her gaze expectant.

"She wasn't there."

Her shoulders curved inwards as she reached out to clutch Rabin's arm.

Row's head dropped, his hair falling around his face.

They all sat quietly for a moment before Zarya spoke. "Then, I don't know if she's still alive. I almost didn't want to tell you about her because I didn't want to..."

"Get my hopes up?" Row asked, and she nodded.

"I'm sorry. This is all my fault. If the gods hadn't chosen me. If I hadn't been born, you would have been together." Tears coated her cheeks, and she wiped them away.

"No," Row said. "You are not blaming yourself for any of this. You weren't given a choice."

She nodded as he wrapped an arm around her shoulders and tugged her against him. He kissed the top of her head, and then their gazes drifted to the castle as if they might see her through the stone walls.

"Go and look for her," Zarya said.

He shook his head. "I spent twenty years hoping she was alive, and I'm not sure I'm ready to end this chapter yet. For now, I can believe just a little longer."

Looking back at Zarya, he touched her cheek. "Besides, you need me," he answered. "We can't finish this without the Chiranjivi. Everyone will die."

Rabin saw the truth in his eyes. He was scared. Terrified to learn that after all these years of searching, he'd come so close only to lose her again. Zarya didn't argue. She just nodded.

"Maybe we should take Ekaja up on her offer?" Yasen asked. "Get a few hours of sleep at least."

Rabin glared up at the city walls. "I never want to set foot in there again."

Yasen nodded. "Understood. Then we'll freeze our asses off in the snow."

Rabin laughed. It was a boisterous sound that echoed through the forest. He must be losing his mind. Everyone turned to him with a shocked look.

"Did you just laugh?" Yasen asked, and Rabin shook his head.

"Of course not."

That brought a brief smile to their faces.

A few minutes later, several palace servants appeared with clothing and food. Rabin noticed Zarya touching her throat. Their tattoos were gone. It had worked. This hadn't all been for nothing.

Urvi appeared before them, and Zarya jumped to her feet.

"Urvi," she whispered. "It's gone."

Urvi nodded. "I... they're all gone."

"I know you said you didn't want this, but—"

Urvi shook her head. "I did want it. Of course I did. I was afraid, but... they're *all* gone. What will the king say?"

"The king is dead," she said. "Soon, everyone will know it. Whatever happens, he is no longer your concern."

"Dead?" she said. "So, you... are our queen, then."

Zarya's mouth opened and then closed. "No. I..."

"Zee!" Yasen called. "We need to go!"

"Take care of yourself," Zarya said as she hugged the other woman and accepted the clothes.

Once they were ready, Rabin searched for a clearing where he could shift.

"Rabin!" Ekaja called before he got far. "I'm sorry. I want to make this up to you."

He glared at her, his teeth grinding. "I'm not sure how you ever could."

She grabbed his arm. "Will I see you again?"

"I don't know."

Then he pulled away and stalked into an open space before turning to see Zarya and Row walking up to Ekaja.

"Find my mother," she said. "If she's still alive..."

Ekaja nodded. "Of course. I'll take care of her until you return. Anything you need."

"Be careful," Zarya said.

"You, too."

Then Zarya, Row, and Yasen climbed onto Rabin's back. He flapped his wings and took a few steps before launching into the sky. He watched the demons marching in every direction, thankful for the long, arduous journey ahead of them.

With any luck, it would slow them down.

Rabin looped around Andhera, lifting his head and roaring before he turned east and towards Gi'ana.

With any luck, they'd arrive in time.

FORTY-NINE

Rabin coasted over the miles as they watched nairatta snaking down the mountains. He flew as hard as he could, pulling ahead until they finally disappeared from view.

After several long days and nights, Ishaan appeared in the distance. He looped over the city to witness the destruction of the past few weeks.

The sky-blue palace stood pale against the smoky sky where a red sun bled across the horizon. His nostrils flared at the acrid scent of smoke curling in the air. He dipped, sailing over the buildings and the palace, where he spotted the courtyard filled with hundreds of soldiers wearing black.

Andhera's army. Abishek had betrayed everyone.

Rabin dropped into an empty square, waited for the others to scramble off, and then quickly transformed into his rakshasa form.

"Did you see them?" Yasen asked. "That shithead king was planning to release an army of demons, and he just left his people *defenseless*?"

Rabin was already stalking in the direction of the palace.

They all stopped when they reached the gates and stared at the army arranged into neat lines.

"Should we be standing here?" Yasen asked. "This feels a little dangerous."

"We have to warn them about the nairatta," Zarya said, though there wasn't much confidence in her statement.

Rabin nodded and once again focused on the front of the plaza, where he recognized a few of Andhera's generals. Gods, how could he ever forgive Ekaja for any of this?

Several people stood on the royal balcony, including a woman wearing a veil over her head; Kabir, the king consort; and the younger of the two Madan siblings. Someone was speaking—a man dressed in the silver-white uniform of the queensguard.

"Gi'ana thanks you for your assistance!" he shouted. "The rebels have ruled this nation for too long, and it is time to bring order to our land!"

He bent down to confer with the veiled woman, who Rabin assumed was Princess Dishani, before addressing the crowd again. "The queen is in your debt! Head into the forest and root them out! Let no one be spared. Man, woman, or child—deal with these rebels without mercy!"

His words rang against the stones as hundreds of soldiers pressed their fists to their chests.

"Queen," Zarya whispered. "She is no queen. She is a tyrant."

An Andheran general began shouting orders before the soldiers turned in unison.

"No!" Zarya screamed. "They can't do this. We have to stop them!"

"*Ready!*" came the call. "*March!*"

They stomped on the spot for several beats before moving towards the gates.

"No!" Zarya screamed. "Stop this!"

She ran into the square, skirting through their lines as Rabin followed with Row and Yasen on his heels.

"Stop!" Zarya shouted as the soldiers marched. The army ignored her as they simply curved around her like water against a rock in a stream.

The soldiers bled into the streets of Ishaan while Zarya and Rabin continued pushing their way through. "Please!" Zarya screamed as they approached the balcony, where the royals looked down at her with surprise.

"Arrest her!" shouted one of the queensguard, recognizing her immediately.

Zarya didn't hesitate, using a thread of magic to silence him. He grabbed his throat, his mouth gaping. "Listen to me! You are all fighting one another when the *real* threat is on its way."

The royals all shared wary looks until Kabir finally approached the railing and peered down with a curious look.

"The nairatta are loose," she shouted. "They're marching across the mountains and will be here in a matter of days, if that. The resistance is not your enemy. The collars are off. You've lost this battle. Gather your army and protect the city, or we're all dead! Do you hear me?"

Rabin watched Dishani the entire time. He couldn't make out her face, but the angle of her head told him she was listening intently.

"You have to listen!" she screamed when they hesitated. "They're coming and will destroy *everything.*"

Rabin watched Kabir confer with the queensguard.

"Do you speak the truth?" shouted Talin, the younger Madan brother. Rabin watched him glance at Yasen before addressing Zarya.

"I do! Why would I lie about this?"

"I will speak with them," he said to his family before pushing away from the railing and disappearing off the balcony.

Rabin and Zarya exchanged a wary look as they waited.

A minute later, Talin appeared in the doorway, flanked by his guards. Then another figure appeared, and Rabin heard Yasen's soft gasp.

"Miraan," Zarya said. "What are you doing here?"

"Our father convinced my sister not to kill me, though she continues to resist any and all efforts to hear out the Rising Phoenix. I tried to stop this." Rabin noticed the prince share a look with Yasen before he took a step closer and leaned in to Zarya. "Are you the reason for the collars?"

She nodded. "Yes."

He breathed out heavily and ran a hand through his hair. "How?"

"I'll explain everything if we survive but freeing them also released the nairatta. They're coming."

"We held them off in Andhera for now," Rabin added. "But only because they didn't hit us with their full strength. You must rally every able-bodied fighter you can. Prepare for a battle on a scale none of us could have ever imagined."

"Nairatta," Talin croaked, his pallor turning ashen.

Miraan held out his hands. "And what will you do?"

"We must gather the Chiranjivi to end this," Zarya said. "I don't know how long it will take or if our plan will even work, but if we're lucky, we'll kill them all."

"Then we'll do everything we can to hold them off," Miraan said.

"I'll help you," Yasen added, and Miraan nodded.

Zarya reached out to squeeze Yasen's hand before he drew her closer. "Whatever you do, Zee, you'd better come back to me."

She looked up. "I'll try. But if I don't, just know how much I love you, Yas. Thank you for being my first best friend."

Yasen wiped a tear from her eye with the tip of his thumb.

"And thank you for being the very best friend a man could ask for," he whispered.

She tipped her head and studied him. "Not your second best?"

He smiled and shook his head. "You were never second, Zee. You've never been second."

At that, she burst into tears and threw her arms around him. He returned the hug and kissed the top of her head. They stood like that for several moments.

"Zee?"

"Hmm?"

"There's an army of demons marching this way."

"There is."

"So, we should all probably deal with that."

She laughed and pulled away, wiping the corner of her eyes. "Be careful out there. You'd better come back to me, too. And thank you for saving me."

"You did it yourself, Zee."

"I don't mean just today."

Yasen pressed his mouth together, looking like he was trying not to cry.

Rabin had never seen him like this before, but Zarya had a way of drawing out the parts of yourself you were too afraid to share.

"I would do it again a hundred times, Zee."

They hugged for another moment and said their goodbyes.

Then Rabin left the courtyard with Zarya and Row. As they passed through the gates, he glanced over his shoulder one more time.

Abishek had lied to them over and over again.

He'd felt almost nothing when Row had killed the king. He wasn't even angry. Just numb.

They hadn't talked about the fact that Zarya was asking them to kill her. He couldn't do it. He wouldn't. He didn't care about himself, but the world would be darker without her.

She met his gaze as they prowled through the streets, planning to make their way to the hideout in the forest.

As if reading his mind, she offered him a soft smile. "Everything will be okay."

"I don't think so," he answered.

FIFTY

Zarya and Rabin followed Row through Ishaan until they reached a quiet corner and exited through a hidden gate. They entered the forest, winding through the trees until they heard the sounds of the rebellion in the distance.

She exchanged a glance with Rabin as they turned another corner to discover the encampment. They'd clearly been hard at work evacuating vanshaj from the city. Her eyes burned with tears. She was so proud of everyone. They'd all come so far since the day she and Yasen met Ajay and Rania and were recruited to this cause.

She couldn't think of a better way to spend her final moments.

People stopped to watch as they made their way through the temporary village. She noted the glasses in their hands and that a few had been dancing.

Celebrating. They were celebrating.

"Zarya!" Vikas called. "You're back!" He ran towards her with Ajay in tow. They both hugged her.

"We were so worried," Ajay said.

"We're okay," she said, even though that wasn't really true.

He greeted Row and Rabin before Farida, Rania, Suvanna, and Apsara also appeared.

"The tattoos," Vikas said, gesturing to several people watching their reunion. "We were training, and suddenly, they all just... disappeared. Do you know what happened?"

Zarya nodded and quickly explained everything except for the whole killing her thing because she didn't have the energy to argue with anyone else. She could feel Rabin's furious gaze burning up the back of her neck.

"An army of nairatta are headed this way?" Ajay asked as the blood drained from his cheeks.

She nodded. "We've alerted the palace, and they're readying themselves."

"This is what we've been preparing for," Farida said. "It's not the enemy we predicted, but the Army of Ashes hasn't been idle during these weeks."

"We have hundreds more Aazheri, freed from the collars," Vikas said. "Surely, that gives us an advantage."

"It might be dangerous using brand-new Taara Aazheri," Row cautioned.

"Rabin will lead them," Vikas said. "It will be fine."

"No," Zarya said. "He can't. He's needed elsewhere."

She reached out and grabbed Vikas's hand. "You became the face of this movement. You were the first to show them what was possible. And now you'll have to do this next part on your own."

They finished discussing their plans while they filled in the others on what it had been like to battle the demons. They might have no choice but to rely on the Taara Aazheri's new magic.

"Are people safe here?" Rabin asked. "The children—anyone who can't fight."

Farida exchanged a look with Vikas.

"We'll do everything we can to protect them," she said.

"Good," Zarya said before turning to Suvanna and Apsara. "We need your help."

"Of course," Apsara said.

"Then let's go somewhere and talk."

After saying goodbye and sharing their hopes of seeing one another alive on the other side, they headed for Zarya and Yasen's flat in the city.

Her heart squeezed when they entered the quiet space. She'd been so happy here with him. She'd wanted to see the world so badly, and it had been even better with her best friend at her side.

She'd found the Rising Phoenix, and she'd made a difference. She'd forgiven Rabin, and they were married, and she loved him more than she could put into words.

But she was about to lose him.

She was about to lose all of this.

"Tell us what's going on," Suvanna said, wasting no time.

Zarya nodded and twisted her fingers together in nervousness.

"Zarya, please," Apsara said. "You're worrying me."

She then explained the rest of Abishek's deception and how Loka had visited her in her dreams. She avoided meeting Rabin's gaze while she talked, knowing she couldn't bear what she'd read on his face.

"You want us to kill you?" Suvanna said after Zarya was done talking, her expression hard. "No. Absolutely not."

"There's no other way," Zarya said. Finally, she ventured a look in Rabin's direction. A muscle feathered in his jaw, and his eyes were as dark as midnight.

"Zarya, I cannot support this!" Row said. "I'm sorry. I've been holding my tongue since we left Taaranas, but you can't really mean to go through with this."

"What choice do we have?"

He couldn't answer, and they all fell silent. Zarya's gaze wandered to the window and the balcony where she'd sat with Yasen staring at the distant view.

She'd spent so many years waiting for her life to begin. But she couldn't have known what fate had in store.

"Supposing we did this," Apsara said and raised a hand when it was clear she was about to be met with a chorus of objections. "I'm only asking. How do we kill the Ashvins without you? If all the Chiranjivi are needed?"

Zarya blew out a breath. "That's where the paramadhar bond comes in."

She paused as she let everyone put it together.

"This is why he was given to me," she said. "Loka said I would need him at the end."

"But won't he die, too?" Suvanna asked, throwing him an apologetic look.

Rabin blew out a long sigh. "Not right away. I'd remain alive long enough to possibly save her. True death doesn't come for a few minutes."

"A few *minutes*?" Row asked. "This is madness! What if he can't revive you?"

"Row," Zarya said. "*Everyone* will die if we don't do this."

He roared in frustration. "I know that!"

"So, we..." Apsara swallowed. "Kill Zarya, wait for the Ashvins to exit her body, and hope Rabin can revive her quickly enough. And while he's doing that, we contain the Ashvins until you return, and then we kill them so that an army of ancient demons doesn't consume all of Rahajhan."

Zarya winced. "When you put it like that..."

"This is a terrible plan," Row said. "This can't be the way."

"It is the way," she insisted.

"Are you so ready to die?" Row shouted. "Your life finally has begun, and now you want to throw it all away!"

"Of course I don't!" she screamed. "I don't want to die. I wanted to live. That's all I've ever wanted. I've found everything I wished for. I'm married to the love of my life. I just..."

She broke off, sobs wracking her chest as she turned to Rabin, burying her face against him. He'd been so quiet during all this, but he was angry with himself for believing Abishek's lies, and she knew exactly where he stood about her death.

She felt a hand on her back a moment later, followed by Row's low voice. "I'm sorry," he said. "I just... I can't bear to watch you die. We already lost Aarav and..."

She pulled away to meet his gaze. "I know. And I'm sorry that I might leave you, too."

He shook his head, and Zarya hugged him for a long moment.

"We'll need Kindle," she said, pulling away, hoping Row wouldn't continue arguing.

"He's been in contact with us," Apsara said. "He's ready to help if we need him."

Their gazes fell on Row, the only one who could retrieve him quickly.

"Please?" Zarya said, and he exhaled a sharp breath.

"Fine."

"Then we'll do it once you both return," she said. "I was meant to free the vanshaj, but there will be no point to their freedom if the nairatta overrun us. We have to finish this."

When no one argued any further, she took that as their silent confirmation.

FIFTY-ONE

After Row left, everyone retired to their separate spaces to rest for the night.

Zarya and Rabin closed the door to her room. He turned around to face her, and his expression was so full of misery that she thought her heart might burst from her chest.

"I'm sorry," she whispered. "I have to…"

He strode across the room and wrapped her in his arms as she broke down, sobbing against him and letting everything out. He trembled as he squeezed her, pressing soft kisses to the crown of her head.

"I hope you know…" she gasped. "I wanted more time. I wanted to do everything with you. See the world. Be together. I just…"

"Zarya," he murmured softly, cupping her face in his hands. "It's not over yet."

"The odds of surviving are almost nothing," she said.

"But they aren't zero."

She nodded, even if she knew it was hopeless. "I'm sorry this is the end for you, too. You should never have agreed to bond with me. This wasn't worth it."

He lifted her chin with a finger. "Zarya. Don't you dare fucking say that. I entered this bond willingly. Openly. I knew what I was signing up for. From the very start, I understood your destiny would take us somewhere important, and it might mean sacrifices along the way."

He wiped an errant tear from her cheek with his thumb.

"The first time I saw you, I knew there would never be anyone else. I knew I would die with you, one way or another. You've brought me the greatest happiness I've ever known, and if it could only be for so short a time, then I need you to understand it was worth *every* moment I got to spend with you."

He paused, searching her face, his dark eyes sparking with gold. He leaned down and pressed a kiss to her lips. "I would have made the same choice over and over, even knowing what I know now. I would have made the same choice no matter what. Loving you and spending even a moment with you was worth all of it."

Her tears were flowing freely now, coasting down her cheeks as her shoulders heaved with the weight of the emotions she was carrying in her breaking heart.

"What do you picture after this?" Rabin said. "If we survive?"

"You and I together," she whispered. "I want to go to university, and I want to live in Ishaan. I want Row and my mother to get another chance, and I want us to be a family."

He exhaled a soft breath. "Then you'll have all of that. Do you understand me?"

He cupped her face in his hands and stared at her until she finally nodded. "I can't wait."

He gave her the softest smile that cracked through the center of her chest.

"I love you," she whispered, clinging to him. "I don't care if the gods chose you for me, I would have loved you until the end."

Then he kissed her in answer. They clung to one another as if trying to hold on forever.

Suddenly, she couldn't get enough. She surged up, pressing her mouth harder to his. She needed him. She needed to feel all of him against her. Inside her. She needed his hands and his touch. This might be the last time they'd ever do this.

In silent agreement, they began undressing, sliding off layers, pants, shirts, boots, cloaks, everything hitting the floor until they were both naked, their warm skin pressing together and heat rising between them.

They kissed and kissed like the world was burning around them. He lifted her, wrapping her legs around his waist. Then he lay her on the bed before he began planting soft kisses down the length of her body.

He pulled up and looked down at the space between her heart where the silver dragon Kishore had inked on her skin sparkled. She touched it, but there was no magic anymore. No power left to control them. It would only be a reminder of everything they survived.

He traced her iridescent black dragon and then the silver, his expression contemplative. Zarya thought it looked like they were reaching for each other.

Then Rabin gave her a soft smile and then leaned down to suck on the curve of her throat and kiss her collarbone, followed by the valley between her breasts. His mouth dragged lower, skating over her stomach and down over her navel. He spread her legs as he fell to his knees, and this reminded her so much of the first night they'd been together.

She forced her mind towards the good memories. The moment he'd told her that he loved her. When he'd saved her from falling to her death in Dharati. She thought of the moment when she'd finally forgiven him. Of the day Row and Koura walked in on them in the haveli.

She giggled, and Rabin peered up from between her legs with an arched brow.

"What are you smiling about, Spitfire?"

She told him, and he barked out a laugh.

"That door is locked, right?"

"I hope so," she answered as his head dove between her thighs, and he licked her with a long stroke. She moaned as her head tipped back and her hips arched.

He continued tasting her as his hands slid up her thighs and stomach, cupping her breasts. With the tip of his tongue, he circled her clit as he pinched her nipples. She was somewhat conscious of everyone else in the apartment, so she did her best to muffle her cries, but they might both die tomorrow, and surely everyone would understand.

She felt herself winding tighter, and it didn't take long before her release exploded as she gripped the bedspread so hard she felt the fibers give. She hadn't stopped shaking when he crawled up her body and lined himself up with her entrance, slowly easing in.

"Zarya," he said as he thrust his hips, his voice low and dark. "I love you."

Then he leaned down to kiss her, and she felt the message he was trying to send. She felt the moments they'd spent together in the depth of that kiss as he made love to her. This was a letter written with their bodies and the hope—the *hope*—that they'd live through this to see another day.

She held his face in her hands as they stared at one another while he slowly drove into her. Their gazes locked for several minutes as they found strength in each other. She felt him thicken inside her, and they came together, moaning softly.

When it was over, they said nothing as they lay tangled together.

What was left to say?

A tear slipped down her cheek, and she decided it was the

last one until this was over. There would be no more crying until this was done.

She would face this head-on. She had vowed to do this. She had been chosen for this. She was duty-bound to fulfill her mother's prophecy and free the vanshaj.

The collars were broken, and now it was up to Rahajhan to finish what had been started.

She hoped they wouldn't waste this opportunity for peace.

She hoped for so many things.

Zarya heard Rabin's breath turn into a steady rhythm as they lay in silence.

She was asking everyone to do the unthinkable.

Zarya might have to take this into her own hands.

Slowly, she extricated herself from Rabin's arms. She hunted for some clothing while he remained asleep and dressed in the dark bathroom.

Then she tiptoed across the room and eased the door open. She was relieved to find the common area empty. On light steps, she crossed the flat and then headed outside.

She passed homes with the curtains drawn and the windows dark and whispered a prayer that everyone else would survive this, too. Then she stole through the city's ruined streets, navigating herself to a familiar place.

After about twenty minutes, she knocked on the door she'd been looking for. It was late, and Zarya hoped she would answer. It took a moment before she heard movement on the other side.

The door popped open to reveal Thriti, her expression wary.

"What are you doing here?" she asked, scanning Zarya up and down.

Zarya swallowed the knot in her throat. "I need your help."

FIFTY-TWO

Zarya, Suvanna, Koura, and Apsara gathered inside a large, deserted plaza as the sun hung over Ishaan the next afternoon. A dark shadow crossed the sky, and they peered up to track Rabin's path as he swooped overhead before dropping into the plaza. A second later, he dissolved into smoke before shifting into his rakshasa form.

"They're close," he said while jogging towards them. "Moving faster than we thought."

"How long?" Apsara asked.

"Another hour or two at most. I've already alerted them on the front line."

They all shared a grim look as two familiar figures appeared in the square.

Row stood with Kindle, their hands clasped, and they all rushed over to greet them.

"Kindle," Zarya said as she hugged him tightly. "Thank you for coming."

They pulled apart, and Kindle looked around the circle. "Row filled me in on everything, but are you sure about this?"

"I'm sure," Zarya said before anyone could interrupt.

"Zarya," Row said, his tone full of pain.

She willed herself not to cry. She'd promised herself no more tears until this was over. "Please don't make this any harder," she whispered.

Row rubbed a hand over his face and then nodded. "I'm sorry... I just..."

"I know." She turned to face the others. "It's up to you to ensure the Ashvins don't escape before Rabin can revive me."

Everyone fell silent as they considered the question no one could bring themselves to ask. But Zarya had to give voice to it. She couldn't just pretend this wasn't the end.

"And if he can't, it will be up to you to save everyone. Somehow."

More worried looks passed around the circle.

She stood surrounded by friends, by her father—her true father—and the man she loved. By a group of people who she now called friends. There was no choice but to face it and hope she was coming back.

Row strode over, throwing his arms around her in a tight hug. They clung to one another as she buried her face in the curve of his shoulder.

"Thank you for everything," she said. "I want you to know I always wanted you as my family."

He pulled away and gave her a bemused look.

"You said that to Abishek when you were fighting. That I didn't want you, but that isn't true."

He brushed a strand of hair from her cheek, his eyes filling with tears, and shook his head. "Thank *you*, Zarya. For coming into my life. For giving me a purpose I didn't even know I wanted."

Zarya swallowed. "Promise me you'll look for my mother," she said. "I hope you get another chance."

Row wasn't her father by blood, but in a way, her parents *had* been in love just as she'd always imagined.

"She was calling for you," Zarya said. "She..."

"Needed me," he answered, his voice hollow.

And then, a single tear slipped down his cheek. She'd never seen him cry before.

"It wasn't your fault. I'm so sorry."

Row inhaled a deep breath. "When you survive this, we will find her together."

Zarya nodded and pressed her mouth together, shoving back the tears she refused to shed. *If* she survived this.

"I love you," she said, hugging him one more time.

"I love you, too." They held on for another moment and then pulled away.

Zarya looked at the others. The brave and kind Apsara. The fierce Suvanna. The gentle Koura. And Kindle, who'd been a father when Row had gone missing.

"Thank you," she said. "You all helped me on this journey more than you can ever understand. When I came to Dharati, I was so lost and bewildered. You showed me kindness and taught me what honor looks like."

Her voice cracked as Apsara, Kindle, and Koura all swept in for a hug, wrapping their arms around her. They embraced for a long minute before pulling away. Suvanna watched them with a serious expression.

She tipped her head and scanned Zarya from head to toe. "When I first met you, I thought you were just a silly little girl," she said. "I'm sorry I called you that, and Rahajhan is lucky to have you."

Zarya stared at her for several seconds and then barked out a laugh. She was truly on the very edge of breaking down completely. "Thanks," she said.

Finally, she willed herself to face Rabin, and her heart split in half.

She walked over and laid a hand against his cheek.

"I'll find you in another life," he whispered. "No matter

where the winds scatter us, I will search across continents and swim through oceans, and I *will* find you again."

She nodded. "I know."

Then she tipped her head forward, pressing it against his chest as she inhaled a deep shuddering breath. Everyone gave them another moment before she forced herself to back away.

They all surrounded her in a circle, looking at each other.

"So..." Kindle said. "What was the plan here?"

"I'm not killing her," Row said.

"Me neither," Apsara and Koura chimed in.

"Well, I don't want to do it," Kindle argued.

Everyone then looked at Suvanna. She blinked. "What? I don't want to kill her, either."

"Well, it can't be Rabin," Row said.

Zarya listened to them argue, strangely touched.

But she had anticipated this.

She reached into her pocket and pulled out the vial Thriti had given her last night. The mystic hadn't argued—simply offered what Zarya asked.

Zarya unstoppered the bottle while they were all debating, and her gaze met Rabin's, who watched on in silence. She lifted the bottle as his eyes widened, and then before anyone could stop her, she tipped the contents into her mouth and swallowed.

"Zarya!" he roared as everyone's attention swung towards her.

Her vision swam, her mind floating away.

She saw them.

These people who had become her family.

Her father.

And her husband. The love of her life.

Gods, how she hoped she'd see him again.

Then she collapsed, and everything went dark.

FIFTY-THREE

Yasen stood shoulder-to-shoulder between Miraan and Vikas, facing northeast as they waited for the nairatta to appear.

Andhera and Gi'ana's armies spread out before them, forming a line of defense. When Dishani finally listened to reason, they were called to cease terrorizing the vanshaj and meet the larger threat. In an ironic twist, their army was now double the size thanks to the Andheran's presence.

Further down the line stood Ajay, Rania, and Farida.

The Army of Ashes had mostly pulled itself together, and what they lacked in elegance, they made up for in heart.

Every Aazheri in Ishaan had been called upon and stood ready to offer their strength.

"How much longer do we have?" Ajay asked.

"Rabin predicted they'd be here by late afternoon," Miraan answered.

His gaze met Yasen's, and he couldn't help admiring the prince in his armor. His dark hair shone under the sun, and his dark eyes brimmed with promise and determination. They'd spent last night together, appreciating each other from every angle and position his filthy imagination could come up with.

On his other side stood Talin, also armed to the teeth.

Dishani remained in the palace with Advika and Kabir, still too weak to do much. Yasen was in the room when she'd conceded this threat was more important than the war they'd been fighting for months.

Though she was the absolute worst, he had to admire her frustration that she couldn't join them on the battlefront today.

"Soon then," Ajay replied from Yasen's other side, and Miraan nodded.

"Soon."

They all turned towards the horizon as the breeze blew off the mountains. It was so quiet, so still, everyone paralyzed with fear and the uncertainty of what came next.

Over the next hour, they waited.

Thanks to his enhanced senses, Yasen was the first to hear it: the sound of marching, chanting, and the gnashing of teeth and fists—the sound of their deaths.

"I hear them," Yasen said, his voice dropping. "They're coming."

Everyone gripped their weapons as word passed through their ranks.

And then... the nairatta appeared.

A black blot stretching over the horizon.

More terrifying than the worst nightmares.

They wore beaten leather armor, and their tough skin glistened a dull grey under the sun. Nearly as tall as trees, their arms and legs were thick and muscled. Horns and teeth and muzzles came together to form these twisted creatures: part human, part animal, and all monster.

"Ready!" Miraan shouted to the sound of hundreds of blades withdrawing. "Wait for my signal!"

They shuffled together, shoulders back, weapons ready, prepared to die.

The demons advanced, sweeping over the landscape almost as if they had wings.

Some of them did.

"How do you think Zarya and the others are doing?" Yasen asked, focused on the advancing line.

"I don't know," Miraan answered. "But we can't rely on them right now."

Yasen glanced at Miraan, to see his eyes were glassy with tears.

"I want you to know I love you," Miraan said. "I didn't want to say it like this, but you are the best man I've ever known. You are brave and fearless. Kind and giving, even if you pretend you are none of those things. Maybe *because* you pretend you are none of those things. But you are worthy of love and everything the world has to offer, Yasen Varghese, and if I die today, I wanted you to know that."

Yasen blinked, stunned into silence for once in his life. He had no idea how to respond. No one had ever said anything like that to him before.

"If you survive," Miraan added, "I want you to be happy. Allow yourself that. I want you to understand that you deserve everything."

Miraan searched his face while Yasen stood there like a stunned ass, unable to form a single sentence. The prince looked away and raised his sword over his head.

"Soldiers of Gi'ana and Andhera! Taara Aazheri who are now free! This is *your* land and *your* country, and today, you will defend it until your very last breath! Don't let the efforts of the resistance have been in vain! I want you to live!"

They shouted in response, raising their fists as their cries rose into the sky with a thread of hope.

Yasen had faced many foes in his life, but this was the first time he'd ever truly worried about dying. Maybe it was due to the strength of the enemy they faced, or maybe it was because he finally had something to lose.

And even... something to live for.

Then Miraan gave the signal.

Together, they charged, finally united.

Working as one.

They picked up speed, racing across the plains.

Yasen lifted his sword, calling out a battle cry as he crashed into the line of nairatta and hoped he'd see the sun rise again tomorrow.

FIFTY-FOUR

"Zarya!" Rabin shouted, running towards her and catching her in his arms as she collapsed and her body went limp. The vial tumbled from her hand, rolling along the stones with an ominous clink.

Row snatched it up and sniffed the contents. "Poison," he said. "She..."

"Killed herself," Kindle said.

Rabin couldn't breathe. He couldn't think. He lay Zarya on the ground, her skin already turning cold. He leaned down to press his ear to her chest. Nothing.

"Zarya!" he roared. "Come back to me!"

"Rabin!" Row said. "You have to save her!"

Rabin nodded. His vision tipped and went blurry. He wiped his eyes with the back of his hand, and it came away wet. He couldn't remember the last time he'd cried.

He'd never done this before. She'd only been *near* death when he'd saved her, not actually dead.

But this was the one that counted most.

He reached for her hand when suddenly, she began to glow. Silver starlight burst around her in a flash, curving her body off the earth. They all watched a silver shadow slowly emerge, peeling out of her skin.

Rabin's chest constricted so tight he thought he might pass out as he watched the silver swirls morph into the shapes of two men.

The Ashvins.

After a stunned moment of disbelief, everyone burst into action.

"Stop them!" Suvanna cried, and together, five Chiranjivi called on their unique powers to surround the Ashvins. Bands of golden and fiery magic, twisting with fluid ribbons of water and air, wrapped around the twins, trapping them where they hovered.

"Zarya," Rabin said, falling to the ground and stretching over her like he'd done in that swamp in Dharati when he'd saved her from the brink. Like he'd done only days ago when her own father had tried to murder her.

Dimly, he registered the struggle around him, but all he could focus on was Zarya, her ashen cheeks, and cooling skin. He took her hand and wrapped it with his. She felt so small and delicate. He'd have only minutes before he'd also start to drift away.

The Bandhan pulsed at his side like a second heartbeat. It ached, and it burned, searing against his skin. Almost like it felt her death, too. Rabin closed his eyes and entered the mind plane, seeking her out. He had to find her. Not only was everything resting on his shoulders, he *had* to save her.

He didn't care about himself. He had never cared about himself, but she needed to live.

"Zarya," he called, searching through the muddled layers of their connection, seeking out that bright spot that signaled her presence. He filtered out his magic, allowing it to flow through her in glowing threads of copper surrounding them both.

It was borne on instinct. Something deep inside his subconscious called to him, and he sought her out. He wandered through the paths of their connection, turning through dark, shadowed corners and halls as he hunted for the glimmer of her life spark.

In his mind, he saw himself running, tripping over endless corridors and careening around corners only to be met with long stretches of nothing. But he wouldn't give up. He would fight for her until his very last breath.

He reached blindly into dim shadows pressing against his copper light. The darkness seemed to have no end, and he fell through it like he was sinking to the bottom of the sea.

It didn't take long before he felt his heart slowing, his pulse turning sluggish. His chest grew tight with gasping breaths as sweat beaded on his forehead. It had been too long. He was dying, too.

"Zarya," he gasped as he tripped, reaching out to save himself. His hands met with nothing, and he tumbled in an endless black void, end over end, as his head throbbed and his vision spun.

Still, he fought. He kicked, wrestling against an invisible current. He righted himself and landed once again on solid ground with a thump, his knees melting out from under him.

His pace was slowing, and his heart along with it. He collapsed onto all fours and began crawling, dragging himself deeper, seeking out the shimmer of Zarya shining in the dark.

He plodded slowly over cold stone as he felt death closing around him. His ribs tightened, and he choked on his dwindling breaths as his heart skipped several beats.

How much longer could he last?

Finally, the tiniest speck flared in the distance. It felt a million miles away, but he pushed forward. One hand. One knee. Again and again, he fought against the waves of death threatening to take him over.

The spot grew brighter as he gathered the last of his

strength, heaving himself closer. Then he saw her. She lay on the ground with her eyes closed and her arms limp at her sides.

She was pure starlight, glowing in silver, the reflection so bright he had to shield his eyes. A wash of nausea crested over him, and he curled inwards as a wave of pain shot through his chest.

He clutched his heart as he dragged himself closer, using his arm to push himself, his feet scrambling against the ground.

He propelled himself forward with a groan born of every ounce of strength he'd cultivated through thousands of hours of training during his life—every battle he'd faced, every war he'd lost, every moment of triumph.

Each of these events had come together to mold him into the man he'd become.

When he'd fought against the kings and queens of Rahajhan, claiming land in the name of his home, when he'd stood up to his father, when Gopal had those words carved into his skin, and when he almost died trying to escape, Rabin had been preparing for *this* moment.

For her. He hadn't known it until recently, but everything had been leading him to Zarya and the destiny she had to fulfill. But Rabin had a destiny, too. He'd been chosen as her protector. As the one who would save her at the end.

And fuck, it would be a cold day in hell before he failed at the one and only thing he'd been put on this plane to do.

With a final heave, he swung his arm up, wrapping his hand around her wrist, and then... they both exploded in a burst of silver starlight.

FIFTY-FIVE

A rush of power surged through Zarya's blood. *Magic*. But it wasn't magic she'd ever experienced before. Rabin had saved her from near death twice, but he'd never saved her from this blackness swallowing her whole.

Her thoughts were clear, but her body felt like it was floating inside nothing a hundred miles away. She could feel her life draining away. A humming, a strange resonance echoed in her ears. She felt no pain. She was adrift in a sea of emptiness, hovering through blackness, her mind tumbling through her skull.

She was supposed to be doing something.

Waiting for something, but it felt so distant. So far away.

Something touched her. A warm hand wrapped around her wrist, and she recognized that touch like she knew her own heartbeat.

She had only a moment to register that either she had reached the end... or this was another chance.

Light exploded around her, silver and searing her eyelids. That muted numbness of a moment ago suddenly morphed into the greatest pain she'd ever known. She screamed, her back arching as a cresting wave of agony slammed into her flesh, squeezing her bones so hard they creaked.

She screamed and screamed as the light grew brighter and brighter, but she *felt* it.

Her life returned, flowing through her veins, her blood swirling, her dead heart stuttering to a steady pulse.

Memories rushed towards her. The seaside cottage. The day she finally escaped. Meeting Vik and Yasen. Her first kiss. Then Rabin. Everything he'd meant to her. His betrayal and her forgiveness. Falling in love and marrying the only man she'd ever truly want. She craved this life so much. She wanted everything that came next.

So, she fought for it. For this beautiful life she'd found and the beautiful people in it.

And then... her breath exhaled with a soft puff as she came back.

She blinked up at the sky as a tear escaped and slid down her temple.

With another blink, she felt a warm body closing around her. She smelled the earth and fresh, green things. She felt his tears coating her throat and how hard he shook.

But what she felt the most was the endless depth of his love.

She peered down to the top of his head, his dark hair gleaming in silver light.

She lifted her hand, almost surprised when it obeyed her command. She stroked him with the barest touch, causing him to look up.

Her gaze met his, and at that moment, she knew he'd done it.

He looked nearly dead himself, but he'd saved her.

"Zarya," he growled, and then he was on her, his mouth crashing into hers as her arms folded around him. They kissed and kissed. They'd nearly been lost, but he'd done it. His voice cracked as he whispered her name over and over, kissing her nose and her eyes and her cheeks, then her throat and her hands as he ran his palms over her as if to ensure every piece of her was accounted for.

It took another moment for her to realize they were in Ishaan. The sensation felt like waking up from a very long dream. The sky looked wrong. Black fog hung around them, flashes of dark lightning streaking across the horizon.

Finally, Rabin pulled away and tried to help her sit up. He swayed, stumbling back before she reached out to catch him. They sagged against one another trying to settle their breathing. And that's when Zarya took in their surroundings.

The five other members of the Chiranjivi stood in a circle, magic flowing from their fingertips. Swirls of shadow, lightning, and starlight crashed around the two men hovering in the middle.

The Ashvins weren't fully corporeal yet—their translucent forms rippled where they hung, but they had full control of their magic. Streams of nightfire burst from their hands, striking into the fortified walls of the Chiranjivi's power.

Zarya blinked as her head spun.

So much electricity flew through the air that the hairs on her arms stood up.

"We have to help them," Rabin said, clutching his chest as his breath sawed in and out.

"Right," Zarya said, trying to move. Her limbs felt like lead as she heaved onto her hands and knees. Her vision tilted as she sucked in sharp breaths. Gods, neither one of them was in any state to help.

They shared a look, and another bright flash drew their attention.

Apsara screamed as one of the twins flung out a hand, knocking her back. Her magic sliced off as she was thrown from her feet. They tossed Koura through the air next while

Suvanna, Row, and Kindle drew deeper into their magic with gritted teeth.

Another strike and Kindle went flying.

A bright flash blinded them all, and Suvanna and Row were hurled back. The twins wasted no time, spiraling high into the air, coasting overhead, their arms raised and their chins pointed up.

They spun in a circle, disappearing as a silver line streaked across the sky towards the mountains.

"They're heading for their army," Row croaked.

The Chiranjivi spun around to find Zarya and Rabin on the ground.

"Zarya," Row breathed, falling to his knees to embrace her. "You're alive. You're alive."

He rocked her back and forth as she clung to him, her head still spinning.

She pulled away. "What happened?"

"The Ashvins appeared as soon as you... died," Row said. "We tried to contain them, but they're too strong."

Their gazes wandered north, where the ominous sounds of fighting and death floated across the distance.

"We have to get to them." Zarya struggled to sit up, her limbs like jelly as her legs collapsed under her. Rabin pushed onto one knee with his head bowed and one hand planted on the ground as he inhaled deep breaths.

She touched his face, laying a hand on his cheek.

"Did you..." she asked.

"I almost didn't make it," he answered.

She nodded as a tear slipped down her cheek.

"Thank you," she whispered.

Everyone helped Zarya and Rabin stand on shaking legs.

"I'll take the two of you," Row said. "The rest of you follow."

He held out his hands, and Zarya and Rabin grabbed one each.

A few seconds later, Zarya felt like she was being squeezed from every side. She'd never traveled with Row like this and wasn't sure she ever wanted to again. The world around her compressed and bent before the pressure released.

They arrived in a flash on the northeast side of Ishaan to witness a sight of chaos.

Hundreds of nairatta battled the armies of Gi'ana and Andhera, but they were bigger, stronger, and far more vicious. The fighting stretched over the plain under a blue sky choked with ash.

In the distance, the Ashvins hovered over the turmoil, surrounded by the same death and destruction they'd unleashed a thousand years ago, changing the face of Rahajhan forever.

Their ghost-like bodies had turned more corporeal, but they weren't of this world just yet.

Zarya felt a blast of wind at her back as Apsara dropped from the sky a moment later. The winged warrior took in the scene with a grim expression.

"Can you control them?" Row asked Zarya. "That's what Abishek planned, wasn't it?"

"I'm not sure," she said. "I think he planned to take them over first."

"Try it," Rabin said, still hunched over with his hands on his knees.

She swallowed and faced the twins. They hadn't noticed her, so she cast her mind towards them. She could sense a tether still loosely binding them like they weren't completely free of her yet. Maybe it would work.

Her eyes fluttered closed, and she pushed against the wall of their thoughts. It wasn't different from the experience of reaching into Rabin's head. It resisted her initially—her mind slipped against the surface while she searched for a crack.

She became only dimly aware of the screams and the clash of steel echoing around her. Her limbs trembled from the force, and she gritted her teeth against a wave of nausea. She'd been dead only minutes ago.

The tiniest fissure appeared in the barrier of the Ashvins' mind. She realized they were one—their spirits had joined at some point during their endless lives. This is why she'd seen them both in her visions.

She shoved against the striation and *felt* the moment she slipped into their subconscious. Their inner plane was a dark and tumultuous place, scattered with ashes and bones. Black forks of lightning flashed against midnight black, sparking like millions of points of brilliance. She ordered them to stand down and felt their shock and surprise and annoyance at her intrusion.

Her eyes peeled open to discover one of the twins scanning the horizon—looking for her. It took him a minute to find her standing half a mile behind the battle. Their gazes met, and her stomach dropped to her feet when his mouth stretched into a wicked smile.

With a toss of his hands, he hurled her from their minds with such force that she stumbled.

"What happened?" Row asked, catching her fall.

"I think they've become too strong for me."

Kindle and Koura arrived a moment later, panting heavily from their flight across the city.

"So, what do we do?" Apsara asked. "How do we fight them off? Is there another way?"

"Loka told me it had to be all of us," Zarya said. "That we could stop them together. I think we need to join our power like we did when we saved Amrita from the blight."

Everyone shared an uncertain look.

It seemed like a long shot, but all they could do was try.

Zarya began walking closer to the battle while the others

followed a moment later. In the distance, she spied Yasen and Miraan fighting back-to-back against a pair of snarling nairatta.

She limped towards him, clutching her chest, nearly on the verge of collapse. Yasen arced his sword over his head and brought it down, slicing through the demon's shoulder before it collapsed at his feet.

"Yas!" she called, her voice cracking.

He looked up immediately and started running. "Zee!" he shouted. "What happened?"

She collapsed against him, squeezing his biceps, and pressed her forehead against his chest to catch her breath. When she was steady, she looked up. "I'll explain everything if we get the chance. I need you to protect us."

She gestured to the Chiranjivi, and he understood her request immediately.

He began shouting orders to form a circle around Zarya and the others. Everyone shuffled in quickly, weapons ready. Zarya caught sight of Vikas and she lifted a hand to wave as he dipped his chin before he spun around to ward off another demon attack.

She looked back to Row and Rabin and then continued deeper into the battle with the line of Chiranjivi behind her.

As they passed, she could feel the weight of everyone's stares.

The hope in their eyes.

Gods, she hoped she wouldn't let them down.

When they'd reached the center of the clearing, she stopped. The Ashvins noticed her immediately, and she held their twin dark glares as she stretched her hands out. Rabin and Row took one on each side, and they formed a chain one by one as her eyes never left the twins.

One cocked his head, studying her carefully as she inhaled a deep breath.

Their army circled them in a barrier of protection, but she knew they couldn't hold on long.

"Ready?" she asked the others.

"Ready," they answered back.

For what? She wasn't sure yet.

Her anchors had weakened. But her magic was the key.

Nightfire.

None of this had been an accident or a coincidence.

All of this had been carefully orchestrated for this moment by the gods. Did she care that they'd manipulated her life? She didn't. Not when it meant she could save them all. Not only the vanshaj, but now *everyone*, too.

She turned to Rabin. "I need you," she whispered.

"Anything, Spitfire," he rumbled.

Through their paramadhar bond, she felt the surge of his strength flow into her. It pulsed in her chest, bringing her anchors back to life. They spun and sparkled in her heart, and she had only a moment to recall the first time this had happened and knew everything was about to change.

Then she started to glow.

Silver starlight surrounded her before spreading to the six others, casting them all into brightness like a line of brilliant stars.

She watched the Ashvins' smug expressions drop from their faces as their eyes flashed like inky pools of midnight.

They attacked. Beams of nightfire hurtled towards them, streaking over the plain.

Zarya watched them barreling closer, almost as if in slow motion.

"Steady!" Zarya called. "Don't move!"

The Ashvins' magic rushed towards them while the Chiranjivi obeyed her command despite the fact they now stood in the path of certain death.

But the gods had chosen her for this.

Why? She might never know the answer, but she wouldn't fall, not as long as there was a single breath in her body.

"Hold!" she screamed again as she shook, her limbs trembling and sweat dripping into her eyes. Her magic flared, her anchors spinning faster as the seven Chiranjivi grew brighter.

The Ashvins' magic streaked across the plain and struck their line in a flash of silver.

Zarya felt it like a coal burning through her chest. She screamed as pain shot down her spine and radiated through her limbs.

She shook harder, but she held.

And then... the Ashvins' nightfire dissipated into nothing.

She blinked. They'd stopped it.

"Yes!" she screamed as she bent over squeezing Row's and Rabin's hands. "That's it!"

That's when she noticed the inhuman sounds of the demon's screams. The nearest were clutching their heads as they sank to their knees, and the seven Chiranjivi grew brighter and brighter. The starlight spread to engulf the nairatta, turning them to dust.

The Ashvins retaliated immediately, firing more magic in their direction.

Zarya screamed as blast after blast burned through her like she was being torched from the inside. Her head tipped up, and she screamed at the sky. It was a sound of rage and the certainty that she was on the right path.

It was a sound that ripped from her chest with the force of all her hopes.

Their line held, and that's when Zarya noticed fear enter the twins' eyes.

"They're weakening," Suvanna shouted. "Don't let go!"

Zarya stared the Ashvins down. She didn't blink. She didn't move.

Their eyes were wild, full of malice. Their souls long dead.

But they wouldn't give up yet, either. They'd been feeding off the darkness and their wrath for a thousand years.

Again, they attacked.

"Hold!" Zarya screamed as her magic flowed through her in waves, spreading out in a circle as agony seared through her limbs.

She pushed the twins back.

Finally, they were weakening. They weren't strong enough. She just had to hold on a little longer.

Now it was her turn to gloat. She turned a smile towards them.

But the Ashvins—they, too, were smiling again.

Another dark line crested over the horizon. She exhaled a small gasp.

More demons. More monsters. Thousands of them. So many more than they could ever stop.

"Gods," she whispered.

The Ashvins threw out another wave of nightfire. It struck her in the chest, but she could feel her resistance weakening. Her anchors were dimming again, flickering to only dim points of light.

The sphere of her silver light began shrinking, and the demons recovered as they shook off her ebbing power. Horror swirled in her gut as more nairatta advanced, their roars echoing across the mountains.

They were lost.

She'd come so close.

"There are too many!" Row shouted. "We can't stop them all!"

Zarya gritted her teeth as another flash of the Ashvins' nightfire struck her in the heart, and magic ripped through her bones and organs.

She didn't know how long she could hold on.

"What do we do?" Apsara called. "This is burning her out!"

Zarya bent in half, her eyes squeezing shut and the muscles in her neck straining as she tried to cling to her power.

How could they be losing? She'd done everything the gods had asked of her.

Why hadn't it been enough?

"Zarya," came Row's deep voice. "Look."

She lifted her head and opened her eyes at where Row was pointing.

Vikas fought at the end of their circle, trying to keep the nairatta at bay. Ribbons of shadow magic swirled from his fingers and wrapped around the throat of a massive demon to cut off its air. It clawed at its neck as it choked on a scream. It took only a minute for the monster to collapse and stop moving altogether.

But Vikas... *Vikas*... was outlined in the faintest silver light.

"The Taara Aazheri," Zarya whispered as she understood everything all at once. "We need them, too."

"Vikas! Vikas!" she shouted. "Vikas!"

At first, he didn't hear as he swung his sword and lopped off the head of a demon. The silver outline flared brighter as the creature succumbed.

"Vikas!" Row shouted, and then Vikas turned to look over his shoulder.

"Get in the line," Zarya screamed. "Get everyone! We need all the Taara Aazheri! Join the line!"

Vikas shook his head as his brow furrowed.

"Please! I'll explain it all later!"

He nodded and came running over, slipping his hand into Koura's.

Immediately, she felt a surge of strength, her silver light spreading to include him in the protection of her magic.

The Chiranjivi began shouting for everyone to join hands.

The message filtered across the field until they all caught on.

They trickled in at first, and Zarya's magic grew stronger with each addition. It filled her up, ballooning across the growing line.

That's when she noticed the Ashvins watching her. Watching all of them.

They worked together, flinging out nightfire, sending it in every direction. A beam struck her in the chest, and she screamed, but the pain diminished in the face of her new strength.

Finally, the Taara Aazheri came in droves, forming a snaking line across the field. Hundreds of them. Maybe even thousands. Without her magic, without the Phoenix and the dream they fought for, none of this would have been possible.

Once she was sure it had to be enough, Zarya dropped her head and focused on the spinning anchors in her heart. She acknowledged each one and the role they had played. Then, she whispered to the darkness, knowing she would need it now more than ever.

Gathering each thread into her heart, she twisted them together with the full force of her magic, and then her nightfire erupted in a blinding flash.

It raced along the line, touching every person whose hands were linked, and then... a wave, a wall, a tide of pure sparkling black magic exploded from their army, racing over the land, spreading like ink.

The demons screamed as swaths of midnight death consumed them whole.

It took the Ashvins, burning through them like acid until they were nothing but dust tossed into the wind.

The magic sunk into the earth, spreading across soil and roots and water. Zarya felt it. She felt it reach from where they stood, just like the day they'd saved Dharati.

It sped over the miles, through mountains and forest, through farmland and lakes. Pure starlight purified the earth that had nearly been taken. It buried deep into another world where two evil kings had once been banished. She felt it strip away their taint and the horror they'd brought upon their own people.

This wasn't the end anymore.

The vanshaj were finally free.

The Ashvins would soon be dead.

And *this* was finally a beginning.

She lifted her head as another roll of power slammed into the twins.

They screamed. It was a sound that spoke to the darkest part of her soul. They writhed and twisted as her magic burned through their clothes and then their skin, peeling it away to expose bone and sinew, blood and viscera, until their bodies glowed like the sun.

Zarya dug further into her power, focusing another blast straight into their depths, tearing them apart.

They shattered, exploding into pieces before dissolving into nothing but puffs of white.

She exhaled a choked sob of victory as her magic continued surging and flowing. It rolled from her in waves, spreading over the plain and across Rahajhan, touching everyone who had stood together and tried to change the world.

FIFTY-SIX

Yasen clutched a sword, dripping with dark blood as he watched Zarya's magic spread over the horizon. It shattered through the nairatta in a flurry of screams and agony. They dissolved under Zarya's light until nothing was left but the barest wisps of smoke.

They hung in the air, suspended for several seconds before the breeze carried them away.

That was it. They were gone.

Zarya dropped her hands and fell against Rabin before they collapsed to the ground, both unconscious.

"Zee!" he cried, running over and dropping to his knees. He rolled her over onto her back while Row did the same for Rabin.

"They used a lot of magic after Zarya died," Row said, feeling for Rabin's pulse. "They're alive, but they're very weak."

"Take them to the palace," Miraan said, crouching next to Yasen. "They'll see my best healers. I don't know what happened, but I have a feeling we owe everything to them right now."

He shouted orders to some nearby guards, and a few minutes later, a row of palace healers appeared with stretchers. They laid Rabin and Zarya out before spiriting them away.

"Will they be okay?" Yasen asked Row.

He shook his head. "Let's hope so. They both went through so much."

"They saved us?" Miraan said, his hand over his heart. "I... can't even imagine what might have happened..."

"You have no idea," Row said. "But yes. They saved us all."

Everyone turned towards the torn-up landscape. The dead bodies and the scarred earth. But in the end, it could all have been so much worse.

"Let's focus on cleaning up," Yasen said. "Give everyone their due."

"And then what?" Miraan asked.

"Then we figure out what's next. We've all just been given a second chance. Let's hope we use it more wisely."

Over the next many hours, they collected their dead as the sun set and then rose again. When everything was finished, Miraan insisted Yasen rest in the palace, and he was too tired to argue.

Plus, he wanted to be near Zarya to keep an eye on her.

They entered the courtyard to silence and stared up at the sky-blue palace.

"I was sure I'd never see this place again," Miraan said.

"It's a miracle," Yasen agreed.

"We still need to deal with my sister," Miraan said, then paused. "She cannot rule Gi'ana after colluding with Andhera and the Jadugara to wipe out the vanshaj."

Yasen studied the prince's profile. "What will you do?"

He shook his head. "I'm not sure. I'll be able to think clearer after some sleep."

They crossed the courtyard and entered the palace, where they were greeted by a flurry of servants no longer wearing collars. Their expressions and the fact that they kept touching their throats suggested they were still understandably bewildered.

"Your Highness," a woman said, pressing her hands before her heart and dipping at the waist. "You're okay?"

"We're fine," he said and then turned to Yasen. "Come. You're staying with me."

Yasen followed him through the palace and entered Miraan's wing.

With the chaos now behind them, Yasen recalled what Miraan had said before the fighting began.

He loved him, and Yasen... loved Miraan, too. He'd been trying to deny it, but nothing could be the same again once Miraan uttered those words. Yasen had never said 'I love you' to anyone before, and he wasn't sure he was ready yet.

"I'm not expecting you to say it back," Miraan said as he stripped out of his blood-soaked clothing.

Yasen blinked, giving him a confused expression.

"What I said out there," Miraan continued. "I meant it then, and I mean it now. But I don't expect you to say it back. I only want to know if there's a chance that you'll ever feel the same."

Yasen exhaled a soft breath. How could he read his mind like that?

He took in the scope of Miraan's room. The opulence. The riches. The sheer grandness of it. This man was a prince, and Yasen didn't belong here. They'd freed the vanshaj from their collars, and it was time to move on.

"I think I should check on Zarya," Yasen said, stepping back and pointing his thumb over his shoulder.

"Yas—" Miraan said, his brows drawn together.

"Get yourself cleaned up and get some sleep."

"Are you coming back?"

"Um, I'm not sure."

Then he spun on his heel and left, walking very fast. Gods,

he was such a fool. Miraan didn't see things clearly. When they'd been working with the resistance, they'd been equals of a sort, but here in the palace, Yasen was nobody.

He asked a servant where to find Zarya and Rabin and then made his way through the palace. Entering their room, he found them lying on separate beds with about two feet of space between them.

The curtains were closed, and the room was dark, and he approached on light steps, stopping between them. He studied their faces, relaxed in sleep, and laid a hand on Zarya's wrist, squeezing it gently. She didn't react, and Yasen's stomach twisted with worry.

He looked around, noting a long divan against the wall that should be large enough to accommodate his height. He needed a shower and probably something to eat, but all he craved was sleep. He dropped onto the cushion and lay back with one arm tucked under his head and the other resting over his heart. He stared up at the ceiling as the sun began to set.

He couldn't quite believe *any* of them were alive.

Zarya had saved them.

He smiled to himself, thinking of that day in the swamp when she'd leaped out of the bushes like a feral cat. She'd been reckless and impulsive, but she'd grown so much since then. The only thing she'd wanted was friendship and love, and just when she had it, it was nearly taken away.

But she'd obviously gone to almost fatal lengths to fulfill her destiny, and he was so proud of her.

No, Zarya had never been second best.

And Yasen, well, he was the luckiest asshole in the world to be her best friend.

FIFTY-SEVEN

Zarya's entire body hurt. Even with her eyes closed, lying on her back, it felt like the world was spinning. Slowly, she blinked awake to find a darkened room she didn't recognize. Above her, a sky blue ceiling was carved with ornate scrolls and flowers. Curtains hung around the room in gauzy white, and the scent of jasmine and sandalwood filled her nose.

She flexed her fingers and toes and winced. Her limbs felt like lead. Slowly, she turned her head to the left. Her breath hitched at the sight of Rabin lying in the next bed. Watching him for several seconds, she noted the steady rise and fall of his chest.

She thought back to the last moments she remembered. Her magic had been stretched to its very limit, and she couldn't feel her anchors. Not the tiniest flicker or glimmer. Would they come back?

Someone appeared in her vision. Row dropped into a crouch, putting him at eye level.

"Zarya," he whispered. "How are you feeling?"

She tried to open her mouth, but even that felt like too

much, so she just whimpered. Row brushed a piece of hair from her face and gently placed his hand on her forehead.

"You passed out after the battle ended," he said softly. "I've never seen anyone use that much magic at once."

She stared at him as a tear slipped down her cheek.

It represented so many things: the battle they'd fought, the terror of realizing Abishek had tricked them, her death, and Rabin's fight to save her. The fear of running through Taaranas as Rabin hunted her down. It represented these people who'd become her family. The love in her heart for her husband and for Row, this man who'd raised her.

They'd survived, and she was alive.

Somehow, she'd come out the other side.

Another shadow fell over her, and she looked up to find Koura with a soft smile on his face.

"I'm glad to see you awake," he said, leaning over and placing a hand above her heart. He held it there for a few seconds, concentrating before he nodded and pulled away.

"Your pulse is strong. It was touch and go there, but you'll make a full recovery."

She blinked and finally opened her mouth. "Rabin?" she whispered, and Koura smiled again.

"He'll also be fine," he said as relief relaxed the tension coiling in her body. "Your magic, too," he added. "It will take a week or two to recover, but I'm confident it will return."

She nodded as someone knocked on the door. Row opened it to reveal a servant bearing a silver tray with a small gold cup. Koura took it and held the cup towards her.

"Drink this—it will help you get the rest you need," he said. "While you sleep, I will use my magic to help replenish your anchors."

"Thank you," she whispered as Row cupped a hand behind her head and lifted it up so she could drink. The cool tonic slipped down her throat, leaving a taste of cinnamon on her tongue.

Immediately, she felt the effects as Row laid her head on the pillow and her eyelids slid closed. She heard them talking for a moment, and then, she was gone.

Zarya wasn't sure how much time had passed as she drifted in and out of consciousness. She was aware of Row and Koura at her side, caring for her as they helped bring her back to life. Yasen appeared a few times in the haze of semi-consciousness, and she savored the comfort of his presence somewhere in the depths of her exhaustion.

It must have been days later when she awoke to a dark room and, for the first time, felt like she could move. The tiniest spark flickered in her chest, and she closed her eyes, pressing her hand to her heart.

Eventually, she turned her head to meet a pair of dark irises flecked with gold.

"Rabin," she whispered.

"Spitfire." His voice was raw, but the way he said it filtered through her blood and filled her back up.

"Can you move?" she asked.

"Not really. You?"

"A little," she said. "I miss you."

At that, he simply lifted his arm with a wince, pulling up the corner of his blanket. She sat up slowly and placed her feet on the floor. It took a moment to heave herself up, and then she stole across the space and climbed in beside him.

He wrapped his arms around her, and she pressed her face into his chest, inhaling his familiar scent. They lay together for a long time, saying nothing while Zarya listened to the beat of his heart and the soft sounds of his breath.

He rubbed a hand down the back of her head and kissed her temple. "How are you?" he whispered into her hair.

"So glad you're alive," she said.

She looked up to meet his pensive gaze.

"What are you thinking about?" she asked.

He shook his head and blew out a sigh. "I'm sorry, Zarya. I'll never forgive myself for what he did to you."

"It wasn't your fault. He tricked us both."

"I brought you there. I should have hidden you. I should have protected you." He slid his hand up the back of her shirt to run his fingers across the scars he'd inflicted. "But I hurt you." His voice deepened, and his eyes turned black.

"Please don't blame yourself for this," she said. "I want to put this behind us."

"I'm not sure I can do that."

"Please?"

He exhaled a soft breath. "I can try."

She pressed her mouth together, knowing that he'd probably have to work through this himself no matter what she said or what assurances she offered.

He blinked and tucked a lock of hair behind her ear.

"Are you ready for the next part?" he asked. "This fight is over. We were married in the middle of a hurricane and never had a chance to build a life."

She gave him a watery smile. "I always want to be surrounded by people."

He grimaced, and she laughed.

"All right, how about sometimes?"

"You still want to remain in Ishaan?" he asked.

"I do, but what about your home? Do you want to return to Dharati?"

He shook his head. "Maybe, but I'd have to mend bridges with Vik first. And I don't know if I'm ready to be near my father again."

"Do you think they're okay?"

"I'm not sure."

She looked up at the ceiling and then back at him. "What if we lived at your manor sometimes?"

He smiled. "I'd like that."

"I don't care what we do, Rabin. I just want to be with you."

He hugged her tighter and kissed her softly before they snuggled into each other and eventually drifted off to sleep again.

FIFTY-EIGHT

Yasen stood in the throne room of the Madans' palace. The walls were made of the same sky-blue stone, inset with tall, narrow windows framed with jewels. The floor stretched for what felt like miles, covered in various shades of pale blue and white tiles, reaching towards a single silver throne at the end.

Gi'ana only had one ruler—its queen.

Dishani sat in a chair at the foot of the dais, flanked by two healers. Thanks to Koura's magic and around-the-clock care, she'd improved considerably. She no longer wore the veil and was moving with ease. Scars still marred her face, and a cloth covered her missing eye, but she was healing. Koura said they'd done all they could; the only thing left was time.

Also in the room were Miraan and about a dozen high-ranking nobles, including Rudra and the others who'd come to the prince's aid. About two dozen guards, including the queens-guard, stood along the perimeter in their pristine white uniforms.

And finally, the royal siblings and king consort also stood facing Dishani.

The room was so quiet that it felt like the very air had solidified. Yasen shifted where he stood near the wall. Technically, Zarya should have been here, but she was still too weak to get out of bed. She'd asked Yasen to report back on everything that happened.

Miraan had been secretly convening with officials and the nobles for the last few days. Yasen had been avoiding him, so it was for the best. They hadn't talked about Miraan saying "I love you" and they definitely hadn't talked about how Yasen had run away.

Finally, a man wearing a long robe stepped forward, stopping in the center of the room with all eyes on him. Yasen didn't know his name but recognized him as the royal council leader. Gi'ana's queen wasn't required to submit to their authority, but she often consulted with them on complex matters to ensure a stable outcome.

"After many hours of deliberation, questioning, and testimony from those closest to Princess Dishani, she has been found guilty of war crimes committed against the people of Ishaan, particularly the vanshaj."

He went on to list her sins, including colluding with Andhera, abusing the vanshaj, and using the Jadugara to do her dirty work. Had Dishani reached her coronation, making these charges stick would have been far more difficult. But despite her best efforts, she was not the sovereign leader and, therefore, was still under the jurisdiction of those who made up Gi'ana's council and ruling class.

"The Jadugara are also disbanded," continued the man. "Its members are to be jailed for their lies and deception. Those who've escaped will be hunted down and imprisoned without trial."

Yasen listened with a skeptical ear. It was the very people in this room who had allowed the Jadugara to act with impunity. These people had supported Dishani, and every single one of them had also used vanshaj for their gain.

But Miraan claimed people wanted to be on the right side of history, and with the collars gone, it was obvious everything was about to change.

"Princess Dishani is to be stripped of her crown and is no longer heir to Gi'ana's sacred throne." He paused and exchanged a look with Miraan. "It has also been brought to our attention that Queen Asha may yet be alive."

A chorus of shocked whispers circled around the room. Miraan had already shared the news with his family, who'd all broken down in tears. Now they stood with straight shoulders and stoic expressions, though Yasen sensed they were all on the edge of cracking.

"A delegation has traveled to Andhera, where she was kept prisoner by King Abishek, who is now dead." More gasps of surprise chorused around the room. "She is still the rightful queen, and we will wait on any further decisions until she returns. Until then, Prince Miraan shall act in her stead as the second eldest of the Madan siblings."

When the man fell silent, Miraan stepped forward and bowed to the nobles first and then his family. He approached Dishani, who listened to her conviction without expression.

Miraan looked down at her.

"Her necklace," he said. Dishani blinked with her good eye, her mouth turning down. "I know you still have it."

She paused and reached into her pocket, pulling out Zarya's chain. It dangled from her hand, the turquoise jewel flashing in the light. Miraan reached for it, and she released it into his palm before his fingers closed around it.

"The punishment for your crimes is execution," Miraan said, and Yasen watched everyone in the room shift uncomfortably. "But I will allow you the privilege of living in exile because you are my sister, and I still find it in my heart to love you despite everything. I believe you aren't the wicked person you became. I believe you let your fear get the best of you. My hope is that you will reflect on the choices you made and try to do better with the rest of your life."

Dishani exhaled a soft breath as her hands gripped the armrests before slowly turning towards her family. Every time Yasen looked at her, all he saw was what she'd done to Zarya. She didn't want Dishani dead, but Yasen and Rabin certainly did. Miraan was a better man than either of them because as he stared at his sister, there was only compassion in his eyes.

Dishani's shoulders slumped, and a tear slipped down her cheek.

"You will be comfortable," Miraan said, his voice thick. "Provided with anything you need, but you will not be welcome here again."

Yasen watched the faces of the other Madans. Advika was quietly sobbing while Talin looked like someone had ripped into his chest and stomped on his heart. Kabir's posture remained straight with his hands behind his back, but a shine reflected in his eyes.

Yet, they did not come to Dishani's defense, and Yasen wondered if they'd all suffered at her hand.

Finally, Dishani nodded, and the relief in Miraan's expression was obvious. He had no desire to sentence his sister to death.

"Then say goodbye," he replied. "This will be the last time you see any of us again."

Miraan gestured to the queensguard. "Your things have been packed, and a ship is waiting to take you to Salayana," he said, naming an island a week's journey away.

Dishani said nothing, her expression neutral as she was helped up from her seat. Slowly, she limped across the floor with a member of the queensguard holding each arm.

As she approached her family, she stopped and watched them as another tear fell.

"I'm sorry," she whispered before looking back at Miraan. They stared at one another for several long seconds.

Then she turned away and continued out of the room.

No one spoke. No one moved.

It felt like no one even breathed until she reached the door and passed out of sight, never to be seen in Ishaan again.

FIFTY-NINE

Zarya and Rabin were feeling more themselves a few days later. They'd heard about Dishani's banishment, as well as the arrests of the Jadugara. Miraan was busy drawing up new laws that would see the vanshaj freed for good.

She was trying to reconcile how she hadn't been able to confront her half-sister, but perhaps it was for the best. Zarya didn't need a reminder of the cruelty she'd suffered thanks to Dishani. It was time to forget her, and Zarya truly hoped the former princess would find happiness despite everything.

They were eating lunch in their room while Row paced back and forth, muttering to himself. Several members of the queensguard had secretly traveled to Andhera days ago to retrieve Asha—assuming she was still alive.

Zarya wrapped her hand around the stone hanging from her neck. Yasen had returned it after Miraan recovered it from Dishani. She'd sobbed uncontrollably as Rabin had clasped it around her neck, and now she couldn't stop touching it.

Zarya wished she could have joined the mission to retrieve Asha, but she couldn't travel yet. Row had been split between staying with Zarya and finding the love of his life. Zarya had insisted he go, but in the end, he couldn't bring himself to leave her side.

Now he anxiously waited, knowing the queensguard was due back at any minute.

"Come and have lunch," Zarya insisted. He'd barely eaten in days. While she'd been touched that he'd wanted to take care of her, he was also driving her a little nuts.

A knock came at the door twenty minutes later, and Yasen entered. Row stopped in his tracks with a sharp breath.

"They're back," Yasen said before he turned to Rabin. "You should know that Ekaja came, too. She insisted."

Rabin grunted and then nodded before pushing his chair back from the table. He hadn't said much about her betrayal, but Zarya could tell it was eating at him.

Zarya also stood as Row turned, and their gazes held.

This was it—the moment when they'd all *finally* be reunited. Ambition and fear had torn them apart, but soon they'd be together again.

Never in her wildest dreams did Zarya ever imagine this might happen.

Never did she imagine that she'd find both a father and a mother at the end of this.

She crossed the room and held out her hand. He took it and inhaled a deep breath.

"She isn't how you remember her," Zarya warned. "Don't expect the woman you knew."

He nodded. "I'm sure she's in there somewhere."

They all followed Yasen through the palace and into the queen's wing. All of Dishani's things had been removed, and Zarya's heart beat faster, knowing they'd placed her in here. But it made sense.

Despite everything, this was where she belonged.

She was still Gi'ana's true queen.

Queensguards flanked the doorway, and as Zarya, Row, and

Rabin approached, they immediately opened a door to allow them inside.

The room was dim, with the curtains drawn and dozens of servants scattered about. In the center of the room sat a long, curved divan, and on it was a woman—Asha, her *mother*.

She looked much healthier already; Zarya could only assume Ekaja was responsible for that.

At their entrance, Asha looked up. She was surrounded by her family, who glanced at Row and Zarya and then moved away to allow them a chance to speak with the queen. Zarya nodded a thank you and then turned to her mother.

Her breath caught at the reflection in her dark brown eyes. It felt like she could see lifetimes buried in their depths. Pain and loss and sorrow. But also... hope.

Asha spotted Row first. So many emotions flashed across her expression as she sat up straighter and blinked several times as if willing the sight to be real.

Zarya's chest squeezed.

So many people had told her how much she looked like Asha, but now she really saw it. Cleaned up without blood and dirt covering her face, Asha truly was Zarya's near mirror image.

"Row," Asha whispered on a breath that seemed to echo all the years they'd been separated.

Zarya watched him. This man who'd been her father. He couldn't seem to move as he stared at Asha like she'd risen from the ashes. In a way, she had.

Asha was crying, tears coating her face. "I never thought I'd see you again."

Zarya moved closer to Row and gave him a little nudge.

That snapped him back to reality.

"Asha," he said, his voice cracking. "My love. My heart."

He crossed the room and fell to his knees, laying his head on her lap and wrapping his arms around her waist. She dropped her head to his, her shoulders trembling.

He was sobbing. She was sobbing. Almost everyone in the room was sobbing.

"I searched for you," Row gasped. "For twenty years, I looked for you. I almost gave up hope." They shook as they clung to one another. "I had no idea he had you," he continued. "I'm so sorry. I should have found you."

"It wasn't your fault," she whispered. "I never gave up hope I'd see you again."

Zarya met the gazes of the Madans: her half-siblings and Kabir. In amongst the turmoil of the last several months, she'd gained another family, too.

"I did what you asked," Row said, looking up at Asha. "I protected her. Abishek nearly killed her, but I stopped him. I made so many mistakes, but she's safe now."

"I knew you would," she said, brushing her hand down his face. "There was no one else I could trust."

Row turned to face Zarya, pride shining in his eyes.

"I'd like to introduce you to your daughter," he said, almost choking on the words and gesturing towards her.

That's when Asha's gaze fell on her, and Zarya felt the ground shift beneath her feet.

"Zarya," she whispered as tears spilled down her cheeks. She stared at Zarya and shook her head. "You're so beautiful. Can you ever forgive me?"

Zarya moved closer. "There's nothing to forgive," she whispered. "None of this was your fault, any more than mine. Row cared for me, and I couldn't ask for anyone better. I understand why you had to do it."

Asha sobbed harder. She could barely catch her breath.

"Please," Asha said, holding out her arms. "I haven't held you in twenty years."

Zarya broke down and tripped towards her, falling against Asha as they cried together. Row wrapped her from behind, and they hugged and cried for a long time.

A family—*her* family. Finally.

Zarya eventually pulled away and stared up at her mother, hardly daring to believe this was real.

"There's someone else you need to meet," she said.

She stood and took Rabin's hand, dragging him towards the divan.

"This is Rabindranath Ravana, my husband," she said, and Asha's face fell.

"You're married?"

Zarya nodded.

"I missed everything," she said as she looked about the room. "My children grew up, and I missed it all."

Zarya didn't know how to respond as Talin, Miraan, and Advika all drew closer.

"*Commander* Rabindranath Ravana?" Asha asked a moment later.

Zarya held her breath, remembering Abishek's story about Asha losing favor thanks to Rabin and his armies.

"Yes," he said with his hands clasped behind his back.

Asha exhaled a laugh. "Fate is a strange thing, isn't it?"

Rabin dipped his chin and looked back up.

They shared a look before she addressed her other children. "I will make this up to you. And Zarya, I will never be able to express how much I hated sending you away."

"Mother," Talin said. "We're just happy you've returned. And we have so many years left."

Asha pressed her mouth together and nodded.

Then she focused on Rabin again, assessing him from head to toe. He held still as Zarya glanced between them. "Welcome to my family, Commander. I can't wait to get to know you both."

SIXTY

Rabin bowed to the queen of Gi'ana as more tears welled in her eyes. When she'd asked if he was Daragaab's former commander he had no idea how she might react. He'd spent years fighting her armies and claiming their land at his queen's behest.

But maybe that was all in the past.

Because she'd just welcomed him into her family, and it was everything he could do not to break down. Asha watched her children with such love that he felt his heart twist.

Eventually, she grew tired, and it was time to let her rest. Advika, Talin, and Miraan all hugged her tightly and they promised to have dinner together when she was feeling better. Kabir dropped to a knee and took her hand to kiss the back before pressing his forehead against it.

Rabin remembered Miraan saying Asha and Kabir had never loved one another, but it was obvious something existed between them. They were good friends at least. "We're all so happy you're home," he said.

She ran her hand down the side of his face. "I never thought I'd see any of you again."

Rabin wrapped an arm around Zarya, and she turned and buried her face in his chest. He didn't deserve this. He was shocked Zarya was still speaking to him after everything he'd done. He was putting on a front because she didn't deserve his anger, but inside, he was churning with rage about how much he'd fucked up.

His hand cupped the back of her head, and finally, the healers insisted everyone leave to allow Asha some sleep.

"Stay with me," Asha said, holding her hand out to Row. "Please."

They all watched Row as he blinked and inhaled deeply. He looked like an entirely different man already. Rabin couldn't even begin to imagine what it must feel like to have this second chance.

"Of course," Row said, sinking down next to her. He tentatively wrapped his arms around Asha and kissed her temple as if afraid she might shatter under his touch.

Then Zarya and Rabin followed the others out with their hands clasped. Zarya stopped and peered over her shoulder one more time, and Rabin glanced back to witness Row and Asha hugging as they sobbed against one another.

Zarya turned to look at Rabin with a smile on her face. They were getting the second chance she'd wanted.

"I'm so happy," she whispered. After they left the room, Zarya added, "I know we almost died in Andhera, but if we hadn't gone to see the king, we might never have found her."

Her expression bordered on hopeful.

Possibly, but he still couldn't forgive himself for what he'd done.

"Let's go back to bed," he said, taking her hand again. "You need rest, too."

"Rabin," someone called behind them a moment later. He stopped in his tracks, recognizing Ekaja's voice. Her rapid footsteps approached, and he spun around to face her.

"Can we talk?" she asked. "I'd like a chance to speak with you alone."

Dark circles ringed her eyes, and her normally straight posture was curving in on itself.

"Anything you have to say to me, you can say in front of Zarya," he answered, his hand tightening around hers.

Ekaja dipped her chin. "Very well. I wanted to speak with her, anyway. Is there somewhere private we can talk?"

"Our room," Zarya said, looking up at him for confirmation.

He nodded and headed down the corridor, tugging Zarya along. At the sound of Ekaja's sharp footsteps, it took everything in him not to look back. Her betrayal was one of the worst hurts he'd ever known.

Finally, they reached the room where Zarya and Rabin had been recovering for the past week. Their single beds had been removed, and now they shared a large one against the far wall. Zarya fell asleep against him every night while he stared at her beautiful sleeping face, hating himself for nearly getting her killed.

Zarya sat beside Rabin on a divan under the window while Ekaja took the armchair across from them. Rabin said nothing, waiting for her to start.

Ekaja swallowed nervously and rubbed her palms on her thighs.

"I'm sorry," she said. "I made a huge mistake. I let him talk me into it. I truly didn't believe he would hurt you."

Rabin exhaled a derisive breath. "What did he share with you? How much did you know?"

"That... he was sending you into Taaranas. That he would use Zarya to break the seal."

"And you didn't think *any* of that might hurt us?"

Ekaja stared at him, her lip quivering as a single tear slid down her cheek. He'd never seen her cry before. Until this moment, he didn't even think she was capable of it.

"I made a mistake," she said softly. "One I will regret for the rest of my life. You have every right to be furious, but I only hope that someday you might find it in your heart to forgive me."

Rabin's jaw ticked. It was obvious she was feeling a lot right now. She was sorry, and she'd been right that Abishek would have found someone else if she'd been unwilling to help. Still, it didn't mean he was ready to forgive her yet.

"I'm not sure if I can," he said. "I'll need time to think about it."

She nodded as another tear tracked down her cheek. "I'll do anything to make it up to you. I tried to talk him out of it. That's why he made me ride with you in the carriage... he was punishing me."

Rabin braced his elbows on his knees, considering that information. They were all silent as his thoughts tumbled with memories of Ekaja and the moments they'd shared. She'd been his rock when it felt like his world was falling apart, and he knew he would miss having her in his life.

"You said you wanted to speak to me as well," Zarya asked after a few moments.

Ekaja sniffed and wiped her cheek with the back of her hand. "The king is dead, and you are his heir. Andhera is now yours. When will you return home to take your crown?"

Zarya blinked. Rabin could tell from her expression that this hadn't occurred to her yet. The last thing in the world he wanted to do was to return to Andhera, but if that's what she desired, he would follow.

"No," she said, shaking her head. "I don't want that. I never wanted that."

"Then who will lead?" Ekaja asked, a worried groove forming between her brows. "The king's death means the nobles are already maneuvering to take Andhera from you. They will succeed if you don't return to claim what is yours."

Zarya looked at Rabin and studied him before turning back to Ekaja. "I have no desire to return to Andhera ever again. My father nearly killed me, and he kept my mother locked up for decades. It holds only dark memories for me."

"You could make new ones," Ekaja insisted. "It's your home. Andhera is your blood."

"He wouldn't have wanted that," Zarya said. "Maybe..." She shook her head. "I never wanted to be a queen. I want a different story for my life, nor can I expect Rabin to return."

She reached out and took his hand. He covered it with hers and smiled softly, grateful that she knew him so well.

"I want you to do it," Zarya said. "It was my understanding that if my father died without an heir, you were to take up his position."

"I couldn't," Ekaja said, shaking her head.

"But you will," Zarya said. "Don't worry—it will be only temporary."

Rabin frowned, wondering where Zarya was going with this.

Ekaja appeared equally confused. "What do you mean?"

"I mean, it's time for a different kind of future. One where every citizen is represented. I want you to create a place where the Taara Aazheri have rights and a say in how Andhera is run. I want the nobles to share what they have with those who barely survive the winter. Seek out Dav and Suria at the inn. This was their vision, and they are more than capable of helping you."

Ekaja's mouth opened in stunned shock. "I couldn't. I wouldn't know how."

"You'll figure it out," Zarya said. "You are strong and smart. Brave. And I suspect kind, as well."

"I—" Ekaja started to protest when Zarya raised a hand.

"It's the least you owe me," she said matter-of-factly, and Ekaja snapped her mouth shut. "I will never return, but I need to know the people my father left behind are in good hands."

Ekaja exhaled a sharp breath and then dropped her head. "I will do my best." Then she slowly stood as her gaze swept over Rabin. "Will I see you again?" she asked.

Rabin breathed out a heavy sigh. They'd shared so much over twenty years. She'd been there for him when no one else was. He understood better than anyone what it was like to fall under Abishek's spell.

Slowly, he nodded. "Maybe..."

She exhaled a soft breath. "Thank you."

Then she turned around and stalked out of the room.

When she was gone, Zarya laid a hand on his arm. "Are you okay?"

"Yeah."

She glanced at the closed door. "Do you think what I made her do is unfair?"

"Not at all," he answered.

"Do you think she can do it?"

He exhaled a laugh. "If anyone can, it's her."

Zarya pressed her lips together. "I can't go back."

"Neither can I."

She wrinkled her nose. "I figured as much."

"Andhera isn't your responsibility, Zarya. You have no obligation to become its queen."

She nodded. "Then I hope she succeeds."

"I do, too," he answered, truly meaning it and hoping that someday Ekaja could find the peace and the life she deserved.

Yasen stood in the solarium of Ishaan's palace, staring out over Rahajhan and towards his home. Former home.

They were preparing to leave for Daragaab tomorrow. He didn't especially want to return, but after what they'd seen in Taaranas, they had to check on Amrita and Vikram. Tarin had sent a letter claiming they'd both fully recovered, and Amrita was due to give birth any day.

With any luck, they'd get a chance to see the baby, too. He liked the idea of being an uncle.

"Yas," came a voice, and he turned around to find Miraan standing in the doorway.

Yasen had been waiting for this and knew he couldn't avoid it any longer.

"You've been hiding from me," Miraan said as he approached. There was no accusation in his voice, only a touch of hurt.

"I haven't," Yasen said, though his lie was obvious.

"Where have you been sleeping?"

Yasen pressed his mouth together. "First, in Zarya and Rabin's room while they were recovering. But when they were feeling better, they kicked me out." He pulled a face, and Miraan laughed.

"And after that?"

"I found an empty bed."

Miraan nodded. "I scared you. That's why you're avoiding me."

Yasen blew out a breath and ran a hand down his face. "You did, but it's not because..." He broke off. "It's not because I don't feel the same."

The words hung between them, and a spark of joy flared in Miraan's eyes, there for a moment and then gone.

"Then what is it?"

Yasen waved a hand up and down. "You're literally a king now. I am nobody."

"You are *not* nobody, Yasen Varghese. Why would you say that?"

Yasen made a sound of disbelief. "Compared to you, I am. You can't be with me. You need to be with some rich noble."

Miraan's jaw turned hard, and he stepped closer, cupping

Yasen's face in his hands. "You are not nobody. You are worth a thousand rich nobles. Do you hear me?"

Yasen blinked, emotion pressing at the back of his throat. The way Miraan said it with such steadfast conviction almost made him believe it.

Miraan released him and stepped back as he smoothed down the front of his jacket. "Just promise you won't leave. Stay with me, and let's try this."

"You might break my heart," Yasen said, his voice raw with an emotion he'd never felt before. It was probably the most vulnerable thing he'd ever said out loud.

Miraan's forehead creased. "I vow to do everything in my power not to."

Slowly, Yasen nodded.

"Besides, it may be you who breaks mine," Miraan said. "But I need you to understand that it would be worth the risk."

Yasen exhaled a long sigh. Was he brave enough for this?

"Yeah, me too," he finally said with a nod.

"Then you'll stay?" Miraan asked, hope in his voice.

"I'll stay."

He smiled at the prince—not a prince, a king.

Miraan tugged his forehead towards his. They stood in the sunlit solarium as the sun beat through the windows and warmed his skin.

Yasen had always been a coward when it came to his heart. The only two people he'd ever truly loved were Vikram and Zarya. But maybe he deserved more than that.

He pulled up to look into Miraan's dark eyes, reflecting with a possibility of a thousand things.

Maybe Yasen *was* ready for this.

Maybe he couldn't wait to find out.

SIXTY-ONE

Zarya and Yasen clung to Rabin's back as he soared over the sprawling green forests of Daragaab. She watched the landscape race below, happy to be returning. Not only had she grown up here, she'd met some of the most important people in her life.

He landed on the outskirts of the Dharati with a heavy thump. It seemed unlikely Vikram's sentries hadn't seen them coming. But he'd pardoned Row, and she hoped they would be welcome.

Zarya and Yasen slid off Rabin's back before he shifted into his rakshasa form.

They began weaving through the trees until the city walls came into view. Both Rabin and Yasen stopped and stared ahead with wary looks. She understood why neither wanted to return. They had so many dark memories here.

She held out her hands, taking one on each side.

"It'll be okay," she promised. "I'll protect you."

They each looked down and smiled.

It had been almost three weeks since the battle with the Ashvins, and Zarya's magic had completely returned. In fact, it was stronger than ever, almost as if she'd absorbed the Ashvins' power as her own.

The darkness was now a part of the fabric of the continent, and Zarya hoped it would be a very long time before anyone succumbed to its evil possibilities again.

"No one would dare cross you," Rabin said in a low voice, and she grinned.

Rabin still blamed himself for everything Abishek had done. She understood he was putting on a mostly content facade for her sake, but sometimes she'd catch him when he didn't know she was looking, and the darkness in his expression told her everything. There were days she worried he'd simply disappear when it finally became too much to look at his mistakes.

"Let's go," she said, tugging them along.

They entered the city to find it at the height of its midday bustle.

When the sky-blue doors of the Jai Palace came into view, she sensed Rabin's hesitation. She squeezed his hand to assure him she was here to support him however he needed.

The guards instantly recognized their entire group, but arriving with Yasen, their former commander, had its advantages. They bowed and allowed them through, but something appeared off. Zarya caught a troubling hint of worry and sorrow in their expressions.

The hairs on the back of Zarya's neck rose. What was going on?

The green doors to the Jai Tree stood slightly ajar.

Zarya entered, followed by Rabin and Yasen.

She scanned the leaves and roots overhead, searching for the rot Yasen had described. She checked in with him.

"It's gone," he said, also peering up. Thank the gods for that.

Amrita looked mostly like herself, but... she was crying? Great streams of sap dripped down the front of her body as her chest heaved in and out.

They approached the dais in a line as their eyes fell on Vikram. He sat on the steps with his elbows on his knees and his head buried in his hands.

"Vik?" Yasen asked, slowly moving closer and kneeling on the tiles. "What's wrong?"

Vikram's head snapped up, peering at them with bloodshot eyes and a pale and sickly complexion. He took Yasen in, scanning him up and down.

"He took her," he said. "Nidhi was born two days ago, and *he* took her."

Zarya exchanged a look with Rabin and sunk down next to Yasen.

"The baby? Who took her?"

Vikram opened his mouth and shook his head before he broke down in sobs. Yasen leaned over to rub his arm as he answered, "Gopal. He said he planned to 'raise her.'"

"What?" Zarya said. "He kidnapped her?"

A shadow fell over them, and Zarya looked up to find Rabin staring at his brother with fire and rage in his dark eyes.

"Father took your child?" he said, his voice low and full of menace and his hand clenching at his side.

Vikram inhaled a sharp breath as tears coated his cheeks. "I couldn't stop him."

Rabin exhaled a long, slow breath, nodded, and stepped back. "Zarya, stay here and watch them." He turned to Yasen. "You, come with me. We have a date with my father that's long overdue."

Slowly, Yasen rose to his feet. Zarya watched a message pass between the two men. They'd never been friends until the last few months, but the abuse they suffered at the nawab's hands bonded them in a deeper way.

"Then, let's do this, Commander."

Rabin clapped him on the shoulder. "Just call me Rabin.

That isn't who I am anymore. I haven't been that man for a very long time."

Yasen laughed softly, and they both turned to Zarya.

"We'll be right back," Rabin said, and she nodded as they left the room, their quick steps echoing against the walls.

"Where are they going?" Vikram asked Zarya.

She looped her elbow through his. "To get your daughter."

Several hours later, Rabin and Yasen landed in the Jai Palace courtyard. It hadn't taken long to arrive at the Ravana estate, where Rabin had found the baby in the nursery with her nannies.

They screamed when he'd reached into her crib and lifted her up, carefully nestling her in the crook of his arm. Then he'd gone with Yasen to find his father.

The nawab was alone in the library when Rabin found him. That was his father's first mistake. He'd demanded the child be returned to Vikram, but Gopal refused. That had been his second mistake.

Now, Yasen slid off Rabin's back with the little girl cradled in his arms. Rabin shifted and then retrieved her, peering into the tiny face of the child. His niece. When he'd found her helpless in her crib, a fierce sort of possessiveness overtook him.

He'd never thought much about becoming a father but holding this precious life in his arms opened his heart to the possibility.

Zarya had never talked about children, but maybe they'd consider it someday. She had so much love in her heart and would make an amazing mother.

"You, okay?" Yasen asked. "You're getting blood on her blanket."

Rabin looked down at himself. "I think that was you," he answered, nodding towards Yasen's blood-spattered coat.

Blood.

His father's blood.

"Come on," Rabin said, and they entered the Jai Tree. Zarya sat on the steps next to Vikram with his head still buried in his hands.

At their approach, she stood, her eyes widening, clearly noting their state.

"What happened?" she asked as Vikram looked up.

When he saw the bundle in Rabin's arms, he let out a choked breath.

"What did you do?" he whispered.

Rabin was quiet as he lowered Nidhi into Vikram's arms.

"You are now the beneficiary of the Ravana fortune," he said roughly.

"What?" Vikram asked as he accepted the bundle and hugged her tight while he rocked her.

"Father is dead. I swore I'd kill him someday, and stealing your child was the last straw."

"And I helped," Yasen said with a thumb pointed at his chest.

Rabin turned to give him a crooked smile. He certainly had.

Vikram blinked and then dipped his chin. "Good."

All three men shared a grim look.

"But you are the heir," Vikram said a moment later.

"I renounce any claim I have to the Ravana line," Rabin said, and he felt a thousand pound weight lift from his shoulders. "Use the money to care for our mother and help the Taara Aazheri find new lives."

Vikram nodded. "Of course."

"Gi'ana is already making changes. I hope Daragaab will do the same," he continued.

"Are you staying?" Vikram asked, addressing all three of them.

"No," Rabin answered. "I just wanted to make sure you

were okay." He crouched onto his haunches and looked down at the child before lifting his gaze to his brother's. "I'm sorry I left. I'm sorry you had to deal with all this alone. I live with that regret every day."

Vikram hugged his daughter closer. "I know what he did to you. I don't blame you anymore. And now you have Zarya, and I know you love her, and I have my beautiful girl." He touched Nidhi's cheek with a gentle finger and so much love in his eyes. "Had I not become Amrita's steward, we wouldn't have met. I fell in love with her the moment I laid eyes on her."

Rabin exhaled a long sigh. "Maybe we can get to know one another again."

"I'd like that. Please come back and visit." Vikram turned to Yasen. "You, too. I'm sorry I let him hurt you. I should have been stronger. I... only ever wanted you to be happy."

Yasen gave him a half-smile and wrapped Vikram and the baby in a hug.

"Thank you for being my friend when I had nothing," Yasen said softly. "And I'm sorry I left you, too."

Vikram shook his head as Yasen stepped back. "I never blamed you for that. I understand why you needed distance from this place."

"Thank you," Yasen said.

A look of understanding passed between them, filled with so many things: love, hope, and the chance at a different future. Then Rabin held his hand out to Zarya and pulled her close.

"Zarya," Vikram said. "Promise me you'll come and visit with my brother sometimes?"

She smiled. "Of course. Thank you for taking a naive girl under your wing."

"It was my pleasure, and I'm happy for you both."

"I hate to leave, but we need to be off," Zarya said. "We have a wedding to attend."

"Who's getting married?" Vikram asked.

"Some friends we met in Ishaan. Rania and Farida. They're kind of the reason all this began."

Vikram gave her a watery smile, and they all turned to Amrita.

Zarya walked over and lay a hand on the bark as the queen blinked.

"She says thank you for saving her child," Vikram said. "And that she's happy to see all of you."

Zarya peered up. "I miss you," she said. "Thank you for being my friend."

"She says you are a remarkable person and that she's grateful you came into her life."

Zarya's eyes shone with tears as Rabin walked up and wrapped an arm over her shoulders.

"I am, too. I promise to come back and see you soon."

Then Zarya, Rabin, and Yasen said their last goodbyes before they entered the courtyard.

Without saying a word, Rabin passed through the gates to stand at the end of a long boulevard stretching into the distance. He inhaled a deep breath, studying the city as Yasen and Zarya walked up behind him.

He'd experienced so much pain in this place, but Gopal was dead, and it was time for a new beginning. One that included Zarya and Yasen and the friends they'd found.

"You okay?" she asked, and he peered down to look at her. Gods, she was so beautiful.

He had to find a way to stop blaming himself for what Abishek had done.

For her, he would try to move on.

"I will be," he answered. "Let's go home."

SIXTY-TWO

ONE YEAR LATER

Zarya and Vikas shoved the heavy double doors open and bounded down the university's front steps. Their grueling semester had just ended, and they were both looking forward to a few months off.

"Did you get that last question?" Vikas asked. "I almost ran out of time."

"I'm not sure," she said. "I think so."

"I'm sure you did," he said wryly. "How many hours did you study?"

"A million," she joked, and they laughed.

With their elbows linked, they headed down the path leading to the gate, where she found a most welcome sight.

Rabin leaned against the fence with his arms crossed and one ankle over the other.

She broke into a run and threw her arms around him as he lifted her up and spun her around.

"How did it go?" he asked as Vikas approached.

"She aced it," Vikas said, and Zarya grinned.

"Maybe," she answered with a wrinkle of her nose, and the two men started laughing.

"Come on," Rabin said, taking her hand. "Everyone will be arriving soon."

They hopped onto their horses and made their way into Ishaan and to the haveli they'd purchased shortly after the battle with the Ashvins. Rabin had agreed to live in the city, and she'd agreed they would spend time in the forest whenever he needed a break from the noise.

Their home was beautiful, stretching three stories into the sky and made of the palest pink marble. It sat on the edge of a square with a giant crystal astrolabe in the center, and Zarya loved sitting at their bedroom window to watch the way the stars and moon would make it sparkle at night.

They entered the main floor to find a flurry of people scurrying back and forth, along with a harried woman shouting orders with a pen tucked behind her ear and a clipboard in one hand. They'd hired a party planner to make all the arrangements for tonight's celebration. It had been a year since they'd been to Taaranas, and today, they would gather with everyone who'd worked at the heart of the resistance.

Thankfully, their house had more than enough room.

Zarya went upstairs to change. She chose a beautiful purple sari with pink beading. Standing in front of the mirror, she traced the silver dragon on her chest and thought about how far they'd all come.

In the past year, Rahajhan had become a completely different place. The rulers of each realm had traveled to Ishaan to meet with Miraan, who had been crowned king of Gi'ana eight months ago.

They'd spent days discussing the future of the Taara Aazheri. While some were reluctant at first, they eventually agreed to amend every law still keeping them beholden to the citizens of the continent.

They were to be paid fairly for their work and afforded the same rights as every citizen. Every realm also set up a fund that any Taara Aazheri could access to help build new homes, receive an education, start a business, or support those who simply wished to live a peaceful life.

Vikas had chosen to enroll in the university with Zarya, and they'd learned all about their magic together. She loved every moment of it.

When she heard the door open downstairs, she finished dressing and ran down to meet Row and her mother. They'd purchased a haveli a few blocks away and they all had dinner together at least once a week.

Even after a year, the sight of Asha still caught her breath nearly every single time. She'd gained some weight, and her hair shone like a midnight river. The best healers in Rahajhan had been working for months to erase some of her worst scarring and, by all accounts, she was thriving.

But every once in a while, Zarya would catch a haunted look in Asha's eyes. It would take some time to lock away the hurts caused by the former king of Andhera.

The queen of Gi'ana had chosen to renounce her crown, wishing to live a quiet life with the man she'd never stopped loving. And they were *so* perfectly in love. Row was so different around her. Now she understood why they'd butted heads so much during her childhood: he, too, had been nursing a broken heart.

Zarya threw her arms around them both, and they hugged her back.

Over the next hour, everyone else drifted in.

Ajay, Rania, and Farida arrived together. They still lived together in their flat, and Rania and Farida were so happy together that Zarya's throat tightened whenever she saw them. It had been *their* love that had set the Rising Phoenix in motion.

The door opened to reveal Apsara and Suvanna. They'd come from Vayuu where Suvanna had been staying with Apsara. Zarya and Apsara had exchanged a few letters, and while Suvanna still wasn't quite set on the idea of commitment, she was apparently warming up to the idea.

Finally, Koura and Kindle also arrived from their respective realms to offer good news and updates about the Taara Aazheri.

News coming in from Andhera suggested Ekaja was hard at work making Dav and Suria's dream of a democracy come true. Rabin had been in touch with her once or twice, and he was considering a visit. Perhaps they'd revive their friendship one day.

Vikram and Amrita were doing well. Nidhi was almost walking now and causing Vik all kinds of trouble.

Rabin had returned a few times to help bring the forest of Daragaab back to life alongside his brother and a team of rakshasas. Soon all evidence of the swamp where Zarya had lived would be gone. The seaside cottage still remained, and maybe one day she'd find it in herself to return.

The seven Chiranjivi toasted to one another and the battles they'd fought together.

"When do you think we'll all be needed again?" Kindle asked.

"Let's hope never," Row said, and they all laughed.

The door opened again, and Yasen appeared with Miraan in tow. Despite his reservations about becoming attached to the king, he'd stuck around like he'd promised, and Miraan was very clearly winning him over.

Then came the other Madans. Her family.

They all hugged and caught up as the night continued. Food and drink were passed around as music played into the early morning.

Zarya couldn't remember the last time she'd felt so... content.

This is what she'd craved all those years living by the sea. To be surrounded by friends and family. To laugh and never be alone.

Tired on her feet, she sat on the staircase and sipped her wine as she watched the people she loved so much having fun. The royals' presence had thrown off a few members of the resistance at first, but they seemed to be adjusting as they sang and danced.

She looked up when Rabin appeared above her. He sat down as they both watched everyone in silence.

"Thank you," Zarya said as Rabin looked over. "For giving me this. This is all I ever wanted."

He tipped up a half-smile. "I plan to spend the rest of our lives giving you everything you want, Zarya."

She gave him a quizzical look.

"What's wrong?"

"I was worried... when you were being so hard on yourself for Abishek's lies that you'd leave me."

His brows furrowed. "Why would you ever think that?"

She shrugged. "You were so angry, and I know you were trying to hide it but..."

He took her chin in his thumb and forefinger. "I was angry," he said. "It might have been one of my darkest moments, and I did try to hide it from you, but I learned to forgive myself for your sake. That day in Dharati, when I killed my father, I decided I would always be everything you need. And I would *never* have left you."

"Good," Zarya whispered as she wiped the corner of her eye with the back of her hand. "Because I could never bear it."

"You can't get rid of me that easily, Spitfire."

He winked and they looked back at the party and the dozens of people crowding the space.

"Can we head to the manor after this?"

She laughed and touched his cheek. "Is this too much for you?"

He cocked an eyebrow as he surveyed the crowd.

"Maybe it's not so bad."

She made a sound of surprise. "So we can have more parties?"

"Let's not get ahead of ourselves. I'll need at least a month of silence first."

She giggled. "Then we'll leave first thing."

"Sounds perfect," he said and kissed her softly.

She pulled back to study his face, remembering the very first time she'd seen him. He'd taken her breath away, and as she stared into his dark eyes and the sparkling golden flecks, she knew he would take her breath away every day of her life.

"I can't wait," she whispered.

A LETTER FROM NISHA

Dear Reader,

I want to say a huge thank you for choosing to read *Queen of Shadows and Ruin*. If you enjoyed it and want to keep up to date with all my latest releases, just sign up at the following link. Your email address will never be shared, and you can unsubscribe at any time.

www.secondskybooks.com/nisha-j-tuli

If you loved *Queen of Shadows and Ruin*, please consider leaving a review on your favorite platform. And if you'd like to get in touch, I love hearing from readers! You can join my Facebook reader group, send me an email on my website, or message me on Instagram.

Love,

Nisha

www.nishajtuli.com

facebook.com/NishaJT
instagram.com/nishajtwrites
tiktok.com/@nishajtwrites

PUBLISHING TEAM

Turning a manuscript into a book requires the efforts of many people. The publishing team at Bookouture would like to acknowledge everyone who contributed to this publication.

Audio
Alba Proko
Melissa Tran
Sinead O'Connor

Commercial
Lauren Morrissette
Hannah Richmond
Imogen Allport

Cover design
Andrew Davis

Data and analysis
Mark Alder
Mohamed Bussuri

Editorial
Jack Renninson
Melissa Tran